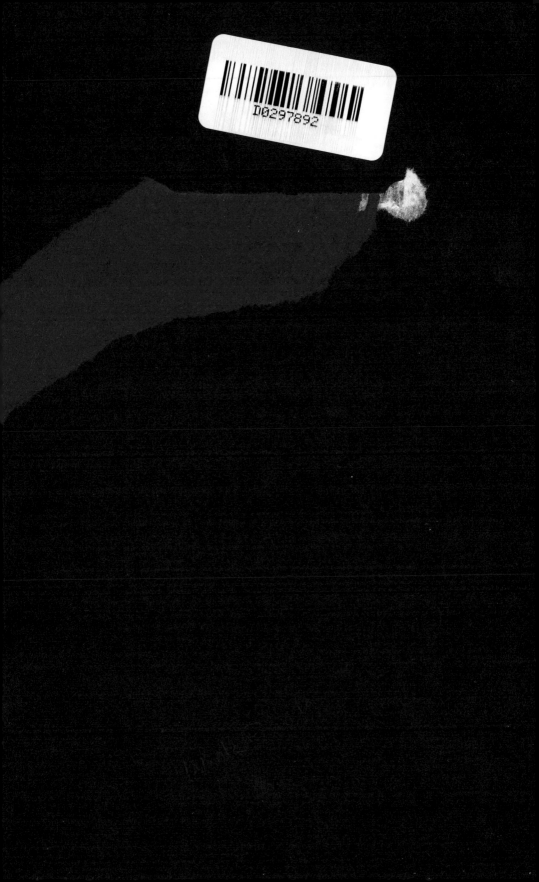

The Winter Palace

www.transworldbooks.co.uk

The Winter Palace

Eva Stachniak

Doubleday

LONDON · TORONTO · SYDNEY · AUCKLAND · JOHANNESBURG

TRANSWORLD PUBLISHERS
61–63 Uxbridge Road, London W5 5SA
A Random House Group Company
www.transworldbooks.co.uk

First published by Doubleday
an imprint of Transworld Publishers

A CIP catalogue record for this book
is available from the British Library.

ISBN 9780857520531

Addresses for Random House Group Ltd companies outside the UK
can be found at: www.randomhouse.co.uk
The Random House Group Ltd Reg. No. 954009

The Random House Group Limited supports the Forest Stewardship
Council (FSC®), the leading international forest-certification organization.
Our books carrying the FSC label are printed on FSC®-certified paper.
FSC is the only forest-certification scheme endorsed by the leading
environmental organizations, including Greenpeace.
Our paper-procurement policy can be found
at www.randomhouse.co.uk/environment.

For Szymon and Chizuko

ST. PETERSBURG, OCTOBER 17, 1756

Three people who never leave her room, and who do not know about one another, inform me of what is going on, and will not fail to acquaint me when the crucial moment arrives.

—from the letter of Grand Duchess of All the Russias (later Catherine the Great) to Sir Hanbury-Williams, British Ambassador to the court of Empress Elizabeth

THE
WINTER
PALACE

he spies you learn about are either those who get exposed or those who reveal themselves. The first have been foolish enough to leave a trail of words behind them; the second have reasons of their own.

Perhaps they wish to confess because there is nothing else they have but the arid memories of their own importance.

Or perhaps they wish to warn.

I was a *tongue,* a *gazette.* The bearer of "the truth of the whispers." I knew of hollowed books, trunks with false bottoms, and the meanders of secret corridors. I knew how to open hidden drawers in your escritoire, how to unseal your letter and make you think no one had touched it. If I had been in your room, I left the hair around your lock the way you had tied it. If you trusted the silence of the night, I had overheard your secrets.

I noticed reddened ears and flushed cheeks. Slips of paper dropped into a musician's tube. Hands too eager to slide into a pocket. Too many hurried visits of a jeweler or a seamstress. I knew of leather skirts underneath fancy dresses that caught the dripping urine, of maids burying bloodied rags in the garden, of frantic gasps for air that could not frighten death away.

I couldn't smell fear, but I could see the signals it sent. Hearts speeding up, eyes widening, hands becoming unsteady, cheeks taking on an ashen hue. Words becoming abrupt, silences too long. I had seen it grow in rooms where every whisper was suspect, every gesture, or lack of it, was noted and stored for future use.

I had seen what fear could do to your heart.

ONE

1743–1744

I could have warned her when she arrived in Russia, this petty German princess from Zerbst, a town no bigger than St. Petersburg's Summer Garden, this frail girl who would become Catherine.

This court is a new world to you, I could have said to her, a slippery ground. Do not be deceived by tender looks and flattering words, promises of splendor and triumph. This place is where hopes shrivel and die. This is where dreams turn to ashes.

She has charmed you already, our Empress. With her simplicity, the gentle touch of her hand, the tears she dried from her eyes at her first sight of you. With the vivacity of her speech and gestures, her brisk impatience with etiquette. *How kind and frank Empress Elizabeth Petrovna is*, you have said. Others have, too. Many others. But frankness can be a mask, a disguise, as her predecessor has learned far too late.

Three years ago our bewitching Empress was but a maiden princess at the court of Ivan VI, the baby Emperor, and his Regent Mother. There had been a fiancé lost to smallpox, there had been other prospects derailed by political intrigues until everyone believed that, at thirty-two and without a husband, the youngest daughter of Peter the Great had missed her chance at the throne. They all thought Elizabeth Petrovna flippant and flighty then, entangled in the intricacies of her dancing steps and the cut of her ball dresses—all but a handful who kept their eyes opened wide, who gambled on the power of her father's blood.

The French call her "Elizabeth the Merciful." For the day before she stole the throne of Russia from Ivan VI, she swore on the icon of St. Nicholas the Maker of Miracles that no one under her rule would ever be put to death. True to her word, on the day of the coup, she stopped the Palace Guards from slashing Ivan's infant throat. She plucked the wailing baby Emperor from his crib and kissed his rosy cheeks before she handed him back to his mother and packed them both off to live in prison.

She likes when we repeat that no head has been cut off since the day she took power but forbids us to mention the tongues and ears. Or the backs torn to meaty shreds by the knout. Or the prisoners nailed to a board and thrown into a freezing river. Mercy, too, knows how to deceive.

Here in the Russian court, I could have warned the pretty newcomer from Zerbst, life is a game and every player is cheating. Everyone watches everyone else. There is no room in this palace where you can be truly alone. Behind these walls there are corridors, a whole maze of them. For those who know, secret passages allow access where none is suspected. Panels open, bookcases move, sounds travel through hidden pipes. Every word you say may be repeated and used against you. Every friend you trust may betray you.

Your trunks will be searched. Double bottoms and hollowed books will not hold their secrets for long. Your letters will be copied before they are sent on their way. When your servant complains that an intimate piece of your clothing is missing, it may be because your scent is preserved in a corked bottle for the time when a hound is sent to sniff out your presence.

Keep your hands on your pockets. Learn the art of deception. When you are questioned, even in jest, even in passing, you have mere seconds to hide your thoughts, to split your soul and conceal what you do not want known. The eyes and ears of an inquisitor have no equals.

Listen to me.

I know.

The one you do not suspect is the most dangerous of spies.

As soon as she seized the throne of Russia, Empress Elizabeth made no secret of her resolve to rule alone, without a royal husband. Since she would have no children to succeed her, she sent for her sister's orphaned son, Karl Peter Ulrich, the Duke of Holstein. When the young Duke was brought to her, lanky and bone-thin, his eyes blood-shot with exhaustion after the long journey, she pressed him to her heaving bosom. "The blood of the Romanovs," she announced, as he stiffened in her arms. "The grandson of Peter the Great." She presided over his conversion to the Orthodox faith, renamed him Peter Fyodo-rovich, and made him the Crown Prince. He was fourteen years old. She didn't ask him if he wished to live with her. She didn't ask him if he wanted to rule Russia one day. Now, right after his fifteenth birth-day, she didn't ask him if he wanted a bride.

Princess Sophie Fredrika Auguste Anhalt-Zerbst. It was her por-trait that arrived first, and I recall the grand moment of its unveiling. Portraits of this kind are not meant to render a likeness, but to entice.

"Her?" I heard Chancellor Bestuzhev say when the Empress men-tioned Sophie for the first time. "But why her?" The Chancellor men-tioned the need of crafty ties, and hedging one's bets. Europe required a careful balance of power, he cautioned. The Prussians were growing too strong as it was. "Your Highness should consider a Saxon prin-cess."

The Empress stifled a yawn.

"I've not decided anything yet," Elizabeth told him. Her nephew Peter was sitting at her feet, his long white fingers turning the tur-quoise ring around, as if he were tightening a screw.

In the weeks that followed I heard Sophie's father referred to as a prince of quite exceptional imbecility, a Prussian general not able to control his foolhardy wife for whom the shabby Court of Brunswick had become the measure of all grandeur. The Anhalt-Zerbsts were well connected but poor, shamelessly clamoring for Empress Elizabeth's attention, reminding her that she once almost married one of them, this tenuous link to Russia their only real hope of attaining significance.

When a footman parted the red velvet curtain, we saw a portrait of a slim and graceful figure standing by the mantel, a girl of fourteen, summoned from her studies. We saw the pale-green bodice of her gown, the dainty hands folded on her stomach. Whatever rumors may have reached us, Princess Sophie was not a cripple. No childhood illness had deformed her spine. There was an air of lightness around her; she seemed on the verge of breaking into a cheerful dance. Her chin was pointed, her lips small but shapely. Not quite pretty but fresh and playful, like a kitten watching a ball of yarn unfurl. The painter made sure we would not miss the exquisite pallor of her complexion, the softness of her eyes, the blue flecks of her pupils so striking a contrast to her raven-black hair. Nor could we overlook her ardent will to please.

Murmurs, hesitant and vague, filled the room. Courtiers' words mumbled and slurred so praise could still be retracted, blame turned into a veiled compliment. *The art of deception*, I thought, the eyespots on a butterfly's wing flickering for a lifesaving second. Grasshoppers that change their color with the seasons to match the fading leaves.

The grand gentlemen and ladies of the court were still looking at the portrait, but I knew there was something far more important to watch. The face of the Empress of Russia taking her first measure of this princess child who, if she willed it, would become her nephew's bride. The face I had learned to read.

There was a sigh, a slight twitch of Elizabeth Petrovna's lower lip. A moment of pensiveness, the same that descended upon her before the time of prayers. A tear slowly rolling down her rouged cheek.

My eyes returned to the portrait, and I knew what the Empress had perceived. In the painted features there was a slight but unmistakable hint of manliness, a distant echo of another, older face. The fiancé long dead. A memory that lingered and still moved her to tears.

"Lord be merciful. . . ."

When I heard the Empress of All the Russias whisper the prayer for the departed souls, I knew the Anhalt-Zerbsts had scored their first victory.

The chorus of voices rose, still hesitant, still unsure. No courtier wanted to risk Elizabeth's wrath. Like me, they had seen objects flung at anyone near her, a powder box exploding in a cloud of white dust, a silver statue of Amor and Psyche making a jagged dent in the floor. Like me, they had seen the quivering stump inside a mouth from which the tongue had been cut.

"Her dress is green," the Grand Duke Peter said. In German he drew out the vowels in an almost musical manner. It was only in Russian that he sounded awkward and harsh.

All eyes turned to him.

The Duke himself was dressed in a green velvet suit, embroidered with gold. At that time his face was not yet marred by smallpox. It was lean and pale but not unpleasant. The day before I had seen him stare at his hand, examining each finger as if it held some mystery worth pondering.

"What do you think, Peter?" Elizabeth asked the Grand Duke. I watched her smooth the sleeve of her dress, the rich burgundy brocade gown, play with the pearls that adorned it. "Does she look anything like this picture, Peter?"

"This is a good likeness," the Grand Duke said. "This is how I remember my cousin Sophie."

"Your *second* cousin, Peter."

"My second cousin," he agreed. "She is not a cripple."

"Who said she was a cripple?"

"I don't remember."

"Who told you she was a cripple, Peter?"

"I don't remember. My Blackamoor heard it. But it's not true. Sophie is very strong. In Eutin, she outran me every time we raced in the garden."

"Such display of vigor might not be such a good sign, Your Highness," Chancellor Bestuzhev remarked.

I looked at him. At the gray powdered curls of his wig, the bushy eyebrows, the soft lines of his smooth face. His velvet jacket was new, I noted, smartly cut, becoming. It was the color of dry blood. A miniature portrait of the Empress was pinned to his chest. More than once, I had seen the Chancellor leave Elizabeth's bedroom at dawn, his clothes rumpled, buttons undone, embers flickering in his black eyes.

A slippery eel? An old fox?

Had he missed what I had just seen? Was he still hoping the Empress had not set her mind on Sophie?

"Why not, my dear count?" Her Majesty frowned.

"Strong legs? A pointed chin? Women like that tend to be bossy. I've formed this opinion based on significant personal experience, Your Highness," Chancellor Bestuzhev continued, with a gracious bow. A slight titter traveled through the back of the room. The Chancellor's wife, known for her frequent storms of rage, had been endowed with a pointed chin.

Like an actor contemplating his next triumph, Bestuzhev added, "Experience I'd be pleased to tell Your Highness about at another, more opportune, time."

The Empress turned away from him.

"I've decided to invite Princess Sophie here," she said. "With her mother. Nothing official. The Anhalt-Zerbsts have received enough favors from me to show their gratitude."

I could see shoulders dropping in relief. Courtiers hurried to express their agreement, to offer reasons why they thought the Empress had made an excellent choice.

She was very cheerful that day. The embroidered trim of her gown shimmered as she moved, and I remember wondering who would get it, for the Empress never wore the same dress twice.

The portrait of the little German Princess with an eager smile was moved aside. Stretching on the daybed the footmen had fetched for her, Empress Elizabeth ordered Count Razumovsky to sing. There was no impatience on her face when he plucked the strings of his favorite bandura to tune it. She didn't even scold the Grand Duke when he stuck his thumb in his mouth, probing his gums. A week before, he had lost another rotting tooth.

If Chancellor Bestuzhev was disappointed about the imperial decision, he did not show it. I saw him bend to murmur something into Elizabeth's ear. She smacked him playfully with her folded fan. He took her hand in his and kissed it. Slowly, his lips lingering over her fingertips.

I didn't look away.

I was sixteen then, rosy-cheeked and nimble, and already stripped of illusions, one of the countless, nameless girls in the Empire of the East. Pretty enough to pinch or pat on her buttocks as she passed by or to whisper lascivious words into her ear. I knew that "a ward of the Crown" was but a fancy name for a beggar whose luck could run out at any time.

So many of us, orphaned or abandoned, were left at the Empress's feet. Clamoring for a nod of her head or her amused grin. For a chance, however slight, that she might think us worthy of another look. That we could be of use.

Count Razumovsky, a Ukrainian choirboy who had once charmed his Tsarina with his hooded black eyes and rich baritone, cleared his throat. The Emperor of the Night, we called him, the most forgiving of all Elizabeth's lovers. The thick curtains were drawn, the candles lit. In the flickering light, Elizabeth's face took on a silvery glow, and the room filled with the soothing, mournful chords of her favorite *duma*.

If you find someone better, you will forget me;
If you find someone worse, your thoughts will bring me back.

My father was a bookbinder. In Poland, where we came from, there was not enough work for him—a young man with a wife, children, and an ambition to move up in the world.

We would have gone to Berlin, where my father had once been an apprentice, had it not been for Prince Kazimierz Czartoryski, Castellan of Vilnius, who had given him his first commission. Impressed by my father's craft, the Prince promised to remember him. He kept his word. When Empress Anne of Russia wanted precious old volumes restored, the Prince said, "I know just the man. An artisan of true grace and imagination, especially skilled in gold tooling."

It was the spring of 1734. I was seven years old and my baby brother had just been born.

"Tell him to come to St. Petersburg," the Empress said. "Here a good man always has a future."

A city willed by one man, my father called St. Petersburg. The new capital of Russia, he told me, had been built in defiance of the unruly waves of the Neva and the ruthless darkness of northern winters.

We came by ship in the fall of 1734. Only three of us. My baby brother had been buried in the Warsaw cemetery. Yet another son who would not grow to learn his father's trade and inherit his father's business.

"This is our chance," Papa told us, pointing at the flat line of the land from which, out of the morning haze, I discerned wavering shapes of buildings as if drawn by a child's hand. Behind us, all I saw was the ship's foamy wake.

"God willing," Mama said, her voice softened with hope. In Warsaw, a fortune-teller had told my mother that she would live long enough to see her daughter marry a great and powerful man. "A noble," the woman had said, giving Mama a lingering look. It was all hidden in the crisscrossing lines of Mama's palm, loss that would come and go, joy that would shine after a long journey. My father frowned when he heard these predictions, but Mama was so happy that she gave the woman a silver coin.

My mother was of noble blood, although her family was too poor to make much of their status. "A house, a barn, a few cows," my father used to say and laugh. "You could tell they were not peasants, for before your grandfather set off to plow his few acres, he put on his white gloves and his saber."

My father liked to talk of the day he surprised my mother in a relative's parlor, as she was bending over a length of lace, needle in hand. He had been summoned to pick up some old books for binding, and Mama had been sent there by her widowed mother in hope of better prospects. Feeling his eyes on her, she faltered and pricked her finger. "You frightened me," she exclaimed, and sucked on her wound.

He fell in love that very instant.

When he returned, a few days later, he gave her a book he had bound himself. *La Princesse de Clèves*, Mama told us, teasing him laughingly about his choice, proud of her polished French. The story of a wife in love with another man? A husband spying on his wife? What were you thinking then, she would ask Father.

He wasn't thinking. He was besotted. He wanted no one else but her.

"A clever girl like you shouldn't be mending lace," he had said that day.

She took the book he'd brought. He watched how reverently she opened the gilded pages. How she raised her eyes to take in his smart figure, compact and fine-boned, his brown, determined eyes. The silver buttons he had polished. The hands that knew how to give a new life to a tattered volume eaten with mold. She listened when he told her of Berlin, where he had seen his first cameo bindings and where he had heard his first opera.

"A bookbinder's wife," my grandmother said and sighed when, a few weeks later, my father asked her for my mother's hand. My grandmother didn't care for my father's learning, or his skills. He was in trade. Her only daughter was going down in the world. It was to appease her that my parents named me after her. She died before my first birthday.

Barbara, or *Basieńka,* my mother called me. In Polish, as in Russian, a name has many transformations. It can expand or contract, sound official and hard or soft and playful. Its shifting shape can turn its bearer into a helpless child or a woman in charge. A lover or a lady, a friend or a foe.

In Russian, I became *Varvara.*

Days after we arrived in St. Petersburg, my father began working for the Imperial Library. "The writings of wise and learned men," he called it. "A collection worthy of a great monarch." Peter the Great had amassed fifteen thousand books during his grand tour of Europe; many of them were now in dire need of my father's skills.

My mother was beaming with pride. Her mother had been wrong. She had chosen her husband well. What was impossible in Poland would be possible here in Russia. Empress Anna had asked to see the new bindings as soon as they were finished, and in her mind's eye Mama already saw me at court, catching the eye of some noble.

"She is still a child," my father protested.

"More time for you, to make a name for yourself," Mama would retort. For her the tattered, moldy volumes from the Imperial Library were a promise, a sign of future favors, so richly deserved.

By the end of our second year in St. Petersburg, we were living in our own house. True, it was on Vasilevsky Island with its long-abandoned, silt-choked canals, with its brush-covered fields where wolves still roamed at night, but it was far better than what we had in Warsaw.

The house was wooden but spacious, with a cellar for my father's workshop. He took on apprentices. We had maids and footmen, a cook, a carriage and a sleigh. My mother hired a French and a German tutor for me, and then a dancing and deportment master who assured her that he had once taught Countess Vorontzova's niece. When the time came, Mama was determined her daughter would be ready for a good marriage.

⌒

Every day, as soon as my lessons ended, I sneaked into my father's workshop. Seated on a small stool in a corner, I watched the slow, deliberate movements of Papa's hands as he chose the right piece of leather from the pile he kept by the door. "The best part of a skin is near the backbone," he would tell me. "The rest is not as even in color." I loved watching when he placed the pattern for the binding on the leather, moved it so as to avoid imperfections, and, using the softest parts of the skin, finally cut it.

He had shown me books touched by lesser craftsmen, books he was now obliged to repair. "This should never have happened," he would say, shaking his head and pointing to where gold leaf had come unglued or had tarnished from too much heat. His secrets were simple. The sharpness of a paring knife, he would tell me, was far more important than the strength of the hands. Like his apprentices, I was to learn that forcing a dull knife would only damage the leather.

"Will you remember what I'm teaching you, Barbara?" he wondered.

Breathing in the workshop odors of vinegar and soot and glue, I promised that I would.

"Having aspirations," my mother called it. She was a practical woman. Her dreams were always rooted in possibility. Wasn't her husband a man of exceptional talents? Empress Anna had not yet received him, but hadn't a princess of the court summoned him to the Winter Palace once already?

It was Mama's favorite story. In a small garret room in the upper reaches of the palace, Princess Elizabeth had handed my father her treasure, a tattered prayer book with large letters that did not strain her eyes. "A gift from someone dear to me," she'd told him. "I don't even know if it can be repaired."

Gingerly, my father took the book and caressed the cracked leather of its cover. He examined the rubies and sapphires that made the shape of a cross, pleased that none were missing. He took note of the loose pages and thinning stitches.

"Yes," he told Princess Elizabeth. "It can."

She kept looking at him.

"Not a speck will be lost," he promised the Princess, extracting a handkerchief from his breast pocket and wrapping the book.

Over the next two weeks my father polished and secured each jewel, glued in loose pages, and stiffened the fragile covers. When the layer of grime was wiped off, the leather turned out to be mostly un-damaged. Good calfskin, the color of rust, he would say, needed but a touch of birch oil to last forever. In the end it was the prayer book's gilding that suffered the most from time and touch, but gold tooling was my father's greatest skill. When he finished, no one could tell where old pattern ended and new began.

Elizabeth took her prayer book in her hands, turning the pages, carefully at first, marveling at how sturdy they were. The daughter of Peter the Great put her hand on Papa's shoulder and let him see the tears of gratitude that shone in her eyes.

It had happened before, Mama reminded us. Serve the Tsar well, and you can rise through the Russian Table of Ranks. Promoted to the fourteenth grade, a commoner becomes a noble. A minor noble at first, but when he reaches the eighth grade, his noble status extends to his wife and children.

"And then?" I'd ask.

"A princess of the court always needs beautiful and clever girls to serve her, Barbara. Once you are at the Winter Palace, nothing is im-possible."

The Imperial Library was housed in the west wing of Kunstkamera, the Tsar's museum, for it was not just learned books that Peter the Great wanted to display but also his curiosities. There were precious stones and fossils, herbaria with plants from the New World, and his collection of monsters: glass jars with specimens of human and animal deformities the Tsar had ordered his officials to bring him from all across Russia.

"A museum is a temple of knowledge," my father told me, "a lit lamp that sends its rays into the darkness, the proof of the infinite variety of life."

For Peter the Great had a mission—to enlighten his people. There was no evil eye, no spells capable of transforming a healthy fetus into a monster, because, as the Tsar's words inscribed on a Kunstkamera wall declared, *The Creator alone is the God of all creatures, not the Devil.*

"A cursed place," our maids called the museum, crossing themselves every time they passed the Kunstkamera's heavy doors. They spoke of rooms in which eyes of the dead stared at the living, where body parts were waiting for their rightful owners, who would— they believed—come to fetch them and give them the burial they deserved.

Year after year, every Monday morning, my father went to Kunstkamera to select the books he would work on that week. When he returned home, his garments smelled of mold and dust. The maids soaked them overnight before washing, and said that they still stained the water black. I saw them cross themselves the Orthodox way, with three fingers touching, left shoulder first, before they picked up my father's clothes. "The Devil's work," they said, "never brought anything good."

"Are you not afraid of monsters?" I asked my father once.

Papa answered with his own question. "How can anything on this earth be unnatural, excluded from the laws of creation?" In his eyes I saw a flicker of disappointment in me. "You should never say the word *monster*, Barbara."

I thought about this a lot. I still do. I watch for words that shape our thoughts, our destiny.

A tongue.

A gazette.

An Empress.

A spy.

Six years after we arrived in St. Petersburg, Empress Anne died, having named baby Ivan VI her successor and her German minister, Biron, Regent. The Palace Guards did not approve. Scheming foreigners, they muttered, were taking hold of Russia, grabbing what wasn't theirs. What would they do next? Strike out at the Orthodox faith? The Regency swiftly passed from Biron to the baby's mother, Anna Leopoldovna, but the rumors of foreign masters did not stop. When a year later, on November 25 of 1741, Princess Elizabeth, the only surviving child of Peter the Great, stormed the Winter Palace, Russia rejoiced. It was high time, everyone said, for a wholly Russian princess to claim what was still left of her inheritance.

As soon as Princess Elizabeth seized the throne she had exiled the German advisers. A triumphant decree announced the end of "degrading foreign oppression." Another imperial ukase forbade anyone to mention Ivan VI's name. All coins with his image had to be returned to the mint and exchanged for new ones. Anyone defying Elizabeth's order would have their right hand cut off. By April of 1742, the princess who once asked my father to bind her precious prayer book was crowned the Empress of All the Russias.

"Go to her," my mother urged my father. "Remind her who you are. Offer your services at her court."

My father hesitated. Even though the work at the Imperial Library ended with Empress Anne's death, he had built up enough of a reputation to get plenty of private commissions. "We are doing fine," I would hear him tell Mama. "We are happy. What else do we need?"

"Do it for your daughter's sake," she replied. "So that we won't have to worry for her future."

Papa did not refuse my mother's bidding, but he always found reasons for the delay. The Empress was getting ready for a pilgrimage. The Empress was weakened by the Lenten fasts. Easter was coming.

The court was awaiting the arrival of the Empress's nephew; the court was too busy with the coronation; too many petitioners were lining up outside the Throne Room.

And then on a bright April morning, when Mama came to my bedroom to wake me, I saw her falter, clutch her hand to her stomach, and wince. "It's nothing, Basieńka," she assured me, forcing a smile. "I must've eaten a bad oyster." The whites of her eyes were flecked with red.

"I'm better already," Mama said, as she helped me put on the morning dress the maid had laid out. "Hurry up, Papa is waiting for us."

Our Easter had passed, but in the old-style Orthodox calendar, the Holy and Great Friday was still a week away. Our maids were already fasting, while we sat down to our usual breakfasts.

That April morning, the kitchen smelled of fresh coffee and burned bread. The scullery maid, ordered to warm up a loaf on the stove, had left it on for too long, and the thick slice on my breakfast plate had a hard, charcoal crust. Papa told me to scrape the char off with a butter knife. I did, but it still tasted bitter.

After breakfast, my father went downstairs to his workshop and I waited for Mama to ask me to read from one of her favorite French novels while she embroidered my new dress. But she didn't. A shadow descended on her face. She moaned.

"It's nothing." Words broken in mid-breath, clipped with pain.

I remember the faint squeak of doors leading to the room where rows of bottles filled with herbal infusions stood on a shelf, each labeled in my mother's neat handwriting. I remember the sharp scent of mint on the glass stopper I held as Mama measured out thirty drops that sank into a lump of sugar, staining it green. She let the sugar dissolve in her mouth before swallowing it and then, still trying to smile, she adjusted the golden chain with a Virgin pendant on my neck. As she led me to the parlor, I thought of how soft and warm her hand was, with tapered fingers, just like mine.

In the parlor Mama said that she needed to lie down, for just a short while. I shouldn't bother Papa, for he had important work to do. Without him, the apprentice would surely damage the bindings.

"I'll feel better before the cannon is fired at Petropavlovsky Fortress at noon," she whispered. "I promise."

"Can I lie beside you?" I asked.

"Yes," she said, and made room for me on the ottoman. I must have looked frightened, for she stroked my cheek and made me swear I would not worry. I was fifteen years old and didn't know of promises that cannot be kept, of shivers that would not go away.

By the evening she was dead.

In the days after my mother died I tottered through hushed rooms, frightened and lost. Silence rang in them, but I was consumed by a belief that I could still catch her if I hurried. Sometimes I could feel her presence, her silky kiss, the gentle squeeze of her hand. "I have something to tell you, Basieńka," her soft voice promised. "Something important. Something you need to know."

I didn't turn in the direction of the whisper. I didn't want to see that she was not there.

It was in the long empty days after Mama's death that I learned to listen.

"Take them," I heard a servant urge another, pointing at my mother's knit silk stockings embroidered with roses. "Master won't know!"

Balls of dust gathered in the corners while the maids gossiped in the alcove as if I was not there. In the street I saw a woman wearing my mother's bonnet and her sash. Two of Mama's silver jugs had also disappeared.

People betray themselves so carelessly in front of children. Clues drop like fairy-tale bread crumbs that mark a path through the forest. Sometimes they whisper, but my hearing has always been superb. Sometimes they switch languages, but I have always been clever with words.

"What does it matter?" Papa said, when I begged him to search the maid's trunk. "It won't bring your mother back, will it?"

The maid who took the knit stockings sickened first. She complained of pains in her stomach, and her face flushed beet-red with fever. "Nothing good ever comes from working for foreigners," her father muttered when he came with a hay cart to fetch her body. Before leaving, he spat on the ground and waved a fist at my father and me. Then the butcher's apprentice, two houses away from us, woke up with his back covered in a red rash, as if the bathhouse demons had flayed his skin.

It was all our fault, I would overhear in the days that followed. Poisonous, hushed voices stalked me in the kitchen, the alcove, our garden with its flimsy fence.

We were foreigners. Roman Catholics, Poles. We didn't eat carrion or beaver tails as other Latins had done, but we were up to no good. We had come to Russia with falseness in our hearts, wishing to convert Russians to our Latin faith.

The maids recalled my mother's sins. Hadn't she said that there was nothing wrong in depicting the face of God the Father? Hadn't she scolded me when—in my innocence—I crossed myself in the Orthodox way like them, with three fingers touching, from left to right? Was it a wonder that she was struck dead? "Just as she reached for bread," I heard the maids gossip. "On the day of *our* fast."

I do not recall when I heard the word *cholera* first, but suddenly everyone repeated it. A furtive, menacing word I thought it, like a curse, drawing a circle around Papa and me that few dared to cross. Before leaving, the cook asked to have her last month's wages forwarded to her brother-in-law. A footman packed his trunk and departed the same day. Two of the maids followed. Then the oldest and most experienced of Papa's apprentices disappeared. Deliveries were left at our doorstep; people crossed to the other side of the street at the sight of us. Many of Papa's clients avoided us, too, and soon my father had to let the remaining apprentice go.

"It's nothing but fear," Papa kept telling me. "We have to be strong, Barbara. This will pass."

I tried to believe him.

Cholera did not strike us, as the maids predicted, and there was no epidemic. No one else died in the following month, or the month after that. By mid-summer the talk subsided, yet our fortunes did not improve. Since we could no longer afford tutors, my father made me read passages from his German books as he worked, correcting my pronunciation. I thought them tedious, the descriptions of differences between grades of leather, or types of precision tools, but I didn't complain. As soon as I had finished reading, he showed me how to keep accounts, and I was glad to be of help.

"A few more lean months, Barbara," Papa would say, each time I finished adding up his meager commissions. In the evening, sipping his favorite drink, hot milk sweetened with honey, topped with a thick layer of melted butter and sprinkled with crushed garlic, he assured me that soon he would be back on his feet. He had not lost his skills, had he? The new Empress was Peter the Great's daughter. Soon, in Russia, books would be important again.

One morning in October, after I finished my daily reading, I watched my father bend over his workshop table in silence, to apply gold-leaf lettering to the spine of a book. He had often shown me how a shadow was cast on each side of the spine where it curved to the sides. These shadow lines marked the limits of the space that could be used for the letters. If gold tooling were to reach beyond them, after the book had been held open a few times, the gold would crack.

"I've been at the palace," Papa said. He paused before he continued. "Just as Mama wanted."

I held my breath.

"There were many petitioners. I lined up for hours before I was allowed into her presence. I didn't tell you before, for I wasn't sure it would make any difference. But your mother was right. The Empress had not forgotten the prayer book I restored for her when she was still just a princess."

He told Elizabeth of Mama's death, of how cholera had decimated his business and depleted his savings. "But it did not break my spirit, Your Majesty, or my faith in Russia," he assured her.

The new Empress was pleased. So pleased that she ordered her Quartermaster to send my father the Court Journals to bind. And she had asked about me.

"Bring your daughter here so I can see her," she had commanded.

My father turned his face away when he said these words, so I could not see the expression on his face, but his movements were unusually hesitant.

I still remember the title of the book my father was working on that day. Tacitus, *The Annals and the Histories*. It was the only title I ever saw him work on where the letters crossed the shadow lines.

In the middle of November, seven months after my mother died, on a murky day veiled in chimney smoke, my father took me to the palace. The hackney coach took the Isaakovsky pontoon bridge, which—by the end of December—would be replaced by the winter ice road across the river. Nestled against my father's side, I imagined the Empress smiling at me, extending her hand to be kissed. Inside the carriage, the fur blanket gave off a faint smell of birch tar and kvass.

Before we set off, my father sat me on his lap and kissed the top of my head. He said that he wished to secure my future in case God called him, like Mama, before his time.

"You have no one but me to look after you, my child. I cannot sleep in peace when I think I might die and leave you all alone," he whispered.

He held me tightly. I breathed in his smell, not the familiar whiff of vinegar and glue but the rare scent of eau de cologne and snuff.

Empress Elizabeth. I thought of angels when I first saw her, of the glittering messengers of God, their winged arms herding lost children to safety. In a silvery dress, a single white feather crowning her forehead, she floated on the aroma of orange blossoms and jasmine.

"Come here, child," she said, her voice especially sweet as she pronounced that last word.

I hesitated. One does not approach angels without fear.

"Go on," my father urged me, his hand pushing me forward.

I walked reluctantly toward the Empress of All the Russias, my
gaze cast downward, fixed on the hem of her dress sewn with gold
thread and pearls. I prayed the curtsy I had practiced for days did not
betray my unease.

The Empress took my chin in her hands and raised my eyes to
meet hers. "What a pretty smile," she murmured.

I felt her fingers on my cheeks, a smooth, soft caress. I let her words
thicken around me, like the warmth radiating from the white-and-
blue-tiled stoves of the palace. My father had told me that the Empress had a good heart, that she, too, knew how it felt to lose a mother
and fear the future. Didn't she bring her sister's orphaned son to her
own court? Hadn't she just made him Crown Prince?

"What's your name, child?" she asked.

"Barbara," I said.

"Varvara Nikolayevna, Your Highness," my father corrected, offering my name in the Russian way, with his name echoing after mine.

"Your father has asked me to take care of you if he dies, Varvara. Is
that what you, too, wish?"

"Yes, Your Highness," I said.

"Very well, then," the Empress said to my father. I saw her folded
fan touch his shoulder. "I'll take good care of her. You have my
promise."

My father stood a little stooped and motionless as the Empress
departed, with courtiers crowding upon her, praising her benevolence.
He lowered his head when a few of them stopped and inspected me
through their monocles, the looks you give a caged bird. His hand
when he squeezed mine was cold and moist with sweat.

Did he guess what would happen to me?

I stood by my father's side, silent and trembling until the last courtier disappeared and the guards closed the gilded doors. I longed to ask which one of them was the Grand Duke Peter, but I didn't dare.

It was beginning to snow as we left the palace. The hackney carriage was waiting for us, the driver greeting us with a broad smile and vodka breath. By the shore of the Neva, the wind played with stray litter, a torn straw hat, a scrap of burlap, a wooden toy wheel with broken spokes.

Convicts with shaved heads were being marched along the embankment, a whole group of them in shackled pairs. Many had their nostrils slit. Some, with the narrow eyes of Tartars, were missing a nose or an ear. As the soft, wet snow intensified, their bare heads turned white.

Our carriage pulled onto the Isaakovsky bridge. Now that I had seen the inside of the palace, the fur blanket seemed even more threadbare, the smells of birch tar and kvass harder to ignore.

My father said, "It doesn't mean I'm going to leave you, Barbara. I'm just being prudent."

This is when I started to cry.

I didn't see my father die. One evening at the end of December, he pushed away a bowl of kasha and sour cream. He was not hungry. All he asked for was his usual cup of hot milk. He would take it in his bedroom, he said.

We had just had our first Christmas without my mother. Days seemed fragmented, broken into odd pieces, a plate too full, a pinching shoe, an empty chair. The hollow, choking feeling overwhelmed me every time I had to admit that, by then, even the shawls hidden in Mama's closet smelled of nothing more than dry rosemary.

In a few days we would welcome the new year. The year I would turn sixteen, and would no longer be a child.

The new maid who took the milk upstairs screamed when she opened the door. She wouldn't let me inside but made the sign of the cross over my head and tried to hold me in her arms, muttering her incantations against fate, as useless as hope. Her apron still smelled of Christmas baking, of raisins, vanilla, and cloves.

"Call your priest, Varvara," she insisted, barring the door with her body. "For pity's sake, send someone for your priest!"

I pushed her away.

When our priest arrived with an altar boy, Papa was lying on his bed, his face ashen and still. His fingertips were purple, as if he had bruised them in the last moments of his life. On the desk there was a sheet of paper with his writing on it. A quill lay next to it, the nib chipped.

"His heart broke," the priest said, and I imagined my father's heart shattered into razor-sharp, transparent slivers.

My father's last words contained no message for me. Instead, he had jotted down some reminders for the following day. Ever since the news of Empress Elizabeth's patronage of him spread, orders for new bindings had been pouring in. He planned to buy two more jars of glue. His tools needed repairing, knives had to be sharpened. The tip of his favorite polisher was broken. A new place should be found for storing leather, for he spotted signs of mildew on the pigskin. *Sweet almond oil*, he had written, *works best for greasing the surface.*

The priest knelt and intoned the Prayer for the Dead. I too fell to my knees. *Wieczne odpoczywanie*, I tried to repeat after him, *Eternal rest*, but my voice caught on these solemn words and broke.

Useless, I thought, for on that dark December evening all that mattered were silence and tears.

The new commissions had not been enough. My father had too many debts, I was told. Our house and the contents of his workshop had to be auctioned off. I saw my mother's favorite carpet rolled and taken away. I saw my father's books stacked in crates on a wagon. My whole inheritance amounted to a small bundle and a few rubles wrapped in a piece of cloth.

The Empress, I kept thinking, promised to take care of me.

It was February of 1743, the coldest month of the year, when I arrived at the Winter Palace. The footman with sour breath who had brought me told me to wait, leaving me in the servants' hall. No one took any notice of me but a palace cat, which kept rubbing itself against my ankle. I saw servants scurrying back and forth, chased by fear. I heard slaps, curses, invisible feet pattering up and down service corridors. An icy draft of air touched my cheek. Fear swelled in my throat.

I shrank inside my skin and waited.

When dusk fell, a tall, silvery-blond woman entered the room. Her dress looked heavy and must have been warm, for I caught a pungent whiff of her sweat. She gave me an impatient look. Pushing away the cat, she began complaining of smudged doorways, marks on window-panes, and fur on the ottomans. The German vowels gave her Russian a sharp, accusatory sound.

"I'm Varvara Nikolayevna," I ventured. "The Empress sent for me."

"I know who you are," the woman snapped, her dark eyebrows drawing together, a dismissive smile on her lips. I decided that her face looked like a turtle's, far too small for her big body. Later I would learn her name: Madame Kluge, the Chief Maid, charged with my welfare.

"Come, girl," she ordered, and I followed her, cradling my bundle, noting the worn floorboards under my feet, the chinks in the paneling, the balls of dust gathering in the corners. A thought came that I was nothing but a fly, allowed a few steps before someone would bring down the swatter.

We didn't go very far. In the palace kitchen I was given a plate of thin gruel and a tin cup of kvass. I was to eat quickly, for Madame Kluge had no time to waste. I was not to speak, for Madame Kluge did not care for what I had to say. When I finished, Madame Kluge led me to the servants' quarters. There were seventeen of us in a room reeking of chamber pots and mold. Mice scurried under the beds, hid in our shoes. The Empress's cats, I heard, were fed too well to bother with vermin.

"Be ready when I come for you in the morning," Madame Kluge told me and was gone.

I sat on the hard, narrow bed, the only empty one in the room. I kissed the Virgin pendant my mother had given me. At first the other girls cast curious glances at me, but when they saw me cross myself the Latin way, they looked right through me.

I slept badly, the noises of the room stealing into my sleep: grinding of teeth, moans, wind smacking the frozen windowpanes. The room was icy. Once I woke startled, feeling someone's hand sneaking underneath my thin blanket. I sat up in my bed, my heart thumping, and looked around, but everyone in the room seemed sound asleep. I bit myself on the arm to see if I had not dreamed the clammy touch. Next to me, a girl groaned.

When I finally fell into deep sleep my mother came to me and brushed my hand with something wet and warm. "Let's go, Basieńka. The Empress is waiting for you," she said, and I followed her ghostly, flickering form through the darkness.

In the morning, when I thought no one was looking, I hid the coins I brought with me under a loose floorboard next to my bed. That evening, when I lifted the floorboard to check on my inheritance, I found the rag limp and empty, my money gone.

Madame Kluge returned later in the morning, just as she had promised. She had found a place for me in the Imperial Wardrobe. She hoped my mother had at least taught me how to sew.

She didn't even stop to hear my answer.

I walked behind her, her voice a scolding din in my ears. She knew my kind. Stray cats expecting bowls of cream. People were having children right and left, and then wanted others to care for them. Far too many people were taking advantage of the Empress's good heart. Rubles didn't grow on trees. Sausages and loaves of bread didn't fall like rain from the sky.

In the Imperial Wardrobe, Madame Kluge told me to make myself useful. "And don't let me hear any complaints about you, girl."

My embroidery brought me no praise. My stitches were crooked, and I mixed up my colors. My mother did not raise me well, I heard. When I was given buttons to sort and sew on, I struggled to thread the needle, making a knot at the end that was too big and did not hold.

No one spoke to me, except to give me orders. The other seam-stresses, deft and fast, bent over their work, busy talking of Russia's new Crown Prince. They pursed their lips and called him a poor or-phan deprived of his mother's love. I heard that he was witty, and kindhearted. That he remembered the name of everyone he had ever met and every tune he had ever heard. Merely a year since he arrived and his Russian was good enough to give orders and understand what people said to him. His Orthodox name, Peter Fyodorovich, fitted him so much better than the German Karl Ulrich. He liked *bliny* and sturgeon soup. He liked kasha and mushrooms. In the Winter Palace the grandson of Peter the Great was growing healthier and stronger with each day.

Now that Russia had an heir to the throne, the seamstresses pre-dicted balls and masquerades. The Empress would need many new outfits and gowns. There would be no idle moments in the Imperial Wardrobe.

By the end of each morning, my feet were numb from the cold, my fingers swollen with needles' pinpricks. I had but a slice of black bread to eat, with nothing but a weak tea to soften it in my mouth.

"Is that all you've accomplished?" Madame Kluge scolded, snatch-ing the dress I had been working on and waving it like a standard to spark a chorus of giggles.

I bent my head and wept quietly. Madame Kluge handed me a knife and watched as I cut off the buttons I had sewn. I would not get my supper that night, I heard. I didn't deserve a proper meal until I learned to do a proper day's work.

On my way back to the servants' room I peered through a small opening in the window glittering with frost. In the palace yard a mule was pulling a big cart filled with slabs of frozen meat, its driver hurrying to make room for an imperial sleigh. As soon as the sleigh stopped, a young man jumped out and rushed inside the palace. I wondered if it could have been the Crown Prince himself, but there was no one I could ask.

I thought of a basket filled with buttons, of rows upon rows of dresses enveloped in lengths of silk and kept in large leather trunks, dresses I would never be allowed to touch. I thought of the web of wrinkles around Madame Kluge's narrow lips, her sour voice, the drop of yellow pus that gathered in the corner of her right eye.

I slipped into my narrow bed. My stomach rumbled, and I pressed it with my fingertips. A palace cat walked by without casting one look at me. I didn't think I slept, but I must have, for I dreamed of eating steaming dumplings from a plate as big as the moon.

When the Empress was cold at night, the seamstresses claimed, she summoned twenty guardsmen into her bedroom to warm the air up with their breaths.

When the Empress gave masquerades, all women had to dress in men's clothes and men had to wear hooped gowns and totter on high heels. And none of the court ladies could match Her Highness for the grace of her shapely legs.

Threading their needles, pinching the folds of the satin trims and frothy lace, the seamstresses gossiped about what would become of the handsome soldier who played a serpent in the palace play. The Empress, they said, asked about him twice already. The cats that slept on her bed wore velvet jackets and hats. They feasted on fried chicken breasts and lapped milk from silver dishes.

I kept my eyes on the sewing, but the basting I was given to do came out crooked. My stitches were too long. I had to rip off everything I did. The dresses were heavy and slid off my lap to the floor, gathering dust. Another sign of my clumsiness.

And I was slow, far too slow.

"Do as you are told," I heard, when I tried to defend my efforts. "Don't speak back to your betters."

This is what they all wanted from me, I thought, bitterness lashing at me like a spring shower. Leave no mark on the sheets I slept on, on the rags that passed for towels in the servants' room. Shrink so their eyes could slide over me without noting my presence. They wanted me to disappear, to crumble into a handful of dust, so that some maid could brush me off the floor, wipe my traces away, and not even remember she did so.

Once you are at the Winter Palace, nothing is impossible. Now that I was an orphan, my mother's words tormented me. There was nothing frivolous in wishing to advance in the world. It stopped one from becoming invisible.

Every morning the Mistress of the Wardrobe dressed up wooden dolls for the Empress, clothes dummies, like the ones textile merchants put in their windows to display their wares. At court these dolls were called "pandoras"—little pandoras if they modeled day or informal dresses, big pandoras if they were draped in ceremonial robes and evening gowns. Madame Kluge carried the pandoras to the Imperial Bedroom, for the Empress to decide which outfits she would wear that day.

I thought of my mother's aspirations. I thought of what the Empress had promised to my father.

I gathered my courage and pleaded with Madame Kluge to remind the Empress of my existence when she presented the pandoras. I could read in French and in German. I had a good voice, pleasant and steady. I could sing, too. My hands were clumsy with sewing, but my handwriting was neat and even. Could she not ask the Empress to let me serve her?

Madame Kluge didn't even let me finish. I saw her hand rise, I felt the stinging pain of her slap across my cheek.

"You are a nobody, girl. This is who you are. A *nobody*. And a no-body is who you'll always be."

I didn't wait for another slap. I hurried back to my place and picked up the dress I was working on. My cheek stung, and I pricked my finger, drawing a bead of blood.

Behind me I heard other seamstresses mutter about how the Empress didn't care much about either books or writing. And even if she cared, didn't she have more important people than a Polish stray to assist her?

I could feel my heart harden. I knew myself smarter than Madame Kluge, smarter than the maids who were now laughing at me. I imagined the Empress coming in and seeing me bent over her gown. As beautiful as I remembered her from that first day I'd seen her, smelling of orange blossom, a feather in her powdered hair.

"What are you doing here, Varvara Nikolayevna?" she would ask. "Why has no one brought you to me? What fool gave you this sewing to do?"

I imagined Madame Kluge's unease, her lips stammering apologies and pleas for forgiveness. "She is my ward," the Empress would dis-miss it all in anger, "and I shall take care of her, just as I promised her father."

Madame Kluge, the color drained from her face, her eyes cast low, would bend her head. And then her turtle's face would flush with fear, as the Empress ordered her out of her sight.

My own fate would be assured. I would wear silk dresses with wide sleeves that made my hands look slender. I would sleep in the alcove by the Imperial Bedroom. No one, ever, would pass me by without seeing me.

Weeks went by, and in the Imperial Wardrobe I found myself more and more awkward and slow. The blisters on my fingers never got a chance to heal; my shoulders ached from constant bending. Other seamstresses were praised for their stitches, while my efforts were never noticed. Each time Madame Kluge saw me, she gave me a haughty look of scorn.

The daily bowl of kasha with a thin sauce kept the worst of hunger away, I had a roof over my head, and yet none of it mattered. I was an orphan at the mercy of strangers who kept me away from the Empress. If I was able to talk to her, remind her who I was and what she had promised my father, my luck would surely change.

One raw April day, emboldened by despair, I wrote a note to the Empress and pinned it inside the shawl wrapped over the big pandora's dress. I reminded Her Imperial Highness of the prayer book my father had restored for her and of her promise to assure my future. I wrote, *I lie awake, day and night, thinking of the day Your Majesty touched my face.*

Madame Kluge brought the note back with a triumphant smirk. She made me read my own words aloud to the titters of other seamstresses. The bit about my father, especially. *An artisan of true grace and imagination*, I had written, *a man who had always believed in the greatness of the Russian heart.*

"We like big, fancy words, don't we?" she said and sneered, before tearing my note to pieces.

I didn't answer.

"A stray will always be a stray," she hissed. If I persisted in my underhanded ways, she predicted a future collecting horses' dung in the street. "Which your illustrious father would be doing now, had he not hurried out of this world."

I did not know how to hide the hatred in my eyes.

Madame Kluge took out her horse whip and lashed it across my shins. I felt a searing flash of pain, then another. I watched the skin of my legs turn white first, then red.

I clenched my teeth and vowed never again to cry.

A month later I was still waking up long before dawn. I would slip out of the chilly room where the sewing maids slept, and wander through the corridors like one of the palace cats. The Empress, I had heard, didn't sleep much at night. Perhaps, if I kept walking through the palace corridors, I would run into her or the Grand Duke. I heard of the liking he had taken to a Blackamoor his aunt gave him as a welcoming present. He had made the black-skinned man his adjutant. Wasn't I as worthy? All I craved was a chance to remind the Empress of my existence.

At first I sneaked into the palace kitchens, tempted by the smells of the rich food that never made its way onto the maids' table, but the pantries were always locked, and in the storage rooms all I ever found in abundance were cheap tallow candles. Sometimes the guards asked where I was going or coming from, but I would look them in the eye and say something saucy, like that I was not in the habit of divulging my mistress's secrets. A few younger guards always tried to steal a kiss as I passed, but I was nimble and all they ever managed was to brush my gown with their groping hands.

I didn't encounter the Empress, but I discovered rooms where tables were covered with carpets and where the cupboards were full of odd-looking musical instruments, rooms crammed with discarded furniture, paintings piled against walls. In such a room, I found a crate full of old books.

One by one, I took them out and wiped each clean of dust. They were mostly science books, on astronomy and medicine, books about tools and plants I had never seen. The bindings were simple, without adornments. My father would have frowned at the loosening seams and dark spots of mold on the pages.

It was on such a night that he found me—Count Bestuzhev, the Chancellor of Russia.

"Who are you?" he asked.

I hadn't seen him enter the room, absorbed as I was by the volume I'd pulled from the crate. Above its musky odor, I could detect the scent of vodka on his breath as he towered above me. There was another smell about him, too, an acrid smell of something I had no name for yet.

I knew who he was, for I'd often seen him walk through the palace corridors as if he were the lord of creation. His velvet ensembles, I heard, came from Paris. The handles of his canes were made of silver and whalebone. The seamstresses whispered that he frequently warmed the Imperial Bed and speculated how he looked in a woman's gown when he danced at the Empress's masquerades.

"I'm a palace girl, a seamstress," I replied.

"A seamstress who reads German books?"

In the room's semidarkness, I could feel his eyes on me. His fingers pressed under my chin as he tipped my head up and examined my face.

"Do you know who I am?" he asked.

"You're a slippery eel, a cunning fox," I answered evenly.

He laughed.

"How do you know that, palace girl?"

"I listen when I sew."

"And what is it that you hear?" He touched the nape of my neck, stroked the chain with the Virgin pendant my mother had given me. "Tell me."

"Chevalier Duval is lusting after the stable boys," I said boldly.

"Is he? How do you know?"

"Anton says so."

"And who is Anton?"

"The Grand Duke Peter's footman. The tall one, with crooked teeth. Anton is sweet on the Chief Seamstress and always tries to kiss her, but she thinks him a wastrel. All his talk is for nothing, she says."

My heart pounded. The book slid from my lap and fell to the floor, but I didn't bend to pick it up.

"The Saxon Envoy has had his mercury cure," I continued. "That's when the doctors make you drink lead and pray to the Greek gods."

"Is that so? And tell me, palace girl, do your ears ever hear talk of the Empress?"

"Sometimes."

"And what is said?"

"Madame Kluge says that the Empress shouldn't forget that Count Razumovsky loves her. I think Madame is in love with him herself. She blushes every time anyone mentions his name. I've seen her hide in the service corridor to hear him sing."

"Madame Kluge? That fat German nobody who fancies herself so important?" the Chancellor asked.

"She pinches her lips to make them look fuller. She pads her breasts with sashes."

He laughed again, a soft, throaty laugh of amused delight.

How deceptively simple and easy are the steps that change our lives. I didn't know the habits of the Empress then—the changing bedrooms, the eager lovers who awaited her midnight summons. Luck had brought the Chancellor of Russia here, I believed, into this forgotten part of the palace. Luck had made him talk to a clumsy seamstress of the Imperial Wardrobe. And luck would take me to the Empress's side.

There were more such nights in the months that followed. Nights wide-eyed and hopeful, nights of easy laughter and confessions I offered the Chancellor willingly, grateful for the luxury of his attention.

Madame Kluge kept a bottle in her drawer. She said it was eau de cologne, but I saw her and the Mistress of the Wardrobe take sips from it. Many sips.

Anton, the Grand Duke's footman, said he wished to crack the Blackamoor's skull against the wall.

Countess Golovina kept a serf girl under her bed at night to tell her stories when she could not sleep.

It wasn't hard to learn which of my stories pleased the Chancellor.

"Can a palace girl keep a secret?" the Chancellor asked me once.

"Yes," I told him.

"There is more to this palace, Varvara, than the Imperial Wardrobe."

I nodded.

"And there are more important stories. Only you must know where to look."

The Chancellor of Russia put his hand on mine.

I lowered my eyes, fixing them on the silver buckles of his shoes. They were square, encrusted with gems.

I listened.

He told me of godless people who plotted against our Empress, who wouldn't hesitate to raise their hands against her. Cunning and shrewd, they knew how to hide their thoughts, to bury them in false professions of friendship and loyalty.

They were everywhere, but they were hiding. The Empress had to know who they were and what evil they were trying to do.

There was no laughter in his voice. His eyes did not leave me when he spoke.

The righteous had to be rewarded, the evil punished. The wheat had to be separated from the chaff. My father had brought me here to the Imperial Palace for a reason. My father had trusted his Empress. His daughter could learn to be more important than he had ever thought possible—she could become the eyes and ears of the Empress.

Her tongue.

Her gazette.

The teller of the most important of stories.

"Someone the Empress can trust, Varvara," the Chancellor said. "And someone I can trust, too."

I was sixteen years old. I still believed in the common fantasy of the powerless that rulers would rule differently if only they knew what was concealed from them. I believed that eternal stuff of teary narratives in which kings or queens, sultans or emperors, change their hearts after learning the joys and sorrows of the common man.

"Look at me, Varvara," the Chancellor said. The hand that covered mine was heavy but warm and soft on my skin.

I raised my eyes, high enough to take in his clean-shaven face, the dimples at the corners of his mouth.

He had been watching me long enough, he told me. I was clever with languages. My Russian was impeccable. He had heard me speak German to one of the Grand Duke's footmen. I knew French, too. And Polish.

"Do you want to learn what I can teach you?"

I moved closer toward him, close enough to see tiny shapes of my own pale face reflected in his eyes.

I nodded.

Excitement rose in me like my mother's sweet raisin dough. I thought it easy, childishly simple. All I had to do was to learn from him and my life would take a turn for the better.

I didn't know yet how dangerous stories could be—that Chevalier Duval was already paying for the favors of stable boys with the secrets of the French king or that Anton would soon be interrogated and dismissed from the Grand Duke's service. But even if I had known, I wouldn't have stopped telling the tales that made the Chancellor of Russia see me.

Not then.

Not yet.

The white nights had barely ended when my lessons with the Chancellor began.

The first one was short.

The Chancellor pointed at a spying hole in the paneling.

"Stay here and watch," he said. "When I come back, you will tell me what you've seen."

Alone in the service corridor, I looked eagerly through the spyhole. I glimpsed the shadowy figure of a woman, sitting alone at her escritoire, reading by candlelight. There was nothing remarkable about her appearance or actions, and after a while I found it tedious to keep watching, but I did. An hour later, the woman put the book away, yawned, extinguished the candle, and left the room.

I thought of abandoning my hiding place to follow her, but I didn't know my way out of the secret corridor, so I stayed where I was. The day had been hot; the corridor was stuffy. My throat felt raw from breathing in the dusty air. A rivulet of sweat was running down my spine. I kept pinching my arm to keep myself awake.

The Chancellor asked me many questions when he came to fetch me. Did the woman wear a beauty spot? On which part of her face? Did she toy with her bracelet as she read? With her chatelaine, perhaps? How many buttons were there on her sleeves? How often did she turn the pages of the book?

With each unanswered question, my hopes sank. I felt tears sting my eyes. Nothing would ever change for me, I thought, bracing myself for my dismissal.

But the Chancellor of Russia lifted the sleeve of my dress, to display the bruises my pinching had left.

"Impatience is the only flaw you cannot afford," he said, smiling. "Everything else I can teach you."

There had been many lessons since that first one. Soon I knew how to pick locks with a hairpin, how to tell by the grain of wood where concealed drawers were hidden. I knew how secret pockets could be sewn into belts and traveling sacks, letters hidden in secret compartments of clocks or in the lining of shoes, tucked away in chimneys, the vents of stoves, beneath windowsills, inside cushions, or in the bindings of books.

I learned how to trail someone without being seen, to tell the true smiles from those that masked treason, to sneer at the flimsy hiding places underneath loose floorboards or under the pillows, places even the least apt of thieves could find.

I learned the virtues of distraction and the blessings of routine. I learned how to make my face blank, how to fade into the background.

Being invisible, I learned, was a virtue of spies.

A secret passage, narrow and steep, led up to the Chancellor's rooms. When he wanted to see me, a red kerchief appeared under my pillow, but on this chilly August night the Chancellor of Russia had sent one of his own footmen for me. I shivered with anticipation. The Empress had just moved back to the Winter Palace after the summer months spent at Peterhof. Could it be that the Chancellor would finally take me to her?

Quietly, careful not to wake the sewing maids, I slipped into my best dress, of white muslin, one of my mother's. The seamstress my father had hired before he died had to take it in, but when I caught the glimpse of myself in the mirror, the dress looked as if it was made for me. The shoes I wore were less accommodating. My mother's feet had been smaller than mine, and my toes felt pinched.

He was waiting for me in his chambers, the Chancellor of Russia, sitting in an armchair by the window, watching with narrowed eyes as I approached. He had taken off his wig, and I thought that without it, his head looked smaller, less imposing. I took in a bald patch on top of his head, the thick golden ring on his finger. I decided that the black velvet with silver trim suited him more than red, and that the lace collar looked particularly fine.

Was he the powerful man from my mother's dream?

"Come, palace girl."

There was a playful note in his voice that made me feel important, marked for grand things. My timidity peeled off like onion skin. Now he will take me to the Empress, I decided, but I knew enough to hide my joy. Hadn't he once said impatience is a flaw?

To break the chill of that August night, a birch log was burning in the fireplace, wet, for the wood hissed and smoked.

"I've sent the servants away," the Chancellor said, waving toward a small table set for two. "But you will not leave hungry."

I made a step toward it. It looked like an ordinary table, and the plates were empty.

"It's a mechanical table." The Chancellor laughed, seeing my bewilderment. "Just like the one the Empress has in her suite. You better learn how to use it." He motioned for me to sit. I did.

"Lift it," he said, pointing at a china plate. Underneath, there was a wooden lid.

"Open it," he said.

Inside, there was a pencil and a piece of paper.

"I know what mushy gruel Madame Kluge feeds the maids, so write what you fancy most," he told me. "Don't be shy."

Sturgeon soup, I wrote. *Roasted pheasant*.

"Anything you like. Go on." I smelled vodka on his breath.

Oysters.

Angel cake.

He pulled the strings that made the table descend down the shaft concealed beneath the floor. The boards closed over it. When the floor opened again, the table was laid with dishes, covered with silver lids. He lifted them one by one.

"Eat," he said. "The Empress doesn't like skinny girls. They make her feel clumsy."

His plate remained empty.

He watched me fumble with the oyster shells, fork up the morsels of cold, lemon-scented flesh. The fish soup was hot, and I ate too fast, scalding my tongue. Strands of smoked sturgeon lodged themselves between my teeth. I tried to loosen them with the tip of my tongue, but they wouldn't budge.

Two glasses stood by a half-empty bottle of cherry vodka. He filled them both to the brim.

"A gift from the Empress," he muttered. "A sign of imperial appreciation and gratitude."

If there was bitterness in these words, I ignored it.

"Her favorite drink, Varvara. Taste it!"

I took the glass in my hands, as carefully as I could, but I did spill some on the table. There was no tablecloth to absorb it, so I wiped the wood with my sleeve.

He laughed.

"Go on," he urged, his voice softer now. "It's really good."

I tasted the pink-colored liquid. It burned my throat. I put the glass down hastily.

He leaned toward me and raised his glass, emptying it in one gulp.

"Only a sip of imperial gratitude?" he mocked me. "You need to drink more of it."

I drank more. I felt a surge of dizziness. The room swirled and wobbled. I dug my fork into a thick slice of cake, smeared in whipped cream and covered with chocolate.

The warmth in my stomach filled me with pleasure. My lips tasted of sturgeon and whipped cream.

Where does destiny end and choice begin?

He was watching me when I finished my meal, when I wiped the silky grease off my lips, when I tasted the sweetness of molten chocolate, when I drank more of the cherry vodka. When he spoke, his voice was smooth and fluid.

"You are a pretty girl, Varvara, but the Empress doesn't care for women in that way. You don't even know what I'm talking about, do you? You should.

"You should know that she is at heart a peasant's daughter. She likes her men simple and strong. She likes to be flattered and desired, but she also likes novelty more than anything else.

"I can make the Empress summon you, but I cannot make her interest in you last. You'll have to know what to tell her. And for that you'll need me more than you think you do."

I watched the bald patch on the top of his head. His jacket was open, his chemise loosened. Something thickened in my throat, and I closed my eyes. He rose and came up to me. I felt his warm hands sliding inside my dress, touching my breasts. I felt the stone of his ring snag the lace on my mother's dress.

"I won't hurt you," he murmured.

I let him pull me toward the ottoman. I felt my skirt rise, then my petticoat. Through the thin cambric of his shirt, I felt his heart beat so hard and so fast that I was terrified he would die. What would I tell his servants when they found me in his dead arms? Would the footman have to break them to free me?

His fingers closed harder on my wrists. Something in me closed and folded.

He guided my fingers to the scar on his chest. Three white lines just above his heart, and the fourth, the deepest of them, where my whole finger could hide.

He guided my hand inside his breeches, closed my fingers on his member. My hand was all wet and sticky. Then he put his hand between my legs, and I felt something soft and sinking give in, like soot falling down the chimney.

When it was over, he asked, "I didn't hurt you, did I?"

"No," I said. "You did not hurt me."

I believed it then.

"Nothing happened. I didn't take anything from you, Varvara. You are still a virgin."

He slurred his words.

I watched his head loll on the ottoman, his red-rimmed eyes heavy with sleep.

I stood up, wobbly on my legs. My mother's dress was wet with his seed. My shoes were lying under his desk. I bent to pick them up but did not put them on. As I walked to the door in my bare feet, I could hear the Chancellor snore. I turned toward him. My eyes avoided the opening in his breeches. In candlelight, the bald patch on his skull shone like a polished shield.

Outside the Chancellor's room I could no longer hold off the sickness of my stomach. I vomited into a giant vase that stood in the corridor, but my head was still spinning from vodka, and the sour taste in my mouth did not go away.

By the time I got back to the room where I slept, the vodka rush had worn off. My hands were sticky, and my fingers smelled of vomit.

The jug in the room was empty, so I peed into a chamber pot and washed my hands as best I could in my warm piddle. Then I took off my mother's soiled dress and tied it into a bundle. When no one was watching, I would scrub it clean.

I fell into a shallow sleep, and when I awoke that night I saw the moon, its face veiled with luminous mist.

I do not remember my dreams. In the morning, when the chambermaid filled the water jug, I hurried to it, pushing the other girls on my way. I tried not to think of the Chancellor's hands on my breasts, of my mother's dress, crumpled and soiled.

Nothing happened. You are still a virgin.

I dipped my hands in the water and washed them with soap. Then I washed them again. Through the palace window I saw the Neva, the edges of the gray waves sparkling in the morning sun.

"Spying, Varvara," the spymaster of the Russian court would tell me later, "is the art of using people who do not believe in loyalty, whose appetites are enormous and unpredictable, and whose motives are always suspect. Anyone working for us can be bought by a higher bidder. The best spies are not those who work for money or out of fear. The best spies are those whose deepest desires are fulfilled by their master."

There were so many lessons. There were so many such nights. Nights soaked with promises, rewarded with praise. I was smart. Clever. Pretty. I was nimble and quick. I knew when to keep silent, and when to speak up. I listened and remembered all I had heard.

I was no longer a seamstress, a nameless palace girl, a stray without a soul in the world who cared if I lived or died.

My future was bright, the moment of my triumph near.

In the corridors of the Winter Palace, on my way from the Chancellor's chambers to the Imperial Wardrobe, I warmed myself with such thoughts.

The summer was long gone, the court had settled back in the Winter Palace, but I still had lessons to learn. Nothing was quite what it seemed. Those who wouldn't deign to look at me in the hallways had secrets dirtier than mine.

If I had any doubts that there were other, faster ways to the Empress's good graces, the Chancellor dispelled them: "The Empress is fond of weddings," he would say. "If she doesn't find you irreplaceable, she will marry you off to the lowest of her lackeys and dance with the bridegroom. Anyone you fancy already?"

"No."

A caress, a warning, a promise. And then, underneath it all, the conviction of my own importance, dulling my senses, pushing me where I would never have gone alone.

"Listen.

"Watch.

"Remember.

"Lie to anyone, but never to me and you won't regret it.

"Come back."

I never refused. It is like opium, the power of knowing what others believed hidden.

I didn't know then that the Chancellor's voice would grow louder in me and more insistent, suffocating my own thoughts, insisting it was the only voice worth hearing.

Don't say too much. Watch out for those who ask too many questions. Follow the sweaty palms, the nervous looks. Remember that there are no safe places and no room can be entirely sealed. Do not believe the displays of kindness: All gifts and smiles are bribes.

I didn't know then how addictive secrecy is, how impossible to escape.

On the last night of September the Chancellor took me to the Imperial Bedroom.

The heavy curtains were drawn. On a marble tabletop I saw a bottle of cherry brandy, half empty, slices of lemon gleaming in the spilled liquid. The cat that stretched by the fireplace wore no velvet jacket. The Chancellor's cane rested against the mantel, the silver tip of its handle reflecting the flicker of the flames.

I thought the bedroom empty, until, in the semidarkness that hid the canopied bed, I heard a dance tune whistled.

"There she is, Your Majesty," the Chancellor said. "Just as I promised. This one will not disappoint."

"Bring her closer," the Empress ordered, emerging from the shadows, shielding her eyes from the pale beam of light sneaking in through the crack between the curtains. I noted her scarlet lips and her nails, stained pink with rose-hip oil.

How she differed from the resplendent figure I recalled from that day, more than a year ago, when my father had brought me here to the palace. Her loose hair now seemed thin and limp, her face bloated. Her pink muslin negligee revealed the wrinkled skin of her breasts. When she settled into an armchair I saw a slipper dangle on her bare foot.

"Your father was a handsome man," the Empress said, playing with a golden bracelet on her wrist. I caught a sour whiff of brandy on her breath. "Very handsome. What was it he did, again?"

"He was a bookbinder, Your Highness."

She giggled. "You have his silky eyes."

I knelt and kissed her hand, soft, fragrant with the attar of roses. She brushed my shoulder, smoothing the sleeves of my dress, and waved me away.

From the corner where I removed myself I heard her lower her voice as she spoke to the Chancellor. I knew they were deciding my fate. I heard the words *Grand Duke* mentioned, and *maids-of-honor*. Questions were followed by swift answers, which I took for assurances of my skills. Once or twice the Empress cast a glance in my direction, as if to test the truth of the Chancellor's promises. I waited, my heart beating wildly, my hands clasped, straining my ears.

Finally the Chancellor bowed and turned toward me.

"You may thank Your Majesty, Varvara," he said. His face was flushed with pleasure.

I turned my eyes to the Empress. I saw her nod.

This is when I rushed toward her and threw myself at her feet.

When we left the Imperial Bedroom, the Chancellor told me I would be assigned to the Grand Duke's court. "A maid of the bedchamber," he said. The work was not too taxing, as the Grand Duke cared little for his clothes and never allowed bedchamber maids to touch his military uniforms.

"Watch his maids-of-honor, his footmen, his valets," the Chancellor said. "Know who is cheating him at cards and who is trying to gain his trust. Remember, you are watching a future Tsar."

I nodded.

"The Empress will send for you at night," the Chancellor continued, his words punctuated with the thump of his cane against the floor. "When she does, make sure you have good stories to tell her. You are not the only one of her tongues."

I nodded again.

I felt his finger lifting my chin.

"I've kept my word, haven't I?"

"Yes."

"And you are grateful?"

"Yes."

His hand caressed my cheek for a brief moment, and then fell limp.

"The Empress wants her stories, and I want mine, Varvara. I protect, provide. You listen and obey. You are my eyes and ears, too. Keep them open. Lie to anyone, but never to me."

I thought it such an easy promise to give.

From the Empress's bedroom came the sound of a man's bold laughter followed by the plucking of guitar strings. Whoever he was, he must have come through the secret passage as soon as we had left.

I followed the Chancellor of Russia, along the empty corridors of the Winter Palace, to his rooms.

In the morning, in the Imperial Wardrobe, Madame Kluge's face seemed even more sour than usual. Back at my seat, my eyes red and smarting from too little sleep, I began ironing the ribbons for the new gown.

Madame Kluge didn't look at me.

Ever since the court had returned from the summer retreat in Tsarskoye Selo, the seamstresses gossiped about how the Empress frowned when she heard her Chief Maid's name mentioned, or how she called Madame Kluge "a German blockhead who could never do anything right." There were more and more mornings when Madame Kluge returned from the Imperial Bedroom in tears, with the pandoras smashed, the clothes torn off them and crumpled. On such occasions the Mistress of the Wardrobe ordered us to drop everything and hurry to dress another set of dolls for Madame Kluge to present.

This morning, to everyone's relief, the pandoras came back intact, and we all busied ourselves with the hurried preparations of the Empress's newest outfit, snipping off all loose threads, ironing the hem, feeling the fabric for a forgotten pin. When the gown was ready, swaddled in a length of silk, Madame Kluge took it to the Empress.

I watched her hurry out of the room. I watched her when she came back, to fetch one of the seamstresses for some last-minute adjustments. For a time I feared that nothing would happen, that the Empress had forgotten her promise.

But then Madame Kluge returned and I saw her say something to the Mistress of the Wardrobe, who nodded.

They were both looking at me.

I began basting ribbons to a crimson evening gown. I smoothed the ribbon in my hand, placed it on the silk, and began threading a needle as Madame Kluge approached me.

"The Empress wishes you to take care of the Grand Duke's wardrobe." Her voice was strained and uncertain, and I did nothing to hide my delight. "When you are done here today, pack your things."

I heard the other seamstresses whisper.

The ribbon and silk slipped from my hands to the floor, but neither Madame Kluge nor the Chief Seamstress scolded me or told me to wipe the smile off my lips.

That evening, when I finished my work in the Imperial Wardrobe, Madame Kluge led me to a small room in the west wing of the Winter Palace, next to where the Grand Duke Peter's maids-of-honor slept.

I was to empty my own chamber pot, she told me, but I could have as many tallow candles as I needed, as long as I brought back the melted ends. A scullery maid would fetch me a jug of water each morning for my toilette.

"You can have a shelf, too," she said, as she walked me to my new lodgings. On the stairs, I noted, her hand was clutching the railing with more force than necessary.

"A shelf, a table, and a wooden chest for your things, Varvara Niko-layevna," Madame Kluge said when she opened the door.

I felt a surge of pleasure at the sound of my full name.

The room was an old alcove, boarded up with thin paneling. I looked at the bare floor, the ceiling streaked brown with damp, the thick dust on the windowsill and a little table. There was no fireplace. From behind the flimsy wall came the easy laughter of the maids-of-honor, getting ready for the imperial masquerade, where all women would dress as men and all men would wear women's gowns. In another room someone was playing the violin.

Madame Kluge took a few awkward steps, then turned toward me. Her lips were drawn in a thin, straight line.

There were two other maids of the bedchamber, she informed me, both charged with keeping the Grand Duke's wardrobe in order. There was hardly enough for them to do, as it was. The maids-of-honor kept their own servants. "You better ask the Grand Duke himself what he wants you to do around here," she said. "Tomorrow, scrub yourself well, and present yourself to him."

I could hear the old haughtiness in Madame Kluge's voice. If I wished her to fumble, lose herself in guessing, to be awed by the outrageous possibilities of my changed position, she refused to oblige me. The Empress wished a Polish stray to serve the Grand Duke. So be it. It was not the first time the Empress had puzzled the Chief Maid with her orders.

Madame Kluge gave me one last look and took her leave.

I wiped off the mouse droppings with a piece of old rag I found under the table. My new bed was as hard and narrow as the one before, the blanket as threadbare.

Squeals of fawning laughter from behind the wall told me that the Grand Duke must have come into the room. The old paneling was loose enough for me to peek through, and I saw him, tall and lanky, in a hooped dress of white silk and a woman's wig, his lean face powdered and rouged. The maids-of-honor—all in dark-blue Holsteiner uniforms—flocked around him.

He was turning to a round of giddy applause. I saw him curtsy and cover his face with an ostrich feather. I heard him giggle and say something in Russian. His high-pitched voice, I thought, sounded squeaky and very foreign.

When they all left, I wiped the dust off the wooden chest and opened it. It did not smell of mice. I put the few things I owned into it—my mother's dress, a pair of her shoes, a few books my father had bound. I closed the lid of the chest and looked for the key, but there was none.

In the morning, before I presented myself to Grand Duke Peter, his Blackamoor warned me to be quick; Master was tired after the masquerade and wished to get on with his day.

The Grand Duke had just finished his breakfast. I thought him thinner than he'd been in the rare moments when I had caught sight of him in the hallways. There was a white, pasty smudge on his forehead. His blond hair was heavily powdered in what I heard described as "the Spanish fashion," and he was reciting Russian place-names, in the girlish voice I had overheard the day before. A list of fortresses, it turned out to be, along the eastern border.

Books full of plans and pictures were spread across the table among the breakfast dishes, and being my father's child, I flinched at the damage greasy fingers would cause.

"Speak," the Grand Duke said, lifting his eyes from the map he was studying. In German, his voice sounded less shrill than it was in Russian.

I thought it wise to speak in German, too. I said that it was Her Majesty's wish that I would make myself useful to him.

"What can you do?"

I didn't expect to be asked, but seeing the newspapers that lay on the side table, I saw my chance. "I could read from them, Your Highness," I answered. "To spare your eyes."

The Duke gave me a curious look and blinked a few times. His eyelashes, I noticed, were oddly pale. He had a milky skin, and later I would see how readily it flamed red with sunburn every time he was exposed to sunlight for too long.

"I have to ask Professor Stehlin," he answered. "He is my new teacher. From Prussia."

I expected to be dismissed, but the Grand Duke pointed at one of the maps on the table. His fingernails, I noticed, had been tinted with red oil.

"Do you know where Prussia is on the map?"

I nodded, and saw that it pleased him.

The Grand Duke asked me many questions that morning. He wanted me to tell him where I was born and why my parents had come to Russia. He was disappointed to hear that my father had been a bookbinder, not a soldier. "Don't the Poles like to fight?" he asked.

When I said I didn't know, he told me not to worry. Life carried many surprises. He'd always thought he would be the King of Sweden. "You may still marry a soldier," he said.

This is when I noticed a hoop skirt lying on the carpet, flattened and stained.

To my relief, Professor Stehlin did not object to a reader. And so, every morning, I arrived at the Imperial Study, ready for my new duties. "Keep your eyes opened," the Chancellor had said. "Remember, you are watching your future Tsar."

There was a lot to read. Excerpts from foreign dispatches and newspapers, descriptions of fortresses from *Sila Imperii* or from *Galerie Agréable du Monde*. Passages about the habits of various animals, and the anatomy of plants, about the layout of St. Petersburg canals and the treasures of Kunstkamera.

Every passage I read became the theme of a lesson. A military fortress called for an explanation of a mathematical formula, a dispatch for tracing the boundaries of foreign lands and positions of various countries on the map. And—if the Grand Duke became restless or tired—Professor Stehlin ordered a walk: to the gardens, to the streets of St. Petersburg, the city his famous grandfather Peter had coaxed out of the marshes and the sea.

The future Tsar, I thought, had a wise teacher.

"Speak," the Empress commanded the night when I was summoned into the Imperial Bedroom. On my way there I had seen a sobbing maid, her arms huddling her thin body. The door through which I entered was hidden in the carved paneling; it opened without a sound. A tongue was not to be seen.

Her Majesty was lying on her bed, poultices on her eyelids. Two cats stretched beside her, fast asleep. I seated myself beside the bed on a small embroidered footstool. "Flatter her. Tell her stories she wants to hear," the Chancellor had urged me. "Make her wish you hadn't stopped talking."

"Professor Stehlin said Your Majesty looked ravishing in the Preobrazhensky uniform at the last masquerade," I began.

"To whom?" She did not remove the poultices from her eyes.

"To Count Lestocq. It made him bite his lips."

It seemed easy enough, the fine curl of Elizabeth's smile urging me on.

From behind the door came the shuffling of feet. Elizabeth's courtiers were eagerly awaiting their turn.

"Is my nephew making good progress at his lessons?"

"Yes, Your Majesty."

"Does he fancy any of his maids-of-honor?"

"No. He never singles out any of them over another. But they imagine that he does. Especially Mademoiselle Gagarina."

There would be no dearth of stories. From my tiny nook of a room with its flimsy wall, I had spied on the maids-of-honor and heard their foolish chatter. In the Grand Duke's rooms, their eyes slid over me as if I were made of air, but their thoughts were already mine. This one tried to tempt the Grand Duke with the sight of her bare breast. That one sulked, for the Grand Duke complained she couldn't sing a note. I had heard their childish confessions of first kisses and secret vows; I had carefully weighed their desires and their fears.

They were such easy prey. Too pampered to watch behind their backs, too sure of themselves to take note of anyone not like them.

The Empress sat upright, wiping the poultices off her eyes. "Light another candle, Varvara. It's too dark in here."

I rose from the footstool. I lit a new candle from the old one and placed it on a side table right beside the Imperial Bed. I heard a cat's husky purr. The Empress was running her long, tapered fingers through its coppery fur.

"Mademoiselle Gagarina, Varvara?" she said, chuckling. "Tell me: What does the silly goose want?"

The Grand Duke had many visitors, I told the Chancellor.

Prince Lev Naryshkin made the Grand Duke titter with his loud farts and imitations of street whores. Count Vorontzov had presented him with a silver traveling set, encrusted with tortoiseshell and mother-of-pearl. "Fit for the best of soldiers," he said. Madame Kluge was inventing excuses to visit. She was finding fault with chambermaids, making them scrub the grate of the fireplace over and over again. Always managing to appear when the Grand Duke was alone, speaking of Eutin to him, telling him she had been born there.

The Empress came, too. She'd watched as the Grand Duke busied himself with his maps, patted his head when he explained to her the movements of troops in some obscure battle. "Your grandfather would have been proud," she told him. I told the Chancellor of the promised spring bear hunt, with the trackers and running hounds. And of the teasing. About Mademoiselle Gagarina, her prancing about, her mincing steps. "I'm looking for a bride for you," the Empress had said, pinching her nephew's cheek. "I have to, before it's too late."

At the word *bride*, the Chancellor bristled. I took note of the sharp twist of his head, the tightening of his lips. I thought of a bird, swooping.

"Has she mentioned anyone yet?"

"Princess Marianna of Saxony, a few times. But the Grand Duke doesn't like hearing about her. *Horseface*, he calls her. So now the Empress mostly speaks of the Princess of Anhalt-Zerbst."

"As if we needed another German! As if the one we have was not trouble enough. Does he still wet his bed?"

"Yes. The maids complain of washing his sheets."

The Chancellor did not hide his irritation with Peter the Great's grandson. The world was not a plaything of Dukes. Russia needed an alliance with Saxony or Austria. The Prussian King was getting too strong. It would be better for everyone if the heir to the throne understood that much.

There was weariness in his voice. On his desk, papers were turned facedown, arranged in clusters of two so that none could be removed unnoticed.

The Chancellor sighed. "Am I asking too much of him, Varvara?"

A spy does not need to answer such questions.

A spy needs to speak of the letter hidden in the secret drawer that opens only when the carved column on the right is pushed. A letter calling Frederick of Prussia the cleverest monarch in history. A letter complaining that Russia is a barbarian land where people worship idols and kiss their pictures hoping they would cure them from all ills. A letter in which the heir to the Russian throne writes: *If I had not left Holstein, I would by now serve in Your Majesty's army and learn what being a true soldier is all about.*

A letter Madame Kluge agreed to put in the right hands.

In the first days of October, Professor Stehlin began marking passages from the history of Russia for me to read to the Grand Duke. The description of the Grand Embassy of 1697, Peter the Great's European journey, where the Tsar learned the intricacies of shipbuilding and during which he bought his books and treasures. The Battle of Poltava of 1709, where the Russian troops defeated the King of Sweden and captured the land that gave Russia precious access to the sea.

Look at him, I read, *this God-like man, now enveloped in a cloud of dust, of smoke, of flame, now bathed in sweat at the end of strenuous toil. Through God and Tsar, Russia is strong. For the Sovereign is the father of all people, like the Earth is their Mother.*

"With Peter the Great," Professor Stehlin told the Grand Duke, "nothing was ever left to chance."

The Grand Duke did not roll his eyes.

The visit to Kunstkamera—Peter the Great's famous museum on Vasilevsky Island—was to be like a puzzle the Grand Duke was to solve by himself. Why had his grandfather opened it? Why make people come and study his famous collections? What did Russia's greatest Tsar wish his people to learn?

The Grand Duke jumped up and clapped his hands at Professor Stehlin's announcement. "Will she come, too?" he asked, pointing at me.

"If this is Your Highness's wish."

My knees nearly buckled. My hands trembled. Even though the island was easy to spot from the palace windows, I had learned not to look past the waters of the river. It is not that I didn't remember that I once lived there. The thread that linked me to my memories was always tugging at my heart—if I let it tug any harder, the hurt would choke me.

My father's voice came back to me first: *"The power of reason . . . breaking down fear and superstition . . . Kunstkamera is a temple of knowledge."* And then I remembered our maids calling Peter's museum a cursed place, one that would bring bad luck on our heads. Were they right when they sneered at my father's words?

I pushed away these thoughts. I would not cry, I vowed.

The first thing Professor Stehlin pointed out to the Grand Duke in Kunstkamera was a glass dome covering a hill made of skulls and bones. Two baby skeletons propped on iron poles looked as if they were preparing to climb it. Beside them another skeleton, bow in hand, seemed about to start playing his violin. A wreath made of dried arteries, kidneys, and hearts hung above them, with a calligraphed inscription that said: *Why should I long for things of this world?*

"Anatomical art," Professor Stehlin called it. "So why should we think of death when we are still in our prime?" he asked his pupil.

The Grand Duke rubbed his hands and grinned. He remembered word for word what I had read to him days before.

To make us aware of the brevity of life. To remind us that we will have to account for our deeds well beyond the moment of death.

Professor Stehlin nodded with a smile.

They were in the next room we entered, motionless creatures with pale, leathery skin, floating in glass jars, their pensive faces suspended in clear liquid. Two heads fused into one, a face lacking eyes, legs locked into a mermaid's tail. Fetuses with stumps for arms, babies with two faces.

The dead staring at the living, the maids in my parents' house had whispered.

I tightened the shawl about my shoulders. Beside me, the Grand Duke shuffled his feet.

"These are deformed fetuses born in Russia from human and animal mothers. Your grandfather ordered them to be collected and brought here," Professor Stehlin explained, his voice rising in excitement. "Look at them carefully, Your Highness. Ask yourself, *Why?*"

The Grand Duke was staring at the jar with twins, one reduced to a few folds of shriveled skin clinging, frog-like, to the back of its bloated brother.

He was silent.

Professor Stehlin answered his own question. Peter the Great wanted to teach his subjects. Monsters were merely damaged fetuses. "The fruit of illness and abuse," he said. "Or mother's fear." And then he pointed to an inscription on the wall: *For a mother can pass the imprint of her fear to the life she carries in her womb.*

"Repeat these words, Your Highness," he said.

The Grand Duke turned his eyes away from the jar he had been staring at all this time. I saw his lips move, but no words came. And then I heard his scream, piercing, thick and dark, followed by the sounds of his footsteps fading away.

I looked at the Grand Duke's tutor. He was blinking, bewildered at the effect his words had.

"Don't just stand there, Varvara," he ordered. "Go after him."

I made my way to the bottom of the stairs, where the Grand Duke crouched and shivered. He hid his face in the palms of his hands when he saw me. "They'll kill me here," he sobbed. "I know they will."

I tried to put my hand on his shoulder, but he shook it off.

"There have been omens," I heard him whimper. "Just like when Mama died. They don't want me to know, but I do." A rivulet of vomit leaked through his fingers, dripping to the floor.

I thought of a nestling, its wings flapping aimlessly, too paralyzed with terror for flight.

"Get a footman, Varvara," Professor Stehlin's voice commanded behind me. "Hurry up, girl."

I hadn't even heard him come down, but he was now at the bottom of the stairs, helping the Grand Duke stand.

"You've seen the monsters, Your Highness. You've seen what fear can do. Don't let it rule your thoughts. We cannot know the future," I heard him say as I rushed outside. "But with the help of reason, we can prepare for what might happen."

In the silence that shrouded the rest of that day, I turned those words in my head, examined them for stains of doubts, the way my father examined the leather for the bindings of his books.

We cannot know the future.

Reason can conquer fear.

But that night, alone in my bed, I could not shut my ears to the Grand Duke's muffled sobs in the room next to mine.

A hundred times I almost rose, almost went to him. But every time I came up with excuses. He would just send me away. He would soon stop. The future Tsar has to learn his lessons like everyone else.

Lessons hurt.

There is no other way.

The sobs quieted down in the end, and I, too, drifted into sleep. *Look*, the Kunstkamera monsters urged me in my dreams. *Look at our webbed fingers, our fused legs, our eyes squeezed shut.*

Why are you not looking?

Are you afraid that you can see too much?

People like to think they can hide behind their faces, mold them like masks for a costume ball. They hope that their eager smiles or haughty looks do not betray thoughts they prefer to keep hidden. A courtier's corrosive envy. A lady's contempt. A child's piercing longing.

I was not the only one of the Empress's tongues, but I could read her face better than others could. Her pupils widened when a man's bold look pleased her. A slight frown always preceded the surge of her impatience. A sweep of her arm signaled interest. If it waned, she would start playing with anything her fingers could reach.

The sins of others made the best of stories. The bowels of the palace were dark and deep, like the waters of the Neva. Something was always moving there. Something was always washed ashore. Secrets were like cast-up corpses, warped coins, polished shards of glass covered in mud. Useless to those who didn't know where they came from. Treasures to those who did. All I had to do was watch and remember. All I had to do was listen to those who thought themselves alone.

Princess Golubeva kept her serf hairdresser locked in a cage in her bedroom alcove, so that he would not betray her baldness. In Count Sheremetev's library, in a locked cabinet, books had titles like: *Venus in the Cloister* or *The Nun in Her Chemise*. There were pictures there, too, with secret levers hidden in their frames. Once pulled, they revealed their hidden doubles: shepherds and shepherdesses frolicking naked in a meadow. A stern court lady lifting her dress to show a little dog licking the spot between her legs.

It didn't take me long to become the most popular of imperial tongues.

That night a bracelet on the Empress's wrist captivated her, the glow of gold glittering in candlelight, the clinking of the jeweled pendants attached to it.

"There is something about Madame Kluge that Your Highness should know," I said.

"Madame Kluge?" the Empress said idly. "What about her?"

"An old *Baba* came to her."

The bracelet stopped moving. The Empress sat mute when I said it all: the old *Baba*'s toothless mouth muttering her incantations, a candle that sputtered and smoked even though there was no draft.

How swiftly my words flew, how easily.

Rubles changed hands. Charms were given. Foul. Unspeakable.

Take this bottle. . . . Fill it with your piddle. . . . Smear it on the four legs of your mistress's bed. That will stop her affection from slipping away.

Hairs, nail clippings, flakes of skin were to be gathered. Mixed with charms and potent herbs. Bundled up in old paper. Tied with a black ribbon freshly ironed. Placed in secret so the charms could work their way.

The Empress drew a sharp breath. I didn't know then how much she feared witchcraft, but I wouldn't have stopped talking if I'd known. Her eyes widened, her hand gripped mine, pulling me closer. No one has ever listened to me like that before.

"Where is it?" she demanded.

I pointed at her bed, hoping I had heard it right. Hoping Madame Kluge had done what she was told to do.

"Show me," the Empress said.

I walked to the bed and lifted the mattress. I should not have doubted the force of desperation. It was there, a small bundle of paper, tied with a black ribbon.

The Empress ordered me to open it.

I did. It smelled of dust and herbs. Inside, beside nail clippings stained pink, there was a bone, a ball of hair, a wilted carrot, and a bunch of dried flowers.

The Empress crossed herself, again and again.

"Put that thing there," she commanded. I could hear the tremor of fear in her voice. "Careful. Don't drop it."

I placed my finding on a table by the window.

"Cover it."

I placed a silk kerchief over the package.

"Now go," she said.

I made a step toward the secret door. But to my surprise, she stopped me and motioned for me to approach.

"You did well, Varvara. The Chancellor was right about you. You did very well."

I felt her fingers touch my hair.

I didn't think much of the Chancellor or Madame Kluge that night, when I reached my spartan room. I didn't ask myself what would happen. I fell asleep with the memory of that touch.

A sable pelisse covered Her Majesty's shining gown, the edge of her green velvet hood revealing a black feather in her hair. From the balcony where she stood, the Empress watched as two guards brought Madame Kluge to the palace yard, freshly cleared from the first November snowfall.

The Grand Duke was absent. The Empress forbade her nephew to leave his room, for he had awakened with a sore throat. When I came to ask if he wished me to read to him, he was straddling his dog, teasing it with a bone. "Leave me alone," he snapped gruffly.

The crowd had been gathering since dawn. People huddled by the walls of the Winter Palace, stomping their feet, pounding their chests to make the blood flow faster.

Madame Kluge's fat face was pale and clenched, her eyes downcast. *German traitor* . . . I heard the shouts . . . *wishing misfortune on our heads.*

Feet shuffled on the frozen ground. Rumors flew, dark and menacing. *Worshipping the Dark One* . . . *biting the merciful hand that fed her.*

Someone threw a rotten cabbage. It splashed into a slimy puddle on the snow. Madame Kluge's eyes shrank with fear.

Caught red-handed, I heard. *Exposed when she least expected. Serves her right. Spying for the Prussians. Her hands greased with German gold.*

Wasn't she always sneaky and underhanded? Always asking questions when she should've been quiet?

A dog snarled. I heard a single beat of the drum.

All eyes turned to the balcony, its railings covered with a flag on which the double-headed Russian eagle was spreading its wings. The Empress did not move.

When the drum sounded again, the Empress turned toward the Captain of the Guards. Her gloved hand rose and, for an instant, I thought that the plea in Madame Kluge's eyes would soften my mistress's heart. But the Empress of All the Russias nodded and lowered her hand.

The guards pushed Madame Kluge onto the makeshift scaffold, hastily assembled from a few pieces of timber and a plank. I felt drops of falling snow melt on my cheeks and lips. Behind me a man complained that he could not see anything.

How meager the trifles one clings to, to keep guilt at bay: the memories of an unkind word, a face distorted with anger, the lash of a whip. How welcoming the thought of punishment deserved, of justice meted out. How easy the contempt for those who fall from grace.

"No one will be put to death under my rule," the Empress had vowed on the day of the coup that gave her the throne, two years before. Madame Kluge would not die, I told myself, knowing that death was not all a soul could fear. Under the strokes of the knout, skin turns to meaty straps. Muscles tear. Backs break. It didn't take much to turn a woman into a cripple.

Someone behind me tittered. I heard Madame Kluge scream. Before I could turn my eyes away from the scaffold, I saw her body go limp.

The Empress nodded again. The guard who held the knout raised his hand and the first blow broke the silence. Nine more followed before the verdict was announced—dismissal from court and exile.

Since that day, no one in the Winter Palace was allowed to mention Madame Kluge's name.

"You play the palace game. You lose or you win," the Chancellor would tell me that night, caressing my breast. "You, too, can find yourself back where you came from."

The scar on his chest, he said with a chuckle, was a mark left by a dying hand. He didn't even recall the man's name.

"Keep watching what lurks in the shadows, Varvara. The moment you stop, someone else will take your place."

I made myself believe that there was no other way.

In the small, forgotten rooms at the far ends of the old Winter Palace—dim oak-paneled chambers that still remembered her father's giant footsteps—beds were kept ready for the Empress at all times. The room she chose was never the same from night to night. No one was to know where the Empress of Russia would sleep.

She, too, was afraid of an assassin's dagger.

I had seen many an imperial secret by then. I had seen my mistress in tears; I had seen her sick from lust. I had seen her ripped clothes in a heap on the floor, slashed to free her when she had been too drunk to undress. In the months that had passed since my first summons, I had brought her many stories of foolishness and pride, of hopes and deceits.

It was the measure of the Empress's confidence in me that she told me of the letter her secretary had dispatched to the Prince of Anhalt-Zerbst.

The letter made no promises but asked for his daughter's company. The Empress had every reason to believe the Princess would arrive before February 10, in time to celebrate the Grand Duke's sixteenth birthday.

"We would all be in Moscow by then," she told me, pleased at the thought of the court's approaching journey. Staying in one place for too long made Elizabeth restless. Days were always brighter elsewhere, nights more starry. Besides, she disliked the thought of any of her palaces left to the servants for too long. This is when walls began to peel, silks faded, and carpets grew threadbare.

Master's eye fattened the horse.

There was no reading of reports that night. Instead, I was to write down a list of questions for the steward. Did the furniture the Empress had ordered shipped to Moscow in advance of her trip arrive? Was there any damage from dampness or mice? Had the sculptor been hired to check the condition of the statues and do the necessary repairs? Even away from the capital, her visitors would not be given an excuse to doubt the splendor of the Russian court.

"The grand ballroom of the Annenhof palace would do very well for their first dance," Elizabeth said. Her hand was stroking a purring cat curled on her lap.

The cats were never fooled by the charade of changing bedrooms. They always knew where to find her.

In the Imperial Wardrobe the seamstresses were busy laying out the traveling clothes. In the hallways footmen were stacking up trunks and chests before loading them onto carriages. Crates lined up with braids of straw were still piling up in the main hall. In the stables, the grooms were fitting harnesses and traces for the horses.

From now on I was also to make sure Grand Duke Peter's reading contained suitable passages. "Not so many battles, Varvara," the Empress said. "Some French novels, perhaps. But make sure they are not too frivolous. My nephew is too impressionable. And find him some love poems to learn by heart."

In January of 1744, in the Moscow Annenhof palace, the Empress of All the Russias wanted to hear of nothing but the journey of Princess Sophie of Anhalt-Zerbst.

"What have you heard about our travelers, Varvara?" the Empress demanded as I entered her bedroom that night. It was past midnight, in the darkest of hours. She was lying on the bed, her feet bare, her head propped on pillows. Pushok, one of the cats that came with her from St. Petersburg, the fluffy white one, had settled down beside her, licking its paws.

I seated myself at her feet, the slim, shapely feet of a dancer. Pouring lavender oil on the palms of my hands, I warmed them first, rubbing the skin.

"Prince Naryshkin says that the Princess is not too pretty."

"And what does the Chancellor say?"

"He says that the Princess is very clever."

"Cunning, he means," the Empress said, rolling her eyes. "Meddling. And how does he know that?"

"He has received another letter from Berlin."

The Berlin spies had been busy, and so I could paint for the Empress a picture of the young Princess from Stettin, a grim, black dot at the mouth of the Oder River, far away from anywhere important. I hinted at a dark-haired girl left to her own devices, playing with merchants' children on the slippery cobbled streets, the daughter of a scatterbrained mother who had been disappointed that her firstborn was not a boy.

"Her father, Your Highness, is good at dispensing advice but lacks the means to act upon it. And her mother's temper grows worse with each year."

I told the Empress of the shabby poverty of the genteel, of threadbare carpets that underpaid servants washed with sauerkraut to coax back the color, chairs from which grayish filling always threatened to slip out, silverplated dishes revealing copper or tin at the edges, dresses that had to be mended and darned and were always out of style.

"Is that what Bestuzhev says about her? Does he think I'll send the girl back if I hear about that?"

I could feel her feet tense. I could see the flash of anger gather in her eyes.

"The Chancellor says that poor princesses are not used to power. Elevated above her station, she will be grateful to those who put her there and will therefore be Your Highness's most loyal subject."

Under the pressure of my fingers, my mistress's feet were again growing soft and warm. I rolled the toes between my thumb and forefinger, one by one.

"The Grand Duke," I continued, "asks about the Princess every day."

I was not surprised to feel Elizabeth's feet stiffen again. I had already seen the twitch of her lip when her nephew mangled some Russian name. I had made note of a dismissive sneer after his awkward fall at one of her masquerades, when he tripped in his high-heel shoes.

I poured more oil on my palms. "The Grand Duke wants to know why Sophie is so slow to arrive."

In his bedroom, Peter had spread a map on which a toy carriage moved a few inches every day. Two dolls were sitting inside, the bigger one with a chipped nose ever since one of the palace cats had knocked the carriage to the floor. I did not mention the fact that every time Professor Stehlin told him to stop rubbing his cheek and pulling on his ears, Peter seemed astonished, as if he were not aware of the wanderings of his own hands.

Elizabeth closed her eyes. I kept talking.

The Grand Duke used to worry that his fiancée would be skinny. But Professor Stehlin told him not to. The Princess would take on more flesh as soon as she started eating excellent Russian food. "Women," Stehlin said, "should be plump and soft like our Empress."

"Is that what the old flatterer really said?" my mistress asked, just as I knew she would.

"Yes, Your Majesty."

"And what did Peter say to this?"

"He was pleased."

The curtains let in the first light of dawn. I was keeping my voice low and steady, hoping Elizabeth would finally drift into sleep.

The Grand Duke had wanted to know what to do with a fiancée. Would he have to kiss her, he had asked me three times already. When I said that he would have to, he blushed crimson.

There were more questions: Would he still have to take dancing and deportment lessons when he was married? Or would he be allowed to concentrate on his regiment? Would Princess Sophie like to watch him drill his troops? Wasn't she, too, a soldier's daughter?

The Empress closed her eyes.

Everyone in Petersburg was waiting for the arrival of the Princess of Anhalt-Zerbst, I continued. Jugglers were perfecting new acts, fortune-tellers prophesied joy.

As soon as I heard the first light snore, I made sure the silver-fox-fur blanket covered the Empress's feet. I wiped the oil off my hands and slipped out of the room. I knew better than to snuff the candle.

The Secret Chancellery's dispatches about Princess Sophie's progress on her monthlong journey to Russia came in hand-bound folders tied with green ribbons, their ends sealed with wax. They contained unflattering stories of darned stockings and chemises of coarse linen. The Anhalt-Zerbsts lived in a palace no one in St. Petersburg would look at twice.

When the invitation from Russia had arrived on New Year's Day, it was reported, Sophie's father hesitated for three full days before giving his consent for the trip. He objected to the change of religion that a marriage to the Russian Crown Prince would bring. "How can we risk our daughter's salvation for earthly glory? Allow the worship of idols?" he had asked. "If I listened to you, we would still be in Stettin," his wife replied, but even she attempted to hide the news of Elizabeth's summons from her daughter. "So as not to excite her too much when nothing is certain yet," she told her husband. There had been talk of Sophie's secret engagement to her own uncle, but the Anhalt-Zerbsts were no fools. They knew a better match when they saw one. The Princess may have been too fond of sitting on her uncle's lap, but she was still a virgin.

"They come in four carriages, and even that expense has to be paid out of the imperial coffers," the Chancellor had scoffed, as he thrust the dispatches from his spies at me.

The spies reported on petty squabbles over lost combs and bedbugs. A German maid confirmed that Sophie had worn a corset to straighten her spine until she was seven. But there was no sign of dislocations now, the spies confirmed.

The Princess and her mother were traveling in unmarked carriages under the names of Countess Reinbeck and her daughter, Figchen—little fig—plump and sweet and filled with tiny seeds, Sophie's childhood nickname. Her mother, Princess Johanna, complained ceaselessly that winter was a bad season for traveling.

The ruts in the roads were frozen solid. The bedchambers at post houses were often unheated. Figchen suffered from swollen legs and had to be carried during their stops. More than once, the travelers had to sleep in the postmaster's room, with his children, dogs, and chickens. So much for the famed comfort of the Prussian inns, Princess Johanna grumbled.

For the spies watching them day and night, no detail seemed too trivial to report. Each tidbit made the Empress chortle with delight.

By the time the travelers reached Riga, the charade of incognito had been abandoned. The family's unmarked carriages were sent back to Prussia, replaced with a Russian gift of an imperial sleigh. "Isn't it like a big bed, Maman?" Sophie reportedly exclaimed. "Have you ever seen anything like it?" She learned fast how to get in and out of it and declared that for the first time in weeks she was warm right down to her toes. She kissed the sable furs, touched featherbeds and fur blankets and declared "our dearest Empress Elizabeth" the most generous of all people on earth.

"Clever flatterers, the Anhalt-Zerbsts. This much I grant them," the Chancellor told me, his hand sliding inside my chemise. "But still, our little Figchen with her pointy chin won't last longer here than a few weeks."

Chancellor Bestuzhev was not pleased with the steady stream of dispatches about Princess Sophie's gushing adoration for Her Benefactress and with the Grand Duke's growing impatience to meet his intended bride. In the Empress's presence, like everyone else, the Chancellor praised the Princess of Anhalt-Zerbst with all the flattery he could muster, but from me he did not hide his anger.

What the spies were sending him were pitchers of warm spittle. What was he to do? Drink it and smack his lips?

I watched his black eyes, gleaming with indignation and stifled fury. I listened when he complained that reports took forever to arrive.

His spies were repeating themselves, sending accounts of the same incidents with insignificant variations, most of them useless. Rulers can be blind and deaf to what is the most important, but the best courtiers cannot be.

"See if there is anything in those the Empress might need to hear," he said, throwing a bunch of papers on my lap. This, too, was a skill he had taught me—fishing for the important detail buried in the trivial.

I glanced at yet another account of the solemn morning prayers for the health of the Empress and the Grand Duke, of stockings worn three days in a row, one darned at the toe but not too skillfully, of a loose stool and a regular one, of a birthmark on Sophie's thigh. *Using the pretext of having to treat her swollen legs, I examined the Princess,* Elizabeth's surgeon wrote. *She has already had her menses. With full authority I can state that she has good bones and will have no trouble giving birth.*

Only Princess Johanna could always be counted on to brighten the Chancellor's mood. I reached most eagerly for the copies of her letters home and the daily scribbles in her journal.

I was received by Prince Vladimir Dolgoruky.

It never occurred to me that all this was for poor little me, for whom in some other places they hardly beat the drum and in others sound nothing at all, Johanna wrote about her reception at Riga.

"Poor Figchen might have fallen out of the carriage," the Chancellor muttered. "And no one would have even noticed her absence!"

I giggled.

I braced myself for his usual tirade about apples and the apple tree, vain mothers and their daughters, but it didn't come. I had found a letter that had pleased him more than the sound of his own voice.

Being one of the generals entrusted with the task of welcoming Princess Sophie of Anhalt-Zerbst to Russia, I feel it my duty to inform Your Excellency of a conversation I had with our illustrious visitor.

It was the following demand that I hasten to inform Your Excel-

lency about. Princess Sophie asked if I could supply her with details on the characters and habits of key courtiers. Her questions
were: Does the Empress like them? Are they rich enough? Do they
have wives and children? Who are their closest friends?

"If you make notes on them," the Princess added, "and give them
to me, I will remember you well, General."

Knowing that if I refused this unusual request the Princess
would find someone else to do it for her, I prepared the notes. An
exact copy of them is attached to this deposition. As Your Excellency may be so kind as to observe, they include only the most obvious and easily obtainable facts. If, as in two instances, I included the
name of a favorite dog, it was at the Princess's specific request.

The Princess is *very* fond of dogs.

This was the letter I read to the Empress that night when the
maids had been sent away. I read it slowly, the way the Chancellor
instructed me to. "Planting a seed of imperial doubt," he had called it.

The Empress was seated at her dressing table, staring at the coils
of her golden bracelet glittering on her wrist.

"Where is Sophie now?" she asked, as if she did not hear a word of
what I had just read.

"In St. Petersburg, Your Majesty. For a quick rest before hurrying
on to Moscow."

"Does she like it there?"

"She says it is so much bigger and grander than Berlin. She clapped
twenty-five times when Prince Repnin took her to see Your Majesty's
elephants. She could not believe such giant beasts could dance so
gracefully."

"She will make it here in time for Peter's birthday, won't she?"

"Yes."

I saw the Empress bend closer to the silver-framed dressing mirror, lick her finger, and run it along her brow. She was waiting for a
night visitor, I realized, someone for whom she was now dabbing per-

fume behind her ears and on her wrists, someone who would come through the secret passage that led all the way to the courtyard.

"Go now," she told me.

I set the folder on the small side table by the Empress's bed. But before I opened the door, she called me back.

"How long have you been at the palace, Varvara?"

"Almost a year, Your Highness."

"How old are you now?"

"Sixteen, Your Highness."

"You could be her friend. An older friend she could trust."

"If this is what Your Highness wishes," I replied, and paused, waiting for her to say more, but she waved me to hurry out.

The travelers were taking their time. By February 6 the Empress no longer cared to hide her impatience, not even in the Chancellor's presence. She had hoped that Sophie and Peter would spend a day or two together before the birthday feast. How long could "a quick rest in St. Petersburg" last? Didn't they know she was waiting?

On February 9 a sleigh passed through the grand entrance of the Annenhof palace and stopped in front to the jingling of harness bells. A sliver of a girl untangled herself from the furs and quickly followed her mother inside the grand entrance, past a throng of chamberlains and Guards officers waiting to greet them.

"How warm it is here, Maman!" she gasped, clapping her hands. "Warmer than the Zerbst palace is in the summer!"

In the grand hall it was Marshal Brummer and not Chancellor Bestuzhev who welcomed the imperial guests.

"An honor," Princess Johanna said, her voice loud enough for all to hear. "And a source of our greatest joy."

They were whisked to their rooms to freshen up before meeting the Empress. In the palace corridors, courtiers and chambermaids, cooks, valets, and stove stokers hovered on tiptoes, craning their necks. Having pushed my way forward right behind the guards, all I could see was a disappointing glimpse of a sable pelisse and a brown head-dress.

I hurried to the Empress's side. She was seated in the Throne Room surrounded by her ladies of the court. The Grand Duke Peter stood by his aunt, shuffling his feet, eyes fixed on the door. Chancellor Bestuzhev was there, too, behind them. The expression of stifled amusement on his thin lips could be mistaken for joy. "You should've been more blunt," he'd snapped when I'd told him the Empress paid no heed to the letter he'd ordered me to read to her. "We cannot let this little *Hausfrau* play her little games."

"They've arrived, Your Majesty," I said, breathless from running, which earned me the Chancellor's annoyed glance.

"So you've seen her, Varvara?"

I nodded.

"Does Princess Sophie look tired?"

"She looks tired," I said. "But she is anxious to meet Your Highness."

"Not as tired as her mother, I presume."

Was there a mean note in her voice? Did I hear a touch of jealousy already, before she had even seen Johanna?

The newcomers arrived a few moments after I had been waved aside, having merely discarded their outerwear. Both were visibly moved and gasped at the sight of their hostess. Princess Sophie wore a tight-fitting pleated dress adorned with plain yellow ribbon; her mother had chosen a modest and bulky outfit, which made her look awkward and dumpy.

A clever touch, I thought.

Resplendent in her hooped gown of silver moiré embroidered with triple gold braid and clusters of glittering diamonds, a single black feather in her hair, the Empress stood patiently while Princess Johanna recited her obviously rehearsed speech. She mentioned her profound gratitude, sacred bonds between their two families, and her joy at finally being able to express it. She asked for contin-ued protection for the Anhalt-Zerbsts, but most of all "for the child whom Your Majesty has deigned to allow to accompany me to your court."

Pleasure glimmered in Empress Elizabeth's eyes. She kissed Princess Johanna on both cheeks and embraced her. There came promises of favors, gasps and praises, a frenzy of protestations followed by more assurances and pledges.

"Now, let me take a good look at her," I heard Elizabeth say.

Sophie stood behind her mother, her hands folded. *No, she is not pretty,* I decided, noting how long and pale her face was, how pointed her chin. It was not a face that would attract, although she had a beautiful complexion, milky white and translucent. The Princess was very slim, too slim. Her bony shoulders stuck out awkwardly in spite of the double thickness of her shawl. And yet there was something appealing about her, something I could not yet define.

Sophie smiled, a timid, girlish smile, and lowered her eyes.

"I've never been so happy, Your Highness," she began softly, in French. "You are even more beautiful than I've been told."

"Oh, but she is *charmante!*" the Empress exclaimed as she embraced the Princess again and again, kissing her on both cheeks.

Chancellor Bestuzhev stirred. I saw him brush invisible specks from the front of his velvet waistcoat.

"And my nephew?" Elizabeth asked, pointing to Peter. "Is he as handsome as he was when you saw him last? Or are you too shy to say it?"

I saw a touch of pink on Sophie's cheeks.

"Enough of this ceremony," the Empress announced, pleased with Sophie's silence. "Come, join me in my suite, where we can be alone."

The Princesses and the Grand Duke followed her out of the Throne Room. The door leading to the Imperial Suite closed with a thump, and soon the courtiers—including the Chancellor—began to leave.

There was a small antechamber outside the Imperial Suite, where, in a garlanded niche, a white-marble bust of Peter the Great stood. Beside it, a tapestry showed fountains of light illuminating the entwined initials of the Empress. I lingered there. I do not know what I was waiting for—a chance opening of the door, perhaps? An order I could offer to fulfill? A piece of knowledge I could carry to the Chancellor?

Sometimes I heard the Empress laugh or Princess Johanna speak, sometimes the Grand Duke. Only Sophie seemed to be silent.

After an hour or so, the door did open and the Empress stepped out, alone. She took no notice of me but stood by the window and parted the curtains. In the long, silent moment that followed, I saw her wipe a tear from her eye.

After the official greetings, the imperial guests were left to themselves. Lent had already begun, the time of confessions, of asking forgiveness of those wronged. For six weeks Orthodox believers would touch no meat, no fish, no butter or cream, not even with tea or coffee.

Yes, it was the time of Lent, but the guests were Lutheran and thus free from Orthodox observances. No fast for them, no morning prayers. They were told to rest after their monthlong journey, to regain their strength.

By then, I had been to Princess Sophie's room.

Her toilet kit was covered in rare French shagreen. Inside, there were porcelain jars and bottles decorated with cameos. Some contained water smelling of barley, some milk of sweet almonds, one was full of *poudre de violette* for her hair, and one had three different shades of rouge. The perfume bottles were most elaborate. There was the one with a carved cupid aiming an arrow into the distance, another with a nymph standing by a tree—the gifts of the Empress, all. I heard the chambermaids say that the German princess came with four chemises only and a dozen pairs of thick stockings.

I had opened the little silver box. Some of the black taffeta beauty spots within were round, some shaped like a heart or a crescent. I placed one of them on my cheek, but it wouldn't stick.

A green notebook with a flimsy lock easily gave in to a hairpin. Too easily, perhaps.

The Grand Duke's eyes are brown and shiny, just like his grandfather's.

The Empress of Russia is the most beautiful woman I have ever seen. And the kindest. She cares little for ceremony.

She was clever, I thought. There was nothing in this room—no evidence of doubt, no fear of loneliness at this foreign court where a newcomer has no friends.

The Chancellor would not like these dutiful displays of her virtue, I decided, anticipating his sour look, his fingers tapping the table with annoyance. There would be more complaints about drafts, more shots of vodka emptied in one gulp.

The thought gave me an unexpected jolt of pleasure.

Princess or not, Sophie was just a girl. There was nothing she could do to stop the Chancellor from sending her back where she came from. He might let her take the gifts, mementos of her futile dreams but nothing more. Until the end of her days, she would mourn what she had lost, this brief glimpse of a life that could have been hers.

You could be her friend, the Empress had told me in January as we all waited for the Princess to arrive. It was the first week of March and I was still peeking through the spying hole of this Moscow palace, watching Sophie and her new maids-of-honor, four Russian girls from the provinces, daughters of low-ranking nobles.

I saw how the maids-of-honor clustered around Sophie, asking her how she liked Russia and what she thought of their dresses and hairdos. I saw how gracious the Princess was with these trivial questions, how eagerly she praised their taste, their choice of trinkets.

Even for a petty German princess, they were better company than a bookbinder's daughter.

A few days later, from the murky dusk of a walled-up service room, I watched Princess Sophie of Anhalt-Zerbst, sitting on her bed, alone, in a silvery muslin dress, too light for the Russian winter, a shawl around her narrow shoulders, rocking her body to and fro.

I watched her pick up a book and begin to read. I made a note to check for letters between its pages as soon as I got a chance.

The dead air in the service room was making my head spin. From between the cracked boards of the floor seeped the smell of cooked cabbage and dried mushrooms. I tugged at the tight collar of my court dress, thinking of the elephant parade in St. Petersburg I would miss this year.

When I peeked again, Sophie stood in front of an opened door, not into the main hallway but to the corridor used by her servants. Footmen and maids rushed every which way with breakfast trays, coffeepots, baskets. One of the maids was trying to tell her in Russian that she was not supposed to open that door, that this was not the right passageway for her.

"Please, please, Your Highness," the maid pleaded, her cheeks rosy with excitement. I could imagine the stories she would tell in the servants' hall that evening.

"*Spasiba.* Thank you," Sophie kept repeating, but she did not move.

The main door opened, and I saw Princess Johanna come into the room. Or rather whirl inside, with the nervous energy of a storm. She had bruised shadows under her eyes, not yet masked with powder. "What are you doing, foolish girl?" she screamed at her daughter. "Close that door at once!"

Princess Johanna accused her daughter of indifference, lack of charm, absence of feminine lightness. The Grand Duke had not been pleased lately, and she could see why.

"Why don't you show more interest in what he has to tell you?"

"But all he wants to talk about is Holstein, Maman."

"Then talk about Holstein, stupid girl."

More accusations followed. Her daughter was not walking with enough grace. She was neglecting her duties to her father, though what duties these were it was impossible to tell. Sophie stood, head bowed, her fingers fondling the small pendant around her neck.

The main door opened again, and Bairta came in, crying loudly. She was a little Kalmyk girl the Empress had given Princess Sophie as a welcoming gift, after hearing the child singing in the street. Her voice, the Empress declared, was like the purest of chimes. Bairta's father had asked only for a good horse in exchange for his daughter.

Seeing her, Princess Johanna snapped, "Why can't you keep this wretch in your own room, Sophie? She is giving me a headache with her constant wailing."

Bairta scurried into a corner and made herself invisible.

Luckily, Princess Johanna got exhausted by her own tirade. Stretching her lips in a forced grin, she took a close look at herself in her daughter's mirror, adjusting her hair and a beauty spot on her chin. For a moment she stood motionless, listening to something I could not hear. "Don't tell me that I didn't warn you," she said to Sophie before leaving.

As soon as her mother was gone, Sophie wiped her eyes and shook her head like a wet dog. She made a few hesitant steps around the room, practiced curtsying in front of a mirror.

You could be her friend, the Empress had told me. *An older friend she could trust.*

In the corner of the room, Bairta began to sob. *This is my chance,* I decided.

I slipped out of the service room and knocked on the door.

"Come in," I heard.

I entered.

Princess Sophie smiled at the sight of me, a smile of recognition I did not expect.

"You read to the Grand Duke, don't you?" she asked me. "What is your name?"

"Varvara Nikolayevna."

"Varvara Nikolayevna," she repeated. On her lips, my Russian name seemed oddly harsh. "Has the Duke sent you?"

"I was just passing by, Your Highness," I lied. Disappointment flickered across the Princess's face but quickly vanished. "I thought I heard someone crying," I added.

She pointed to Bairta. The poor child was squatting, her face hidden between her knees. "She cries all the time. I try to ask her what's wrong, but she doesn't understand me."

Bairta made a sound that was half sigh, half sob, her shoulders hunching.

I knelt beside her.

"Why are you crying?" I asked in Russian.

Reluctantly, the weeping girl lifted her eyes. "I want to go to my Mama," she sobbed.

There was little comfort in the silent look Sophie and I exchanged then. How do you tell a child that not even a princess can oppose the wishes of an empress?

"Tell her I'll show her something if she stops crying," the Princess said.

I did.

Bairta watched, curious but still teary, as the Princess puffed up her cheeks and narrowed her eyes. She growled, meowed, and hissed like angry cats readying for a fight. Then came the screech of the battle, so real that if I closed my own eyes I would think two of the Empress's cats had crept into the room unobserved. Sophie's face flushed with the effort, but she didn't stop until the tears on Bairta's face stopped flowing.

I still remember that first sweet warming of my heart, lingering like perfume.

"How did you learn to do it?" I asked in amazement.

When Sophie laughed, her whole face lit up. Her blue eyes brightened. She didn't look like a little *Hausfrau*, I decided, and her chin was not that pointed.

"My father taught me," she answered.

And then she added, "But I won't tell you about him, for it will make me sad. And it would be pretty useless if I began to cry now, wouldn't it?"

Professor Stehlin had been ordered to shorten the time the Grand Duke spent on his lessons. The two children, the Empress said, were to be given time alone, before the court returned to St. Petersburg.

She told me to watch them.

The Grand Duke visited his fiancée every day, in her rooms, for two full hours, just as the Empress wished, but there was little to report.

Sophie asked him if he would take her for a sleigh ride, but he said it would only bore her.

"Would you teach me a Russian dance, then?" she asked.

"I don't like dancing."

"Why not?"

"I just don't."

The only time the conversations lasted for a while was when Sophie asked Peter about Holstein, just as her mother had told her to.

The best news I had to report was when the Grand Duke placed an awkward kiss on his fiancée's cheek, a kiss followed by a race down the corridor to see if they could make a Palace Guard on duty laugh.

I was on my way to the Grand Duke's study when Bairta stopped me.

"Come," she lisped, taking hold of my hand. "Mistress wants to see you."

I followed Bairta in silence. The day before I had heard her play the harp in the antechamber to Sophie's bedroom. I didn't ask the child if she still missed her mother.

Sophie was waiting for me, alone, sitting by the window, a book on her lap. I recognized the foot warmer she rested her feet on; the Empress did not think fur blankets enough for Russian winter chills.

I was cautious at first, for I half expected her to start asking me questions about the Grand Duke or the Empress. I wondered what I could tell her without revealing my own secrets. From the adjoining room, I heard Princess Johanna's chirping voice, echoed by a man's laughter.

"Is Varvara the same name as Barbara?" Sophie asked me.

"Yes," I replied.

"Does it mean anything?"

I told her that in Greek my name meant "a stranger, a foreigner," but that St. Barbara, my patron saint, was a learned woman who converted to Christianity in spite of her father's objections. She could protect those who prayed to her from lightning and storms.

"How do you know that?" the Princess asked.

"I read it in one of my father's books.

"He died," I added, before she managed to ask.

She raised her blue eyes. I fixed my gaze on the tapestry behind her. It was of a nymph turning into a tree, twigs entangled in her hair, legs fusing into a trunk, already half covered by bark. Behind her, a man tried to grasp her before she escaped.

"I, too, like to read," the Princess said.

The only book she didn't like was the Bible, because her teacher at home, a Lutheran pastor, required her to learn passages from it by heart. When she made the tiniest of mistakes in her recitations he slapped her, saying, "The joys of the world are not worth its pains."

I studied her face as she spoke, the dark smudges under her eyes, the black hair pinned too tight, unpowdered, bare. For a moment I let myself fall into a memory of the cats' concert and Bairta's childish joy.

"Will you help me?" I heard, unexpectedly. I made a step back. The heels of my new shoes sank into the thick Turkish carpet that covered the floor.

"With my Russian," the Princess added hastily, and handed me a sheet of paper. It was a letter. A draft, rather. She had copied sentences from the exercises her Russian tutor gave her to study, but she was sure they still needed correcting.

She was a foreigner and therefore she couldn't afford errors, she told me. Not in Russian.

Any foreigner who succeeded in Russia, she said, had to be of the highest caliber. The Russians never forgave the slightest transgression by those not of their blood. She had been warned already.

Her voice wavered and hardened.

I didn't ask who had warned her. I didn't want to know.

"We are both foreigners here, aren't we, Varvara Nikolayevna?"

"Yes, Your Highness."

It was a short letter, a note of thanks to someone yet unnamed for a gift of French wine, a whole case of burgundy from the last shipment before the Baltic shores froze. *A thoughtful gift I will find most useful once Lent is over,* Sophie had written.

The errors she made were slight—a few spelling mistakes, a "soft *znak*" omitted here and there. She handed me her own quill, and I made the necessary corrections in the margins.

Every time I pointed out an error, Sophie made a comic groan. "How silly of me not to notice," she would exclaim. "How foolish!" When I finished and curtsied, ready to leave, she stopped me.

"I'm sorry to be such a bother," she said.

I looked at her face, the tensing of her lips. "It's nothing," I muttered.

I watched her turn to the mantel for a small package wrapped in yellow cloth. "I hope you'll accept a gift—a trifle, really."

"There is no need," I protested immediately, but she shook her head. I felt her fingers on my arm; I saw her eyes look into mine.

"Please, Varvara Nikolayevna," she said, handing me the package. "But don't open it now." She stopped me from removing the purple ribbon with which it was tied.

Later, alone in my room, I untied the purple ribbon. The yellow cloth slid off, revealing a piece of amber cradled in white satin.

I took it out and raised it to the light. It was a superb piece of amber that must have cost Sophie far more than she could afford. In honey-colored resin, two large bees were entangled in an embrace.

I admired the bent, stick-like legs, the folded wings, the abdomens with invisible stings, curled and bare.

I wondered how the bees had died. Was it duty or hunger that had lured them to the same sticky grave? Or a curious need to explore what was not meant for them at all? The courage of wanting more? A longing to stand by each other even if it meant death?

We are both foreigners here.

Is that why I did it? My first reckless act of transgression? To hold on to this sweet warmth I had so very nearly forgotten? To make it last for a few more moments, before caution and fear crept back? Or was it mercy, another name for the sin of hubris? A lesson in survival, my gift to her?

For she had been terribly foolish with her writing.

Not with the maxims or ambitious plans for self-improvement, not with her own written portrait in which she called herself a *"Philosophe* at fifteen," even though her fifteenth birthday would come only in May. But with the page I retrieved from the bottom of her drawer.

Memoir of an Elephant

You come in your finery, you see me and you gasp: "How big he is, how strong and yet how docile." You think me reconciled with my captive state; you think yourselves grand, for you have enslaved a giant.

You talk of bringing me a wife, you make plans for my unborn children, foolish plans, for a captured elephant will never reproduce for the profit of the tyrant who has taken away his liberty.

You watch me, but I watch you, too, and I find you small and fearful, a pitiable race I offer this warning:

Accept the virtues of a simple life, of modest and natural customs. Bow to reason and not to fear. Bend your knees before kings but not before tyrants.

Such is the wisdom of elephants.

I held the paper in my hands for a long time, studied the elegant, even loops of Sophie's handwriting, the elongated *f* and *l*. I imagined the Chancellor's glee, his praise for my skills.

I imagined Elizabeth's wrath.

On the silver tray where Sophie kept her bottles with barley and lavender water, I lit a candle.

I let the page burn, watching the fire eat the words she should not have written. Then I doused the flame, leaving the remnants of the blackened sheet on the tray.

I hoped Sophie would know what it meant.

I prayed no one was watching me.

"The little *Hausfrau* must be doing something wrong, Varvara," the Chancellor snapped when I reported how Sophie kept herself awake long into the night to study her Russian vocabulary and Orthodox prayers. "Surely the Princess of Anhalt-Zerbst is not a saint."

I tried not to think how slight and pale she had looked that day when her mother came to scold her, how beseeching her eyes were when she asked me for help. Soon she would make another mistake, write something careless, reveal her disappointment with the Grand Duke or even the Empress herself. And then, bruised and hurting, she would be gone.

I had helped her once, but I could not keep acting against the Chancellor's wishes. One word of his would crush me, and what could she do to stop him?

I had no illusions. I was like a sea creature clinging to a rock. Over me, storms raged while I held on, hoping that the currents and waves would not sweep me off. If I perished, who would notice?

Once it is all over, I thought, *she has her father to go to, but I have no one.* The spymaster's voice in my head warned me to remain indifferent, not to go too far.

Princess Johanna, the Empress declared, had let her daughter grow too thin, too bony. What Sophie needed was the simple goodness of Russian food, the dishes Elizabeth's own mother fed her when she was a girl, the dark rye bread, *shchi*—the sauerkraut soup thickened with oatmeal—kasha with stewed mushrooms. At mealtimes, the Empress took to summoning Princess Sophie to her side, delighted when, after emptying plate after plate, her young guest called this or that dish her favorite until yet another delicacy was urged upon her.

That, I thought, was a good sign.

At the end of February, the Empress began her preparations for her annual pilgrimage to the monastery of Holy Trinity–St. Sergius. There was no reporting of secrets at this time of year. In these days, Elizabeth preferred stories of noble sons living in poverty, striving for holiness.

At the monastery, the Empress, her head covered in black lace, her stomach racked with hunger pains, would beg the Virgin of Smolensk for forgiveness. For each night of drinking, for every guard she took to her bed, she would kiss the Virgin's painted hand and offer a prayer. There had been many such nights in a year. There would have to be many such prayers. All matters of this earth must wait for her return.

We all welcomed this time, not only because of her absence.

The days of fasting and praying forced Elizabeth to think of eternity. For the first two days after her return, the Empress of Russia would speak of nothing but mercy and forgiveness. It was the best time for confessions and pleas for clemency, petitions and requests. The servant lucky enough to be in charge of her appointments would double his salary in bribes.

This year, however, the Chancellor of Russia was not considering the benefits of the imperial remorse.

On the day that the Empress left Moscow for the Monastery of St. Sergius, Princess Sophie was allowed to begin her instruction in the Orthodox faith.

The Grand Duke continued his daily visits to his fiancée, but with the Empress's absence a note of discord appeared between them. Slight, perhaps, easy to ignore, but not to my ear.

It all started when the Princess asked for the Holy Icon to be placed in the corner of her room, the Virgin of Vladimir, which she greeted with a bow every time she entered.

"You didn't have to do that," Peter said, giving her a sour look. "You haven't converted yet."

There was more he disliked. With the Empress away, Sophie didn't have to ask for rye bread and *bliny* for breakfast. She didn't have to drink kvass, either. Or try to speak Russian so often.

"Like some simpleton," he had said.

I often saw tears in her eyes, but she had quickly learned to keep silent. She didn't complain when Peter taught her to march and present her musket. She never repeated a request for a green Preobrazhensky uniform instead of the blue Holstein one Peter had ordered her to wear as he marched her through the hallways with great vigor. "Higher," I'd heard the Duke command. "Lift your legs higher, Sophie. Tempo. Tempo."

She was trying. She stayed up until nearly dawn to study her Russian vocabulary, copy passages from Russian books, pages and pages of them. If there was any time left after her daily lessons, she practiced the loud reading of the Orthodox Creed. I could hear her voice late each night, stumbling over phrases.

On a piece of vellum paper she kept on her escritoire she had written, *Three things are essential. To please the Empress, to please the Grand Duke, and to please the Russian people.*

The Empress had been gone for a week when I heard Princess Johanna screaming at Sophie. "Acting out," Johanna had called Sophie's bouts of nausea and the fainting spells. "Stop behaving like a spoiled child," she scolded when the Princess begged to be excused from her public appearances.

That morning Princess Sophie got out of bed and vomited dark slime into a bowl the maids carried out quickly, covered with white cloth. Her eyes were glassy with fever.

I saw Princess Johanna shake her daughter's thin body and urge her to sit up in her bed, to stop pampering herself. "Make the Grand Duke see that a daughter of a Prussian officer is not a weakling," she snapped.

The vomiting went away after a purging and a day of fasting, but the fever was more persistent. The court doctor who examined the Princess was not alarmed at first. Clear skin meant that it was not smallpox. He, too, was sure that a few days of bed rest was all Sophie needed.

My daughter'll receive Your Highness tomorrow, Princess Johanna wrote in answer to the Grand Duke's inquiry. *She has been touched to hear of Your Highness's concern for her but begs Your Highness not to worry.*

But the bouts of fever continued in spite of ice-cold compresses that the maids changed every hour. On the third day, the Princess did not recognize her mother. "I want to go out," she insisted. And then she fainted. The best of Moscow doctors summoned for a consultation agreed that bleeding was the only cure.

Princess Johanna called them barbarians, ignorant fools used to treating thick-skinned peasants. Russian doctors had killed her brother, she ranted, pushing them out of Sophie's room. She would not let them touch her child.

Nothing would change her mind. No pleading, no arguments that bleeding would purify the blood. Her daughter's constitution had been upset with too much excitement, she insisted, and unfamiliar food. All Sophie needed were a few more days of fasting. She was already feeling better.

Through the spying hole in the service room, I saw little beyond the drawn curtains of the sickbed and the bent figure of the German chambermaid, picking at her fingernails.

The Princess was lucid enough in the mornings, but by the afternoon, the fever returned. The maids whispered that she was too weak to stand on her own. I heard the surgeon declare that soon even a bleeding might be of little use. On the marble floor of the entrance hall, little Bairta was jumping from one square to the next, for hours, trying not to step on a line, for that would bring bad luck.

Days were still frigid, the air brittle with frost. The invitations for the ducal pair to winter sleigh rides had all been politely refused. From its small box I took the amber with the pair of bees imprisoned inside. I turned it in my hands for a long time before returning it to its hiding place.

"What would *you* want with her?" Princess Johanna had shrilled at me when I asked to see Princess Sophie. "You've bothered her enough already!"

"What can we, mere mortals, do to change the will of the Lord?" Chancellor Bestuzhev said and sighed as I reported on Princess Johanna's obstinacy. "The Lord is my witness this is not how I wished the girl to go."

"The Grand Duke'll miss her visits," I said, wishing to believe my own words.

"The Grand Duke will forget her as soon as she is gone," the Chancellor replied. I must have winced, for the look he gave me was sharp. "You are not sorry for her, are you?"

"No," I answered. Too quickly, perhaps.

I had seen enough to know that nothing changed with more swiftness than one's position at court. There were others as eager as I once was to move up in the world. Girls who smiled like cats in the pantry, lingered when ordered to hurry, growing sloppy and careless with their chores.

I saw them enter the Chancellor's room; I heard their stifled laughter. I saw them leave, smoothing the folds of their skirts. I saw them married off so that the Empress—dressed in a peasant costume—could dance at their weddings.

Another day passed with Princess Johanna still refusing to listen to the surgeons' pleas and rejecting the slightest suggestion to send word of Sophie's illness to the Empress. Her daughter was strong. She was young. It was nothing.

In her own chamber, adjacent to her daughter's sickroom, Sophie's mother, her face paint smeared on her cheeks, rubbed herself against a certain Valet de Chambre. Through a spying hole I could see his lips nuzzling her neck. I could hear the Princess giggle.

I waited until they had their fill. I waited for the words that followed.

"That peasant's daughter, happiest in the company of servants . . . fat, vain, jealous . . . must be on her knees praying now . . . asking the Virgin which regiment to choose her new lover from: the Kalmyks or the Cossacks . . . both, I would say . . . to make up for the lost time."

The floor squeaked; the door opened and closed.

In the dusty darkness of my hiding place I watched when, her lover gone, Princess Johanna sat at her escritoire and began writing, hastily, without a pause, filling one page, then another. I watched her when she paused, wiped her forehead, and yawned before she folded her letter and hid it.

A smile stuck to her lips when she rose and left the room. Moments later, I heard her voice next door, scolding the maids. The air was too stuffy. Sophie's pillows were flat and stained. Why was the chamber pot still not emptied?

The flimsy escritoire yielded its secret to me without much fuss. *This is a barbarian land*, the Princess wrote, assuring the King of Prussia, *not the Empire it makes itself to be*.

I recalled how Monsieur Mardefeld, the Prussian Ambassador, his belly quaking, kissed Princess Johanna's hand with far too much ardor. Was he passing these missives to the Prussian King? *Soon,* the letter promised, *very soon, I should be able to inform Your Majesty of many auspicious decisions taken as the result of my direct intervention.*

Who did foolish Johanna fancy herself to be?

I see indolence and chaos, a country weak and petulant, demanding constant praise, she had written.

I slid the letter back into its hiding place. In the corridor, I could hear someone sobbing.

I shivered.

Her child might die at any moment, but all Princess Johanna would ever mourn would be her own deluded dreams.

"So our illustrious Princess fancies herself to be a Prussian spy?" the Chancellor said, laughing at what I had just told him.

He had taken to wearing shorter wigs that revealed the nape of his neck as he walked. His eyes were set in livid rings and his cheeks sagged.

"You've done well, Varvara." The Chancellor clapped his hands and leaned back in his armchair.

I thought of Sophie, rigid, waxy-faced with pain, gulping air through parched lips. I thought of the surgeon's warning, "Only bleeding can break the fever."

I went to see the Grand Duke.

He was building a wooden fortress, one of the models from his Cabinet of Fortification, his aunt's gift.

He had spread out the directions for putting the model together and was gluing two pieces of wood, concentrating on making them fit perfectly. The tip of his tongue was sticking out as he contemplated his next move.

"Your Highness. May I speak bluntly, like a soldier?" I asked.

"Speak."

"If Princess Sophie dies, the Empress will not forgive Your Highness for not telling her."

"She won't die," he said, shrugging his shoulders. "She is stronger than you think. She will outlive me, and she will outlive you."

"What if the Empress asks why you did nothing to save her?"

He hesitated. He, too, lived in fear of Elizabeth's fury.

I had brought paper, quills, and ink.

I had brought a sander to dry the ink.

He sat down with a loud sigh and wrote a letter to the Empress. He sealed it with red wax, carefully, right in the very center.

I thought of the Empress, in a simple black dress, her head covered with a kerchief, looking up at the gilded face of the Virgin. I thought of the messenger's journey along the Yaroslavl' road, to the gold-and-blue onion domes of the monastery.

I'm convinced that Princess Johanna's obstinacy is preventing her daughter's recovery, the Grand Duke agreed to write. *That Sophie needs a true mother at her side.*

A lone horse left the stable, its rider a messenger who would reach the monastery before dawn. The Empress could be back in Moscow by evening the day after.

Hurry, I muttered into the night.

Hurry.

If anyone can still save her, it will be you.

The Empress did arrive, in the dark of midnight, jaws wobbling with mad fury, a sharp foxy smell trailing her as she swept toward Sophie's room.

"Out of my sight, you slut," she hissed at Princess Johanna, who wisely retreated into her room. The maids ordered to bring her meals from the kitchen and empty her chamber pot would later laugh at how she jumped every time they knocked on the door.

Selfishness and greed surrounded her, the Empress kept scream-ing. Fear and ignorance. If it weren't for the Grand Duke's presence of mind, she would have come home to a funeral.

The palace surgeon pleaded that Princess Johanna had refused to let him examine the patient, forbade him to bleed her. "And that was enough to stop you?" the Empress snarled, before dismissing him from her service.

Count Lestocq removed the coverlet from Sophie's bed. The Empress's old lover, once a surgeon at the court of Empress Anne, had been one of the conspirators in Elizabeth's bid for power. On the eve of the coup, Lestocq had shown the hesitant Elizabeth two cards, one with a crown and another with the gallows. "You can choose only one," he had told her.

Count Lestocq took out his lancet with an ivory handle, first sharpened on a whetstone and then honed on a leather strap, like a razor. As soon as the blade released a stream of blood, the Princess stirred and opened her eyes.

For the next hour Elizabeth sat by Sophie's side. She wiped her moist forehead. "I'm here," she murmured. "I'll take care of you now."

When the footman announced the arrival of a Lutheran pastor, the Princess rose on her elbows and murmured something, her voice soft and pleading.

We all watched the Empress bend over Sophie to hear her words.

And then we saw her turn back to us, tears rolling down her cheeks.

"This child . . . this blessed child," she said, her voice quivering, "has just asked me to send the Lutheran pastor away. She wants me to call for an Orthodox priest."

On June 28, 1744, in Moscow, the whole court watched the Princess of Anhalt-Zerbst walk into the chapel of the Golovin Palace to be admitted to the Orthodox faith. In her scarlet gown trimmed with silver braid, with a simple white ribbon in her unpowdered hair, she looked both resplendent and girlish. The Empress herself had put a thick layer of rouge on her face and vermilion on her lips.

The Princess was still weakened by her illness, but her steps were resolute as she walked behind the Empress, behind her mother and the Grand Duke.

She recited the Creed from memory and made no mistakes. When the time came to say the words *Simvola very*—symbols of faith—she said them almost without a trace of an accent.

I heard sobs from the crowd when the Archbishop placed salt on her tongue and anointed her forehead, eyes, neck, throat, and hands with holy oil. She kissed his hand and waited for the Mass to be sung, for the body of Christ to be placed on her tongue in the Holy Communion.

When she turned back to face us, she was no longer Sophie, a petty German princess with darned stockings and threadbare linen in her trunks. She had become Catherine Alexeyevna, an Orthodox believer. The following day, in the Uspensky Cathedral, she would be officially betrothed to the Grand Duke.

I watched the Empress clasp Catherine to her chest, call her her own darling, the solace of her days, her precious girl, her own little doll.

Catherine Alexeyevna. Ekaterina. Katia. Katinka.

The Empress had renamed her after her own mother. Not even an echo of her Prussian father's name was to weaken Elizabeth's claim on this girl whom she had taken as her own, whose life she had saved.

I noted Princess Johanna's bitter face.

The bells were ringing; the flares were lit. On the day of betrothal, there was dancing in the streets. On the imperial orders, oxen were roasted on giant spits and beer flowed from the fountains. When the night fell, fireworks exploded in giant wheels and cascades of falling stars. Russia abandoned herself to pleasure.

In the streets of Moscow, I saw fire-eaters with yellowed tongues and singed fingers. I saw a dancing bear with a bleeding bald patch on its nose. I saw a parrot pluck at its feathers, twittering and squawking when its master ground the hurdy-gurdy. I saw a girl not older than ten balance her lithe body on a rope stretching between two houses. The crowd below gasped when she teetered. There were shouts of joy in the streets. *Long live Peter, the Grand Duke of All the Russias! Long live Catherine, our Grand Duchess!*

I bought a wooden bird that clapped its wings when it was pushed. I would leave it by Bairta's bed, I thought, so that she wouldn't even know where it came from, her going-away present. Catherine had asked the Empress to send the child home to her mother, and the Empress had agreed.

Chancellor Bestuzhev was one of the first to kiss the Grand Duchess's hand and to congratulate the Grand Duke. "Your Majesty was right," he said to the Empress. "She is *charmante*. There cannot be a better choice."

Once, in the midst of the celebration, I saw Catherine slip out into the corridor lined with mirrored panels. Briefly she leaned against the wall and closed her eyes. When I reached her a few moments later, she was fogging the mirrored panel with her breath and tracing a letter *S*. Then she wiped it clean and breathed on the mirror again. She wrote a *C* in its place.

She is alive, I thought. *She is safe. The Empress will see to that.*

This was all I could do for her, and I hoped it would be enough.

"Curious how willingly some people dig their own graves," the Chancellor told me, lifting his eyes from the pile of papers. *The Empress listens to me*, Princess Johanna wrote in one of her silly letters. *The Empress agrees on my assessment of the country's vital interests.*

I knew that the messenger of the Prussian Ambassador had been intercepted on his way to Berlin and that an offer of a few hundred rubles for his silence proved far more attractive than the frozen expanses of Siberia.

"Let her write." The gilded chair creaked under the Chancellor's growing bulk. "Let her think no one is watching. I want to know who visits her and where she goes."

I felt his hand trace the line of my neck, linger on the collarbone, before sliding down toward my nipples.

My eyes were still the best, I thought. My ears could still hear what others would have missed. Had I not been at court for almost two years, surviving when others had perished?

TWO

1744–1745

n Moscow the Grand Duchess Catherine Alexeyevna was buying presents.

A length of muslin for Countess Rumyantseva; a marble egg on a golden base for her mother.

A china vase, a porcelain figurine of a ballet dancer. A necklace of peacock feathers. A set of birch boxes, one nestled inside the other, smelling of mushrooms when you opened the lid to sniff them. A riding habit with tapered coattails and long, cuffed sleeves.

A musket for the Duke, a model cannon, a set of plaster-of-paris trees to put outside the fortifications he was constructing in his room.

A helmet stand.

They lined up outside her bedroom, the tradesmen of Moscow, their attendants loaded with bundles and crates. They showed her wooden dolls dressed in the latest Parisian fashions, tempted her with ostrich feathers, lace trimmings, gauzes, and bonnets. They pointed out that Empress Elizabeth thought the world of the Parisian milliners. They coaxed her to touch samples of fabrics, spoke of the luster of pearls, of the stately sheen of rubies, of how the glitter of sapphires around the neck is as subtle as the flutter of butterfly wings.

Didn't the Grand Duke like dark Prussian blue more than any other color? they asked as they spread shimmering fabrics on her floor. They spoke of a little help every woman needed to entice a man—to conceal and reveal. They offered pomades and perfumes, waters to moisten the skin, essences of rose, narcissus, and orange blossom.

"The Russian people are watching, Your Highness. They must not see Your Highness in the same dress twice. Simple straight sleeves are no longer in fashion."

She could not afford to be outshone or thought of as stingy. Her new friends were expecting tokens of her affection. Her servants' loyalty, too, had to be bought. If she didn't do it, someone else would.

They made her buy bags for needlework, powder puffs, beauty spots, snuffboxes, sachets of perfumes, and white gloves by the dozen. It was not extravagance, they argued. It was necessity. Was it true that at the Prussian court King Frederick measured the cheese left after supper and wrote the measurement down in his notebook? That he melted the ends of candles and sold them?

A costly purchase can entice a merchant to wait a few more weeks for his payment. One creditor can be paid with money borrowed from another—but this cannot go on forever.

"Bankers are a happy lot these days," the Chancellor told me merrily. "And I was beginning to think that our little *Hausfrau* would put up more of a fight."

Debts can so easily be turned into reproaches, an accusation that the Empress has been niggardly with her allowance. Catherine was betrothed, but she was still not the imperial bride.

I looked at the Grand Duchess and thought, *There is nothing else I can do for you.*

But then everything changed.

In the middle of December the court was in Khotilovo, on its way from Moscow to St. Petersburg, when the Grand Duke fainted during supper. In his room, revived with salts, he complained of pain in his legs and arms. At first everyone suspected measles, but by the time the fever and vomiting started, the doctors had no doubt. It was smallpox.

Empress Elizabeth, who had been traveling ahead and had reached St. Petersburg already, hurried back to her nephew's side.

We all held our breaths.

The bedside bulletins from Khotilovo spoke of long, feverish nights and of the Crown Prince's will to live. In churches all over Russia, priests led prayers for Peter Fyodorovich and the safety of the Empress. Like a true mother to her beloved sister's child, the Empress nursed the Grand Duke herself, sitting by his bedside day and night. She washed the sores on his face and body. She fed him broth and strengthening tonics. She quieted his cries of pain.

Hushed voices in antechambers considered the possibilities. Death might reshuffle the cards. What would become of that other heir, Ivan VI, the child who had been condemned to a prison cell on the day the Russian daughter of Peter the Great seized the throne?

I heard it evoked often in those days, the memory of that November night three years before when the Palace Guards brought Princess Elizabeth back to the Winter Palace on a sleigh, beautiful like a Madonna from an icon, a Russian cross in her hands, a leather cuirass over her shoulders—triumphant but in need of protection, strong but in need of love. One by one, the soldiers had knelt before her, kissed the hem of her dress, sworn to protect her with their lives.

Elizabeth could have had Ivan killed then, but she didn't. Perhaps for a reason?

As the Grand Duke was fighting for his life, the whispers grew. The Empress was almost thirty-five. There was still time before she would go through the change of life. What if she made Ivan her husband? Perhaps he was soft in the head, but he would be fit to father a child soon enough. A true successor to Peter the Great!

With the Empress and the Grand Duke away from the Winter Palace, official duties were suspended, plans put on hold. Doors once flung open for visitors were kept shut; no music poured from opened windows. In the receiving room, cats were the only guests. They lounged on the ottomans or chased one another across the floor.

Idle footmen and maids sat for hours on the steps of the service corridors, chatting and giggling, scarcely bothering to make room for those who wanted to pass. By the stables, guards gathered to play cards. Fortified with good snuff and shots of vodka, they tried to pinch or fondle any palace girl who walked past.

Everyone waited.

Catherine and her mother had not been given apartments at the Winter Palace but had to take a house on Millionnaya Street. They were fast becoming insignificant, worthy of no more than a passing whisper. If the Grand Duke died, the Empress would have no use of them. The house was two-story, its windows always closed and curtains drawn. To the annoyance of Herr Leibnitz, a German cloth merchant, and the families of Guard officers who lived nearby, day after day creditors banged on the door, cursing their own foolishness in trusting these foreigners, complaining loudly how the mighty of this world did not care to pay their debts.

I thought of the two bees locked in the piece of amber Catherine had given me. *We are both foreigners here,* she had said.

She soon would be gone. What harm was there in showing her some kindness?

I walked to the house on Millionnaya Street and rang the bell. The day was cold and windy, threatening more snow. A sleigh passed by, its bells jingling. A narrow footpath cleared of ice had been sprinkled with sand and ashes.

The maid who asked me to follow her could not resist asking if I'd heard anything about the Grand Duchess moving back to the palace.

I shook my head. The hall smelled of wood smoke and mold.

"This way," the maid said, showing me to a small parlor on the first floor.

The room seemed quite dark with its wooden paneling, its front windows hung with velvet curtains. Cheap cotton velvet, I noted, not silk. The only light came from a narrow window facing the backyard with its bare trees. A tile stove took up the whole corner of the room, radiating a pleasant heat. Beside a clavichord, on a side table I spotted a pile of books in plain bindings. When I opened them, they turned out to be tales of pirates, shipwrecks, and kidnappings.

I took it all in. The armchair with frayed covers, a watery mirror, a sewing box with a lacquered lid on which a beautiful firebird glittered, a woolen shawl draped over the chair by the window, two crossed sabers hanging on the wall above a bearskin. From the corridor came the noise of clanking pots, a patter of feet, the soapy smell of boiling laundry.

I recalled the house on Vasilevsky Island, Papa's measured steps, Mama's voice cheerful and brisk. The memory was so vivid that I could almost inch into her arms.

The door opened quite abruptly. In this house a visitor was clearly a rare treat.

"Oh, it's you," Princess Johanna said when she walked into the room. She didn't try to hide her disappointment.

"I hope I'm not intruding," I said.

Catherine was right behind her, her hair hastily coiffed, half hidden under a lace cap. She smiled and made a step toward me, but Princess Johanna held out her hand to stop her. Did she think me common? I wondered. Or merely of no use to them?

"Any change in the Grand Duke's condition?" Princess Johanna asked.

I repeated the words of the latest health bulletin: There had been another bleeding, but the fever had not come down. "All in God's hands," I said.

Catherine lowered her head.

"All in God's hands," Princess Johanna repeated.

The maid came with refreshments, slices of fruitcake and hot tea with plum preserves but no sugar. The Princess of Anhalt-Zerbst did not think me that important.

It was an awkward visit. Princess Johanna launched into an elaborate tale of her connections with the House of Brunswick, while Catherine kept motioning for me to have more tea and cake. Her fingernails, I noticed, had been chewed to the quick.

"Are you making progress with Russian, Your Highness?" I asked her.

"Not much," she replied. "I have so few people to talk to."

"Nonsense," her mother snapped. "My daughter has made great progress."

"Father Semyon is praying for Your Highness every day," I said, keeping my eyes on Catherine. For her sake, I tried to sound cheerful as I recalled who at the palace inquired about her health and circumstances. The list was not that long, but Catherine blushed with pleasure.

Princess Johanna rose. She was losing patience.

I, too, rose, ready to leave.

"Could Varvara Nikolayevna come back tomorrow?" Catherine asked, giving her mother a pleading look.

"If you wish, Sophie," the Princess replied. Her eyes slid over me, unseeing. "I don't see what harm it could do now."

I was already downstairs when I heard hurried steps and felt Catherine's arms lock around my waist.

"Your Highness," I gasped.

"Please don't mind Maman," Catherine said, her eyes fixed on mine, a frightened bird. "Please."

I felt her slender body quiver against mine. I heard a sob.

"Will you come back, please?"

"Your Highness—" I began, but she stopped me.

"Just Catherine," she said.

"Yes," I told her. "I'll come back."

In the next weeks, every morning I prepared detailed summaries of newspaper articles Professor Stehlin had marked for me the day before, so that I could read them to the Grand Duke once he returned to his apartment at the Winter Palace. By mid-January as the summaries were piling up, unread, I began to arrange them into folders according to subject matter. The Grand Duke's study, I vowed, would always be ready for the imperial lessons. I kept the quills sharpened, the inkwells full. I carefully dusted Peter's model soldiers, making sure I did not upset their positions on the plaster-of-paris battlefield.

And all along I thought of Catherine's joy at seeing me.

"Let's find out if you look good in blue," she would say when I arrived, making me try on one of her dresses, rushing to and fro through the room, in search of ribbons and shawls to adorn it.

Resigned to my presence at her daughter's side, Princess Johanna left us alone. So I have many memories of the two of us in that dark-paneled parlor, two girls trying to ignore what we could not control. We would skip along the corridor, giggling, until the maid chastised us for our foolishness. We would curl up on an ottoman, arms pillowing our heads, whispering in the deepening dusk of a winter afternoon.

Tell me the funniest thing you have ever done.

And the dumbest.

And the thing that you would like to happen again and again.

And the best.

And the worst.

But there were times when Catherine would grow solemn. "Tell me he'll live, Varenka," she would urge me. "Tell me now, quickly."

"He will."

I put all the hope I had into these words to brush aside her terror.

It was so good to talk like that, sitting side by side on the squeaky ottoman, sipping hot tea, eating cucumbers smeared with honey, her favorite dish.

Like sisters.

"I've never had a home, Varenka, a true home where I felt I could be myself. I've always had to think how others see me.

"I'm always a guest, Varenka. A Lutheran among Lutherans, an Orthodox among the Orthodox. German among Germans, Russian among Russians. But who am I when I'm alone? I don't know any-more."

I turned my face away to hide my tears.

"Varenka?" she said, taking hold of my hand.

"I had a home once," I began.

As the health bulletins from Khotilovo became shorter and grimmer, I heard Catherine's name mentioned in dismissive tones. In the cor-ridors of the Winter Palace, the courtiers recalled the days of Empress Anne, spoke of the hated rule of the Germans. The time when an old noble might find himself ordered to cluck like a hen. Or, like Prince Galitsin, be forced to marry a Kalmyk maid and spend his wedding night in a palace made of ice.

Why would this German princess be any different?

Catherine knew of the rumors. "They don't want me here, do they?" she asked me.

"The Russians don't give their trust very freely," I replied. "They want to watch you first for a long time. They want to be sure."

"I think of him so often," she said. "He liked running with me, all the way across the meadow. He didn't even mind when I won. But now, even if he doesn't die . . ."

She took a deep breath before bursting into tears. I drew closer and held her, but the sobs did not stop.

Did the Grand Duke consider closing his eyes and taking his leave in these dark Khotilovo days? Did Elizabeth, always by his side, trick him into returning to life? Did she soften his fear when he woke from nightmares in which his father was pushing him away or his Eutin tutor was whipping him and forcing him to kneel on hard peas? Did she convince him that he could still be loved?

"You have to eat," Elizabeth coaxed him, a spoonful at a time, her ears deaf to Count Razumovsky's pleas that she must spare herself,

deaf even to the warnings about what smallpox scars do to a woman's
skin.

"One more sip, darling."

"One more bite."

"My beloved child."

"My falcon."

If he had died then, in Khotilovo, in his aunt's arms, there would
have been a grand state funeral and a public mourning. The whole of
Russia would have imagined what the good Peter would have done
for his subjects and for the glory of the Empire. His name would be
lovingly evoked for years to come.

A carriage would have taken Catherine and her mother back to
Anhalt-Zerbst, across the plains of Russia, loaded with presents and
memories of splendor that had passed her by. If Peter had died, where
would Catherine be now? Married to some princeling, an empress of
a crumbling castle and a herd of cows? And where would I be, without
her?

But Peter didn't die.

By the end of January, six weeks after his collapse, the Grand Duke
made his first wobbly steps, each of them—the Empress declared—
a proof of God's mercy. She held Peter's hand when the surgeon removed the bandages from his face. She promised him that the ugly
red patches would soon fade.

In the first days of February, the Grand Duke was allowed to return
to St. Petersburg and slowly resume some of his duties. *The Crown
Prince of Russia has fought bravely*, the last official bulletin on the state
of his health read, *like the most valiant of soldiers. He battled the illness
with fierce determination and courage until the Lord granted him victory.*

But victory is not everything. It's just as crucial to consider what
has been won.

When Grand Duke Peter returned to the Winter Palace, the Empress
ordered Professor Stehlin to put aside all the foreign newspapers and

military history books at once. "Let Varvara read him something light," she commanded. "Something to take his mind away from death."

In the palace library, I pushed aside the French novels and history books. No star-crossed lovers, no Tacitus, no stories of ancient Rome. The Grand Duke was not to think of plots and murders. I chose the travelers' tales for him. Sir John Mandeville's stories from the islands of Andaman. Stories of people without heads, who have eyes in each shoulder, and those whose upper lips are so big that when they sleep in the sun they cover their faces with them.

For many evenings, I sat in the corner of his bedroom, illuminated by a single candle, reading aloud while Peter rested on his bed. The curtains were always drawn; not even moonlight was allowed to come in from the outside. Every time I lifted my eyes away from the book, I could barely see his lanky body sprawled in the thick darkness, his face covered with a gauze kerchief. If I stopped reading, he banged his fist and demanded I continue.

Sometimes I saw him pull on his ear until it bled. Sometimes I heard him sob, long, wolfish howls that ended in a choking silence.

He never asked me anything, but he refused to let me leave.

He'll get better, I thought. *For Catherine*. So that the Empress does not send her away.

Once when I thought him asleep I bent over him to adjust his pillow. Under the thin layer of gauze, I could barely discern the redness of swollen skin.

He opened his eyes and stared at me. I kept smoothing the lace of the pillow trim. He didn't stop me, not even when my fingers brushed his hair.

"Your fiancée is worried, Your Highness," I said softly. "She wishes to be allowed to see you."

"I don't want *her* here."

The venom of his words startled me. "Why not?"

"She listens to the Devil."

"Who says such nonsense to you?" I asked. "Who dares to spread such mean rumors?"

Before I could say anything more, I felt Peter's long, thin arms around my neck. Sobs racked his thin body, and he would not be soothed. He wouldn't tell me who spoke of Catherine to him. He shook his head when I described how despondent Catherine had been all these weeks while he lay in fever, how she worried that he still refused food.

He clung to my arm as I tried to soothe him, his fingers digging into my flesh. In the morning I would discover my arm was covered with bruises.

"He is still very weak," I told Catherine in the morning. "But I'm sure that the worst has passed."

One late afternoon, as I was reading to the Grand Duke, the guards announced the Empress's arrival.

I closed the book, stood, and curtsied as she swept in. She did not look at me. Her silk dress rustled as she walked toward her nephew, with the swift, graceful steps of a dancer. He was resting on the bed, his velvet dressing gown tied tight around his thin frame, his face covered with gauze.

She clapped her hands. She had an announcement to make.

"The doctors say that you have been cured," she told Peter.

"I feel faint," he muttered.

"You are faint, for you need fresh air," the Empress agreed cheerfully. "No more of this darkness, no more lying around all day."

"My throat still hurts."

But the Empress refused to listen. In spite of Peter's protests and pleas, she forced him to stand up. She ordered the chambermaids to fling open the curtains, to admit the last light of the day.

The afternoon sun was bright enough to make us squint.

From where I stood I saw the back of a silver-framed mirror the footman had brought. The maids were holding it in front of Peter.

"There," the Empress said, and lifted the gauze from his face. "Look."

"I don't want to," he mumbled, and covered the scars with his hands.

But the Empress would not stand for it. She peeled his hands away and held him firm so that he could take a good look at himself.

"This is not me!" Peter screamed.

I stole my first glimpse at the gaping mouth, the lips fat and earthworm-pink. His cheeks were swollen, covered with pockmarks, each a bloody stamp of pus. Puffed folds hooded his eyes, made them smaller and empty.

I recognized that vacant gaze.

The Grand Duke recognized it, too—the dead eyes of his grand-father's monsters. I heard a scream, a long, piercing wail of agony.

"This is not me!"

The Empress held the Grand Duke in her arms as he cried. It would all pass, she crooned. The redness and the swelling. Soon he would put on weight. Of course, not all the scars would disappear, but he was not a woman. Why should he cry over a blemish or two? A man did not have to have pretty skin. A man needed to be strong. Invincible.

I slipped out of the room as swiftly as I could without drawing attention to myself.

I sat on the chair outside the Grand Duke's bedroom and took a shaky breath. From behind the doors came a wail, and another one, and then nothing but the Empress's voice, singing a lullaby.

Spi mladenets, moy prekrasnuy
Sleep, my young one, my beautiful

As soon as the doctors declared the Grand Duke cured, the Empress ordered Catherine and Princess Johanna to move back to the Winter Palace.

Slowly, the court returned to its old ways. In the Empress's suite, doors were left open again for visitors, and music filled the evenings. There was talk of a ball, a masquerade, and a display of fireworks in honor of the Grand Duke's recovery.

Catherine spent most of the time in her rooms, alone, or praying in the palace chapel while Princess Johanna, eager to celebrate her return from oblivion, threw herself into rounds of important visits. Chevalier Betskoy, whose ardor had visibly diminished during the time of uncertainty, was back at her side. Johanna always looked the other way when I passed her in the palace corridors, as if it would diminish her worth to acknowledge my greetings.

I saw Catherine almost every day, although our time together was brief. The Empress refused to allow the Grand Duchess to visit her fiancé. Each time we met, Catherine would ask if the Grand Duke ate well, which books he liked me to read to him, if he could stand without holding on to a chair.

He was stronger with each day, I assured her.

The story of shipwrecked seafarers who mistook a giant whale for an island was his favorite now.

He listened to music after dinner.

She never asked me how he looked. And I was grateful for it.

Two more weeks passed before Catherine was allowed to see her fiancé for the first time since his illness.

I had just finished my daily reading when the footman appeared in the doorway and announced the arrival of the Grand Duchess. Peter winced, teeth closing on his fingernails. I could see how hard he fought not to cover his face. That day he was wearing a bushy powdered wig, making his head look bigger than it was. Not a good match for his still-scrawny neck.

Catherine walked in, too fast, I thought, too eager.

"I brought you a present, Peter," she said, halting in mid-step. I saw her face grow pale. I saw her eyes slide away in a revulsion she didn't know how to hide. I saw the blind, raw fear that made her gasp.

"What is it?" Peter demanded.

"A violin."

She held out the case. When he touched her fingers, her hand recoiled.

"Do you like it?" she asked.

He didn't answer.

"I was so worried, Peter," Catherine persisted, her voice too tight. "It was terrible not to know what would happen. I prayed for you. I was so frightened. They wouldn't let me see you."

"Who wouldn't?" He opened the case but did not remove the violin.

"The Empress. My mother. Everyone. I tried to learn to play the clavichord, but I'm not musical like you."

She spoke fast, words meant to cover her unease, but how could he not see the quiver of her lips, the forced smile?

"You cannot stay very long," he said. "I'm still weak."

"I prayed for you, Peter."

"You said that already."

The Grand Duke pushed the violin case aside. He picked up one of his model soldiers. "I may still die. I have to be careful."

"Then you will be careful," she said. "We'll both be very careful. You won't die."

The right words, I thought, but they'd arrived too late.

From the field that stretched in front of the Winter Palace came loud barks. Dogs were chasing one another out there, as they often did. From time to time a squeal marked a moment when play turned to menace.

In the silence that followed, Peter gave Catherine a fleeting, ferrety look.

"Don't come any closer," he snarled when Catherine approached his bed. She stopped.

He knocked a toy soldier from the side table.

"Pick him up."

She bent obediently. When she handed the figure to him, he wouldn't take it.

"Put it where it was."

She set the toy soldier on the table. I could see how she willed herself to look at Peter's pockmarked face.

"Go away. I don't want to see you anymore."

She did not move.

"Go," Peter insisted, his voice higher, more shrill.

She bowed.

"Go!"

Slowly, she turned and walked away.

Later that night, I slipped into Catherine's room. She lay motionless, her eyes wide open. Her left foot, bandaged, was elevated on two pillows.

She had been bled again.

I didn't have to ask her what had happened. I had already heard the maids whisper that as soon as the door to Peter's chambers closed behind her, the Grand Duchess had clutched at her stomach. She had barely made it to the privy before she vomited the omelet she'd had for breakfast. In her room, she vomited again. Her body trembled, her face was flushed, but her hands were chill as ice.

The maids gossiped that her mother had ordered her to stop crying. When she couldn't, Princess Johanna had slapped her daughter's face. "If he sends you away now, you fool, there is nothing but shame for you back home," she screamed.

The Grand Duchess, the maids whispered, didn't calm down until the surgeon opened her vein, until his bowl filled with four ounces of her blood.

I took Catherine's hand in mine. I felt the gentle squeeze of her fingers, still cold to the touch.

I gently wiped tears from her face.

She turned to me. And then in that full, soft voice, she said, "I don't know what I would do without you, my Varenka."

That night, I took out the piece of amber with the two bees. Through the cracks of the paneled walls seeped the smell of incense the maids burned in the Grand Duke's room to sweeten the air. A candle sputtered. An owl hooted somewhere on the palace roof.

Could life ever be simple again? Will I ever wake up with a light heart?

I thought of the Chancellor's hands, the brush of his fingertips on my skin. I thought of Purgatory, where the tally is kept of all our sins to be measured against our good deeds. What would be heavier, compassion or greed? Mercy or betrayal?

I thought of the living praying for the dead.

Would anyone pray for me?

I don't recall falling asleep, but when I woke up the piece of amber was still in my hand.

At midnight of the first Sunday of March 1745, Great Lent began with the solemn tolling of the cathedral bell.

The Bible, the priests reminded the faithful, says that before the deluge man ate nothing but the fruit of the earth, extracted through backbreaking labor. This is why foods not absolutely essential for the maintenance of life must be given up at Lent in penance for human sins.

The Empress, still exhausted after the Great Duke's illness, abstained from her annual pilgrimage and was allowed to eat fish twice a week. The convalescing Duke was fully exempt from the fast and took Communion in his bedroom.

Only Catherine ate nothing but bread and boiled vegetables. She drank water instead of wine and took her coffee without cream. She stood by the Empress's side at Mass and took Communion before gathering her maids-of-honor in her rooms for daily prayers.

She was still sending the Grand Duke presents. A set of model soldiers for his re-creations of the famous battles. A Polish guitar strung with catgut instead of wire.

The Grand Duke refused to see his fiancée. If he spoke of her, he never called her Catherine or even the forbidden "Sophie." It was always "she."

"*She* is here again? Does *she* have nothing else to do? Tell her I am busy with my music. Tell her I have an important letter to write."

I longed to scold him, but you cannot scold a Crown Prince. You can only ignore the petulant sneer on his lips and repeat, "The Grand Duchess asked if she could come back later. The Grand Duchess said she didn't mind waiting."

In the antechamber to his rooms, Catherine sat patiently for hours until he relented and ordered me to allow her in. When he did, I would open the door to the sight of her face, white and drawn.

I hoped I was the only one to notice her tears.

Sometimes he turned his back on her and refused to talk. Sometimes he would order her to make herself useful. That meant arranging troops on the model battlefield he was working on or holding the pieces of fortifications he was gluing together. "You're so clumsy!" he yelled when she put soldiers in the wrong place.

When he told her the visit was over, she left, her pale face serious, composed, impossible to read.

"The redness will go away," she would say when anyone asked her about her fiancé. "The hair will grow back. He is alive. This is all that matters."

To the Empress, she said that the Grand Duke often spoke about his gratitude. "Your Majesty saved his life. No mother could have done more for her son."

She kissed the Empress's hands. "Now it is my turn to make him happy," she told Elizabeth.

I noted the blush, the modest bow, the flash of eyes widened with awe and gratitude. She had learned her lesson: No one would ever again see her disgust or fear.

If you act long enough, acting becomes part of you.

I was not the only one to take note of the changes in the Grand Duchess. Even the Chancellor stopped calling her a little *Hausfrau*, and he no longer smirked when he mentioned her name.

But just when I began thinking that Catherine had a chance, the Chancellor played his trump card, the one I wanted so badly to forget.

I was with the Empress in the low-ceilinged garret at the west wing of the palace when the Chancellor came with Johanna's letters.

"Stay," he said when I rose to leave.

I froze.

"Your Majesty should take a look at this," he said, handing her the pages covered with Princess Johanna's crooked scrawl.

"What is it?" she asked.

"Prussian gratitude," he answered.

She gave him an impatient look but took the letters and motioned for him to hold a candle closer.

He stood beside the Empress as she read, his red velvet jacket unbuttoned, a monocle in his right eye flashing every time he moved his head. The Empress emitted grunt after angry grunt.

Giving us her sweat-stained dresses, as if we were beggars. Making us sing praises of this filthy palace . . . this daughter of a peasant . . . playing an Empress when she would be happier in a stable . . .

"The messenger was stopped," the Chancellor told the Empress. "None of this filth got out of Russia. But that's not everything. Tell Her Majesty what you've seen, Varvara."

I prayed the earth would open and swallow me. I wished I would die before my words would hurt Catherine's future. But I had no choice.

"What is it, Varvara?"

The Empress frowned, both curious and disdainful. In her loose silk dishabille, she looked enormous and fluid, her body threatening to spill its boundaries at any time.

"Princess Johanna, Your Highness—" I said.

"What about her?"

"A midwife came. I saw her leave Princess Johanna's room with bloodied rags and a bowl covered with a cloth."

"Princess Johanna? How do you know that she wasn't bled?"

"The midwife, Your Highness . . . I saw her bury what was in the bowl in her own garden. The Princess paid her a hundred rubles and promised her another hundred after her daughter is married."

"Where does this midwife live?"

"On Monetnaya Street, Your Highness. Her house is painted blue. She buried the thing in the back."

The Empress, flushed, rose from her bed and began to pace the room. Her hand clenched at her skirts.

"A woman who murders her own child!" the Chancellor began. "Who lets the midwife's knife cut up the life God entrusted her with!"

He was driving his point home, without subtlety. *Daughters are like their mothers. Ruthlessness runs with filial blood.* "Is nothing unthinkable, Your Majesty? Is nothing sacred anymore?"

The Empress was breathing heavily, her eyes puffy and red from all the sleepless nights. Hell was on her mind, the sulfurous fumes of eternal damnation, devils in short German jackets poking out the eyes and tongues of sinners.

She picked up a fan, her newest, made of swanskin and black feathers, a gift from Count Razumovsky. She drew her neck down between her shoulders like a giant tortoise.

The Chancellor took her silence as a good sign. The glint of pleasure in his eyes meant that he could already see Catherine and her mother in tears, packing their trunks.

Disgrace brings forth the vermin, he had told me many times. *When the mighty fall, enemies crawl out of darkness.*

I watched the Empress break her fan in half and throw it to the floor, like a bird's wing, maimed, useless.

Russia would soon turn to England or Austria for her allies, just as the Chancellor had wished. All would be well in the mighty Empire of the East.

The spring would come. At night the ice on the Neva would crack like musket shots, and big pieces of drifting ice would float out to the sea.

But I would no longer have a friend.

In the morning, Catherine went for a walk by the banks of the Neva, with just a maid at her side, away from the hollow walls, away from the two-sided mirrors, spying holes, and treacherous ears of the palace. Snowdrops, Catherine's favorite flowers, were beginning to pierce through snow in the meadows, and she was eager to find them.

I waited until the maid with her tarried, her skirt snagged by the sharp prickles of a thistle, and then I approached the Grand Duchess.

"Please, I don't have much time. It's better that no one should see us."

She gave me a playful look. "But why, Varenka?"

"Something terrible has happened. I've come to warn you."

The smile waned on her lips.

The maid was heading back toward us, a crushed thistle head in her hands. I put my finger to my lips.

Catherine asked the maid if she had seen her kerchief. "I must have dropped it," she complained. "The red one Maman gave me."

It was a thin excuse, but the maid had no choice but to turn back to look for it.

I spoke hurriedly. I was blunt. "Your mother has written letters to the King of Prussia. Letters the Empress will never forgive."

Fear gushed into Catherine's eyes.

"How do you know?" she asked.

"I heard the Chancellor speaking with the Empress. A messenger has been intercepted at the border."

Catherine bit her lip, hard.

"The Empress is furious. She will summon you tonight. Both of you. The Chancellor is certain she will send you back home."

Catherine cast a furtive glance behind us. The maid was still far enough away for us to speak.

"I don't want to go back, Varenka." I felt her gloved hand clasp my arm and quickly let it go. "Not in disgrace."

"The Empress doesn't want you to go back. But you have to make her see that you are not like your mother."

I couldn't tell her everything. I could not confess to spying. All I could offer was a gambler's bet. Point to a narrow path away from the brink and pray it would work.

"Fall to your knees, Catherine. Kiss her feet. Cry. Tell the Empress that you have no mother but her. This is what she wants to hear. If you don't . . ."

Catherine flinched.

"Fortune is not as blind as people think, but you have to take your own steps," I insisted. My voice was strong, unwavering, as if I had not just told her to cut herself off from the woman who had given birth to her.

The maid had tired of searching for the phantom kerchief and was approaching fast. I bowed my head.

"I have to go now," I told Catherine.

"Thank you, Varenka. I'll never forget your kindness. I'll repay it, too. I promise." She turned to the maid. "Never mind the kerchief," she called. "I'm so forgetful. Perhaps I didn't take it with me, after all."

I lingered in the antechamber that night, waiting to be summoned, but the Empress was in no mood for gossip. Inside the room where the Empress would sleep, I heard the Chancellor's voice followed by someone's nervous laughter, but I couldn't tell whose it was.

The service bell rang, and I watched a footman, a young, lithe man I had not seen before, go in. "Get both of them here," I heard the Empress yell. "Immediately."

It didn't take long. Footsteps became louder, heels pattered on the bare wooden stairs. A scream, a stumble. Another scream, closer now.

I slipped behind a curtain, my heart hammering. Johanna and Catherine came running, escorted by two sentries, mother and daughter yanked out of their beds, hastily dressed, with buttons and clasps undone—disheveled and terrified, just the way Elizabeth wanted them to be.

Princess Johanna was thrashing her arms about her like a bird shot down from the sky, but I gave her only a passing glance. It was Catherine I watched. Her face was flushed from running, her eyes red-rimmed. Her whole future depended on what would happen next.

The door opened, and the sentries led them in to the Empress.

Outside the antechamber where I hid, the muffled steps of the Palace Guards thickened. Humiliation of the mighty always made for excellent entertainment. In the morning, I knew, everyone would hear of undergarments stained from fright, of fingernails bitten to the bloody quick, of trembling hands unable to hold a cup of coffee.

The Empress's voice was a roar. *Barbarian land? . . . a vain, deluded woman who thinks herself worthy to rule it!*

She had been deceived. She had allowed a viper to coil itself on her breast. Russia had been slighted, maligned, humiliated. By a nobody. By a German whore.

Is this how Germans repay hospitality?

Is this how Germans treat their benefactors?

Is this the German understanding of loyalty and gratitude?

Ungrateful bitch!

Traitor!

Then I heard Catherine's voice.

"Your Highness, you saved my life. You treated me like your own beloved child. Like your own daughter. You have done so much for my family, and I have tried to be worthy of your trust, but now I'm left with nothing!

"I don't have a mother, for I cannot call a mother a woman who has betrayed my Benefactress. I'll leave with her, as Your Highness has commanded, but please do not make me leave without your blessing."

"Listen, you ungrateful wretch!" I heard the Empress scream. "Listen to the words of the daughter you don't deserve! Get out of my sight! Out!"

Something crashed to the floor, and then came the words I, too, had been waiting for.

"Alone!"

The door opened and Princess Johanna stumbled out, humiliation a hard lump in her throat, like a nut swallowed whole.

I slipped out of my hiding place, my heart pounding. I walked past the footman and the guards, ignoring their avid looks. I found myself praying: *Let this be the new beginning, an omen for the future. Let it be a lesson learned and always cherished. A lesson remembered when the times turn black again.*

I walked, the floorboards creaking under my feet. In the dry winter air, the wood was losing its moisture. By the time spring came, the paneled corridors of the Winter Palace would be even more porous and cracked.

Let us be watchful, I prayed. *Let us hide our true hearts from those who think they know us so well. Those who believe they own our bodies and souls.*

I didn't have to see the Chancellor's face to know he had covered his disappointment well. He would have gathered Johanna's foolish letters, bowed, and left. He would be in his room, staring into the flames, a bottle of vodka on a tray.

He would not summon me for a while. He needed lips more pliant, hands more willing to soothe him, thoughts he didn't have to watch and stamp out. He needed to see himself in eyes empty of doubt, in a heart softened with fear.

Don't ever cross me, he had said. *Don't get too clever, Varvara.*

I didn't care. Catherine would not be sent away. She was safe.

I was no longer alone.

That night I waited for her outside her room for hours. Finally, released by the Empress, she arrived, tears glistening on her cheeks. I cradled her in my arms as if she were a child, hushing her sobs, smoothing her silky hair.

"It's all over," I murmured. "You are safe now, Catherine. Everything will be fine. Did the Chancellor say anything before he left?"

"He said that he trusted Elizabeth's judgment. That he knew the Empress had nothing but Russia's precious future in mind. But he kept showing her the letters."

His was the cleverness of a fox, I thought. Guilt by association. Guilt by the ties of kin. He could not oppose Elizabeth's mercy, but he could fan her anger.

"She told him to take his filthy letters away, Varenka," Catherine said. "She threw them to the floor, and he bent and picked them up. One by one."

Catherine raised her head and smiled for the first time. I felt an instant of surprise, for it was the mischievous smile of a child.

For three April days in 1745, to the sound of drumrolls, heralds rode through the streets of St. Petersburg announcing that the imperial wedding would take place on August 21. Soon, by the imperial order, top nobles would receive advances to equip themselves for the great day. As soon as the Baltic thawed, ships began bringing in cargoes of cloth, carriages, French toiletries and wines. In St. Petersburg only English silks were more popular than silken cloth from Zerbst, especially white and light colors decorated with large flowers of gold and silver. Catherine's father sent a shipment of Zerbst beer, but it was declared thin and flat.

The Empress supervised every detail, changing her mind at the slightest pretext. For a time the Amber Room was where she wished to bless the young couple before they left for the cathedral. Then she decided it too small. A *berline* was ordered in France, with glass panels that would make the coach look like a giant jewel box so that the people of Russia could admire the ducal pair as they rode with her in the wedding procession. Should it be adorned with flowers, she fretted, or should the elegance of its golden trim be its only decoration?

Then, on the day she was to sign the order for the carriage maker, a bird crashed against her bedroom window and there was no more talk of glass panels.

The Chancellor had not sent for me since Princess Johanna's humiliation, but the Empress kept me too busy to give this but a passing thought. Losses never stopped him before, and this time—as he always did—he had recovered his balance quickly. With each visit to Elizabeth's receiving room, he praised the soon-to-be imperial bride as if he had never wanted her gone.

You do not have friends, Varvara, he used to tell me. *You have aims and goals. Time changes them all. Learn from both the fox and the lion. For a fox cannot defend itself against a pack of wolves, and a lion does not know how to avoid a snare.*

The Empress decided that Princess Johanna would not leave before the wedding. "I don't want any vile rumors," she said. Not all daughters were like their mothers, her eyes said each time she took the measure of her defeated rival. Betrayal was not contagious.

For her part, Princess Johanna did what she was told. She suffered the sugar-sweet praises of her child and the Empress's sharp looks. She turned away all visitors. Every time I passed by her rooms, I heard the sounds of packing. Maids hurried in and out with baskets; footmen brought trunks and braids of straw.

I spoke to her only once before the wedding day. She had ventured outside of her room on some errand, furtive and uneasy, her pupils enlarged with belladonna. When she saw me she stopped abruptly and—perhaps noting that two Palace Guards were within earshot—forced herself to greet me.

"Are you well?" she asked, her voice tight with strain.

"Yes," I answered. "How kind of you to inquire, Princess. I trust you, too, are well?"

"I am. I'm glad to be going home. I have other children who need me. More than Sophie does."

I fixed my eyes on the moon-shaped beauty spot glued to her upper lip, ignoring the sarcasm in her voice. I didn't even care if she suspected me of betraying her. This woman had very nearly destroyed her daughter's life. And for what? Her own vanity, her own lust.

Princess Johanna glanced in the direction of the guards, and I followed her gaze to see that they were watching us intently. The taller one winked at me and placed an open palm on his heart.

The Grand Duke's face gradually lost some of its redness. But as the swelling subsided, one of his eyes seemed to hang lower than the other. It gave him an air of perpetual bewilderment. I tried not to think that it reminded me of a clown.

Catherine did not look away. She did not flinch when Peter complained that she was too skinny, that her chin was too pointed, or when he told her that the Princess of Courland was the prettiest woman he had ever seen.

She made him laugh with her cat concert. She drew for him the layout of Frederick of Prussia's Berlin palace: the White Hall, the Golden Gallery, the Throne Room. She nodded and smiled when he said that the Prussian uniforms had better cuts and were made of sturdier cloth than Russian ones.

Her visits to the Grand Duke grew longer.

He let her read him his Holstein papers: leases about to expire, a table of fees for disposing of animal cadavers, petitions to lower the toll tax, to build another brewery. Gothic script, he claimed, was hard on his eyes. She offered to write his letters for him. All he would have to do was sign and seal them.

Women are clever that way, he said. They have more patience with what is trivial.

Once, when Catherine suggested he should cross himself more often during Mass—"To make sure the people see you do it, Peter. You'll be their Emperor"—he agreed.

Hearing exchanges like this, I grew bolder. Elizabeth would not live forever. The Grand Duchess would one day be the Emperor's wife.

With her I had a future.

By June, as the wedding preparations intensified, regular palace business came to a standstill. The Empress left documents unsigned; negotiations stalled, foreign diplomats awaited official audiences for weeks, without success. She had no time for such matters, the Empress responded in answer to the Chancellor's pleas. There were guest lists to decide upon, seating arrangements to approve, the composition of corteges to discuss, favors to bestow or withhold. "Splendor is hard work," the Empress said, sighing with exasperation.

I had never seen her in such high spirits. Russian steam *banya* replaced the portable baths. In the morning, she walked barefoot, swearing it improved her circulation. She insisted on keeping the palace windows open, even on the hottest of days, so her rooms held the permanent stink of cow dung from the Tsar's meadow. The vases had to be filled with field flowers—wild daisies, goldenrod, chamomile—the scents, she said, of her childhood.

There was no escape from the planning frenzy. Soon the bushes and hedges around the palace were covered with linen bleaching and drying in the sun. From the kitchens came bad-tempered shouts, clanging of pots and saucepans. Maids rushed around with red-rimmed eyes and reddened hands. From the Oranienbaum orangery, gardeners sent blossoming lemon trees in thick silver pots to keep the palace air sweet.

The Empress's cats were banished to the anterooms, for every inch of the Imperial Bedroom was covered with swatches of fabric, lace, ribbons, leather, skeins of wool. The five footmen the Empress often asked to sing for her were obliged to bring a long bench to stand on.

Pandoras modeling wedding clothes were presented and summarily rejected, as the new Chief Maid stood by, trembling with unease. Didn't she know that frothy flounces were passé, too many jewels on silver cloth would make the gown stiff? Were there no softer hues of white? Watching her bow and withdraw, promising to do better next time, I, too, began to doubt if there was an outfit worthy of Elizabeth's approval. But as the nights began to grow shorter, the Empress summoned Catherine and Peter to announce her decision.

Two big pandoras stood on the table. Catherine's wore a gown of silver cloth, richly embroidered on all the seams and the hem. Over the dress flowed a cloak of web-thin lace. Peter's pandora wore an ensemble of the same cloth, but its sword and trim glittered with diamonds. The Empress leaned the two dolls toward each other in an imitation of an embrace, beaming at the ducal pair.

Catherine touched the fabric of the dress, exclaimed at the intricate silver needlework. The Grand Duke poked his pandora stiffly with his finger.

"What do you think, Peter?" the Empress asked.

The Empress had ordered him to rub a concealing cream on his cheeks and forehead. From a distance it made his face look smooth enough, but up close the cream looked caked and crumbly, and it stained the collar of his jackets.

"Ask her," he said, pointing at Catherine.

Catherine bowed. "The dress is beautiful, Your Highness. The most beautiful I've ever had."

"The moon children," the Empress said. "You will look like a pair of moon children."

They both bowed and left the room together, holding hands.

The Empress sighed with pleasure, but my eyes were on the Chief Maid. She was wiping away a tear. There was nothing in her fresh, trim looks that resembled her predecessor's, but suddenly I remembered Madame Kluge's face, pale and terrified as the guards dragged her to the scaffold. To ward it off, I recalled the red welts on my shins, the lash of her derision, but these memories seemed like bits of fluff gathering under beds.

Her fall had been my gain and my warning. As soon as her back had healed well enough for her to sit up, she had been sent back to Zerbst. "Better than to Siberia," the Chancellor had told me.

Later that day, in his own quarters, I heard the Grand Duke say that he wished his aunt would not insist on horn music for the wedding. Violins were far superior. He also wished Catherine smelled better. She should rinse her mouth with vodka, like he did.

Never mind, I thought.

There will be a wedding.

There will be a wedding, I muttered, as I rushed about on one of my many errands. When the Empress called for me now, it was to look for some lost samples, or to write hastily dictated notes to her jeweler or perfumer. The pantry attendant had been caught stealing partridges. Half of a wine shipment had disappeared.

No task was too trivial for her. She demanded to see the polished tabletops, spotting scratches and chips that had to be filled. She decided which portraits needed to be washed with milk, which cracked windowpanes must be replaced. She interrogated the cooks, the wine merchants, the gardeners; assured herself that there would be no shortage of grapes, pineapples, oranges, or candied fruit. She fretted that the smokehouses were behind with their deliveries of smoked sturgeon and *balyk*. No foreign guest must have the slightest reason to deride Russian hospitality.

Not when the future Tsar married his bride.

Hurrying down the hallway, I heard the Chancellor's voice behind me.

"There is something quite touching about young girls and weddings, Varvara, don't you think?"

I stopped and turned toward him.

"The Grand Duchess is looking splendid these days," he continued. I heard the sarcasm in his voice, a thin note of warning.

"Yes."

"And the excitement has rubbed off on you," he continued, blocking my way. "Well, well, who would have thought?"

He had not summoned me since the day of Johanna's disgrace. Warding off unease, I pressed my lips together, sifting through what his words meant. But I knew. The spymaster of the Russian court had been watching me, and he was not pleased.

I made a step forward.

With a mock bow, he stepped aside to let me pass.

By July, the Empress sent for Catherine every morning, making her sit beside her and showering her with praise. She plaited colorful ribbons into her dark hair, made her try on a red *kokoshnik* adorned with fat pearls that had once belonged to her mother. She made her learn Russian dance steps and taste the dishes the cooks brought for approval. The Empress chose the church for the ceremony, the Church of Our Lady of Kazan, consecrated in the name of her favorite icon. The Kazan Madonna had healed the sick and turned near defeats into victories, crushing the enemies of Russia. Elizabeth craved miracles as much as she craved the embraces of her Palace Guards.

On the nights the Empress dismissed me, Catherine and I made plans. The Grand Duchess needed someone to trust.

She needed me.

"As soon as I'm married, I'll ask for you," Catherine told me. "I'll say my eyes ache in the candlelight and that I need a reader who can read to me in French and in Russian."

I nodded.

"As soon as I can, I'll make you my maid-of-honor, Varenka. I don't know how, but I will. We'll always be together, then. You'll always help me, won't you?"

I pressed her hand to my lips.

Next door, Princess Johanna was ordering her maids around. "Not like that, you fool, be careful," we heard through the thin wall.

I glanced at Catherine.

"Let's not talk about her," Catherine said, and looked away.

She was right, I decided. Her mother was her past, not her future. And the past mattered less and less.

Did I grow careless in these days? Heady with the thought that after the imperial wedding day I—a bookbinder's daughter—might walk behind the Grand Duchess as one of her noble maids?

Did I become too caught up in Catherine's joyful smiles and girlish fears?

"What will he do when we are left alone, Varenka?"

"Kiss you."

"On the lips?"

"Yes."

"And then?"

"On your breasts."

"What do I have to do? Kiss him back?"

"Yes."

"Will it hurt?"

"A kiss?"

"No, you know what! Maman says that it'll hurt, but that it is my duty to endure it."

"It might hurt."

"Much?"

"Not much."

It'll be over quickly, I thought, a groan of his pleasure, his release.

"Soon there'll be a child there," I said, gesturing at her belly. "And then nothing else will matter."

In these nervous days Catherine burst into sobs for the most trivial of reasons—a torn ribbon, a broken tortoiseshell comb she had brought with her from Zerbst. Once she bit her hand so hard that she drew blood.

Diversion was the remedy I sought, a quick walk in the garden, faster and faster until we ran out of breath, a litter of kittens I found in the attic and brought down in my arms, the mother trailing me suspiciously as I put the warm wriggling bodies in Catherine's lap.

I tried not to think how bemused the Chancellor's smile looked.

On the wedding day, Friday, August 21, the Empress herself assisted with the bride's makeup and wardrobe. She dabbed a touch of rouge on Catherine's cheeks, placed the ducal crown on her freshly curled hair, and embraced her before the dressmaker was allowed to do the last fitting.

"A joyful day," Elizabeth declared. "A new beginning."

It was a day of trumpets and kettledrums, of one hundred and twenty coaches leaving the Winter Palace for the church. Palace Guards in rich new uniforms stood at attention. Cheers rose above the din of voices in the teeming crowds. Catherine and Peter rode with the Empress in the *berline*, which looked like a small castle. It was pulled by eight white horses in golden harnesses, tall feathers dancing in their manes.

The wedding was splendid. The priest chanted, "O Lord, our God, crown them with glory and honor," as two glittering crowns were switched over the heads of the bride and groom, crowns that would be placed in a display case over their marriage bed. The rings of plain gold were blessed and exchanged.

The bride and groom fell to the floor to ask for the Empress's blessing. The cannons roared, bells clanged in all the churches of St. Petersburg. Father Theodorsky spoke of the miracles of Providence that united the offspring of Anhalt and Holstein and would protect them as they reigned over the Russian people. The Chancellor of Russia offered his congratulations in a flowery speech, praising Elizabeth's womanly intuition and evoking the legacy of the other Catherine Alexeyevna, Peter the Great's beloved wife, the Empress of Russia. He spoke of the Grand Duke's tenacity of spirit, a clear sign that the blood of the Romanovs was in Peter's veins. This is a momentous day, the Chancellor said, one that filled him with pride and hope for Russia and profound gratitude to His Sovereign.

"Old flatterer," the Empress muttered under her breath.

She was beaming.

There had been no omens. The groom was first to step on the piece of white cloth on which the couple were to stand. The rings did not fall to the floor; the flames of the candles did not falter and die.

From the flurry of balls and amusements that followed on that magical night, I recall an odd array of incidents—a drunken Frenchman insisting that in his travels he had seen a witch that would not burn, a morose-looking Austrian choking on greasy chunks of sausage, the stink of urine coming from the fireplace in the great hall, someone's too eager hands groping my breasts, a cat chased by a squealing piglet across the courtyard.

I remember Catherine's face, her eyes wide with belladonna, her gleaming white dress smudged with soot at the hem. She had a giddy bout of hiccups that wouldn't go away. And I recall Peter's huffy protestations when anyone mentioned his *understandable* impatience for Cupid's den.

Princess Johanna made a show of praising everything around her in a loud voice. The wedding dress is breathtaking. The Empress is most merciful and kind. My daughter is in excellent hands. Russia is a country with a glorious future, a mighty Empire with no equal.

She was grateful, she repeated, for her time in Russia, but now she was looking forward to going back home.

The huge silver disk of the moon hung above the Neva, right behind the Petropavlovsky Fortress. The chill in the air was a faint reminder of the northern winds that would soon come. In the streets, jugglers had long exchanged balls and rings for flaming torches. Fireworks exploded with showers of sparks.

The two wedding crowns had been placed in a sturdy case and nailed to the wall above the marriage bed.

It was the Empress who led the newlyweds to their bridal chamber that night and closed the door.

In the morning, I snatched a bowl with ice from the chambermaid. I knocked softly on the door of the bridal chamber.

"Come in," I heard.

Catherine was sitting on the floor by the bed. Through the opening of her cambric nightshift I saw the flash of white skin and the pinkish round of her nipple. There was no sign of Peter.

"What happened?" I asked.

She shook her head.

"I saw a rat," she said, pointing at the corner near the fireplace. "It came from there."

"It's gone now," I said. I took a chunk of ice and rubbed the skin beneath her swollen eyes. The ice had begun to melt, and a frigid stream made its way down my sleeve.

"I know," Catherine said and sighed. She did not move.

I summoned the lively chatter that came so easy to me in those days. I rattled on about Countess Golovina stumbling on the dance floor, the beatific look on old Count Shuvalov's face every time he caught a glimpse of a shapely ankle.

I let my voice sparkle.

I laughed at my own jokes.

She was not listening.

"It's like a stone here," she said, pointing to her chest. Her voice was anguished. She sniffed her arm, her sleeves, the inside of her nightshift at the cleavage. She looked up at me then, her face nakedly hurt.

I knelt beside her and took her strong, white hand, adorned now with her wedding ring, in my own hand.

"He had a flask of vodka hidden in the folds of his dressing gown. He gave me some to drink. He said that a wife had to listen to her husband, that if on a bright day a husband said to his wife, 'Look how dark it is,' she should say, 'So dark that I cannot see a thing.' And if, a moment later, he said, 'But it is bright daylight,' she should say, 'Indeed, how silly of me not to have noticed.' Then he drank more and more until he fell asleep."

"Did he touch you?"

"No."

"Kiss you?"

"No."

"Not even when he woke up?"

"No. I don't even know when he left."

"Has anyone come in here today?"

"Countess Rumyantseva and Princess Galitsina. They took the sheets away."

I lifted the coverlet. The mattress was bare.

She began to cry.

"It's nothing," I said, lifting her up from the floor, making her sit on the edge of the bed. "It happens all the time."

"How do you know?" she wept.

"Men get scared. They grow soft and uneasy and ashamed of their own weakness. It is just one night. It doesn't matter," I told her. "It means nothing."

At the time, I even believed it myself.

Princess Johanna left three days later, at dawn. I passed by her room and saw the doors opened wide. The room was empty but for a braid of straw, a few broken plates, and some torn lace that even the maids did not want.

Later, I would learn that the Empress gave Johanna a letter to the King of Prussia that demanded the immediate recall of the Prussian Ambassador. Rumor had it that in Berlin a Russian spy was to be beheaded. In St. Petersburg a Prussian agent was being sent to Siberia. As the Chancellor had wanted, there would be no more talk of closeness between Prussia and Russia.

Princess Johanna never said goodbye to her daughter. In a parting note she wrote that she didn't wish to upset a happy bride with the sadness of separation.

Catherine read the note and threw it into the fire.

"Race me, Varenka," she said, and ran down the corridor.

I followed.

THREE

1745–1748

As soon as the excitement of the imperial wedding died out, the Empress lapsed back into her irritable moods. Once again everything was an omen, and every omen was about her. A rattling window, a dead bird falling down a smoking chimney, a riding cloak that had gone missing. Hunts were called off, gowns sent back, questions dismissed with sulky shrugs. Only the cats made her face brighten. She carried them in her arms, called them "her babies," tossed balls of yarn for them to chase. "You love me for myself alone," I had heard her croon into Pushok's silky fur.

The palace rumors swelled. Peter had called his aunt a mare in heat. Then a fat bitch. Words of little wit or imagination, but what can be expected from a half-witted Crown Prince who likes to pour his drinks over his servants' heads? "Does she think I am her caged monkey?" he'd screamed. He brought a box of his model soldiers to the bedroom. He lectured Catherine on the intricacies of some battle for three hours. He fell asleep drunk.

A month after the wedding, the Grand Duchess was still a virgin.

The Empress was not amused. "Heartless ingratitude after all I had done," she screamed. "I've been too good, too indulgent."

They were the Chancellor's words, I suspected, the sweet fannings of revenge, sticky and poisonous. In the Imperial Bedroom I spotted traces of his daily presence: Montpellier gloves scented with nutmeg, his brass spectacles forgotten on the pile of dispatches the Empress ordered me to read to her. Each time he walked into the Empress's room, his eyes slid over me, narrowing slightly, as if I were made of mist and merely obscured his view.

He had still not sent for me. He no longer wished me to touch him. He no longer cared for my stories or for the news I brought to him.

What of it? I thought.

If fear hovered in my defiance, I pushed it away.

The Empress still sent for me. I was still Catherine's only friend.

To the Empress I pointed out how diligent the ducal couple had been with their official duties. I praised Peter's patience and Catherine's grace. In the past weeks they had been asked to become godparents, witnesses at weddings, guests at churchings and consecrations.

The Empress shrugged and pouted her lips.

"Did he come to her last night, Varvara?"

"Yes, Your Highness."

"Did he get into her bed?"

"Yes."

"So why didn't he lie with her? What did she do to turn him away?"

"She is shy," I said.

"Shy?" the Empress repeated, before waving me away. On her lips the word was laced with derision.

Outside, in the corridor, the guards were changing their stations. They were from the Preobrazhensky Regiment; their leafy-green coats were faced with red. The smells of snuff, vodka, and sweat floated through the air. Heels clicked, sabers clanked. Silver bandoliers glittered.

I hurried past, unseeing.

"Countess Rumyantseva wants to know why. What can I tell her, Varenka?"

Catherine was nibbling on a blade of grass. We sat in the palace garden, where I hoped no one could overhear our words.

The previous night, the Grand Duke had come to bed very late. He'd brushed her off when she tried to touch him. Then he turned his back on her and fell asleep.

"Was he drunk again?" I asked.

"A bit," Catherine said, tossing the blade of grass down. Her eyes, I saw, were rimmed with red.

Everyone was plying her with advice. Countess Rumyantseva insisted she open her nightdress more, to show her breasts. The imperial perfumer swore by the essences of cinnamon and sandalwood. Only smell, he insisted, was capable of evoking turbulent reactions in the soul. Even the maids dared to suggest she drink tea brewed from dried oat straw.

It was time to stop all this talk.

I slipped a vial of dove's blood into Catherine's hand, the kind one can purchase for a few kopecks in the back alleys of St. Petersburg. A simple deception, a ruse to buy her time, to send the imperial tongues on another mission.

"Drink some wine with him, make him laugh," I told her. "When he falls asleep, smear that blood on the sheets."

"But he will know—" Catherine protested.

"He won't be sure. And he won't say anything. He, too, wants to be left alone."

This is what they both needed, I believed then. A respite from expectations, from the eyes that always watched. All the Empress ever cared about were her own wishes, and now she wished for an heir to her throne. It didn't matter how she got what she wanted. It mattered only that she did.

"Russia does not forget those who've trusted her, Varvara," the Empress said when I entered the Imperial Bedroom that night and curtsied. "I remember your father's wish."

She was not alone. The Chancellor sat in a gilded armchair by the window, holding a roll of papers, striking it against his open palm. He turned his face toward me, giving me a bewildered smile, as if amused at a puppy trying to bite his shoe. I felt the muscles in my jaw clench.

The Empress ran her hand through her hair. It was still thinning, in spite of the birch-bark rinses and a hundred brushstrokes each morning and night. I could smell cherry brandy on her breath. The candle beside her flickered.

My heart was racing. Was it possible the Empress would make me Catherine's maid-of-honor?

"It's not good for a woman to be alone, Varvara."

As soon as she said these words, the Chancellor clapped his hands.

I still didn't guess, not even when I saw the door open and a young man come in, his leafy-green jacket lined with scarlet. A Palace Guard.

"What a fetching couple you two'll make." The Empress's voice seemed to come from far away, a woman in another room talking to herself.

This is what a cornered animal must feel, the unforgiving harshness of rock at the dead end of the tunnel. Even though it is still there, the fluttering moment of disbelief that this is indeed the end. Even though the blood is still racing. Even though the mind still hopes for miracles—an opening in the wall, the hunter suddenly struck dead.

Egor Dmitryevich Malikin, Second Lieutenant in the Preobrazhensky Regiment, was to be my husband. "A great honor," the Empress continued, certain of my gratitude. I was to marry one of the proud guards of Peter the Great, the elite corps with two-rank seniority over the regular army, the makers of the Tsars who had brought Elizabeth to the pinnacle of power.

A noble, just like my mother had wished.

"He is an orphan, like you. Look at him, Varvara."

I did look. At the mop of his black hair, the thick brows, the row of even teeth his smile revealed. One gloved hand rested on his hip, cradling a plumed shako; the other one, bare, hung loosely. I raged at the thought of this hand touching me. I imagined my escape, dressing in men's clothes, sneaking out of the palace, away from the marriage I had not sought and did not wish. But alone and on the run, a man, like a woman, would end up dead or a slave to masters yet unknown.

"A handsome man, Varvara, wouldn't you say?" Elizabeth asked.

"Yes, Your Highness."

From the murky shadows came a tapping sound. The Chancellor was drumming a cheerful beat on his knee with his rolled papers. Some memories do not want to recede: *I protect and provide, Varvara, you listen and obey. . . . Lie to everyone else, but never to me.*

I cast my eyes down. I tried to make my face show nothing at all.

"You don't remember me?" I heard Egor's voice. Too eager, too pleased.

"No," I said, although of course I had seen him at the palace. Like the other guards, he had teased me and tried to stop me on my way. Why hadn't I seen the danger in the grip of his fingers on my wrist when I'd passed him by? "You won't escape me that easily," he had once shouted after me.

So wrapped up was I with the lives of others that in the corridors of the Winter Palace I had forgotten the choking grip of revenge.

Clad in benevolence, aimed at the heart. This was my punishment. Punishment worthy of a spymaster, punishment for which I had to thank the Empress on my knees. Now I had to praise my mistress's generosity, call her my Benefactress, Russia's "Little Mother" who knows best what is good for those entrusted into her care.

A woman is a vessel to be filled. Her husband's responsibility if she threatens to believe herself important, clever, irreplaceable.

I burned with anger. Anger at myself, at my own foolish complacency. How easy it must have been for the Chancellor to make Elizabeth do his bidding! A few words of doubt dropped in passing to feed her suspicion, a little sigh of warning to make it linger. Isn't the world rife with ingratitude, Your Highness? Isn't loyalty fickle, spoiled by betrayal?

Everyone knew how the Empress liked to marry off her maids,

even if only to dance at their weddings. In a simple peasant dress, just like her own mother, who had once bewitched a mighty Tsar, Elizabeth was happiest in the soldiers' barracks, among dairymaids and stable boys.

If I had paid heed, I could've at least fought.

It was too late now. I was to be Egor's reward for services to the Empress. "Exemplary services," she had said. There was no chink in her words, no secret passage I could sneak through to escape.

"A son, Varvara." Elizabeth held out a Holy Icon for me to kiss. "Come back here with a son nine months from your wedding day."

My hands had gone cold, for it was only at that moment that I realized I would have to leave the palace.

Leave Catherine.

How stiff my lips were when I shaped the words of thanks. How weak my knees when I knelt beside Egor Malikin to thank the Empress and to receive her blessing.

In one of the books in the Imperial Library, I found a traveler's account of an Indian king much skilled in the arts of treachery and deception. From among his subjects, the king selected men who looked like simpletons or could pretend they were deaf or blind. A partially clouded eye was a treasure, a maimed earlobe an asset, reassuring to those who were too foolish to look beyond appearances. Trained in the ancient skills of remembering, these spies were ordered to frequent shops, places of amusement, pleasure gardens and parks. They were to live among beggars and vagabonds, to watch and take note of all the weaknesses of the human heart.

The Indian king also sent out holy spies, trained in enduring hunger and thirst. Taking residence on the outskirts of the city, these men fasted and prayed, read palms, and offered their blessings. To help their fame spread, other spies disguised as merchants and rich men begged for their advice and left praising their insight and divine powers. Soon people thronged to have their fortunes told and to confess their innermost secrets to the king's spies. What better way, the barbarian monarch bragged, to know who among his subjects were the breeders of discontent?

But it was the women in that kingdom of the Far East who truly terrified the author of this account—not the women posing as vendors, selling poisoned food to the enemy, or sprinkling lethal powder on a sleeping man. It was the *vishakanyas*, the maidens of death, who were truly to be feared, beautiful girls fed from childhood with small doses of poisonous herbs or the venom of snakes and scorpions. Their bodies absorbed the toxins slowly, leaving them unharmed. But while the touch of their hands could weaken a man's grip on this world, and a simple kiss could plunge him into a battle for his life, there was no escape from their sensual embrace. The poison seeping through their skin would slow down a lover's heart, thicken his bile, clot his blood.

Vishakanyas were demon lovers, for a night of passion with them meant death.

The Empress didn't like to waste time. The wedding took place the following week in the palace chapel. "A great honor," I was assured by the new Chief Maid, who congratulated me stiffly on my "elevation." She did not call it unexpected and gasped with false cheerfulness as she pronounced the names of the guests to attend the ceremony: "The Empress. The Grand Duke. The Grand Duchess. And the Chancellor himself."

The new Chief Maid praised Elizabeth's thoughtfulness, the size of my dowry, the generous imperial gifts to me. If she knew—as I did—that my husband had managed to borrow money against the prospect of marrying a "favorite of the Empress," money he doubled at faro, she refrained from saying so.

The white satin dress in which I would stand at the altar was one of the Empress's gifts. It used to be hers, from the days when she was still slim. It must have been trimmed with precious stones once, but they had been cut off carelessly, leaving small tears behind. "You only see the holes if you know they are there," the seamstress who did the hasty fitting assured me.

The Grand Duchess came while I was being dressed, the skin beneath her eyes smudged with purple shadows. A new maid-of-honor trailed at her heels, pensive and unsure of what was expected of her.

"My gift is so small, Varenka," Catherine said, handing me a tube tied with a ribbon. "But I hope it will please you."

I was not to open it until I arrived in my new home, she told me.

She was happy for me. Marriage was a blessing, she said. A woman's highest duty, a woman's happiness.

We both knew she could not say anything else.

Was Egor one of Elizabeth's lovers? I wondered. This strapping, lissome man who grinned as he looked at himself in the mirror, like a rat swimming in a bowl of fresh cream, as the saying goes. Earthy, roguish, flushed with his own power. Just what Elizabeth prized in her men.

Did he win me in the lottery of Elizabeth's bedroom on the nights when she was drunk, giddy, and insatiable? Or was I merely a consolation prize?

They all dreamed of it, the guards, as they brushed their uniforms and polished the silver buttons, young men rinsing their mouths with vodka and chewing on parsley sprigs to sweeten their breath. The night duty was the most sought after, an investment worthy of a hefty bribe that would make their commander rich.

I had often seen the doors of Elizabeth's bedroom open silently right after midnight. "Go on," the guards would urge one another, knowing that nothing but humiliation awaited those who did not please her. They had heard stories of naked men clutching their uniforms, dressing hurriedly in the musty dusk of service corridors, ears red with shame. But in the taverns, after a few shots of vodka, no guard spoke of defeat. "You get better broth from an old hen," they claimed. "From the belly down, women do not age."

On my wedding day, as my fingers brushed the smooth white satin of my dress, I promised to honor and obey the man who stood beside me, in sickness and in health. Twice for good measure, once in front of an Orthodox priest and then before a Roman Catholic, for, as the Empress realized to her displeasure after having blessed me with the icon of St. Nicolas, I had never converted from my father's faith.

I felt my husband's hand pulling me down, to my knees. I heard his voice praising the Tsarina's generosity.

Catherine and the Grand Duke came to my wedding. She in a sapphire-blue dress lush with silver embroidery, he in the green Preobrazhensky uniform the occasion demanded, with his wig freshly curled and powdered, a gold-tipped cane in his hand. The Duke said something to his wife. She nodded and gave me a quick look before she lowered her eyes.

He had come, too, the Chancellor of Russia. When the ceremony ended, I saw him tap on his snuffbox, open it, and offer some to Egor. "Queen's Scotch, perfumed with bergamot," he told my new husband, taking a fat pinch for himself. "A gift from one of my new English friends."

I had a swift, piercing memory of my hands touching him and suddenly found it hard to breathe, as if each of my breaths could turn into tears. When the Chancellor stepped toward me, I fixed my eyes on the silver buckles of his shoes, shiny against the scuffed leather.

"Happiness, prosperity, advancement." He delivered his list of wishes as if talking to himself. I turned away, but I was not fast enough. "You can thank me now," the Chancellor murmured in my ear, "for not taking more than you could spare."

I felt color rise from my cheeks to the roots of my hair.

"Pity that you've backed the wrong horse," he whispered, then walked away.

There was no proper wedding feast at the palace; we were not that important, although the Empress had a fiddler brought so that she could dance with the groom. "A good Russian husband, Varvara," she declared, panting with exhaustion when the music stopped and she'd lowered herself into an armchair. "Just the thing to dilute that Polish blood of yours."

I saw the Empress run her fingers through my husband's hair when he bowed in front of her, and only then did I know the depth of my own illusions.

Only a few weeks before, I thought myself indispensable. But in my mistress's eyes, here was the sum of my worth: a discarded lover and a dress she no longer wished to wear.

My husband's regiment threw a celebration for us. There were platters of venison, a roasted piglet with an apple in its browned snout, giant bowls overflowing with *bliny*, buckwheat, sour cream, and caviar, all drowning in an unending supply of vodka and champagne. Increasingly drunken guests demanded we kiss yet again, striking the rims of their glasses with forks as they did so. Egor obliged willingly, more and more intoxicated with his triumph, his bitter tongue pushing its way through my clenched teeth, his hand digging through the folds of my dress. I considered the wisdom of downing enough vodka to feel numb, but something in me urged me to stay sober, to watch and listen, to wait and never forget.

How reckless he was on that day, how sure of his immense good luck, Egor Dmitryevich Malikin, a man of unbounded optimism, secure in his conviction that all obstacles could be eradicated. Had he not been blessed by fate? Rewarded handsomely for his service?

Egor's comrades followed us in a merry convoy to our home on Apothecary Lane just off Millionnaya Street, filling the rooms with banter and jostling. On our way we passed the house Catherine and her mother had occupied during the months of the Grand Duke's illness, and I tried desperately to think of the time I'd spent with Catherine there, the happiest time since my parents died. In our new apartment, Egor's servants lined up in the hall, eyeing me with apprehension, wondering what kind of mistress this new bride would turn out to be. A woman with a lazy eye whom I took to be the cook held out a basket tray with bread and salt. A brown hound growled at me from under the table.

I had been well instructed in my wifely duties. In the bedroom, I knelt to remove Egor's boots. As the custom demanded, a whip was hidden in one of them, to remind me of the price for disobedience. My husband was my master. Without his consent, I could do nothing.

I was not a death maiden. My body did not kill. My thoughts poisoned nothing but my own heart.

"How did it happen?" I could not stop myself from asking Egor that night.

He had been standing guard outside the Imperial Bedroom with others when the Empress opened the door, he told me. She had asked who would like to marry one of her maids. She'd even said my name: Varvara Nikolayevna.

He'd seized his chance.

Like a serf woman auctioned off by her owner to breed more slaves, I thought.

"Why me?" I heard myself ask.

"I can spot a good racehorse when I see one," my new husband told me in a voice he must have thought tender. It was the way I walked through the corridors of the palace. Head high. Chest forward. My eyes bold. My heels hitting the floor with assurance.

He was startled that night to discover how hard-edged I could be, how bitter a reward taken as a right. And I? I waited for the morning. Then, as soon as Egor left, I threw the soiled sheets into the flames, and sat staring at the smoke of the burning fabric, acrid and thick.

I tried to call it home, this high-ceilinged apartment with windows on Apothecary Lane, seven rooms in all. My husband had rented it from a German merchant who assured him that we would smell the sweet air floating from the nearby Summer Garden and, on a quiet morning, even hear the blue monkeys chatter in their cages. All I smelled was soot and boiling cabbage. All I heard was the hammering of the cobbler who rented the cramped rooms in the back of the house.

"Home," I would say to myself, for what had I ever wanted but a place to call my home? But the word sounded hollow, as if spoken into a well. My husband had bought the ornate mahogany furniture, the ottoman and armchairs, in the parlor. The only thing I could call my own was the old trunk I had brought from the palace.

The lid gave a squeak when I lifted it.

I took out my mother's muslin dress and pressed it to my face. I could no longer recall her voice, or the touch of her hand. When I felt tears run hot from my eyes, I blinked them away angrily. I looked at the rose-colored walls, the heavy burgundy curtains, the golden tassels reflecting candlelight. *Not mine*, I thought.

Come back here with a son nine months from your wedding day, the Empress had ordered me when she'd blessed me with the Holy Icon.

I thought of her command each morning when I woke and in the evenings before I fell asleep. Could it be a promise that I would return?

"How often did you have to mount her to get all of this?" I screamed at Egor once. My hand made a circling motion to include the apartment, the servants, his promotion to lieutenant. I saw the shock blaze in his eyes. His lips curled. I saw the glitter of his teeth. His body—the sinewy body of which he was so proud—stiffened.

I thought he would hit me.

Instead, he laughed. A clipped, sour laugh, but in his eyes I saw the flicker of doubt that told me I had won.

It was a hollow victory. I remember the emptiness of waking up every morning, with Egor snoring beside me, muttering something under his breath. I shook off the memory of his greedy touch, even as it etched itself into my breasts, my belly, the pelt of hair between my legs.

I took in the shape of my marital bed, the heavy carved frame, the curtains that could not keep the drafts away. Drawn, our window shutters turned deftly into mirrors that made the room look like a cage, without a way out.

In these first weeks of my marriage, I consoled myself with visions of revenge. I imagined Egor dead, pierced by a sword in a dark alley after some drunken escapade, or, in more generous moments, killed in some distant battle. I imagined the Chancellor's disgrace—some yet unspecified failure of his diplomatic schemes, or a bribe too tempting to refuse—and the Empress's summons. I even imagined my return to court, no longer a tongue, a Polish stray, but the widow of a Russian noble, Catherine's newest lady-in-waiting.

The wedding gift from the Grand Duchess lay safe in my escritoire. It was a drawing in brown ink of a compass, a skull, a roll of paper, and quills, all scattered across the page in a haphazard manner, separated with a thicket of curving lines.

Not a proper wedding present, she wrote, *but something I'm sure you'll like.*

I studied the sketch for a long time, intrigued by the strangeness of the design, but I could not understand it. And then, one day, as I was bending over to pick something up from the floor, my eyes caught the drawing from an angle. The picture was a clever puzzle, one of many I've seen since. The odd objects I stared at for so long, struggling to penetrate their meaning, were all part of a figure: a woman wrapped in a cloak, a roll of paper in her left hand, her right hand holding a quill. She stands triumphant, undefeated, resting her foot on the skull at her feet.

How did we live? Happily, my husband would have answered.

It never crossed Egor's mind that I might not share his enthusiasm. Russia was his Motherland, and she had spoiled him rotten. He was young and strong. "I could eat a horse with hoofs," he bellowed as soon as he entered the house each evening, delighted to hear the cheerful commotion in the kitchen. He patted his belly after meals, to the joy of the cook and the maids. He boasted of his hangovers for which he demanded large quantities of kvass, straight from the cellar—it had to be cool and frothy—and a raw egg that he emptied with a loud suck through a punctured shell. I don't think he ever knew pain that was not inflicted by a sword or a bullet, pain caused by his own decay. Scars of his fights and skirmishes were badges of honor, evidence of how fast his body healed itself. "Feel it," he would urge me, and I'd be forced to run my fingers over a scar on his arm, a curious zigzag he swore came from a knife.

My few attempts to open his eyes to the underbelly of our lives were met with incredulous laughter. "We could be watched? Our servants could be reporting everything we say? Is this what you find in these books you read all day, *kison'ka?*"

Was I but a kitten? My anger but a hiss?

He was my husband, the man of the house; he was taking care of all that was important. "How like a woman, *kison'ka,*" he would tease me, "to argue about what she doesn't understand."

I made sure Egor's uniforms were freshly brushed and mended, his boots shining, piles of white starched handkerchiefs always at the ready. I demanded to see the plates the cook swore were broken and had to be replaced. I chastised a maid for leaving ashes strewn around the fireplace. I sent back soup that was too salty, roast that was too dry. My new servants watched me uneasily, mourning the easygoing life they had had before my arrival, with a master who ate what they served and never questioned their industriousness. "Mistress is coming," I heard them whisper in the kitchen, scattering to their duties with exaggerated eagerness.

The woman with a lazy eye who had greeted me with bread and salt on my wedding day was not a cook. Her name was Masha, and she was our housekeeper, the only one of our servants who faced me without apprehension. Judging by her wrinkled face, she had to be well past fifty, though no one knew her exact age. "Mashenka, *dushenka*," Egor teased her, planting a loud kiss on her cheek every time she warned him he was ruining his health by drinking too much or cutting down on his sleep. "Don't listen to me, and you will listen to a whip," Masha grumbled, as if Egor were still a reckless boy climbing fences, upsetting cucumber frames, chasing partridges through the fields.

Egor's father had found her years ago on some deserted northern road, a girl alone, starved to the bone, clad only in filthy rags. "I wouldn't have lived to see the next day," Masha told me, still awed by the miracle of the stranger's mercy.

Master covered her with his own coat and took her home. Mistress, big with the child who would become my husband, fed her warm gruel and chicken broth. Thick and yellow with silky grease.

It takes a long time to get the chill out of the bones.

"Leave me alone, Masha," I'd say as she trailed me with her stories. But she wouldn't.

"It's not good to sleep so much, Varvara Nikolayevna."

"Don't stare into mirrors. It's easy to get lost in there."

In the world in which I'd once lived, rife with traps and lures, I had lingered in doorways and had not turned away from black cats. I'd paid no heed to the last thought that came just before sneezing. Had I been stubborn? Foolish? Or fatally careless?

I tried to hide from Masha. In my bedroom, I stuffed a handkerchief into a keyhole. I closed my ears to the sound of her shuffling feet. But nothing I did would silence the sharp clucks of her warnings.

The guards were known all over Russia for wild parties and gambling for dizzying stakes. Faro was their favorite game. When his emerald-encrusted snuffbox was pawned, I knew Egor had lost at cards. When he brought it back, I knew that he had won. There had been duels and drunken games of daring, a horse race that almost cost him a mare. I didn't inquire where he spent his days or nights. I didn't mind smelling other women on him. If you don't love, you cannot be betrayed.

"Don't you care, *kison'ka?*" Egor asked once.

"Would it change anything if I did?" I shot back.

Here a memory comes, and refuses to leave. Of Egor sitting on a kitchen stool, hunched up, a thick blanket over his broad shoulders. Of water dripping from his hair and his nose, a murky puddle gathering at his bare feet. Of Masha calling on the servants to stoke the fire and fetch a basin with hot water.

"Like a little boy . . . just like Old Master . . . act first, think later," Masha grumbled as she was drying Egor's hair with a towel, bemoaning the good undershirt, now torn, the town uniform soiled. The missing silver button.

"I'm not sick, Mashenka," my husband insisted. "Just a bit wet."

"What happened to you?" I gasped. "What kind of foolishness—?"

I didn't finish. Masha shot a warning look at me with her good eye. *This is not the time for interrogations. The body has to warm up through and through.*

I didn't give up.

The details came one by one, between hurried sips of scalding borscht. A walk by the river, a wager that grew. A fellow guard who said no one would swim to Vasilevsky Island . . .

Watch me, my husband had said.

"Look at this, *kison'ka.*" Waving aside Masha's protests, Egor demanded his shako. Inside, there was a leather purse. Bulky, heavy with his winnings.

There it was again, the conviction in his voice. A few more months was all he needed. We would leave this rented apartment, the smoky air of the city. Buy a country estate. Small at first, perhaps, but with a pond, and a meadow for the horses to graze. He already had an eye on a steed he would buy. The owner was broke. He would give him a good price.

In the memory that haunts me, the kitchen smells of wet wool and tar. His undershirt is drying by the stove. Egor looks at me, his eyes gleaming.

"There will be mushrooms to pick, *kison'ka*. Partridges to shoot. Masha could have her kitchen garden."

"And how will you pay for it all?" I retort as I turn away. "With your gambling? Or do you still count on the Empress to open the door for you at night?"

In Russia one could acquire nobility, if one rose far enough through military or service ranks. It was Egor's father who earned the right to be addressed as Your Nobleness. But a son of a provincial official could be only a *new* noble. No matter how high the gambling stakes, how loud the denunciations of heirs with ancient names and crumbling fortunes, in the corridors of the Winter Palace, the *old* nobles would still put him in his place.

Is this what Egor had thought of when he'd first seen me at the Empress's side? A wife who knew the palace ways? A wife who would help him assure that his son—if God granted him one—wouldn't have to defend his honor with fights?

I could've asked him, but such thoughts did not cross my mind then.

How tedious I thought it all, instead. Visits to pay and receive. Name days to remember. Soirees and concerts to attend. The dragging talks of rank and four-horse carriages, days reduced to bone-china cups steaming with tea, or watermelon ice melting on hot summer days. What did they know about me? What could they tell me, these "new" friends who praised the cut of my dresses and asked what the Empress was like when she was in her own chambers, away from the eyes of the court?

I answered their questions vaguely. If I could, I slipped away from these gatherings, pleading a fainting spell, or a migraine headache. If I couldn't, I listened and kept silent until the whispers around me thinned and chipped away.

This is not the life I wished for, I thought. *But nothing will change it.*

I had not forgotten Catherine.

When Masha arrived from the Tartar market, I followed her into
the kitchen, praising the cut of the roast, the clarity of broth simmering on the stove. I asked for the servants' gossip. Masha's lazy eye almost disappeared inside her skull as she looked at me, but she did not
disappoint.

There was trouble in the palace, she told me. Too many people
were sniffing around the Grand Duchess's bed. Didn't they know that
a watched pot never boils? Why not leave the young ones alone for a
while?

They were under guard, Catherine and Peter. Their wing of the
palace was like a prison. The Choglokovs, Masha said, were their jail-
ers. Madame and Monsieur Choglokov, high and mighty now. No one
can get past those two to the ducal couple. Acting as if they were roy-
alty themselves, though everyone knows how they got their position.
With a hefty bribe and their eight children. As if the Grand Duchess
could get pregnant by watching a bunch of snotty brats.

At the Tartar market, Masha told me, there had been much laughter at the expense of the Choglokovs. Monsieur pinching every servant girl, while Madame is assuring everyone how her husband sees
nobody but her.

At the end of each day the Choglokovs escorted Catherine and
Peter into their bedroom and locked the door. Until morning.

"They say it is the Chancellor's doing," Masha said.

I didn't doubt it. I could imagine his canny arguments. "Constant
proximity, Your Highness. No distractions. Daily reminders of the
Young Court's supreme duty to their Sovereign. Your Highness has
already done enough."

Having exerted her will, I knew, the Empress would turn her mind
to other things. Once again, pleasure would consume her—a new
dance step, a shipment of French silks, a new Favorite. The "moon
children" would be allowed to visit her from time to time, dressed in

their finery, to declare their gratitude in front of the whole court before being dismissed.

I imagined Catherine alone with her husband, watching the Grand Duke arrange his soldiers into formations or reading to him, perhaps, just the way I used to from the book of Russian fortresses. Were the Choglokovs really that strict in following the Chancellor's orders, I wondered, or would they take a letter to her if I offered them a bribe? Twice I even started to write to the Grand Duchess, just a few words of encouragement, but they both ended in the fire, these notes of mine. I was too aware of the many eyes that would read them before hers.

On Sunday, November 3, I woke up with a feeling that a warm stream was seeping out of me. I reached down between my legs. My hand came away crimson with blood. Then came a sharp spasm of pain. I screamed for Masha, but by the time she came running, all she could do was yank the drenched sheets from under me and take them away. Somewhere in them was the tiny body of a son who did not wish to be born.

"Let me see him," I begged Masha, but she refused. It was not good for a mother to see a fetus yet unformed. "Nothing wrong with him," she assured me, when she saw my frightened eyes. "Just not ready for this world."

But I would not be soothed. As I lay feverish, racked by pain, it came back, the memory of the Kunstkamera monsters in Peter the Great's museum. *Why did you come?* their voices taunted me. *To spy on us? To see what is not meant to be seen?*

Laudanum didn't help. I lost weight and grew pale, for I would not eat. The servants tiptoed around me with grim faces, crossing themselves as if I were already dead. Masha tried to force some bitter-tasting teas into me, muttering that I needed to cleanse my blood, but I spat them out.

I do not recall much of the weeks that followed. Whispers and distant screams, and a wormwood taste on my tongue. Once it seemed that my mother was sitting by the window, bent over her embroidery hoop. She turned her face to me, but when I lifted myself up from my pillows to reach out to her, I saw she had Madame Kluge's eyes.

I heard Egor's voice in the corridor, ordering the servants. I heard his hurried steps and the sound of doors closing. Once I woke to the feeling of his presence. He was sitting on the edge of our bed, his fingers stroking my hand, but I kept my eyes closed until he sighed and went away.

It was Masha who placed the birch box into my hands. "Master said to give it to you," she told me. "The Grand Duchess herself sent it."

"Catherine?" I whispered through parched lips.

On the Empress's birthday, when the official banquet ended, the Grand Duchess had walked up to Master Egor, Masha said, and had asked about me. When he told her I was not well, she gave him this gift to take to me.

Tears stung my eyes.

"Master said you would like it," Masha continued. She must have noticed how I frowned when she mentioned Egor, for she adjusted the nightcap on my head and clucked her tongue, her lazy eye retreating into her skull.

I struggled to gather my thoughts, to break through the fog that muddled them. The Empress's birthday meant that it was December already, that I had been ill for a whole month. Hoping to amuse me, Masha repeated what she had heard of the banquet. The Empress, the Grand Duchess, and the Grand Duke had been seated at the head of the table like three jewels in a crown from which four long tassels trailed, each leading to one of the Guard regiments. The table was adorned with confections made entirely out of sugar, gates opening to wide sugary avenues, wondrous miniature palaces complete with terraces and gardens. "Who gets to eat it afterward?" she wondered, licking her lips. "The Empress herself?"

I held Catherine's gift in my hands. My fingers took pleasure in the smoothness of birch bark, in the shape of a flowery design pressed into it. With Masha's help I sat up. I never would have thought sitting could require so much strength. I felt another welt of pain in my belly and suddenly remembered my dead baby brother, buried in some Warsaw cemetery. *No one,* I thought, *will light a candle for him on All Souls' Day, and my own unformed child will not even have a grave.*

"Open it," Masha urged.

I opened the birch box and breathed in the scent of wild mushrooms, the scent of an autumn I had no memory of because of my illness. Outside, the snow was piling up along the streets, carriages had long been replaced by sleighs. I thought longingly of a ride through icy, silent fields.

Inside the box there were sharpened quills and a crystal inkwell with a silver lid. Catherine's mute invitation for me to write to her.

"I'm thirsty," I said to Masha. "Bring me some hot tea."

Masha turned her beaming face away, to the corner, where a Holy Icon hung, and crossed herself, bending to touch the floor.

"Praised be the Lord's mercy," she said.

For the next months I drank Masha's concoctions without protest; I began eating, and my gaunt cheeks filled with flesh. On the first days of the new year, 1746, I was able to stand up and walk in my room. In April, in the Kazan cathedral, the Empress would celebrate the fifth anniversary of her coronation. Catherine and the Grand Duke would surely be there. I was the wife of a Palace Guard, entitled to witness such a grand occasion.

If I was strong enough to stand through the Orthodox Mass.

In March, Anna Leopoldovna, the mother of the imprisoned baby Emperor, died. The news was repeated in hushed voices, for any mention of Ivan VI's name was forbidden. "Prisoner Number One," I heard him called, or simply "Ivanushka," though even these references were dangerous. Only months before, a wine merchant had been arrested when a dismissed servant denounced him for hoarding old coins with Ivan's image.

Knowing that for Catherine the news spelled trouble, I began waiting for Egor when he came home from his guard duty. Had he seen the Empress, I wanted to know. Was she angry? Had the Grand Duchess been summoned at night again? Was she crying?

His answers were flippant and dismissive. Why should I care if the Grand Duchess was still not with child? Don't I have my own home to care about?

"It's Russia's future," I said once, boldly.

Egor slapped his forearm, as if to swat a mosquito.

"Russia is too great to be weakened by one barren womb, *kison'ka,*" he replied.

On April 25, from the crowded section assigned to the public, I watched the Imperial Family enter the Kazan cathedral. The Empress was all glimmer in her ivory gown, an ermine-lined cape on her shoulders. Peter and Catherine walked right behind. I craned my neck to catch a glimpse of their faces. Peter seemed even more sickly and ashen than I remembered. Catherine looked grave and composed. Dressed in pearly blue, her hair entwined with silver threads, she never once took her eyes from the Empress. Beside them, the Chancellor of Russia, stooping slightly, stood taking his measure of the crowd. His eyes did not dwell long at the spot where I stood.

I felt my head spin. Dark spots fluttered before my eyes, obscuring my vision. Beads of sweat gathered on my forehead. Had I been foolish to think myself cured?

I clenched my teeth. I fixed my eyes on the beam of light that came through the stained-glass window high above. A rainbow of colors whirled and danced. The weakness passed.

Around me the officers' wives honored with invitations to the banquet that would follow the Mass whispered excitedly of tables surrounded by fragrant orange and pomegranate trees, of fountains set up in the palace halls, of a pyramid of fire created by burning wax poured through glass domes.

I would not see any of it. The Grand Duchess, I heard, had been ordered to keep most select company. Only mothers of healthy babies could be admitted to any room she was in.

In the next weeks, with Masha in tow, I began to venture again into the city. I did not care if I rubbed shoulders with soldiers or thieves. I walked quickly past palaces and warped wooden buildings that would not survive the next fire, past brick walls split by winter frost, past churches forbidden to overshadow the buildings of the State.

I wouldn't have admitted it to anyone, but I hoped for the sight of the imperial carriage. Catherine would spot me, too, I dreamed, and she would stop, even if for only a few moments, even if all I could do was urge her not to lose hope.

Masha, her feet swollen from too much walking, grumbled at my recklessness. I was like a northern wind, she complained, blowing any which way, as if ghosts were chasing me.

"And what kind of wind are you, Masha?" I taunted her in anger, but she took my measure placidly with her good eye. Ever since I had "come around," as she put it, she made me wash my hair in kvass to give it a reddish hue. "Master likes it," she would repeat with a sly smile when I protested.

I let her do as she pleased.

In September, when the court celebrated the Empress's name day, I spoke to Catherine for the first time since my wedding day.

As part of the celebrations, the Russian Theater put on a play for the Empress. *Susanin's Revenge* was one of those historical dramas that Elizabeth loved. It was set during the "Time of Troubles," when Russia was teetering on the verge of extinction, before it would be saved, in the nick of time, by Elizabeth's great-grandfather Mikhail. The first Romanov to become a Tsar.

Officers and their wives were invited to the third night of performances.

In the play, a detachment of the Polish army was on its way to

murder the rightful Tsar and put a false one on the throne. The Polish
hetman was haughtily predicting Russia's downfall, the eradication of
the Orthodox faith, and his own rise to glory. Then Ivan Susanin, a
handsome young peasant, offered to guide the Poles through the
swamp. Before the curtain fell for intermission, in a long soliloquy,
Susanin revealed his strategy. The swamp would suck the enemies of
Russia to their deaths.

I thought the play particularly crude but refrained from comment-
ing on it, for I heard that the Empress had relished it. After the opening night the author had been raised through the Table of Ranks and
received a gift of an estate.

The performance must have already started when Catherine arrived,
for only when the intermission began did I hear her voice coming
from the imperial box.

"I need some fresh air," I said to Egor and hurried away.

The door to the imperial box was flung open, and a crowd of well-
wishers had already gathered. I recognized Prince Naryshkin, Countess Rumyantseva, and other court ladies, gushing praises of the actors,
the name-day celebrations, and the Grand Duchess. There was no
sign of the Grand Duke and, to my relief, the Empress's seat, too, was
empty.

I stood in the doorway and waited, but moments passed before
Catherine saw me.

"Welcome, Varvara Nikolayevna," I heard. "What an unexpected
pleasure to see you looking so well."

"I, too, am glad to see Your Highness," I replied carefully. Her face
was cheerful and animated. Perhaps the rumors of Elizabeth's rages
were exaggerated, or perhaps Catherine was with child at last.

I couldn't ask. I could only listen and watch.

Prince Naryshkin launched into some elaborate story of mushroom picking that ended with him and his sister getting lost in the
woods. "Lev, the wanderer," Countess Rumyantseva teased. "Do you
always manage to be so careless?"

Catherine stepped closer toward me. Her scent was all spring flowers: hyacinths, violets, and daffodils.

"How are you feeling, Your Highness?" I asked her, unable to keep my voice from shaking.

"Well," she answered, letting her shawl fall loosely over her shoulders. Prince Naryshkin, tangled in his tale, roared with laughter.

"And the Grand Duke?"

"My husband, too, is well."

This is all we had: a few minutes, a few words. Nothing that could not be overheard, reported back.

"I read a lot now, Varvara Nikolayevna. No more French novels, though. Tacitus." Catherine's smile gave her blue eyes a mischievous tilt. "Count von Gyllenburg suggested I should start reading Tacitus. And Montesquieu. But those books are not easy to find."

"I'll look for them, Your Highness," I promised.

"I'd be most obliged," Catherine said, extending her hand as if to touch me. She withdrew it before anyone could notice.

I watched her turn away from me to greet another visitor, and then I took my leave.

I scarcely watched the rest of the play. Onstage, Ivan Susanin was leading the invaders into the swamp. The Poles discovered his trick too late and decided to kill him before they would perish themselves. Susanin welcomed his own hero's death with a long list of accusations against the enemies of Russia. The Poles were trying to convert the Russians to their Latin faith, to steal their souls and make them their slaves.

"They'll promise us everything to get what they want. In Polish schemes we count for nothing," Susanin declared, hands raised to the heavens, a loud gust of wind bending the stage trees to add weight to his words.

I heard murmurs of approval in the audience, followed by a storm of applause. Beside me, Egor clapped vigorously.

I thought of the brave cheerfulness of Catherine's words, the hand that almost touched mine. When the play ended, I walked out of the theater to our carriage as if in a dream. I was grateful when Egor, spotting a fellow officer in the throng, announced that he would not accompany me home.

For the rest of that week I looked for Tacitus in the old bookstores on the Great Perspective Road. Not finding any of his works, I sent word to booksellers who had once used my father's services. *Germanie* was the first to arrive, followed by *Persian Letters, Annals, Histories.* If I could, I always chose solid leather bindings, strong seams, volumes I hoped my father had once touched, although I never came across the one where the letters of a title crossed the shadow line.

I had no doubts that the Choglokovs carefully examined each book I sent to the Winter Palace. Or that Catherine's notes on the elegant vellum paper with gilded edges assuring me of her gratitude went through the same scrutiny.

One dark November day, Egor returned from the palace with news that the Grand Duke and his wife had departed for Oranienbaum.

"Why?" I could not help asking.

"Bestuzhev's order," he said. "The Chancellor thinks there are too many distractions at court."

He screwed his eyes in mock horror.

"Now, let's see—what distractions could possibly stop the Grand Duke from getting his wife with child? A masquerade? A drill? I can't think of any more. Can you, *kison'ka?*"

I ignored the glee in my husband's voice.

Forty-three *versty* of country roads would now stand between Catherine and me, I thought. A whole day's carriage ride. There would be no theater, no visits. The Chancellor would make sure of that. What would she have to keep her from despair besides books?

The first letter from Oranienbaum was short.

The bearer of this note is a purveyor of many exquisite treasures, many of which would become you. I shall be waiting for the result of his efforts with great impatience. Please remember that I'm as certain of your devotion to me as I'm sure of my friendship with you.

It was not signed, but I recognized Catherine's hand instantly.

A jeweler, Monsieur Bernardi, had brought the note on the pretext of offering his services. After all, I was an officer's wife, a tribute to my husband's rank. Had Egor not been promoted to Lieutenant Captain? He would not want me to be outshone by other ladies. Would I allow Monsieur Bernardi to examine my jewels?

Monsieur Bernardi was not surprised to discover that many pieces had to be cleaned and repaired, clips had to be adjusted, pearls restrung.

He never mentioned Catherine or his visits to Oranienbaum. But every time he came, he slipped a letter from the Grand Duchess into my hand and took the one I had prepared.

You are meant for great things, I wrote in the first one.

Don't trust anyone, I wished to write. *Nothing has changed. You are in a gambling house where every player is cheating.*

But she knew that already.

She knew which of her maids checked her underclothes for the blood of her menses. She knew who went through the pages of the books she read, hoping to find a forgotten note. She knew who spied on her for the Empress and who carried her secrets to the Chancellor of Russia. She had discovered all the spying holes in her rooms and never left her fireplace until the thing she wanted burned had turned to ash.

Even in her secret letters to me, Catherine was taking precautions. She wrote them as if she were writing to a man whose name was never mentioned. She referred to the Empress as La Grande Dame. Peter was the Soldier. The Choglokovs were referred to as the Peacock and the Hen. The Chancellor was the Old Fox. Her awaited pregnancy became "the great event" or "the awaited news."

I'm very sorry, Monsieur, not to have had the pleasure of seeing you for such a long, long time. Even a quick glimpse of your figure would have been a consolation. I long for a time when I will again be allowed to walk up to you and express my happiness at the sight of you.

For these dark days cannot last forever, can they?

La Grande Dame speaks of reading as if it were an incurable disease.

My valet had been ordered to leave my service, because I foolishly thanked him for his kindness in the Hen's presence.

The Soldier's Blackamoor was sent away to St. Petersburg, and two of his valets were replaced, too. We are forbidden to like anyone, Monsieur. We are forbidden to have friends. I pray no one finds out that I'm writing to you. I urge you to burn each of my letters as soon as you read it.

I did what she asked me and burned them. But they are in my memory, as if I still held them in my hands, each word read and re-read, releasing its dose of sorrow.

They kept coming, Catherine's letters. The brood of the Peacock and the Hen were pestering the Soldier to let them play with his model fortress. La Grande Dame came to Oranienbaum accompanied by yet another Favorite, shot twenty-two partridges, and allowed Catherine to take riding lessons. Letters I memorized before they turned to ash.

I was pleased that Catherine was far away from the intrigues of the court. She wrote that the Oranienbaum gardens were giving her unexpected pleasure and a sense of growing calm. There was still no "awaited news" but the long days in the country allowed for a lot of good reading and thinking. She was not wasting time, she assured me, but was using it to reflect on her mission in life, her duties, her obligations. More and more she was convinced that friendship and loyalty were the most priceless possessions she could ever have.

For a time, I took solace in these words.

Another year passed, and the Chancellor of Russia was still in charge of the conduct of the Young Court. By then the Empress let it be known that the wretched scamps, as she took to calling the Grand Duke and Duchess, even in public, had dared to defy the greatest of her wishes.

In the salons of St. Petersburg, the officers' wives talked of little else. It was Catherine whom the Empress blamed, they gossiped.

"I brought her here to breed, not to read," she screamed for everyone to hear when yet another monthly report of Catherine's reoccurring menses reached her. "Who does she think she is?"

The Grand Duchess was becoming the target of malice. Everyone had a theory of why she was not conceiving. "It's because Her Highness refuses to use a woman's saddle when she rides," I heard. "It's because Her Highness laces herself too tight." "What is the use of a barren womb?" people asked. "A fruitless tree?"

There were other rumors, too. At the latest palace ball, the Grand Duke danced with his wife only once. Didn't Catherine notice that her superior airs were making her husband angry? That Peter had begun praising the virtues of his wife's maids-of-honor when he was sure she would hear him? Princess Kurakina had most delicate bones; Countess Vorontzova had the best ear for music of anyone he knew. After all, what kind of man likes a woman who outshines him?

Why cannot she smile more? Make a joke? Drink some wine and stop talking of books?

My father used to say that if a tree is bent, every goat will jump on it.

In her letters to me, Catherine wrote that she had overheard courtiers calling her cold and haughty. Her hand, they whispered, was like a tiger's paw, her smile tight-lipped and cruel.

She was hardly ever allowed to leave Oranienbaum. And when she did, solely to accompany the Empress and the Grand Duke during the most important of court functions, she had to be cautious. *Don't try to approach me, Monsieur,* she wrote to warn me. *This may put in danger one of the few consolations left to me.* And so I saw her only from afar.

She wrote of hours spent alone, staring at a book, often uncut, on her lap. The Empress seldom addressed her, and when she did, Elizabeth's voice was gruff and impatient. *I'm quite convinced that the Old Fox does me harm with La Grande Dame. But what can I do? I've never given him any cause to be my enemy,* Catherine wrote. My few references to the likelihood of the "awaited news" met with either silence or an admonition: *Please, Monsieur, do not ask of what I cannot control. The happiness of friends is the only comfort for those who have no other comfort.*

Dogfights, the faro, the billiards. Fistfights, bears wrestled to the ground. Hours spent sweating at the *banya*, discussing the vagaries of luck.

They cheered one another on, the officers of the Imperial Guards.

Fortune is a woman; she yields only to the bold.

Good luck rubs off.

No one, the officers bragged, knew horses like my husband. Many could spot muscular necks and strong hind legs, heads with large nostrils and well-set ears. Many could point to the cannon bones that were too short, angles of joints that broke the proportions. But it took Egor's master eye to assess which promise would live up to the challenge of the race, which flaw would cause damage on the track.

"Come with us, Egor Dmitryevich," they called from the street, laughing and whistling with impatience. "Hurry up."

A man, unlike a woman, did not have to grow bitter, I thought, sitting alone in our front parlor, flipping cards in the game of solitaire, staring at the unsmiling faces of queens, kings, and jacks.

The clock struck midnight. I pushed the cards away and stood. The sound of scurrying feet came from the hall. There would be whispers in the kitchen. The servants were taking sides, bestowing the blame.

I walked to the window and opened the shutters. Apothecary Lane, silvery with lingering moonlight, was deserted, covered in a layer of thick, wet snow.

In the morning I took a sleigh to the Great Perspective Road. In the French perfumery I bought *eau de fraîcheur*, smelling sweetly of cinnamon and cloves. In the Merchants' Hall I chose a length of muslin and a pair of red silk stockings embroidered with jasmine blossoms.

Only a foolish gambler holds nothing back.

In the afternoon, when Egor came home from palace duty, I ordered Masha to bring us hot tea and some caraway-flavored vodka. I poured some vodka into my tea and drank it. It made my voice soft.

I spoke of the January freeze that painted ice gardens on our windowpanes, of the fox trails on the banks of the Neva I wished he had seen.

I closed the windows and the shutters. I let my hair escape its confining combs.

I laughed.

You have your world, I thought. *I'll have mine.*

I placed my hand on Egor's, and I thought how we might look to someone watching us: a husband and his loving wife, sharing a moment of closeness at the end of the day.

That night, scented with my best perfume and dressed in the turquoise nightdress that set off my eyes, I tempted him to lie with me.

It was a child I wanted. "Only mothers of healthy babies are allowed in the presence of the Grand Duchess" was the Empress's order.

FOUR

1749–1750

y January of 1749, St. Petersburg's salons were rife with speculation about who among the Imperial Favorites would win the battle for a place in Elizabeth's bed. For a while the Empress appeared frequently in the company of the actor who had played Susanin at the Russian Theater. Then some Cossack from Kiev, swiftly promoted to Lieutenant, dazzled her with his "Devil" dance. Next came Nikita Beketov, a choirmaster, rumored to be one of the Chancellor's protégés. Beketov's supremacy seemed assured until he was foolish enough to accept a gift from Countess Shuvalova, a jar of whitening cream, promising to smooth his skin. When his face erupted with bloated red patches, the Countess made sure the Empress feared for the pox. Beketov left the palace in disgrace.

Much was made of the fact that in the Imperial Bedroom, Countess Shuvalova scratched the imperial heels and told the Empress stories. "Might it have anything to do with the Roman nose of her handsome son?" I heard my husband ask with icy glee. He meant Countess Shuvalova's youngest son, Ivan Ivanovich, whose father, Marshal Shuvalov, had once been one of Elizabeth's lovers. There were more Shuvalovs at the court; one of Ivan's uncles was the Chief Prosecutor, two more served in the Secret Chancellery. "Open a coffer and a Shuvalov will pop up," Egor told me, "sniffing for his share of the spoils."

Word spread of Ivan Shuvalov's youthful charm, the soft, dark curls over his high forehead, the absentminded smile on his sensuous lips. "Eighteen years younger than the Empress. Always with a book in his hands. He has written a play. He wants her to rebuild the palace. He corresponds with Voltaire! He has given a pure white falcon to the Grand Duke." St. Petersburg salons resonated with cries of astonishment, accompanied by an uncertain laughter.

The Soldier is like a child, Catherine wrote. *He wishes to play at life while I want to live. He believes all flattery and gets annoyed at me for my warnings. Sometimes, I'm tempted to throw myself at La Grande Dame's feet and implore her to send me home to Zerbst.*

There were too many drunken feasts in Oranienbaum and too many military parades, often interrupted by displays of Peter's rage. Chairs had been smashed, a bottle hurled out of a window. *I believe that the Soldier's heart is good,* Catherine wrote, *but his mind is getting feeble from too much drinking, and then he gets unpredictable.*

I reread her letters greedily before the flames consumed them. Some things should never be written, not even in secret.

If only we could talk, I thought.

When the ice on the Neva thinned and yellowed, the hostesses of St. Petersburg salons repeated the rumor that the Empress changed her dresses five times during the day. Young Ivan Shuvalov was now reading to the Empress, a new play he wished her to stage. Ivan Ivanovich had been spotted walking through the palace with a dreamy look on his face, his hand over his heart as if he were taking a pledge. The Emperor of the Night began spending most of his time in the Anichkov Palace.

Alone.

"Imagine this," I heard.

Imagine the Winter Palace where there is no more late-night switching of bedrooms, no shrieks of anger, no fear of the dark. Behind the bedroom curtains, imagine fiddlers playing, choruses singing old Russian ballads. Imagine a mechanical table always in use for the Empress's late-night suppers. Imagine love's blindness, a woman be-witched.

I tried to, but my thoughts drifted away.

To Masha's delight, I sniffed rot everywhere and gagged at smells: the wet sheepskin coat of our coachman, the frowsy smell of Egor's riding boots. In the mornings I was waking up feeling nauseated. For days I would eat nothing but dark, coarse bread and drink only kvass. The midwife had told me to fill my mind with pleasant thoughts.

I was again with child.

"Our son," Egor kept saying, putting his hand on my still tight-laced belly. "Our little soldier."

I heard the softening in his voice. I felt his hand move up to caress the skin at my throat. I thought of the butcher who had not been paid this month. Of tallow candles that smoked, for we could no longer afford wax ones, not even for the parlor. Of the string of pearls that had disappeared from my jewelry box.

In St. Catherine's cathedral on the Great Perspective Road, where once I listened to Mass with my parents every Sunday, I knelt at the altar and crossed myself the Latin way. It was a daughter I prayed for, a daughter who would not refuse to be born. A daughter I could call mine.

Pregnancy suited me. As the child grew in me, my hair thickened, my skin glowed. I dutifully drank teas the midwife gave me; I never raised my hands above my shoulders, never wore a necklace around my neck. Masha fed me leeks and cooked prunes. I let her massage bear grease on the skin of my belly, tie a red ribbon around my wrist and mutter her incantations.

This time all will be well, she said, and I believed her.

The Chancellor of Russia was waiting for me on Millionnaya Street, his carriage parked a few steps away. I noted the shaggy gray brows, a maze of wrinkles that furrowed his cheeks, the shadow of a double chin. All this talk of imperial love was not to his liking, I thought, with a tingle of pleasure. The Shuvalovs were now openly dismissive of Bestuzhev's anti-French policy, accusing the Chancellor of taking bribes from the English King.

Masha saw the red velvet jacket and gold rings of a grand man wishing to talk to her mistress, the manservant standing behind him, holding his cane, and I heard her mutter a hasty prayer, flustered and uneasy.

"Good day, Madame Malikina," the Chancellor said. Bestuzhev's rust-colored velvet jacket was straining at the seams, and I imagined it cracking open, revealing the white cambric shirt, the scars underneath.

"Good day, Varvara Nikolayevna," he repeated, the missing teeth molding his lips into a grimace.

I walked right past him.

Masha scurried behind me along the Moyka Bridge. Panting, she tugged at my sleeve. I refused to stop. I didn't look back, either, delighting in the sound of my steps on the paved sidewalk.

I heard the carriage door open and close, the horses' hoofbeats on cobblestones, a snarl of a stray dog frightened away. By the time I reached the door of our house the Chancellor was there. Masha hesitated for a moment, but I told her to go inside.

He asked about my health and my husband's.

"We are both well," I answered coldly.

The summer heat brought out the smell of fish and rotting roots from the Moyka River. Without warning, I thought of myself in that first year at court, the child I had been, the scalding pain of my loneliness. "I didn't hurt you, did I?" Bestuzhev had asked then. I pushed back a wave of nausea.

The shrewd eyes of the man who had once been my teacher noted my disgust. The Chancellor flashed me a brittle smile, followed by a grave nod, as if I were still a child in need of chastising.

It's not over. You cannot afford to hate me, the look warned. I knew he was right, but I didn't want to give in.

"I'd like you to assure the Grand Duchess of my respect for her," he said.

I shouldn't have been surprised by his words, but I was. Once again the old palace game demanded a shift of alliances, a shameless turnabout. The Shuvalovs courted Peter, so Bestuzhev had to turn to the Grand Duchess.

"The little *Hausfrau* with a pointed chin?" I could not resist a sneer.

"I was wrong. I willingly admit it."

"How willingly?" I challenged.

The Chancellor gave me an indulgent smile. *You can have your brief moment of satisfaction,* he seemed to be saying. *You have earned it.*

"Most willingly."

"How can I assure the Grand Duchess of anything?" I asked. "I don't ever see her now."

"That mask of ignorance doesn't suit you, Varvara Nikolayevna. Jewels become you far more."

I heard the warning in his words, and I stiffened, knowing I would not sleep that night. I had suspected that the Chancellor might know of the letters the jeweler Monsieur Bernardi smuggled out of Oranienbaum but decided that he allowed them, a wise investment for the uncertain future. Each time I examined Catherine's seals, however, they always seemed intact. What else did I miss that I should've seen?

"I'll pass on your assurances to the Grand Duchess when I have the opportunity," I muttered. A wagon loaded to the brim with birch logs rolled by. An onion seller wearing long braids of onions around his neck was spreading a dirty-looking blanket on a wooden crate. My stomach churned again.

"Good," the Chancellor said, as I opened the door to the house. "This is all I wished to hear. For now."

On November 25 of 1749, the Empress's Accession Day, Ivan Ivanovich Shuvalov was appointed the Gentleman of the Bedchamber to the Empress, the position given to the official Favorite.

Ivan Ivanovich's first invitation from the Empress had been to a pilgrimage. In the salons of St. Petersburg, *praying together* had become a synonym for the sexual act.

The Shuvalovs may have won, I heard, but success is fleeting. Ivan the Devout would not last long. There were limits to even the most ardent of prayers.

Each morning, when I woke up, I placed my hand on my belly, to feel the vigorous thumps of the tiny heels. From the kitchen wafted the smells of roasted kasha and warm bread. Masha made omelets for me with caviar. Egor's commander, Colonel Zinovev, had sent us a basket of gifts. Honey that sweetened my tea came from his country estate. So did the cured hams and smoked sturgeon. Now that his favorite Lieutenant's wife had to eat for two, the attached note said, she had to have the best.

I lowered myself into the rocking chair and let it sway gently. "Swedish," Egor called it, on account of its glossy black finish decorated with red and gold.

He said he would name our son Dmitry. After his own father. Our second son could be Nikolay, after mine.

The dark November days were bitterly cold, the air smelled of sour smoke. The cherry tree outside my bedroom swayed in the wind. Flocks of sparrows descended on its bare branches, only to depart in a swarm of startled wings. "Open the window," I begged Masha, but she refused, muttering of drafts and bad air and the evil eye.

"*Devushka*," the midwife said. "A girl."

Pushed out of the depth of my pain, she was covered with my blood and already wailing. Healthy and alive.

Mine, I thought, bracing myself for Egor's disappointment.

In the street I heard a sleigh come to a stop. Horses neighed. In the commotion that followed I heard whistles, catcalls, and laughter.

As an old custom demanded, Egor's comrades would take him to the *banya* and lash his back with birch twigs. They would taunt him as his skin reddened, as tiny beads of blood mixed with his sweat. The bathhouse demons had to have their revenge on a man whose first-born was not a boy.

On the morning after my daughter was born, I'd fallen into a heavy, dreamless sleep. A murmur woke me. By the window, I saw Egor holding Darya. I was still very weak, but I rose on my elbows.

"You won't have your soldier," I told my husband.

He turned toward me and asked, "But she will live, won't she?" His voice quivered with wonder. I stretched out my hands, and Egor placed Darya in my arms, gently, like the most fragile of china.

"Yes," I promised. "She will live."

Through the closed doors I heard the clinking of cups on a tray. I smelled sweet bread and felt my stomach rumble. Outside, in the street, dogs were barking themselves into a frenzy.

Darya, Egor had named her. *Darenka*.

I did not resent Egor's choice. In Polish, my daughter's name evokes a sumptuous gift, a magnificent offering worthy of the Queen.

Darenka wrinkled her tiny nose and then sneezed. "My little princess," Egor cooed, and I thought that maybe I didn't know everything about him, after all.

In the slow days that followed, as the evenings grew longer, I held my daughter, cradling her in my arms, listening to her breath. She was perfect, I thought, fresh, unspoiled. I touched the folds of the skin that hid her eyes when she cried. I licked her tiny palms with their mysterious web of lines, tracing each tapered finger with my tongue. I kissed the soles of her feet, as smooth as her rosy cheeks.

I marveled at how well her small, warm body fitted into mine as we lay together on our big canopied bed, on the white crisp linen, which seemed to hold the scent of the wind. How wide she opened her mouth in eager search of my breast. I watched the tremor of delight when I placed my nipple, wet with milk, into her toothless mouth. I shivered with love when she closed her gums on it and began suckling, her grip latched just at the edge of pain. I was no longer alone. I was no longer a voyeur watching myself live.

Darya. *Darenka.*

Masha gasped in bewilderment at my refusal to hire a wet nurse. I heard her warn Egor that I'd wear myself out, that he should talk sense into me. "A good strong country girl," she would praise this or that candidate. "Go to your wife," I would hear her urge Egor. "Tell her now."

With Darya snug in my arms, I'd close my eyes and wait for the door to open, for Egor's steps, hesitant, drowning in the thick carpet. For the whiff of the distant stables his clothes always carried, softened by the scent of snuff.

He would reason with me.

"You need rest, *kison'ka.* You need to heal. It's for your own good."

I let him speak, as he leaned over to see Darenka's face, drifting into sleep. I heard his words turn into whispers and wane, and I knew he would let me do as I wished.

Alone with Darenka, her lips suckling on my nipple, I tried to re-member my parents' faces. Not the way they looked in their coffins, wax-like and shriveled, but at these precious everyday moments when they were alive. I recalled the tiny room in Warsaw where I sat, curled by my mother's side, watching her turn the hems of my dresses. I re-called the way her face lit with hope on the day when we arrived in St. Petersburg and the time when she hung the Virgin pendant around my neck. I remembered my father peeling an apple so carefully that the peel formed a long unbroken line and then cutting it into fat wedges that—even in the dead of winter—smelled of autumn sun. How they would have loved Darenka, I thought, promising to take my daughter to visit their graves and to pray for their souls.

Time was gentle to us then. I murmured into my daughter's tiny ear, already ticklish, nudging her into a shadow of laughter, the words of her first story, the story of her birth: *I lay in pain for two days, and you had to be turned inside me before I pushed you out of my womb,* I told her. *Death was lurking, waiting for both of us, my darling, but we escaped. I am your mother, and you are my daughter. With me you are safe. I'll never let anyone hurt you. I won't let you die, and I'll never leave you before you are ready.*

"There cannot be any more children," the midwife had said.

I'd heard her words, but their meaning had not touched me yet.

At the news of my daughter's birth, Egor's regiment presented us with a beautifully carved cradle. At Darya's baptism, Colonel Zinovev stood as her godfather beside Madame Choglokova's oldest daughter, an honor we merited at Catherine's request, since the Empress would not allow her to accept my invitation to stand as godmother herself.

With Masha's help, I arranged the baptismal gifts in our parlor, on a table covered with white damask, so that our visitors could admire them. A golden cross from her godfather. A chalice and a set of silver spoons in an ivory box from her godmother. Catherine's gift, a rosary bracelet of black pearls from Monsieur Bernardi's workshop, came with an inscription: *For Darya Egorevna, whose future will always be in my heart.*

With Egor at my side, I sat through rounds of visits as custom demanded, strangely soothed by the gasps of admiration: *How perfect she is! How tiny! How glowing!* I smiled as our visitors hung over the crib, pointing out resemblances. My nose, but Egor's dark eyes. His lusty bawl, but my smile.

Darya Egorevna.

May she always be with those who love her.

May she prosper and be safe.

I wiped tears off my cheeks.

"May God grant her all this," I whispered.

In our apartment on Apothecary Lane, all locks and hinges had been oiled; our servants were ordered to wear soft slippers and keep their voices hushed. The cradle was beside my bed, but a spare room had already been turned into a nursery with canary-yellow walls and a cedar chest. The room smelled of varnish and paint. My daughter had enough cambric shifts for five infants, half a dozen shawls, a silver-fox throw to keep her warm in the winter, and an expensive china doll with a velvet bonnet.

Her father's gift.

Once, by candlelight, I saw Egor bend over Darya's crib, his voice rising and falling, soothing her whimpers. She gurgled in response, a string of sounds still incomprehensible. He picked her up and held her close to his face, smiling at her in an uneasy happiness I recognized so well.

In the street, a beggar boy was singing off-key, an orphan's song. Soon he would knock at our kitchen door for a bowl of hot soup, a thick slice of buttered bread, and a few moments by the fire to ward off the November chill.

Another gurgle came, muted in bubbly spit.

I watched Egor place Darya back in her cradle and rest his right hand over his heart as if he was making a vow.

The beggar's song ended, and I stepped back, careful not to make a noise.

How dreary this time is, how slow! It stretches endlessly before me, like St. Petersburg nights during the months of winter, chilling the bones and the flesh. Sometimes nothing but a mad gallop through the fields can keep my tears from choking me, Catherine wrote.

For Christmas, the Chancellor of Russia sent the Grand Duchess a case of Hungarian claret and a few rare books acquired for her in Paris.

Both gifts had been returned.

"Was the book Machiavelli, or would that be too crude?" I asked the Chancellor when he came up to me that evening.

It was not the first time that he had sought me out at the Russian Theater, where Egor insisted we show up once a week, ever since I felt well enough to go out. The Chancellor always waited for the time my husband joined his fellow officers, and he always spoke of Catherine. The Grand Duchess, he told me, possessed a rare spirit. She had a unique combination of composure, courage, and quick wit. The Grand Duke would do well if he paid heed to her advice.

Slick words, I thought. *Palace words.*

"Let's give up on blame, Varvara Nikolayevna. Let's try a little more tact. Or even perhaps some Christian forgiveness."

I noted how blackened the remaining teeth in his mouth were, and how long cuffs trimmed with lace were meant to cover the age spots on his hands. There had been talk of mercury cures and far too much vodka, talk confirmed by his reddened nose and bloodshot eyes.

There was such sweet pleasure in the shift of power between us. I dipped into it. I could not resist.

"Have you begun packing already?" I asked.

Ivan Shuvalov, rumor had it, had called the Winter Palace "no better than a drafty dump." A house should be like the setting of a jewel, to match the grandeur of its owner. What was good for Peter the Great when he was still building Russia's glory no longer sufficed for his daughter, who was now ruling over an Empire. Why suffer the sooty walls of times long gone? The low ceilings, the simple furniture any clumsy apprentice could have made? Where is the lightness and light of the present? The new horizons? The new vision? The new pride?

The Empress agreed with her latest lover. Her Italian architect, Monsieur Rastrelli, had already seen his initial plans for the reconstruction of the palace trampled by imperial heels. "Come up with loftier visions," Elizabeth had demanded. "Visions worthy of *my* Russia."

The Chancellor's cheerful smile did not fade at my taunt.

"Packing? Is that what they say I am doing? All I've seen so far are the catalogs of Parisian auctions scattered all over the Imperial Bedroom. And rolls of architectural drawings taking up the surface of the huge desk that is there now. But nothing has been decided yet."

"The carpenters in town have doubled their rates," I reminded him. "The masons have tripled theirs. Does that not signify a decision?"

The Chancellor's eyes narrowed. I could hear his foot tap the floor.

"Perhaps this is the secret of Ivan Ivanovich's success," I continued. "He has the courage of wanting more. The belief in what others snigger at. The ability to pluck the strings others consider long broken."

My breasts were leaking milk. I thought of Darya's lips on my nipple, her tiny hand gripping my finger.

"Ah, the courage of motherhood, Varvara Nikolayevna," the Chancellor replied, dropping his voice. "Indomitable. And always infinitely touching. However, you should consider the fact that your husband has been borrowing quite a bit of money. A wiser choice of friends might alleviate—"

I didn't let him finish.

"I'm not like you," I said, walking away. "I don't judge my friends only by what they can do for me."

Back at the theater seat, waiting for the curtain to rise, I played with the paper leaves of my fan, on which river barges floated among the waves. Beside me, Egor was laughing hard at something his neighbor had just said.

I touched his shoulder. He turned toward me.

"Are we in debt?" I asked.

"Let this be my problem," he said. His fingertips brushed the top of my hand. They were cold, and I pulled away.

On the first day of the new year, 1750, Egor and I lined up with other courtiers in the Throne Room, shining with gilded stars and decorated with intricate arrangements of hothouse lilies—the pride of the Oranienbaum gardeners.

The conversations around me were meant to be overheard, and thus they were useless: wishes for good health in the coming year, predictable gushings over Monsieur Rastrelli's newest designs for the Winter Palace. Beside me, Egor sat in silence. "Wasted," he had grumbled about the hours spent at court. Time, so precious everywhere else, stretched here like strands of hot tar.

I didn't argue. I didn't point out the need to look and to remember what I saw.

Elizabeth reclined on the throne, her snugly fitted satin gown shimmering with diamonds, its ivory white broken only by the crimson-and-silver ribbon across her chest. A golden cape lined with ermine and embroidered with two-headed eagles covered her shoulders.

"A daughter, Varvara?" the Empress asked when I kissed her hand, having recited my wishes of happiness and gratitude for another year of her reign. Up close, the double layer of rouge thickened the wrinkles on her face and neck. There was a hint of rot in her breath, softened with cherry brandy and clover. Where Catherine and the Grand Duke should sit, Ivan Shuvalov, the new Gentleman of the Bedchamber, lounged. "The ducal pair have just stepped out," I had heard, as if one could leave the Throne Room at will.

"Yes, Your Highness," I replied. "A daughter."

The Empress gave me a bleak stare, then a smirk.

"Your husband is a patient man."

I kept my head lowered, but Egor muttered something in response, some promise impossible to keep. Ivan Shuvalov, in scarlet velvet, flicked a curious look in my direction, as if trying to recall where he had seen me before. Behind him, the Chancellor wore an expression of deep satisfaction, as if everything had just gone according to his most wished-for plan.

I hid my disappointment at the Grand Duchess's absence. Catherine had recently received news of her father's death, and the Empress had ordered her to stop crying and forbade her to wear black. Eight days of private mourning was enough for a man who had not been a king, Elizabeth said. *Mourning*, I wrote to Catherine, *you carry in your heart. There will be better years; you only need the courage to imagine them now.*

The order to join the Empress for a private event reached us as we left the third antechamber on our way out of the palace. "Are you sure you got it right?" Egor asked the page who'd run after us. The boy gave him a sulky shrug.

I recognized the room we were ushered to, the cedar panels that could be easily washed with water, the seats, perched on a platform, forming a semicircle against the back wall, turning it into a stage. "The mad room," the Empress used to call it, her own private asylum, where the insane were brought for her to watch. Pictures and ornaments were hung high so that the madmen couldn't reach for them in their thrash-ings. Elizabeth came here often in the first months of her rule. The whisperings of the bad blood, she liked to say, can be quite instructive. God speaks to us through strange channels, so we have to listen to the most puzzling of words.

There were only a few of us present, faces invisible in the darkness, muffled mutterings broken up by nervous giggles. Outside, in the streets banked with snow, the crowds were cheering Elizabeth Petrov-na's glorious reign, wishing her a long life and God's protection. St. Petersburg taverns were serving free vodka and *bliny.*

On the stage the footmen lowered large wooden planks suspended from the ceiling and lit the candles. Now there was enough light to see the stage and the first row, where Catherine and Peter, their absence so jarring in the crowded festivities of the Throne Room, sat. Beside them were the Empress and her Gentleman of the Bedchamber.

From where I was, Catherine's face looked small and narrow, like her waist. I recalled the letter that told me of mysterious pains in her joints. Oranienbaum's climate was not healthy, she'd written.

The Empress clapped her hands. A door, deftly hidden in the paneling, opened. They were led in, her madmen: the monk who cut off his genitals with a razor to purify himself from desire and

who insisted that only castrated humanity could build a true Kingdom of God; a valet who foamed at the mouth and claimed he
had seen a demon woman undress herself before him and call him
toward her.

"She had black teeth and big breasts. She had snakes and twigs in
her hair," he announced when the Empress asked him how he could
tell that she was truly a demon. "The snakes moved and the twigs did
not." He snapped his fingers and smacked his lips. And then he wiped
them with the back of his hand.

The doors opened again and two guards entered, gripping a tall,
beefy youth by the arms. His complexion was ashen, his eyes haggard.
He couldn't keep them still but looked around as if something could
jump out of the shadows at any moment and attack him.

The youth was dressed in a dirty sailor's uniform, torn at the
sleeves. He was barefoot, his feet callused and filthy with mud. When
the guards released his arms, he made a circle around the room, shouting. "Make room for Ivanushka! Make room for Ivanushka!"

He came to a stop, raised his fists to the heavens, and screamed.
The guards stepped back.

Beside me, I saw Egor's hand fly to his heart and pause there.

Was it really him? Prince Ivan, the baby Tsar who had vanished on
that November night more than nine years before when Elizabeth
went to the barracks of the Preobrazhensky Grenadiers, beseeching
them to help her? Or did the Empress of Russia trust the power of
illusion?

"What is your name?" she asked the youth now.

"Ivan."

"Who are you, Ivan?"

"A prince."

"Do you know where you are?"

"No."

"You are in the Imperial Palace."

"Yes. A prince lives in a palace."

"But you don't live here. We've brought you here."

"I live here. This is my room."

"If you are a prince, then where is your court?"

"Here. These people are my court. There are more of them. You don't see them, but there are more. Lots of people. I can hear them. You can hear them, too. They call me Ivanushka. They know."

"What do they know?"

"That God loves me."

"What do you want to do now?"

The youth paused for a moment, troubled by the question. His fingers rose to his lips, and he sucked on them loudly. One of the guards moved forward as if to push him, but he swirled back and thumped his foot. The guard lunged forward. The Empress raised her hand to restrain him.

"What do you want to do, Ivanushka?" she repeated.

"I want to eat."

"Are you hungry?"

He nodded.

"What do you like to eat?"

"Meat. Eggs. More eggs. Give me more eggs!"

"You shall have eggs."

Another signal, and with a squeak the door in the back wall opened again. Three footmen carried in a small table, a chair, and a platter piled with food. Hard-boiled eggs, a whole roasted pheasant, a loaf of dark peasant bread.

Ivanushka did not bother sitting down. He flung himself on the food, ravenous and insatiable. He stuffed it inside his mouth, licking his fingers; he broke chunks of bread from the loaf and dipped them in the sauce. Drippings from the pheasant stained his sailor's uniform; grease clung to his hair. But when an attendant approached with a towel, he shoved him away with a force that was astounding. The attendant was hurled against the wall; the bowl of water smashed on the floor.

"We are going now, Ivanushka. Is there anything else you want to tell us?" Elizabeth asked.

He didn't hear. He had bitten a hard-boiled egg in half, and was plucking out the yolk with his fingers.

Was this public display of madness the Shuvalovs' idea? I wondered. A warning not to pin one's hopes on the ousted Tsar? What were they hoping for? Triumph over Elizabeth's terror of a palace coup? Or a display of their own power?

The Empress rose and turned to the Grand Duchess.

"His mother may be dead." Her lips sucked the words she spoke, the sound of bones emptied of their marrow. "But she had two more children after him. Plenty of heirs, if you don't have one."

Catherine rose from her seat. I couldn't see her face as she walked out. *How easy it could be to get rid of her*, I thought. There was no need for crude methods, such as a thick pillow to cut off her breath. An innocent visit to a house where someone had just died of smallpox could be so easily arranged, a place offered on the ottoman where the sick person had just sat, a gift of a fan that had soothed the fever, or a cup touched by the lips of the sick.

Who would ask what had happened to a barren wife with no friends? Wasn't the first wife of Peter the Great forced to renounce the world? Hadn't she spent her days in a convent, watched at all hours, her guards given orders to slash her throat if anyone tried to free her?

There was no mention of that evening in the mad room in the next letter that arrived from Oranienbaum. Instead, Catherine wrote of the marionettes the Grand Duke had bought from a street troupe, an entire cast of wooden puppets, which he stripped of their rags and decked in the costumes he had designed himself. The play he wrote for his new toys was about a certain Faust, a charlatan, a drunken vagabond who tried to pass for a learned man and a great magician.

The Soldier has ordered a new carpentry tool set and has had long consultations with puppeteers. As a result of his tinkering with the backbones, joints, and pulleys, the Faust marionette can twitch its nose, scratch its head, and move its cheeks in a rather clever fashion.

I told him that I thought it a diversion far better than others.

I sat at my escritoire and took out a fresh quill. With the Shuvalovs growing in influence, with the Grand Duke flattered out of the little sense he still possessed, Catherine needed her allies. The guards? True, they were not happy with the Shuvalovs' ascension. Ivan Ivanovich strutted the corridors like a peacock, I heard them grumble. His hands, so dainty and soft, would not hold a horse. But the guards were in the Winter Palace, not in Oranienbaum.

Only the Chancellor could help her now. As long as she would be careful not to trust him.

"I do not choose my friends by what they can do for me," I had told him that evening. *But I also do not abandon them when they need me,* I thought now.

This necessary new alliance, I wrote to Catherine, *will buy you time in these trying times.*

That night, I dreamed of Madame Kluge, the exiled Chief Maid.

I saw her at the end of some long winding road, alone, a black shawl around her shoulders, walking.

I stopped my carriage and asked her to step inside. "I'll take you where you want to go," I offered.

She gave me a look of great sadness. Then she shook her head.

"I don't want to go where you are going," she told me.

I closed the carriage door and moved on into the darkness, tormented by questions I had pushed away long enough. Had I truly been a mere child led astray? Had I not willingly listened to the spymaster's voice? Had I not touched his flesh again and again?

When I woke, I was choking with tears. Egor was tossing in his sleep, muttering. The sheets were twisted, damp with sweat.

Suddenly I was struck by a terror that Darya might die, her death a punishment for my sins. The fear pierced me with such force that I got out of bed. I bent over my sleeping child. Her cheeks were warm, her breath even.

I knelt beside her cradle. I prayed until daylight spilled into the room.

FIVE

1752

n the first days of the new year, when Egor and his fellow officers came to our parlor for a late-night faro game, I retired to my bedroom. *Lean young dogs,* I called them in my thoughts. Ruffling up their fur, baring their fangs. All muscle and speed, eager for a fight.

Government and the army, I'd hear their voices, *the backbone of empires.* And who does Russia have? Bestuzhev and his protégé Apraxin. Chancellor and Field Marshal. Two old farts, missing their birds at a hunt, growing too fat to mount a horse by themselves, fainting in the heat of *banya.* And trailing behind their backs, rooting in their waste, come the Shuvalovs. They have already pushed Ivan into the Imperial Bed. Now they are eyeing the future Emperor, slobbering at his feet.

I heard my husband's voice rise above the din in an imitation of Countess Shuvalova's syrupy praise: *No one is more generous or more kind, Your Highness. Your memory is astounding. Your military interests a true sign of the Romanov blood. If it weren't for your barren German wife, all would be well.*

I got up and crept to the adjacent room where Darya slept, now that she had outgrown her cradle. Barefoot, for I didn't want to wake her.

That afternoon Egor had brought her a fistful of last year's chestnuts he had saved for her, glossy and plump inside prickly shells. They were now beside her bed, turned into fiery brown horses and soldiers marching to a battle that would vanquish Russia's enemies.

"What kind of games are being played behind our backs?" I heard my husband continue a little drunkenly. "Does anyone at the palace care for Russia's future?"

Darya stirred in her sleep. I opened the curtains and put my forehead against the cold glass. My breath misted the pane. Outside, on the Apothecary Lane, snow drifted.

There is regret in the memory of this moment. Regret that I did not hear the bitterness in my husband's voice.

One moment my daughter was learning to take her first wobbly steps, grasping my hand, steadying herself as she clung to the folds of my dress. Next, she'd run to me giggling when I clapped my hands.

So hopeful, I thought, when I watched her, happily welcoming anyone she saw, a stranger or a friend. Toward her comes the world with all its cruelties and horrors. How can I protect her, teach her to know whom to trust?

Egor warmed to the slightest mention of Darenka. He marveled at the easy grace of her steps, the fierce energy with which she hurled herself into his arms. "Up," she squealed, "up," until he lifted her into the air. It was for her that he turned into a bear lumbering from the forest to snatch the dinner she didn't want to eat, or to conjure up angels from shadows on the walls.

"You stole your Papa's heart," Masha would tell her in the months to come.

"How?"

"Like a thief does. Before he had the time to turn around and catch you."

Children know that to bring people together one has to seduce them, just like one seduces a lover, slowly, patiently, with stories and secrets.

Nestled on my lap, my daughter would call for Egor to sit beside us. Carried in his arms, she stretched her hands to hold on to me.

At night, she demanded stories of a little girl who came to St. Petersburg with her parents from far, far away, and of a little boy who built fortresses out of snow and who ate a bowl of his mother's *bliny* dipped in sour cream until he got sick. She wanted to hear my mother's Polish songs and Egor's *dumy* about the wind in the steppes and the Cossack riding away from home.

I recall Masha asking her once, "Whom do you love more, Darenka—your Mama or your Papa?"

Her little face had reddened, and she burst into tears.

But children do not know that some secrets are too terrible to share and some dreams too powerful to die.

"What kind of future do you have in mind for her?" I'd ask Egor, standing in his path, holding another unpaid bill to his face. Loving a child meant more than spoiling her with gifts she didn't yet need: a dress, a guitar, a set of tiny china cups for a dolls' house, a telescope.

In a year or so a governess would have to be hired, a music teacher, a dancemaster. With what? Empty promises? More talk of yet another country estate we cannot afford?

I could hear it in my own voice, the cold, insidious anger of that first night of our marriage when I envied the death maidens, their bodies laced with poison.

"Do you ever worry what would become of her if you died? What can we count on then? Mercy? Charity?"

He'd stare at me, with Darya's black eyes, before turning on his heel and stalking out.

Do not ask me about the "awaited news," please, and so I didn't. It had to suffice that in January of 1752 the Chancellor had relaxed his rules, that Catherine could write of sleigh rides and new ball gowns. The Grand Duke was busy training hunting dogs and made a terrible racket, but—Catherine wrote—Peter also presented her with a small

English poodle dressed up in petticoats. They went to a wedding and danced rather awkwardly but together. The Empress invited them to her masquerade, and Catherine had a green Preobrazhensky uniform with red facings made for the occasion. One of the court fools handed the Empress a hedgehog she mistook for a mouse, and she almost fainted with fright. A country house collapsed moments after Catherine fled from it. Later she was told that some incompetent foreman had removed a supporting beam. She complained of a toothache, and then—when her tooth had been extracted, together with a piece of her lower jaw—she described how the surgeon's five fingers had imprinted blue-and-yellow marks on her cheeks.

On our birthdays and name days, Christmases and first days of a new year, Monsieur Bernardi brought gifts from the Grand Duchess—a pendant for me, an icon on a silver chain for Darya, a pair of earrings, an amber brooch set in gold. As if these were not enough, whenever I brought any jewelry for cleaning or repairs, the jeweler brushed off my requests for a bill with a gruff "Settled already."

Please refrain, dear friend, from all these expressions of gratitude, for they only embarrass me, Catherine wrote when I protested. *Let me be the judge of what I owe you.*

Nothing, no hopeful accounts of court amusements, no generosity so touchingly offered, could hide Catherine's sorrow. Seven years after the imperial wedding, there was still no sign of an heir.

Regimental affairs began to occupy Egor more and more, peacemaking, resolving disputes that threatened to erupt and soil the regimental honor. Yet another of his officers was nursing duel wounds, the result of some drunken spat. Pointless, Egor called it, vile.

He had expected another promotion, another rise through the ranks, but it never came. He was still Lieutenant Captain while younger men were getting ahead of him, drawing on ancient family connections; once again, the old nobles had overtaken the new.

I'd watch my husband make another circle around the room, the

heels of his boots drumming. The cane chair would crackle danger-
ously when he finally sat down.

"Angry, Papa?" Darya would ask, knowing he would protest with
great force, and that soon he would sing her one of the funny songs he
began making up for her then.

My little heart is full of mud.
My little hand is full of sand.
My little bed is full of lead.
But I have daisies on my head.

*I have received an unexpected gift. I wish I could talk to you about it, but
you'll hear the rumors soon enough.*

In St. Petersburg's salons, the mention of Sergey Saltykov's name
brought knowing looks. He was the master of card tricks, I heard, the
sleight of hand, the cull, the break, the color change. Under Saltykov's
fingers a mixed-up deck straightened itself out, the same card was
revealed no matter where the deck was cut.

St. Petersburg hostesses were all eager to have him as their guest.
A few months before, the Divine Sergey had astounded the court by
marrying one of the Empress's maids-of-honor. He'd seen her on a
garden swing and had been struck with desire. She rejected his advances again and again, until he grew desperate and proposed marriage. A month after the wedding, after some tearful scenes, the new
bride had been dispatched to the Saltykov family estate. "Have I
changed so much?" the rumormongers reported she asked. "What do
I lack that others have?"

You let him win, I thought. *A foolish mistake.*

I saw him many a time in those days. He was a coveted guest of
honor at St. Petersburg salons, Serge with his hooded eyes, the raven-
black thick hair he refused to cover with a wig, his husky voice. When
he entered, the maids moved faster, tea was sweeter, the sour-cherry
preserves he liked miraculously appeared on the tea tray.

He always greeted me with much flourish, inquired about my

health. "What grace, what poise," he murmured, planting a kiss on my hand. I took it for what it was. Serge Saltykov wished to remain in Egor's good graces. Any man-about-town was in dire need of my husband's betting tips.

At first Serge had declared himself merely the Grand Duke's friend. The Empress, he bragged, thought him good company for her nephew, saying that he, a Russian, was "far better than Peter's Holsteiner rabble." This is why she ordered Bestuzhev to cast aside his rules and let the Young Court receive Sergey freely.

Saltykov was penniless, and yet in the spring of 1752 he never arrived in Oranienbaum without presents: an embroidered kerchief for Madame Choglokova, a box of sugared almonds for the Choglokovs' children, a case of French wine for the Grand Duke, a book for the Grand Duchess.

I am being terribly flattered, and I do not believe a word of what I hear, Catherine wrote, *but anything brings excitement into my days.*

Serge's victories were small but significant, a deepening trail in Catherine's letters. The Choglokovs invited him to yet another evening at their hunting lodge. They made him stay overnight, for it started to rain. They insisted Catherine join their guest, to take her mind off all that tedious reading.

She refused to walk with him in the garden, and he wished to know why. Was it because of Madame Saltykova, whom he had not seen for months? Was Catherine jealous, perhaps, and why was that? She wasn't? So why was she blushing?

Then came a reckless horse ride through the fields. A ride where Catherine got so far ahead of him, he had to whip his horse to catch up, drawing blood from his mare's flanks.

I'd guessed it, by then. There had been too many signs.

"It's either freezing your ass in army tents or comforting a lonely *Hausfrau*," I heard Serge tell Egor at one of the soirees. "Can *you* think of other ways?"

Someone must have whispered to the Empress that the Grand

Duke had had more than enough time already, that perhaps it was her nephew, not Catherine, who was barren. The Chancellor, I decided, for the Shuvalovs would not wish for such a turn of events. Was Saltykov the only one Elizabeth considered for the honor of fathering the Imperial Heir? Did she order him on his mission herself?

A son by any means, I thought, was Catherine's only salvation.

Soon the Grand Duchess was writing to me less often, and the letters—when they finally arrived—were brief and vague. *I want to live so much,* she wrote in one of them. *I want to run until I'm too tired to make another step.*

My husband had claimed a small alcove next to our bedroom, and each morning I would see him there, flinching as he lifted a thick metal pole above his shoulders or, his fists padded with layers of quilted cloth, punched a bulky leather bag, training for one of the boxing matches that had become such a rage.

The smell of disappointment around Egor lingered like the sharp odor of singed hair. "Waste," he'd grumble. "So much damned waste."

How tired anger made him look, hardening his features, sharpening his gaze.

Flattery got you everywhere, I heard my husband's voice boom at the nightly faro games. Not merit and hard work. Russia had once again given in to confidence tricks. To lust and wanton greed. In Russia, one could be a hanger-on, but one could do nothing of importance.

Sheer indolence kills the soul.

What Russia needs is a war.

The words I still hear mixed with the sounds of clinking glass and cards flipping, lingering like the smell of cheap tallow candles and sour breaths.

Nations steeped in idle luxury are like cattle led meekly to slaughter. . . . Nations need exertion, iron will. . . . War is like bloodletting . . . indispensable . . . our only cure.

There is another memory from this spring, of Darya trying to slip her small feet into Egor's boots.

"Do you want to be a soldier when you grow up?" I teased her, laughingly, but she didn't laugh back.

"Yes," she answered. "Like Papa."

"But you cannot be a soldier, Darenka," I protested. "You have to grow up to be a lady."

She frowned as though I had given her a puzzle to solve.

"When?" she demanded to know, her hands pulling at the fringes of her dress. "Tomorrow?"

"No. Not tomorrow. Tomorrow you'll still be a child."

"After tomorrow?" There was a wistfulness in her voice that rang like the chimes of Russian bells.

I smoothed Darenka's hair, plaited and tied with colorful ribbons. Curly like mine but black like Egor's. Her body seemed to me so beautifully unfinished, so full of possibilities. No matter how I longed to return to the palace, I knew it would grieve me to clothe my daughter in a stiff court dress and watch her sink into a curtsy.

In the first days of April 1752 a case of claret arrived on our doorstep, the burlap cover soaked with the last of the melting winter snow. A gift from the Chancellor of Russia, the messenger said, when the maids carried it into the kitchen.

The following day the Chancellor's footman delivered a note.

"It's urgent," he told Masha.

I broke the seal immediately.

The Chancellor hoped his humble gift of wine had not been an imposition. There were matters he wished to discuss with me, matters of grave importance concerning someone I cared about. If I agreed, the footman who delivered the note would take me to him right away. His carriage was parked outside my door.

I felt a flare of anger. I was no longer a palace girl, or his tongue. What gave him the right to think that I would drop everything and rush to hear what he had to say?

I held the note in my hand, thick vellum paper with watermarks and gilded edges. The night before, I'd heard Egor denounce the growing Prussian appetite for conquest. The King of Prussia had already swallowed Silesia. Where would he go next before he would have to be stopped? Vienna? Warsaw? St. Petersburg itself?

Someone you care about.

Outside the window the air was misty, the sky leaden with heavy, dark clouds. Over the winter the cherry tree had lost half of its branches. I wondered if it would flower this year at all.

I told Masha to get my hooded overcoat and my gloves.

Chancellor Bestuzhev of Russia was waiting in a private wood-paneled room of an osteria by the Fontanka River, an aging man with sour breath who couldn't hide his smile of triumph.

"What is this about?" I blurted, as he stood to greet me.

I felt his hand on my elbow. Firm but with an unmistakable tremor in it. Behind the closed door, a fiddler plucked the strings of his fiddle. A girl's voice intoned a song about a mother mourning her soldier son.

"A prediction, Madame Malikina," Bestuzhev said, motioning for me to sit. "Mine, of course. Soon our lives will take a different route."

I lowered myself into the chair.

"The Shuvalovs are already celebrating their victory over me," the Chancellor continued. "They forget that a wise Russian proverb warns against selling the skin of a bear that is still roaming the forest."

I stirred, impatient, thinking, *Why does no one but you matter?*

"Listen, Varvara Nikolayevna. Big changes are coming. Big, sweeping changes of constellations that cannot be ignored, not if you still care about where Catherine's star could be heading. And you do care, don't you?"

He didn't wait for my answer. He knew I cared.

"The Empress is not well," he told me. "This is still a secret but not for long. The Grand Duke is nothing but a foolish child, too easily manipulated. The Shuvalovs are already making him dance to their tune. Theirs is a gloriously simple plan: Peter will rule Russia, and they will rule Peter. And Catherine? The fools think she is irrelevant."

The door opened. A skinny boy walked in with a tray, placing it on the table, the cups filled with tea rattling on their saucers. I tried to catch his eye as he served us, but he kept staring at his own hands. In the front room the girl had finished her song and the fiddler had been joined by two more.

The Chancellor waved our server away. I stirred the steaming tea, watching the chunks of sugar dissolve. I took the first sip.

"Saltykov did what he was told," he continued. "Catherine is carrying an heir. The Empress is quite willing to settle for Serge's bastard. 'Not the first one in our family,' were her words. 'Saltykov is good Russian stock.'"

My expression must have darkened, for the Chancellor paused, delighted with the effect his words had on me. My thoughts whirled. So what I'd sensed had happened. Catherine was carrying her lover's child. But why didn't she write to me about it? Did she not trust me? How long had she known?

The Chancellor's voice broke through these thoughts. He wanted me back at the palace. Not among the officers' wives, but at the Empress's side again, whispering into her ear, planting seeds of doubt about the Shuvalovs. He needed me in Catherine's rooms, making the Grand Duchess see how Chancellor Bestuzhev could be of service to the mother of a future Tsar.

"Obscurity is not for you, Varvara Nikolayevna. The game has resumed. And the stakes are even higher now. Isn't your husband anxious to rise through the ranks? Buy an estate? Surely he must be thinking of your lovely daughter's future."

I tried to ignore the sarcasm in his voice.

"Are you listening, Varvara Nikolayevna?"

The clock on the mantel softly struck two o'clock.

I asked, "Why would the Empress want me back at the palace?"

"Because you shall tell her something she doesn't know. Something the wife of a guard could easily have overheard."

"What would that be?"

I studied his face, animated with a radiance that shed years off his life.

"Saltykov swore the Grand Duchess was as good as a virgin."

I must have gasped, for he put his finger on his lips.

"The Grand Duke never got deep enough inside her, and there was no ejaculation. His instrument is bent like a crooked nail. The surgeon swears an incision will take care of it, but we have to be quick before the Imperial Heir is declared the imperial bastard."

Did Catherine not know? I wondered. All these years? Was there no one around her with enough wits to help her? Did our old deception with the bloodied sheets work too well?

Outside the osteria's window, birds were pecking at a slice of lard the tavern keeper hung out for them. My face must have betrayed my confusion, for the Chancellor leaned forward and urged, "Ask to see Her Majesty, Varvara, and I'll make sure she receives you in private."

He rose to escort me to the door. His carriage was at my disposal. He would find his own way back to the palace.

Spring in St. Petersburg sears the eyes with light. The powdery April snow tumbles in the air, iridescent tiny diamonds. The Chancellor's carriage, still on runners, slid through the streets, past soot-covered mounds of old winter snow. Soon icicles clinging to the roofs would begin to drip, although, in the shade, the breaths of passersby still turned to white mist.

I thought of Darya's eyes, round and wet like black pebbles.

If I died, what would happen to her? Would her father's expectations be enough to assure her future?

I thought of Serge Saltykov, of the cards that appeared where he wanted them to. I hoped Catherine didn't love him, hoped that all she wanted from him was a child to quiet Elizabeth.

A child, and a few moments of pleasure.

The Chancellor was true to his word. The following day, a letter from the palace ordered me to present myself to the Chief Steward.

"What is it about?" Egor asked. Sprawled on the floor, he was helping Darya build a precarious tower of wooden blocks.

By then, my husband and I had reached a kind of weary peace. As rumors of the approaching war intensified, he began declaring that the army offered a far superior path to advancement than the Palace Guards. He had not yet applied for a transfer, but he must have spoken of his intention to do so widely enough to extend our credit. The butcher no longer glared at me when he saw me but doffed his hat and inquired about my health.

"Look, Maman, look!"

The block tower was swaying, to Darya's shrieks of delight. Egor's question was still unanswered when the tower crashed. A temptation entered my mind to tell him of my expectations, but it didn't last.

"I don't know," I lied, stooping to help Darya pick up the scattered blocks. "It's an imperial command." My hands, I saw, were trembling.

Egor's eyes rested on me, assessing, but he said nothing.

In the bedroom, I powdered my hair and put the Virgin pendant around my neck. The dress I selected was a cotton one, brown and unadorned, its hem recently turned.

"Again, Papa," I heard Darenka's cry. "Again!"

There is nothing as difficult as escaping what profoundly pleases you, Catherine had written in her last letter to me.

My pulse was racing, my stomach felt hollow, but in the dressing mirror my face looked bright and eager, as though a flash of summer light had come into the room and colored my thoughts with hope.

I waited in the mirrored antechamber. A cold draft seeped through the cracks in the paneling, and I scolded myself for not taking a warm shawl. The courtiers who rushed past me did not stop. One of the Empress's cats kept coming back to rub itself against my ankles.

I was still waiting when the light began to fade, as the palace readied itself for the night. Behind the drafty paneling, I could hear a banging and a shuffling in the service corridors. Something heavy was being moved. My fingers stiffened with cold, and I tried to warm them with my breath.

It was well past sundown by the time I was ushered into the Imperial Bedroom, into the soothing circle of heat radiating from the crackling fire. The Empress was alone, reclining on her bed, a woolen shawl over her pink nightdress. A fat white cat was trying to touch her chin with its paw. Was that old Pushok? I wondered.

"You have astonishing news about my nephew?" the Empress asked as soon as I rose from my curtsy. "Truly astonishing?"

There was a note of derision in her voice.

I spoke plainly.

"There had been no coitus, Your Highness, and there can be none if His Imperial Highness insists on denying his infirmity. It's common talk among the officers. And if the guards know, anyone might question the child's rights in the future. Your Highness understands that more than I do."

"Infirmity?" Her eyes narrowed.

"The surgeon would explain it better, Your Highness. It's the scar that holds the foreskin. Apparently, it's a common enough problem. A simple incision should be enough. But the Grand Duke will not let the surgeon touch him."

There was only one candle burning in the candelabra, but I could see that time had not been kind to Elizabeth in spite of her young lover. Her face looked bloated. I saw her clutch at the carved post as she rose from the bed, her arm trembling with exertion. The white cat slid away into the shadows.

"Why wasn't I told before?" the Empress demanded. "Why was I made to wait all these years in vain?"

She cursed the Choglokovs. Called them idiots who should be flogged with the knout.

She cursed the Grand Duke.

She cursed Catherine. Called her a dim-witted bitch who should have come to her long before with the truth. Why was the stupid girl putting on an act all these years? What was she hoping to hide?

She was coughing now, wiping her mouth with a handkerchief, waving me away furiously.

I bowed and hurried out, knowing that a storm had to run its course.

In the morning the Chancellor sent word that two of Catherine's ladies-in-waiting were hastily packing their belongings. One of the Duke's valets had been sent away, too. Bestuzhev was especially pleased to inform me that the Empress had ordered me back to the palace to rejoin her retinue.

Madame Malikina: Lady in Attendance of the Evening Toilette, the Chief Steward wrote in the Court Journal. I was to present myself in the antechamber of the Imperial Bedroom every evening. Quarters in the palace had been set aside for me and my family.

As the day of our move approached, Darya's excitement grew. She loved running through emptying rooms, hiding in open crates or jumping onto the piles of linen. Masha had taught her to curtsy, which my daughter did with surprising grace, especially in her new gown, of buttercup-yellow silk embroidered with flowery sprigs, Egor's far-too-expensive gift.

I didn't ask what my husband thought of this sudden change in our fortunes. He had been an officer of the guards long enough to know that if an order came from the palace, it must be obeyed. You do not reason with a flood. You look for anything useful that might float your way.

On the day of our move, seeing the apartment on Apothecary Lane strewn with trunks, baskets, and crates, I expected to feel sadness, but there was none. The porters had chipped the doorframes, left scars on the wooden floors. The stripped rooms looked blank and frayed.

It seemed as if I had never lived there at all.

Masha didn't mind that our new quarters were in a distant section of the Winter Palace, close to the stables. She didn't mind the noise, the barn smell of rot and urine that seeped inside every time a window was opened. Instead, she rejoiced that there was no rent to pay, that our five rooms came with a generous supply of wax candles, that we had the right to eat at one of the imperial tables, and an allowance for clothes, which included discarded dresses from the Imperial Wardrobe.

Freed from many of her former duties, Masha found her passion in taking detailed inventory of our new possessions. As soon as our furniture was all in place, trunks and crates unpacked, she would trail me with a sheet of paper, demanding I write down a list of our new acquisitions.

> Two dressing gowns, one of calico and one of striped silk, worth
>   six rubles.
> A pair of white broadcloth pantaloons, five rubles.
> Twelve Dutch linen chemises with ruffles, ten rubles.
> A fox-fur coat, lined with woolen cloth, forty rubles.

To Darya, Masha would point out the rich gilded furniture, the thickness of the carpets, the tall mirrors, the machine that spread the scent of roses as it was rolled through the rooms. She trailed the chambermaids, hoping to learn the secrets of keeping the brass so shiny and the crystal so bright. She did not believe them when the maids told her they used the same water with vinegar she always used.

The surgery was swift. It happened without the Duke's consent or knowledge, for when the Empress took matters into her own hands she did not bother with trifles.

Two of his Holsteiner officers were to suggest a peeing contest. Later, this would become the explanation for the soreness of the Duke's instrument. Opium was added to his wine, though the Grand Duke got quite drunk without it and, after one goblet, passed out. Count Lestocq was waiting next door, his bag with scalpels at the ready. The operation took mere minutes. The cut made the Duke wince and murmur something that caused everyone to laugh. "You must have pulled it too hard, Your Highness," the Holsteiners told him in the morning, when Peter complained of soreness.

But Elizabeth left nothing more to chance. To redeem themselves, the Choglokovs were ordered to find a suitable candidate for initiating the Duke. A certain young widow was contracted, Madame Grooth, big, plump, and of rosy flesh. The court surgeon declared her clean and made sure she understood the nature of her task. She was not to let the Duke withdraw too early.

She swore she would not.

Nothing spreads faster than gossip tacitly encouraged.

The act took place in the Winter Palace. Madame Grooth wore a pleasing gown, laughed eagerly at the Grand Duke's jokes, allowed him to suck her nipple, held him tight until he came inside her.

This was not the time for modesty or silence. The witnesses, four officers from the Preobrazhensky Guards and four Holsteiners, were ordered to watch through a spying hole. No one would ever be able to claim that the Grand Duke was incapable of siring a child.

During the evening toilette, when the Empress received the last visitors of the day, Peter came into the Imperial Bedroom. He seemed taller than I remembered him, and lankier, but also more clumsy.

The Empress pushed away the hairdresser who hovered over her, trying to adjust the embroidered cap that held her powdered locks in shape.

"Peter," she said, turning to her nephew. I saw the French Ambassador edge forward to have a better view. I saw Countess Shuvalova make room for him.

"Do be more discreet in the future," Elizabeth continued. The Grand Duke winced at the sharp tone in his aunt's voice. His pockmarked face reddened with unease. "Not everyone in the world has to know that you have a lover."

What a spectacle it was! Elizabeth at her dressing table, her body still locked in shape by the boned bodice, her eyes bright with glee. "I'm not asking you to refrain, but at least exercise some discretion, my dear child. Think of your wife's feelings. Think of her humiliation, if this becomes known."

Imperial diamonds flashing in candlelight, the scented dress rustling. "Can you promise me that much, Peter?"

I watched the Crown Prince of Russia lick his lips as he nodded. I watched him beam with relief, his mind no doubt already churning up his own tales of the encounter. A hare imagining he had outwitted a fox.

The Russian play unfolded before my eyes, I thought, in all its magnificent artifice. Elizabeth the Terrible, Peter the Fool, and Catherine the Wise had made their appearance. Now the moment came for the spectators to choose whom to fear and whom to despise.

I recalled the Chancellor's words: *Saltykov did what he was told. Catherine is carrying an heir. . . . But we have to be quick before the Imperial Heir is declared the imperial bastard.*

One of the maids began unpinning Elizabeth's hair, a sign for the visitors to leave.

"Go after them, Varvara," the Empress said, when the last of the courtiers had left the Imperial Bedroom. "I want to know what they'll talk about."

Coded secret dispatches reporting on the Duke's sexual performance were sent to all major European courts. They detailed Peter's confident grins, the lively glances cast at any woman who approached him. They reported, too, Madame Grooth's disappointment when the payment she received for her chore proved to be only half what she had been promised.

Cutting Madame Grooth's payment had been the Empress's own idea. "Bitterness," she said, as I massaged her tired feet, "is always far louder than satisfaction with a reward."

The Chancellor's red-walled office smelled of camphor and mold. He raised his eyes from the files he was working on and studied me through his monocle. Then he pushed the papers aside.

"You'll find much changed here, Varvara Nikolayevna. We are more fearful. Less patient. Much is again expected from the intercession of saints."

I had been back at the palace only a few days, but I had already noticed that the confidence with which Bestuzhev used to approach the Empress was gone. There was a new note of servitude in his voice, overflowing with praises for her wisdom and foresight, praises Elizabeth waved off impatiently.

The day was warm, sunny. Through the palace window I could see ice floes on the Neva, strewn with the debris of winter: fir trees from the winter road to the island, a carriage pole with a wheel still attached.

I, too, had changed. I was no longer alone.

"Take a look at this," the Chancellor asked, fishing a print from the documents on his desk.

The print he handed me depicted Ivan Shuvalov, his naked member flagging. The Imperial Favorite was flanked by actresses with ostrich plumes in their hair, their breasts spilling out of low-cut gowns, as he lamented: *My instrument may have taken on more than it can handle.*

The Chancellor laughed softly. "I never underestimate the concerns of the people, Varvara Nikolayevna. Don't you think the Empress should come across this rather soon?"

I folded the print and slipped it inside my sleeve.

There was no need for words. The palace game had not changed. The dangers had not disappeared because the Grand Duchess was with child.

I rose.

"You haven't backed the wrong horse, Varvara Nikolayevna," the Chancellor called, as I turned away. "I haven't hurt you, after all."

When I opened the door I almost knocked over a chambermaid who gave me a frightened glance and blushed to the roots of her hair.

Serge Saltykov was back in St. Petersburg.

I had seen him in Elizabeth's antechamber, his black hair combed back, his eyes brimming with glee, assessing the women who passed by. Country life was boring, he declared. Oranienbaum was a backwater. The Grand Duke was a cherished friend, and one shouldn't question a friend's judgment, but how could he stay there for months at a time? In the company of gardeners and magpies! Life was here, at the Winter Palace. Or beyond it, in the courts of Europe. The King of Sweden, he had been told, kept an excellent stable.

From Oranienbaum, Catherine wrote: *Tell me where he is, please. Find out why he is not coming here anymore. Is it because of his wife? Or has La Grande Dame found out about us? Or is it the Soldier who opposes his visits?*

Serge Saltykov never mentioned Catherine.

His wife was fine, he said, when I asked him. In good health.

"Happy?"

"What is happiness?" Serge replied. "I haven't found out yet. Have you, Madame Malikina?"

He is here, I wrote to Catherine, *making sure no one has reason to blame you. He is keeping silent about his plans, but I'll keep listening.*

It is so easy to lose a child, I thought. Once she gives birth to an Imperial Heir, I'll find a way to help her forget.

"The Grand Duchess is enamored with her new Oranienbaum garden," the Empress answered all official inquiries. "I have no heart to summon her back to the city, when her cherished tulips are in bloom."

The floor of the Imperial Bedroom was still strewn with architectural drawings. Monsieur Rastrelli had again been derided for the smallness of his vision. The new windows had to be far larger, the façade more imposing. One thing, however, was beyond dispute. Before the renovations of the Winter Palace could begin, the court would have to move to a temporary palace.

Not a moment too soon, I thought. In our quarters the warped windows let in drafts, the walls were slimy with mildew. After our first week at the palace Darya began to cough, although she had no fever and the coughing eased when Masha gave her one of her infusions to drink. "No wonder Shuvalov wants this dump razed," Egor grumbled, when a splinter from the floor lodged itself in his foot.

I spent long empty hours in the antechamber to the Imperial Bedroom, awaiting my summons. Other courtiers came and went, giving me unseeing looks, as if I would soon vanish and therefore did not merit closer scrutiny. I heard them inside, on the prowl, offering their clichéd praises, denouncing friends, asking for favors. Grabbing what they could get. When they left I heard the Empress call them good-for-nothing time-wasters or wonder how amusing it would be to let them in all at once, force them to hear their own treachery. I knew when Ivan Shuvalov read her yet another poem or a play; I knew, too, how often he dropped his voice to murmur something he did not want overheard. The Empress addressed her young Favorite as *my sparrow.* At every mention of the spring hunt, she vowed to give the most splendid chase in her lover's honor.

Summoned at last, I'd watch the juicy bits of their intimacy, a show no doubt made sweeter for them by my silent presence. The Empress and her beloved, lying side by side, he with an arm behind his head, chest bare, his hair tied with a green ribbon. She with her nightdress loose, revealing the darkened hollows of her armpits, a lazy smile on her lips, her voice a soft purr.

I didn't turn my eyes away. Of all Elizabeth's sins, those of the flesh were not the worst.

At the end of my third week in the Winter Palace I noticed that the doors to the Grand Duke's apartments were wide open. Surprised that he was not in Oranienbaum, I peeked through the doorway.

The Duke sat straddling an armchair, his long legs stretched out. He was complaining how the rotting beams of the Oranienbaum palace had forced him to move to the ground floor and eat his meals in a tent.

Two of his hounds sprawled on the carpet, asleep, their legs twitching in some imagined chase. The Duke's companions, his maids-of-honor, mostly, though I also spotted the blue uniforms of the Holsteiner officers, spread themselves throughout the room; two ladies sat on a divan, another half lying, half sitting on the floor. The carpet, I noticed, was already torn at the corners, no doubt chewed by the dogs. No one had opened the windows for some time, in spite of the warm weather, and the air was suffocating.

"Varvara Nikolayevna." The Grand Duke waved his hand at me. "Come in, join all my pretty ladies."

I walked into the room and curtsied.

"Where is your husband?" The smile that used to brighten Peter's face had turned into a nervous smirk.

"I don't know, Your Highness," I answered. "He doesn't tell me where he goes." My reply brought a whistle of approval.

Egor Malikin, the Grand Duke announced, was a man of ambition and luck, a fine soldier who would go further if he stopped wasting his time in the *Ladies'* Guard. If he joined the cavalry instead. "That's where the future is," the Grand Duke declared. "No matter how much a wife might object."

"I have no objections to my husband's decisions," I replied.

My answer brought another approving whistle.

"Take the best seat, Varvara Nikolayevna." The Grand Duke pointed at a low chair covered with a bearskin. I hesitated. The head of the hapless beast with its jaws agape was positioned on the floor. I knew I could expect some crude jokes, if I covered it with my skirts.

"Mishka won't bite you," someone said and giggled.

"Unless you wanted him to," a woman's voice added. She stood in the shadows, holding a battledore racket and twirling it in her hand. A shuttlecock, red and white, was lying nearby, too far for her to reach it with her feet, although she tried.

"If he dared," someone else retorted amid more laughter. "But there are some women even Mishka may be scared to touch."

A playing card landed at the toe of my shoe. The ace of diamonds. "Nosy Varvara went to market," I heard a murmur behind me. "Nosy Varvara had her nose torn off."

The woman with the battledore racket began reading aloud what at first I thought was the report of some military conquest. A distant and cold fortress had been stormed repeatedly; soldiers rushed up the hills, only to be repelled by strong defenses. *"Very resourceful defenses,"* she read, and giggled. "Very resourceful," she repeated. The Grand Duke laughed heartily.

I recognized the woman. Countess Vorontzova, the homely, limping niece of the Vice-Chancellor Vorontzov. *Das Fräulein*, as she was called, was one of Catherine's maids-of-honor. What brazen lies allowed this woman to abandon the Grand Duchess in Oranienbaum and come here?

The servants were pouring wine as soon as glasses emptied. A stack of empty bottles was piling up in the fireplace like logs ready to be lit.

"*The fortress*," the Countess continued her reading, "*has often been called proud and icy. Spies sent there spoke of jagged walls and a narrow tunnel.*"

There was no doubt in my mind that it was Catherine she meant, a "fortress" finally conquered by her husband. Seven years after the wedding, if anyone in this room dared to count. Anger rose in me, searing hot, and I struggled to keep my look of indifference.

Das Fräulein gave the Duke another impish glance, jabbing the air with her fist, a not-too-subtle promise that he acknowledged with a titter. This was not some Madame Grooth who could be paid off and sent away. This was a court lady on the prowl. *Das Fräulein*, plain and lame as she was, had been known to hunt down wild boars.

"*Finally the fortress gave in and a torrent of blood flowed, while from the rear bastion a triumphant shot announced to all who watched and listened from afar the completion of the victorious and gallant deed.*"

More laughter and a few loud farts followed these words. The Duke's wineglass was filled again, and he tilted it over the carpet, spilling half of it. *Das Fräulein* clapped her hands.

"May I be excused, Your Highness?" I asked him. The grin of pleasure on his face sickened me. "The Empress awaits me."

He waved me away.

Even before I closed the door I could hear *Das Fräulein*'s shrill voice, mocking my request.

The imperial habits had not changed. The Empress rose late. Days were still a passage of tedious time that led to the evenings, hours filled with endless chatter. It was Countess Shuvalova, the mother of the Imperial Favorite, who led the gossip circle now. Ladies-in-waiting sitting with the Empress in her inner rooms until dusk, embroidery idle on their laps, delivered their accounts of broken hearts and thwarted expectations. The miasma of glee and poisonous malice filled the rooms of the Winter Palace. It was as if the seven years I had spent away from the court were but a flicker of an eyelid.

The arrival of the Imperial Favorite was a sign for the ladies-in-waiting to pick up their work-bags hastily and leave the inner rooms. When Ivan Shuvalov visited, the doors to the Imperial Bedroom were closed. No one was allowed inside. The evening meal was delivered on the mechanical table, pulled up from the kitchen below. Musicians waited in the service corridor for the Empress's summons. If she wished it, they played or sang loudly, so that the music could penetrate the wall.

My time came when Ivan Shuvalov had departed to his own apartment, when all the cats who slept on the Imperial Bed came back from their wanderings. The bedroom was always dark and smelled of smoldering wicks, for most candles were extinguished by then, except the two votive lights under the Holy Icon of the Virgin of Kazan.

The time of imperial unease, I called it in my thoughts. The time softened by old fears. The time that would soon yield under my fingers, like wax. As long as I remembered how thin the walls were, how many ears might be straining to hear what I would say.

The time of caution, of feeling my way. Of learning what had been hidden, revealing what should be revealed.

The Empress still liked the stories of her own grandeur, of who found her ravishing and full of grace, more elegant than Maria Theresa of Austria, lighter on her feet. But she also craved other stories, of the blind *dziad* at the Tartar market who sang the old *dumy* of Romanov glory, of beggars on the Great Perspective Road who blessed the Tsarina's good heart when the alms arrived from the palace.

"You have a daughter, Varvara," the Empress said to me unexpectedly on one such night. "I wish to see her in the morning."

"Mais, elle est charmante," the Empress exclaimed when I entered the Imperial Bedroom with Darya—in her new yellow dress—holding my hand. "You must bring her to me often, now that you are all living here."

"To play?" Darya asked with such joy that even Ivan Shuvalov smiled.

The Empress picked up a purring cat. "Naughty Murka," she muttered into its face. "Where have you been all night? Where do you hide from me, you rascal?"

Before I could stop her, Darya had scampered to the Empress and was running her fingers through Murka's fur, trying to guess the cat's hiding places. "On the stove . . . under the bed . . . in the carriage . . . In there?" she finally said, pointing at the giant vase that stood by the door.

There she was, next to the Empress, my daughter, not yet three years old, utterly at ease.

I was right to return to the palace, I decided, delighting in a glimpse of my child's future: a happy young woman with two or three pretty children about her feet. Behind her, an honorable man, his face still a blur.

Loved.

Safe, even if I died.

The maid entered with ice in a china bowl, for rubbing Elizabeth's face. Behind her, the Chief Maid, followed by a footman carrying the basket with pandoras from the Imperial Wardrobe.

I took Darya's hand and motioned for her to curtsy. My eyes were smarting from lack of sleep. I longed to be in my bedroom, with curtains drawn, to get some rest before the night's summons.

"I'll bring her as often as Your Highness wishes," I promised.

Three days later, at dinnertime, a messenger arrived from Oranienbaum. The Grand Duchess had awakened with a sharp pain. The maid who had lifted her coverlet fainted. Catherine had been ordered to lie absolutely still on sheets wet with her blood until the doctor arrived and declared that there was no hope. The baby was dead.

They all blamed her. For her too frequent visits to the stable with its stench of animal excrement, for breathing in the smoke from extinguished candles, for letting the bad air penetrate the pores of her skin.

The maids whispered that when a black cat dashed across her path, the Grand Duchess had refused to turn back, that she had laughed when the midwife brought her a pregnant stone—inside which small rocks rattled when she shook it—and told her to wear it on her arm. That she sat with her legs off the ground, that she'd played with newly hatched chicks.

No one talked of anything else. Even Darya wanted to know why the Empress was sad. "Does her tummy hurt, Maman?" she asked.

I hid my trembling hands, my voice that threatened to break.

The Empress's inner rooms were crowded with visitors. The ladies from the gossip circle were clucking their tongues in disapproval, echoing one another's vicious words. "Careless . . . Didn't she know . . . How *could* she?"

The Empress sat motionless in a pool of light, her face flushed and creased with exhaustion. Beside her, Ivan Shuvalov shook his head in false amazement, his silver waistcoat shimmering. The maid who brought a platter of *zákusky* had been waved away.

The Imperial Surgeon was delivering his assessment of Catherine's condition. Shifting from foot to foot, he denounced the marshes and the riverbanks exuding noxious miasmas, the legacy of a land not fit for human dwellings. The cold, the lack of light for so many months, they provoked miscarriages and the malformation of fetuses, he declared. He had seen it often enough.

"I cannot stay silent, Your Majesty," he said. "Not anymore."

The Empress gave the surgeon a disdainful look. The fan in her hand jerked.

"My father's city," she said, her voice seething, "is not killing babies in their mother's wombs. It is the mother's thoughts and fears that make them die."

The surgeon attempted to say something, but the Empress was no longer listening. "He might as well start packing right now," I heard someone whisper.

In the silence that followed, Ivan Shuvalov turned to Elizabeth. "The marshes? The lack of light?" he asked disdainfully.

I wished I could make him stop. I wished I could kill the words that followed, scrub his arrogant malice away. With turpentine and salt, I raged, just like the scullery maids wiped the bed frames where bedbugs hid.

"Is this what *she* is saying, perhaps? Are these *her* sentiments?" Ivan Shuvalov continued, as if he had forgotten Catherine's name. "I wouldn't be surprised."

I hurried out of the room, trembling. Then I stopped. Slipping into the Imperial Bedroom, I placed the print of Ivan that the Chancellor had given me in between the sheets.

Let the Empress find that *tonight*, I thought. I imagined Ivan Shuvalov, lips twisting, hands fumbling, a vein throbbing on his temple as he protested his innocence. Swearing that he had never looked at any actresses.

Let him taste his own medicine, I thought.

Let him feel his own smallness. Let him feel the sharp edge of Elizabeth's wrath.

A few hours later, when I arrived in the antechamber to the Imperial Bedroom, I saw maids rushing in and out with jugs of hot water, towels, bottles of smelling salts. A fetid breeze drifted from the open window.

Count Lestocq had been called in to bleed the Empress, a round-faced maid with an armful of towels informed me, her voice brimming with self-importance.

Four ounces of blood.

Dark. Thick.

Her Majesty was calmer now, praise the Lord.

The storm had passed.

Man trouble, I could hear the whispers. *No smoke without fire. Hit the table and the scissors will sound. The cat knows from which bowl of milk he has drunk.*

From the bedroom came the sounds of pleading, broken with a sob.

"No one can see Her Majesty now," the maid told me. "Ivan Ivano-vich has just been allowed back in."

Monsieur Bernardi had no letter for me. The Grand Duchess, he re-ported, is quite weak and has been forbidden all exertions. Her pa-pers, her books, her quills, have all been taken away. All we can do is pray for her swift recovery. She is young; she has always been healthy. Perhaps the harm was not as grave as some are making it.

Your friends see many possibilities where there were few before, I wrote in my letter to Catherine, cursing the secrecy that made me choose such vague words. *Solutions better than the ones lost.*

I hoped she would understand.

This was her chance for another child, a child far less likely to be called a bastard. A child whose birth would repay her with joy for the loss that now seemed the end of everything.

I was right not to tell her of her lover's indifference, I decided. Serge Saltykov would soon be ordered to go to her again, to complete what he had started. It was better for her to greet him with an open heart.

A whole month passed since the news of Catherine's miscarriage and Serge Saltykov was still in St. Petersburg, gambling, borrowing money from everyone. Was the Empress giving Peter a chance to father a child? How long would she wait? I knew Catherine was anxious for news, but I had none.

Hoping the Empress would send me to Oranienbaum to check on the Grand Duchess, I began hinting at reports I would deliver if I only had a chance to see her myself. For days Elizabeth dismissed my promises with grim silence and then suddenly, when I least expected it, she ordered me to go.

It took me nearly a day to reach Oranienbaum. It was a tedious ride along the shore of the gulf, past Peterhof, with screeching seagulls and the smell of rot from the marshes.

In the Lower Gardens, by the canal leading to the sea, the gardeners in their straw hats jabbed at the earth, flattening the hillocks the moles had left. A bird was hopping on the grass, a long piece of straw hanging from its beak. I willed it to stop. The straw fell to the ground. I picked it up and turned it in my hands, releasing the seeds from the pod, scattering them into the air.

Then I saw her. Sitting in a wicker armchair, under a Siberian pine, with Madame Choglokova at her side. Tears welled up in my eyes, and I was glad there was no one to see them.

I watched Catherine pick up a book and cut the pages with a small dagger. The folds of her dove-gray morning dress were loosely draped over her stomach; her black hair was tightly pinned on the nape of her neck. Beside her was a table littered with the remnants of a blueberry tart and cups stained with afternoon chocolate.

Madame Choglokova, the onetime jailer and now the procuress, was embroidering a piece of cloth. There was no sign of her children. At the palace, Countess Shuvalova delighted in reporting Monsieur Choglokov's complaints about his wife's *passage intime*. "As wide as the road to Moscow," he once said to a chorus girl.

Noticing me, Madame Choglokova cleared her throat.

Catherine looked up from her book. She was still very pale from her miscarriage but prettier and more delicate than I had ever seen her before. I didn't like the sadness in her eyes, though, sadness that transcended the loss of the child, sadness that meant the Divine Serge was on her mind far more than he deserved to be.

A magpie descended on one of the branches overhead, screeching, its green-blue trim feathers shining in the sun. *A thief*, I thought, *just waiting for his chance.*

"Varvara Nikolayevna," Catherine murmured. "So you *have* come back. After so many years. And I hear that you have a child."

Madame Choglokova put down the embroidery and joined her fingers at their tips.

"Yes, Your Highness." I lowered my eyes. "I have a daughter," I added, for Madame Choglokova's sake, as if Catherine knew nothing of my life. "She is almost three years old, and already thinks herself a perfect courtier."

I began saying how sorry I was about her miscarriage, but Catherine stopped me. "I do not wish to speak of the past," she said.

So instead we chatted about the particulars of my return to the court. The Empress's promise that Egor and I would move to a bigger apartment in the new Winter Palace, once it was finished. When Catherine asked me again about Darya, I hesitated, thinking the subject too painful for her, but she insisted. She wanted to know of my daughter's delight when the Empress gave her a doll with long black hair she could comb and dress. She wished to be told of Darenka's dimpled cheeks, the lively eagerness with which she welcomed each day.

"She is so trusting, so loving," I said. "Perhaps too much so."

"She has her mother to look after her, doesn't she?" Catherine said.

"Yes," I said.

"Then nothing else matters."

We spoke like that for a while, a court conversation of puzzles and oblique allusions. Some sacrifices are not in vain. One has to do one's duty, first and foremost.

I said I was glad to be back at the palace, to be of use to the Empress and my old friends who had not forgotten me. I talked of the splendor of the new palace that would soon replace the old one, of the architectural drawings I'd seen, harbinger of changes that awaited us all, while in my mind, I cursed Madame Choglokova's stolid presence, her clasped hands and her frowns. Why could she not leave us?

Catherine did not interrupt, although sometimes she rubbed her eyelids impatiently and shook her head, as if something irritated her eyes.

By the Oranienbaum palace, the gardeners were watering giant pots of orange trees lining the terrace. Madame Choglokova planted herself deeper into her wicker chair, her jaw set, giving her the look of a mastiff. Her breasts threatened to spill from her low-cut dress, trimmed with frothy lace. She was determined to play her role to the end. She would not leave us alone. Whose side was she on? The Chancellor had hinted at her cooperation in making sure Saltykov had plenty of opportunities to spend time with the Grand Duchess in the past. But I suspected she was taking bribes from the Shuvalovs, too.

"Perhaps we could all have some chocolate?" I asked. "I heard it cleanses the blood better than nettle tea."

Madame Choglokova retrieved a bell from under the table. She rang it and, satisfied with herself, returned to her embroidery. I watched her fat fingers push the needle back and forth. She was stitching a flower, a green stem with long leaves crowned with a pink bloom.

The servants brought more chocolate and tarts. The commotion was a welcome break I used to touch Catherine's fingers with mine, my silent promise that she was no longer alone at court, that I was back in the Winter Palace to look out for her.

She gave me a quick smile, like Darya's when she was on the verge of bursting into tears.

"The Empress has just returned from shooting cocks and is now determined to give a masked ball in Peterhof, Your Highness," I chattered on. "The display of fireworks will be magnificent. Everyone at court is hoping Your Highness will be well enough to be there. Chancellor Bestuzhev said there is nothing like a public feast to remind us all that the good of Russia is our common goal. And Count Shuvalov agrees."

In spite of Ivan's constant presence at Elizabeth's side, the Shuvalovs had not won as much as they'd hoped for. They, too, had learned that Elizabeth preferred to be courted rather than to surrender. Ivan could have his Russian Academy and his theater, the adoration of poets and scholars, but it was Bestuzhev Elizabeth entrusted with matters of state. How the Empress cherished it: two forces pushing with equal strength, a precarious balance of opposites. Both parties at her feet, unsure, as long as she lived.

At the mention of the Chancellor and Ivan Shuvalov, Madame

Choglokova grew uneasy. Politics was a forbidden subject. Determined to steer our conversation in a different direction, she announced that Oranienbaum was far from being the backwater some courtiers might think. She launched into one of the long and tedious monologues she was so well known for. As I sipped the sweet, thick chocolate I shot Catherine an exasperated look. In response I saw a tiny smile of reassurance flicker on her lips.

"I've been reading a lot, Varvara Nikolayevna." Catherine interrupted the flow of Madame Choglokova's words. There was a glitter in her eyes, that reckless glitter I would see so often later. On that afternoon I thought it such a good sign. "True stories. Useful. I've resolved not to waste time."

Russian history was Catherine's favorite study now. The tales that made our empire grow, she said.

Madame Choglokova jerked her head, sensing she was being dragged into waters beyond her depth. A well-deserved revenge on a jailer, I thought, quite willing to play my part.

"The empire that manages to harness the strength of many nations will never be conquered," Catherine continued. "Don't you agree, Varvara Nikolayevna?"

"Most ardently, Your Highness. And so would our Empress and the Chancellor."

Even now I can still see Catherine on that late afternoon, cheered up by Madame Choglokova's growing unease, a note of spite ringing in her voice. Using phrases like *grappling with the soil* and *weaving of faith into the imperial tapestry*. Asking: "Wouldn't we grow indolent and selfish, if sacrifice were not demanded of us?"

She had been hurt, I thought. She was in pain, but she was not defeated.

The wicker chair creaked. Madame Choglokova was wriggling in distress, a giant fat worm on a hook. Charged with repeating everything she heard to the Empress, she was trying hard to remember Catherine's every word.

The approach of the Grand Duke—his Prussian blue uniform impeccably brushed, brass buttons and black boots shining—saved Madame Choglokova from further indignities. Having just arrived from St. Petersburg, Peter came to seek his wife's advice on the Holstein beer tax. Should it be raised or kept unchanged? And then there was the executioner's petition. . . .

"Good day, Peter," Catherine said, pointing at the empty seat beside her. "Would you like me to pour you some chocolate?"

Peter's tricorne hat cast a shadow over his face as he sat. His Blackamoor, once dismissed by the Empress from the Grand Duke's entourage, was now standing behind him, holding a basket with documents. A sign, I thought, of Elizabeth's satisfaction.

The Grand Duke acknowledged my presence with a nod and a wide smile as if he'd never witnessed my refusal to participate in the merriment at Catherine's expense. *Doesn't he notice that the palace is taking sides?* I wondered. *That one supported either Catherine or Peter? That the treacherous territory in between was narrowing fast?*

The Holstein executioner, Peter said, had protested the illegal dumping of carcasses on the town streets, where it was his duty and his cost to remove them.

"How many people signed the petition?" Catherine asked.

I watched the ease with which Catherine addressed her husband, the rapt consideration with which she listened to his explanations. *Das Fräulein*, I thought, did have her limitations, after all.

Madame Choglokova pulled at my sleeve, motioning for me to leave with her. That, too, was one of the imperial orders: Leave the married couple alone as much as possible. Appearances mattered.

"Shall I read it to you now?" I heard the Grand Duke's shrill voice as I walked toward my carriage. "The man has a point."

"The Prussians are asking to have their noses rubbed in their own filth," Egor announced on one of the first dark afternoons of the fall.

He had just come home from his guard duty and sank into the ottoman in our parlor. His uniform needed a good brushing, I thought. The red facings were smudged with plaster dust.

It was not just him, Egor continued. Such had been the talk of the barracks and *banyas*. Frederick of Prussia—or the Fritz, as the officers called him—could fool the French, but he could not fool the Russians. The Fritz talked peace, for, having devoured Silesia, he needed a rest, but Prussia was still hungry. And hungry Prussia always looked east.

"There will be a war," he said, slapping his knee. "Soon."

The maid had set our silver tea urn on the side table and left to fetch the preserves. Next door, Masha was feeding Darya her dinner, fending off my daughter's high-pitched protests with stories of children refusing to eat, only to be blown into the air and left there hanging, too light to get down. I fussed with teacups on a tray. Two of the saucers were badly chipped. I vowed to pack the china myself for the move that awaited us once the temporary palace was ready.

I sat down opposite my husband, arranging my skirts. A wave of weariness claimed me, and I wondered how many months more my body would endure all those sleepless nights. "You should lie down before you have to go tonight," Egor said, frowning when I stifled a yawn. "What time is it?"

"Not yet five o'clock," I said. Next door, Darya was quiet now, lost, no doubt, in one of Masha's tales.

Egor leaned toward me. The war, he said, meant opportunities. There was a tone of triumph in his voice now. As if he had finally solved a puzzle that had defied him for a long time. "Real opportunities," not empty promises of favors the palace was so full of, all so easily forgotten. There would be promotions, distinctions. Rewards for bravery. Battles he could tell our grandchildren about. Some of the Guards regiments would go; others would stay. In a moment of historical importance, it was essential to know where one wanted to be.

"We might have a future now, *kison'ka*," I heard my husband say.

So that was it. No more hints and promises. My husband would leave the Palace Guards for the army. There was relief in this prospect. It seemed right. The true end to years of aimless floating. Egor could return a Major or even a Colonel. Our daughter would have a proper dowry. We could afford an estate.

"When?" I asked.

"Soon," Egor answered, lowering his voice. "But don't tell anyone."

I nodded. I would not dispute the wisdom of not letting others know what you wished for.

"Any chance for that tea?" Egor was eyeing the tea urn.

The maid *was* taking a long time. I could hear her in the corridor, arguing with the footman.

"Serge Saltykov tried to borrow money off one of the new officers from the Izmailovsky Regiment. Orlov is the name. The man's just arrived from Tver." Egor's tone was cheerful now. "Wants to put fifty rubles on some mare he's spotted. Of rare strength and dexterity, he says. Wants me to check her out."

"Tried?"

"Orlov is broke, like everyone else. Saltykov is going to Oranienbaum to ask the Grand Duke for a loan."

Promising myself to scold the maid later, I opened the spigot, spilling hot tea on my hand; I rubbed it hastily away. "When?" I asked.

"He said tomorrow, but he says many things."

"Let's drink it while it is still hot," I said, filling two cups. In spite of all my rubbing, the tea left a nasty red welt of a burn.

The conversation turned back to the chances of a war, but I no longer listened to what my husband said. Saltykov was returning to Catherine. Finally, she'd been given another chance. And this time, no one could question the paternity of a child that might be born.

SIX

1754–1755

here was to be one more year and one more miscarriage, but then in January of 1754 the Grand Duchess became pregnant again. This time, to my joy, the Empress brought Catherine back to St. Petersburg.

The orders were strict. No physical strain, no horse riding, and no dancing. Catherine was never to raise her hands or make any circular motions. She could walk but only slowly, with small steps. To prevent falls, the maids were to rub her thighs and legs mornings and evenings with a mixture of the oil of Saint-John's-wort and brandy.

There would be no more corsets or masked balls. No wearing of necklaces so that the baby would not have the cord twisted round its neck. No salty foods, for salt could cause an infant to be born without nails or tears. Catherine had to be kept happy, for a crying mother would make a child melancholy.

Elizabeth told the Grand Duke to "approach" his wife at least once a month, to brand the shapeless mass in Catherine's womb with his own stamp.

And Serge Saltykov?

"No need for the Grand Duchess to make a spectacle of her rutting any longer," Elizabeth said, when she ordered Serge to stay away from Catherine. To be truthful, she had been cruder than that. By then the very thought of Catherine provoked Elizabeth to use the language of the tavern. Suddenly it was all about cunts and pricks, fucking and sperm. A German mare and a Russian steed. The mechanics of breeding.

I saw Catherine often in these days but rarely without companions. Still, there were moments when—in search of some lost item from the Empress's *ménagement*—I was able to sneak into her bedroom alone. It was her departed lover she always wanted to talk about.

"Is Serge missing me? Why did he have to go? Why doesn't he write?"

Her voice quivered on the verge of tears. She couldn't believe he had not come to visit her for such a long time.

I thought of Sergey Saltykov's swagger as he walked along the Great Perspective Road, his obvious delight with himself whenever the Grand Duchess was mentioned.

I spoke of the future of the Imperial Heir, of sacrifices. "Serge cannot see you," I told Catherine. "He has to keep appearances." But then she demanded the truth from me.

"She ordered him to stay away from me, didn't she, Varenka?"

"Yes."

"Why?"

"The baby—" I began, but she did not let me finish.

"Why is everybody always talking about this baby, Varenka? Am *I* not important at all?"

She knew why. In her womb she was carrying a future heir, the ruler of the Empire, the son Elizabeth wished to command her Russia one day.

I often wonder what would have happened if I had not lied about Catherine's faithless lover. But I, too, believed in the Kunstkamera warning: A mother's thoughts and fears shape her child. I didn't want Catherine to torture herself with jealousy and doubt. I wanted her baby to soak up the hope from her heart.

In monasteries and churches throughout Russia, crowds prayed for the safe delivery of the imperial child.

With each month of Catherine's pregnancy, the Empress grew more hopeful. Her rages shrank into mere bursts of anger, short and fiery, burning themselves out as quickly as they erupted. As soon as the blessed event was mentioned, Elizabeth's slaps and curses turned into the sign of the cross.

A boy or a girl? Everyone sought to penetrate the secret of Catherine's womb. Was she favoring her right foot or her left? Was she picking up objects with the right or left hand? When she sat down sideways, which leg touched the ground?

She favored the right side of the body, the noble, stronger side, everyone said. She was carrying a boy.

The Empress bargained with God and fate. Ivan Shuvalov had not been barred from her bed, but more and more often, as soon as he left, Elizabeth called for her confessor. Any time, day or night, a servant might be dispatched to give alms to the poor. A night of drinking would be redeemed with a day of strict fasting and prostration in the chapel. On her knees, in front of the Holy Icon, the Empress of Russia beseeched Our Lady for the safe birth of *her* child.

Elizabeth called on Catherine every day. She asked if the Grand Duchess slept peacefully through the night. She made certain Catherine was fed rhubarb and stewed prunes; her bowels should not retain waste matter for too long, since this could cause premature labor. She sent Catherine goose lard to smear on her belly, believing it far better than almond or linseed oil. She ordered that the dogskin pregnancy girdle be washed in rose water and softened with fresh butter.

There would be no separate nursery. The Empress could not think of the *blessed* baby left alone with wet nurses far from her watchful eye. Catherine's child would sleep in the Imperial Bedroom; the move to the temporary palace would be postponed until the baby was strong enough to bear it. The imperial diviner declared the Imperial Bed-room free of hidden currents, and an old woman was brought to pu-rify the space every Friday with incense of wild herbs, "to keep the Prince of Darkness away."

I found myself in the heart of these whirlwind preparations. Serf girls about to give birth were brought to the Winter Palace daily, each hoping to be appointed imperial wet nurse. The Empress screened every one of them. They had to be young, healthy and pretty, patient and mild-tempered, with sweet breaths and big breasts. I watched each of them kiss the crucifix and swear they would feed the imperial infant with love and tenderness and never use the herbs and roots of the Devil.

The pillows, quilts, coverlets were ordered, though not yet deliv-ered, for fear of tempting bad fortune. Silver fox fur would line the ornately carved cradle; soft lace trimmed tiny bonnets and silken gowns; new curtains of quilted velvet would keep the draft away.

When the child is born, the old saying warns, *beware the gust of cold air.*

Catherine had become a vessel, a womb. But as Darya snuggled at my side, as I felt her warm, plump arms around my neck, I truly be-lieved that the moment Catherine held her own child would repay her for all the betrayals of these days.

In the summer, when Catherine was six months pregnant, the Em-press refused to let her out of her sight. She ordered the ducal pair to move with her to Peterhof, where she could see Catherine every day. A midwife was to stay with the Grand Duchess at all times.

I spent most of that summer in St. Petersburg, where Monsieur Rastrelli, ordered to postpone the grand rebuilding for yet another season, was hastily completing the most pressing repairs of the Win-ter Palace. Charged with the preparations of the confinement room in the Imperial Suite, I watched the progress of repairs with growing concern. After weeks filled with noise and dust, in the Imperial Bedroom plaster still fell from the mold-eaten ceilings, newly laid wallpaper peeled off from dampness. By the end of August, when it became clear that the repairs would not be completed on time, the Empress abruptly changed her orders. Catherine would give birth in the small Summer Palace at the edge of the Summer Garden.

Egor was still awaiting his transfer to the army. His request had been languishing on yet another desk. Colonel Zinovev had died unexpectedly in a riding accident, and Egor's new commander created difficulties. A commendation was lost. Yet another copy of his service record had to be ordered. My husband had already spent a small fortune in bribes.

With so much talk of the imperial baby, Darya was getting jealous. She wanted to know why she did not have brothers or sisters. Ever since Masha told her that storks brought babies through the chimneys, she checked our chimney daily. Once I saw her leave an apple there, for the stork. She was ecstatic to find that the next day it was gone.

It would be a painful delivery, I heard, every time I visited Peterhof to report to the Empress on the progress of the preparations. The mother's body would be slow to adjust. The first child carried an extra duty of charting the way for its brothers or sisters. Once I overheard the Empress tell the midwife that in the event of unforeseen trouble, the child's life was to be saved at all cost.

That, too, I kept to myself.

Catherine's gowns grew fuller, their folds more supple. Her face was pinched with worry. In the Empress's company she hardly ever stood up from her chaise longue. For fear of startling her, all loud noises were forbidden. The courtiers moved carefully, spoke in whispers.

Serge Saltykov was still at court, in the Grand Duke's entourage, though the Empress had threatened to send him away. *I see him*, Catherine wrote to me, *but never alone.*

This was not for the lack of Serge's trying, she assured me. The midwife, *the dullest woman imaginable*, as Catherine described her, was spying on her for the Empress and never left her long enough for anyone to come in unobserved.

Autumn had come early that year. On the last day of August the wind from the river was already biting and raw, tearing leaves off the trees. I was in the yard of the Summer Palace when I saw a carriage stop. Catherine's voice called my name.

"I couldn't let you know, Varenka," she said, seeing my surprise, once Prince Naryshkin helped her from the carriage. Her little white dog, Bijou, was jumping about her ankles, happy to be let out.

"He kidnapped me, you know." Catherine pointed at Prince Naryshkin. Her eyes were impish with mischief, making the dark stains under them disappear. She arched backward as she walked toward me, and I caught a glimpse of peach-colored silk underneath her woolen traveling cape. Loose and bulky—the child was a mere month away.

"Entirely my idea," Prince Naryshkin said, laughing, as he described his clever subterfuge. He'd persuaded the Empress to permit this trip from Peterhof so that Catherine could see for herself the progress of preparations. Then he'd invited the Grand Duchess for a brief stroll with her dog so that the midwife would let her out of sight. Together, they had rushed to his carriage.

It was a washday. In the yard of the Summer Palace, giant vats were heated over outdoor fires. The air smelled of suds. The servants were everywhere, carrying baskets of sorted and unsorted linen, bringing out the washboards and barrels for the leftover soapy water that would then be given to the poor.

I led Catherine into the room that was being prepared for her delivery. A room with a small antechamber, alongside the Empress's apartments, crimson damask on the walls, a table. A bare mattress stuffed with horsehair lay on the floor, as the imperial custom demanded. Bijou sniffed it again and again, making me wonder if the mice had not nestled in already.

"The linen will be soft, Your Highness," I said, trying to sound cheerful. "Well worn. And there will be a bed, for the time after. . . ."

Catherine surveyed the room, frowning. After the splendors of Peterhof, I knew how stark it seemed to her. In the corridor, someone was scolded for treading on table linens. Bijou began to bark.

"If I die, Varenka . . ." Catherine said. Her face turned so pale that I felt a stab of fear.

"You won't die. You are strong."

It was Prince Naryshkin who took her by the arm and led her to the window.

"Look," he said.

In the Summer Garden, Serge Saltykov in a purple velvet ensemble bowed very low. His plumed hat swept the ground. Catherine gasped softly and clapped her hands.

"My second surprise of the day," Prince Naryshkin announced, throwing the window open so that Serge could climb inside. "Remember this, Princess. Reward me with at least one smile."

It took one jump, a quick turn of his lithe, muscular body, and Saltykov was in the room with us. His smile was triumphant.

"Serge!"

I saw Catherine throw her arms around her lover's neck. I heard her pleading, "I wait every night . . . I cannot . . . please . . . it hurts so much. . . ."

"But I'm here now."

Catherine's fingers adjusted the embroidered edge of her lover's collar, lingering there. Beside them, Bijou stood on his hind legs, ignored, dancing for a treat.

I gave Prince Naryshkin a warning glance and stepped back. As we left, I caught a glimpse of Serge Saltykov, his handsome face soft with concern. He took Catherine's hands gently and clasped them between his.

"Shh ..." I heard his thick murmur. "Haven't I found a way? Just as I've promised."

"It has begun."

The midwife sent her message at dusk. With it came a request for fresh butter, ashes, rhubarb water, wine and vinegar.

The Empress rushed to the delivery room. The midwife was proud to announce that the waters in which the child had bathed in his mother's womb were reddish, a sure omen that Catherine would deliver a boy.

In the Empress's rooms the court ladies-in-waiting gathered to wait and pray. They were all from Elizabeth's entourage, I noted, when I took my place in the corner, awaiting my summons. Only five of Catherine's maids-of-honor were there, heads bowed, prayer beads slipping through their fingers. The crowded room smelled of jasmine and candied orange peel, the Empress's latest weakness.

The walls of the Summer Palace were thin, and we could hear Catherine groan. Sometimes she gave a yelp of pain like a dog struck with a sharp stone. A few times the Empress urged her to be brave, but mostly we heard the midwife's voice instructing her to breathe deeply, to swallow what she was given to drink, and to push, push.

It was a cool September night. Restless, I rose and parted the curtains. Through the crack I could see the moonlit branches of an oak swaying in the wind.

Let this child come fast, I prayed. *Let it bring her peace.*

The Grand Duke arrived. I could hear him step noisily into the delivery room, mumbling something that I hoped was encouragement. I heard the Empress ask him where he had been and why he was not wearing his Russian uniform.

He said he had been mustering his Holsteiner troops. They had to be ready for a parade. "For there will be one, won't there?" he asked in a petulant voice.

Minutes later we heard him depart.

After an hour, the Empress, warned that the waiting would be long, emerged from the delivery room. Countess Shuvalova hurried toward her with a small comfit pot.

She would retire to her bedroom, the Empress announced, slipping a piece of candied peel into her mouth. She would wait there until the labor came to fruition.

By midnight we were still waiting. Unable to sleep, the Empress had called her ladies-in-waiting into her bedroom, to pray with her, but Catherine's maids-of-honor had been sent away. The Summer Palace, Elizabeth declared, was not built for crowds. The baby would need air to breathe.

By two in the morning I ventured into the delivery room, to ask if anything might be needed. The mattress on the floor was circled by ten thick wax candles, and I crossed myself, unable to stop the thought that it resembled a catafalque. Moonlight bathed the room. Apart from the midwife and her attendant, a young kerchiefed woman, no one else was allowed to stay while the labor was in progress.

The crisp, clean sheets that had been laundered and scented for the imperial delivery were now crumpled and stained. Catherine, her robe opened, her dark hair loose and matted with sweat, lay shivering. Her flesh was pasty, her breasts swollen.

Seeing me, she gasped and tried to lift herself. "No one told me it would hurt so much," she said and moaned, pointing at the huge mound of her child. "Do you think I'll just burst?"

"A few more hours and you won't even remember."

"When will the Empress come?"

"Very soon."

"Varenka, please. Don't you lie to me. Not you."

The midwife clicked her tongue in annoyance, so I didn't reply. Her reddened hands were gently bringing the baby down the birth passage.

"No danger of breech birth," the midwife told me. "You can tell that to Her Highness."

The floor squeaked as I knelt beside the mattress. On the table, by a porcelain basin, lay white swaddling clothes.

"Be off with you," the midwife snapped.

I rose and left.

Two of Catherine's chambermaids lingered in the hall, pretending to dust the railing or wipe some invisible stain from the floor. I wondered which one of them was a tongue.

"What do you think you are doing?" I snapped. They scattered like rabbits chased by a hound.

No one but the Empress, the Grand Duke, and five of Elizabeth's ladies-in-waiting were allowed to witness the final moments of the delivery.

The whispers grew still, and then I heard it: the baby's first shaky cry, drowned in explosions of joy.

In the Imperial Bedroom I crossed myself and gave thanks. It was a boy.

I imagined what I couldn't see: Catherine's son placed between his mother's legs, the cord around his body. The midwife waiting for the first cry so that the cord could be cut and removed.

There were three knots on it, I heard, predicting three future pregnancies. The afterbirth was expelled swiftly, without much pain. The infant was given a spoonful of warm red wine sweetened with honey to cut through the phlegm. He was washed and swaddled.

Through the wall I could hear Catherine's joyous sobs.

In the Imperial Bedroom the curtains were pushed open. The dawn was milky and shrouded in fog. Outside, cries of joy mingled with musket shots and cheers. And then the church bells rang, one by one, announcing the good news.

There are so many words for love: *my dove, the apple of my eye, my honey, my falcon, my hawk.* The Empress muttered them all as she came back to her bedroom, the swaddled newborn in her arms, her ladies-in-waiting behind her. I had never seen her look so ecstatic.

A tiny reddened face, eyes squeezed tightly shut. A whimper chased away with a kiss.

I lingered as visitors arrived, declaring themselves speechless with awe. The little Tsarevitch, Peter the Great's great-grandson, was a marvel of strength and beauty. Russia's great future was secure. *"So handsome . . . so peaceful . . . a little man already."*

They all crowded around the Empress, making sure she was aware of their presence. Princes, counts, courtiers. The Chancellor of Russia peeled off his gloves, easing them off finger by finger, before making a sign of the cross over the infant's head. Ivan Shuvalov, newly appointed the curator of Moscow University, his voice rich with emotion, recited an ode *To the precious one who brought Minerva joy.*

Satisfied, Elizabeth waved them all away. Even Ivan Ivanovich was told to leave. In the gray light of dawn, the canopied crib where she carefully placed the baby seemed to take up half of the room. Settling in a chair beside it, she began rocking it gently.

I turned to depart with the rest, but the Empress stopped me.

"Go to her now, Varvara," she ordered, in a small, strained voice.

I thought: *She cannot even bring herself to say Catherine's name.*

"What shall I tell the Grand Duchess, Your Majesty?"

"Tell her that I'm pleased with her."

I nodded.

"Tell her that I'm tired. That she kept me waiting all night."

The baby was quiet. The Empress rose and let her loose velvet cape slip off her shoulders. In a white shift of quilted cambric, she looked like an awkward moth. From the shadows of the bedroom came the rustling sound of a mouse scurrying along the wall. *Where are the cats when one needs them?* I thought.

Then came the words I dreaded.

"This child is mine. And you make sure *she* doesn't give me any trouble."

This is what it means to be Empress. Take what you want, discard what you no longer need. Live in a world that allows you to do as you please, for in this world fortunes and lives depend on your whims.

I knew it, and yet I still lingered, hoping the Empress would offer some consolation I could take to Catherine. A time for her visit, perhaps, a promise of a swift reunion with her own child.

For a moment, Elizabeth looked as if she might toss Catherine some scraps of her benevolence, but then the baby whimpered in his crib, and she turned away to bend over him.

I entered the delivery room with a heavy heart. I had not expected Catherine to be alone, but to my astonishment she lay without even a maid to assist her, shivering from the cold. The bed linen was soaked from her sweat. Even the candles had vanished.

She had wrapped her arms around her chest, her empty arms.

I smoothed Catherine's moist hair and tried to comfort her sobs. "He will die," she insisted. "He'll die without me."

"The Empress won't let any harm come to him," I assured her. "He's safe and warm. His cradle is lined with silver fox." I described her son to her. The tiny face, the pink lips, the big, gray eyes.

"Did she say when I can see him?"

I shook my head.

"Why, Varenka?"

"You know why."

Catherine's fingers dug into my arm, deep into my flesh. I heard her gasp. I heard her wail.

She had been robbed and left for dead. She was bleeding, not the woman's blood that had to flow but the man's blood that called for revenge. In the chilly light of dawn, I caught a glimpse of her hatred.

"I want her to die, Varenka."

She let go of my arm. I covered her lips with my hand, to silence these dangerous words, but she pushed it away.

"I want to see her take her last breath. I want to look into her eyes when she does it. I want to watch when she struggles for air that will not come."

I made another gesture of warning—the walls were too thin, the shadows not dense enough—but Catherine would not be silenced.

"I don't care if anyone listens. I want her dead. I can't live like this anymore."

I let her cry in my arms until we heard the steps of Madame Vladislavova, the Chief Maid, who entered and declared herself on an imperial errand to check on the Grand Duchess.

She gave me a reproachful look. "The Empress wants you back with her, Varvara Nikolayevna," she said sharply.

Already? I thought. *Another whim? Or suspicion that I might disobey her?* No—I was certain it was merely the desire to hear that I had carried out her cruel wish.

Of all the time's currents, I decided, the imperial ones run swiftest. Patience is not an imperial virtue.

My hand was still smoothing Catherine's hair, and I could feel the velvet softness of her ear underneath my fingers. I knew that in my absence she would not be able to ask anyone about her child. If she did, her questions would be reported to the Empress.

"Tell the Empress I'll be there soon," I told Madame Vladislavova, knowing I was merely buying a few more moments. "The Grand Duchess still needs me here."

An hour later when I returned to Catherine's side from Elizabeth's room, I discovered that Madame Vladislavova had been of no help. "The midwife will come soon" was all the wretched woman had said. She didn't order the wet linen changed. Later, I learned that she didn't even give Catherine a drink of water or help her move to a bed away from the drafts. I returned to find Catherine still on the blood-soaked mattress, shivering from exhaustion and pain.

Ringing for maids, ordering fresh linen, water, and a heavy throw, I raged. Where were they now, I thought bitterly, all these grand friends of hers? Those who fed on her largesse? Where was Naryshkin or his sister? Where was Saltykov?

Did they all wish her dead?

I kept these questions to myself as I helped Catherine rise from the mattress and wash. Her emptied belly still swollen, a brownish streak running like a gash from the navel down. Leaning on my arm, she got into a freshly made bed.

"Varenka?" she asked.

"She named him Paul Petrovich," I answered, knowing what she sought.

"Paul," she repeated.

"He is strong. He is not crying. He would not suckle, though. He fell asleep as soon as the wet nurse pushed a nipple into his mouth."

Catherine's eyes were on me, greedy for every word.

"The wet nurse is clean," I assured her. "Not a spot on her body. Her milk is plentiful. Everyone rejoiced at the full moon last night. It will bring him strength. He has tiny, perfect fingers, with rosy nails."

"Perfect," she repeated. Her smile trembled.

"Are you in pain?" I asked.

She shook her head, but I could tell by the pallor of her skin that she was lying.

I thought of the moment the midwife had placed Darya in my arms, my daughter's first soft whisper of a breath. I couldn't be the one to tell Catherine that these would not be her pleasures.

"I'm strong, Varenka," she said huskily. "For I have you. I ask for nothing more." She took my hand in hers and kissed it. "You will help me. And my son."

"Yes," I said. "I will."

Journal of the Court Quartermaster reported that on September 20, 1754, toward morning, Her Imperial Highness Her Majesty Grand Duchess Ekaterina Alexeyevna gave birth successfully to a son. God has sent His Imperial Highness Grand Duke Paul Petrovich.

The cannonade from the Petropavlovsky Fortress announced the birth of an Imperial Heir. Throughout the city, banners were raised. Jubilant crowds cheered.

In the eleventh hour—the *Journal* reported—in the presence of Her

Imperial Majesty, the child was carried from the chambers of Their Imperial Highnesses to the inner chambers of Her Imperial Majesty.

A lie, I knew.

Not *in the eleventh hour*, but the moment the cord that attached him to his mother had been cut.

"Tell me everything, Varenka," Catherine pleaded. "I don't want you to spare my feelings."

The Grand Duchess is making a spectacle of herself. . . . Poor Saltykov is trying his best to free himself, but a man has his limits. . . .

At the beginning of November the court moved back to the Winter Palace, patched up for the coming months, awaiting the time when proper renovations would begin. Half of the Imperial Bedroom had been turned into the nursery, and this was where Elizabeth spent her days, with the baby, jealous of the wet nurses. Little else interested her. I even saw her shake off Ivan Shuvalov's hand.

When the Grand Duke Peter visited, the Empress allowed him to hold his son for a few moments, until the first whimper, then sent him away. He didn't mind, he had told Catherine. Infants belong to the women. His time would come. His son would grow up a soldier. "His son," Catherine said to me, bitterly. "As if I didn't count."

"The pride of Their Highnesses, their greatest achievement and mighty Russia's hope," the Chancellor of Russia had called Grand Duke Paul Petrovich in his speech at the baptismal feast.

In the Empress's antechamber, my conversations with the Chancellor followed the usual court exchanges of vague illusions. It is easy to be distracted from what is important, but awakening always comes in the end. In Russia one takes what looks like the worst road and it turns out to be the best.

"I have something for you to take to the Grand Duchess, Varvara Nikolayevna," he said, when I was alone with him. "My own elixir of gold, tincture *toniconervina Bestuscheffi*. A remedy for catastrophes of love and strewn nerves. Indispensable in such trying times."

When he'd left me to retrieve what turned out to be a small bottle filled with a yellow liquid, I took a quick look at his desk. There was a large folio sheet there with headings printed in bold type:

Sergey Vasilyevich Saltykov . . . age: 26 . . . handsome physiognomy . . . a lecher who has had Madame . . . Countess . . . Princess . . . amiable character . . . inclined to pedantry . . . for his mission received 6,000 rubles from the Empress and a promise of an appointment at the Court of Sweden.

I visited Catherine each day. She was still feverish, staring for hours out the window at the river, Bijou at her side. My assurances that Paul was thriving did not ease her worry. "Go back to him, Varenka," Catherine would plead. "They wouldn't tell me even if he were dying. You know they wouldn't."

In the Winter Palace, Catherine's bedroom was three doors away from the Imperial Suite, close enough for the Empress's spies to keep an eye on her. This is where she stayed most of the time, in the company of her maids-of-honor. Sometimes I slipped in there at dawn, sometimes in the middle of the night. I cultivated opportunities that allowed me to be alone with her, even for an instant, enough to whisper a quick reassurance.

Once or twice I could smell a man's scent around her, snuff and wet leather of the road. "Serge was here. No one saw him," would be all I could get out of her.

Outside the Winter Palace, the first snow fell on the city, blanketing the frozen roads, the roofs, and the Neva. The sun set early. By afternoon only the torches burning in wall brackets and the bonfires of the sentries made the palace yard visible. Darya had just turned four, and she liked to finger through old books, looking for pictures. "Is it me, Maman?" she'd ask if she spotted a child in them, relieved when I assured her she was not among the innocents slain by Herod's soldiers and that the mother throwing her hands out in despair was not me.

At the end of November, at the churching ceremony when Catherine was allowed to take Communion for the first time after giving birth, she could stand without pain. She was healing, I told myself. All poison has an antidote. She would soon forget Saltykov.

At the beginning of December, Serge Saltykov left St. Petersburg for his country estate. His departure, surprisingly, was not by the Empress's order. "Too many women chasing him here," the Chancellor told me. His eyes were full of malice.

What did I tell Catherine in these last weeks of the year?

That fortune is not as blind as people imagine; it requires a long series of well-chosen steps.

That the Shuvalovs had not yet triumphed. For now that she had her heir, Elizabeth might turn her back on Peter.

"She has choices now she didn't have before," I reminded Catherine. "If she chooses Paul Petrovich over his father, you will be Regent."

"Is that what Elizabeth says?" Catherine asked. There was a flicker of hope in her eyes.

"No," I said. "But that's something to think about."

"I don't need such consolations, Varenka," Catherine said with a frown of disappointment. "I need to know what the Empress says."

The last days of the old year demand the settling of debts. In the Church of Our Lady of Kazan, the Empress gave thanks for the blessed year that had brought her the infinitely precious Imperial Heir.

Her gifts were worthy of a Romanov: a new *oklad* for the Holy Icon, studded with pearls, diamonds, rubies, and sapphires; a jeweled gold altar cross; an engraved censer. In the final days of 1754, we were all summoned to admire her offerings, to exclaim over the clarity of the fat stones, the perfection of silk needlework, the intricate patterns etched into the blue enamel.

Catherine was seldom seen in public. Claiming that she was still sore from her labor, and that migraines plagued her, she had obtained Elizabeth's permission to abstain from attending court balls and masquerades.

The maids whispered that the Grand Duchess sobbed when she believed herself alone. The Empress was not concerned. All she wished from me was one thing: "If anyone dares to call the Grand Duke Paul Saltykov's bastard, Varvara, I want to know right away."

I found Catherine in bed, cradling little Bijou. "Is it you, Varenka?" she asked as I entered, her voice blurred with laudanum. "Have you got something for Bijou? The little darling has been waiting for you." Bijou slipped his wet nose inside my palm, in search of a treat. I pushed him away.

"Varenka is so mean to my little Bijou," Catherine murmured, picking the dog up and raising him. "So mean."

I watched her smile at the sight of Bijou's legs dangling helplessly in the air. The dog was staring down at her with big, astonished eyes, patiently waiting to be restored to dignity. "Don't ever go to mean Varenka," she crooned. "Stay with me."

The bed smelled of camphor. Beside it, Catherine's petticoats lay in a disorderly heap. She must have dismissed the maids in a hurry.

"Your son slept most of the day, without crying," I told Catherine, picking up her silk underclothes. Her petticoat was yellowed and torn in a few places. I resolved to have a talk with her chambermaid.

Catherine lowered Bijou. The dog began licking her nightshirt, stained from the milk. Her breasts were still swollen. She didn't move him away.

"The wet nurses change every two hours," I said. "They pick him up the moment he starts crying. The Empress sits by the cradle. The nursery is kept very warm; the stokers have been ordered never to let the stoves cool. Little Paul is covered with a satin quilt filled with cotton wadding, and then with another, of pink velvet lined with ermine."

I put the folded petticoats on the chair. I ran my finger over the night table, checking for dust.

"They carry him around too much," Catherine murmured. "It's not good for a baby to be always rocked to sleep."

Serge Saltykov returned to St. Petersburg. I saw him in Elizabeth's antechamber, awaiting summons. He did not come to see Catherine.

"Please, Varenka," Catherine begged. "He knows I'm being watched. He doesn't want to put me in danger. Let him know that I can get out of the palace. I need to see him, Varenka. Take a note to him. From me."

My chest grew tighter.

"No need for a note. Let me talk to him," I said.

I found Sergey Saltykov in the guard room, showing off a card trick to a young officer. With his impudent glee, smelling of vodka, snow, and juniper-scented smoke, Serge looked as if he had just risen from a bonfire at some winter hunt. As I walked in, he was motioning for the guard to lift the card on top of the deck. A sigh of bewilderment greeted the appearance of an ace.

"One word with you, Monsieur Saltykov," I said. Our eyes met. I felt his assessing my low-cut dress.

"Will you excuse me, Grigory Grigoryevich?" he said to the guard, and rose.

"She is waiting for you," I said through clenched teeth after he had followed me to the corridor.

"Is she?"

His hand was on my arm, and I felt his fingers brush the nape of my neck. Serge Saltykov believed no woman could resist his presence.

"Then why is she hiding in her room? I'd hoped to see her at the last ball."

Catherine would ask me to repeat his every word, every excuse Sergey Saltykov could invent. She wanted to hear of confessions of disappointment, fear of the Duke's jealousy, the danger to her. "Does the baby look like me at all?" she kept asking me. "Does anyone say he might not be Peter's? Is this why Serge doesn't want to see me?"

She knew what a stain on her son's birth would mean. Any pretender could rise from the shadows and claim to be the forgotten Tsar, the true descendant of Peter the Great. Any pretender could gather the troops and proclaim Grand Duke Paul Petrovich Saltykov's bastard. And yet she was still waiting for her lover's visit. Passion had replaced reason, had made her desperate.

"She is alone now," I told Saltykov. From another room I heard Egor's voice commanding the guards to shape up. "I'll take you to her. No one will see us. Please."

Serge Saltykov gave my arm a gentle squeeze. His wrist, I noticed, was covered with a mat of fine black hair.

"I'm not the master of my time, or my affections," he said. "Tell her that, Varvara Nikolayevna. It's better for the Grand Duchess to know."

In the streets of St. Petersburg, the fortune-tellers pointed to the double five in the coming 1755. It meant hope, openness to new experiences. Five is an adventurer, they said, pushing life to the limits. Five is "five senses." Five longs for freedom.

Before the celebrations began, the Empress—her evening gown stiff with diamonds and bristling with golden thread—blessed baby Paul and presented him with a large crystal pendant. Hung in the window, it would delight his eyes with bouncing rainbows.

The Empress decided to greet the new year in the Amber Room. She wished to feel its healing powers one more time, she announced, before Monsieur Rastrelli moved the amber panels to Tsarskoye Selo, the first step of the renovations that would begin soon.

Lit by five hundred candles, the walls of the Amber Room, a gift from the Prussian King to Peter the Great, glowed with golden and brown flecks. The air was thick with perfume, snuff, and spirits. A small army of footmen hovered by the door, like crows on carrion, swooping on the slightest traces of sawdust carried in from the restrooms. Darya had watched with rapture as I dressed for the ball. She made me promise I would let her dry the flowers of my corsage. Now, in my tightly laced court gown, I stood beside my husband, making plans for the future. Egor's transfer to the army had finally been approved; his new commission would soon follow. It would mean long absences Darya was not yet aware of. It would be just me and Masha for her for a long time.

Catherine had once again asked the Empress to be excused from a public appearance. The request had been granted with a few caustic comments about her haughtiness. "What is she moping about now, Varvara?" Elizabeth asked me. "She doesn't think herself mistreated, does she?" The mockery in her voice made me cringe.

Radiant and sumptuous, the Empress scrutinized the courtiers. Ivan Ivanovich Shuvalov stood at her elbow, whispering to her from time to time. I saw him kiss her hand and press it to his chest with a triumphant grin. In the last weeks he had kept to himself, praising the Imperial Heir loud enough for everyone to take note, mocking those dim-witted enough to believe that the Shuvalovs' star might be fading. To the Chancellor's annoyance, Ivan Ivanovich had chased away the dark-eyed beauty Bestuzhev had sent to seduce him. "You can't touch me," the Imperial Favorite had told the woman. "And neither can he who sent you here."

At midnight, fireworks exploded with sparkling cartwheels, shooting stars, and turning wheels. Molten wax was poured over cold water to reveal the future. When the wax hardened, we turned it in our hands, looking for clues in its shape or the shadow it cast. A sword for the Empress, a horseshoe for the Grand Duke. A letter for me.

War? Journey? Good news? Or bad?

Right after midnight the Empress asked the Crown Prince to open the ball. She was pleased when he danced with Countess Vorontzova. *Das Fräulein* burst into giggles of delight every time Peter looked at her.

I danced and lingered in the antechambers, among tinkles of epaulettes and roars of laughter, collecting gossip the Empress would demand from me the following day. Who had to use the reviving salts? Whose dress needed last-minute letting out? Who still looked plebeian in spite of the latest change of wardrobe?

In her room Catherine was waiting, but Serge Saltykov had no intention of going to her. I watched him dance with Princess Lenskaya, two times in a row. Then I saw him slip out with Prince Naryshkin. "I think the gentlemen are a bit merry," a chambermaid whispered to me with a sly grin.

The thought of Catherine alone, still believing Sergey would come, was too cruel. I slipped out of the ballroom and knocked on her door. She opened it quickly, too quickly, her French dressing gown of pale blue silk opened at the front, revealing the curve of her breasts. A soft scent of birch leaves from the *banya* was floating in the room.

"Oh, it's you, Varenka," she said, her voice flat. I resolved to check how much laudanum was still left in the last bottle.

The wind was howling outside. The Winter Palace was never more aptly named than at this time of year, when all its windows froze into crystal ice gardens. Outside, the cannon shots boomed.

My mother used to say the first person who entered your home in the new year foretold your fate. A dark-haired man brought good luck. A woman was always the harbinger of bad news.

I thought: *Forget Sergey. He is not worthy of you.*

"May I stay here?" I asked.

"If you wish," she said, looking away.

I pulled Catherine down on the rug by the fire. Bijou gave us a tired look and curled into sleep at her side.

"I still remember seeing him for the first time, Varenka." Catherine's voice was slow, lingering. "At the stables. I had just come back from a long ride. The horse stopped and neighed. Serge was bending over something the groom was showing him. Then he straightened and looked at me. Just an instant, and I knew that he knew."

Love was like an illness ravaging her body. If, at that moment, Sergey opened the door and walked in, she would not have resisted him. There was enough poison in her to make her listen to some tall tale of why he could not come. A chance encounter, an order from the Grand Duke that he could not disobey.

Catherine lifted her head. Her hair, escaping her combs, covered her neck and shoulders, thick and dark and silky. Shadows danced on the walls, waves of warmth touched us from the flames.

We both heard the sound of steps outside the door. Had Sergey come, after all?

Catherine froze.

The steps continued past the room, toward the Grand Duke's apartments. A knock on the door was followed by a howl of laughter. I recognized *Das Fräulein*'s giggling.

"Did you know, Varenka?" Catherine asked softly.

"That he wouldn't come tonight?" I asked. I leaned over and placed my hand on her forehead. It was hot.

"You know what I'm asking. Did *she* order him to seduce me? Was this her plan all along?" Tears were rolling down her cheeks, but Catherine made no effort to wipe them.

I couldn't speak. On the night table, a half-burned candle was smoking, for the chambermaid had not trimmed the wick. *Is it so important to know everything? Aren't lies sometimes the kindest response?*

"Look at me, Varenka. I'm her cow. Worse than a cow, for even a cow does not have her newborn calf stolen from her right away!"

She put her hand on mine, her skin hot and dry. "Did you *know*?"

I nodded.

"Why didn't you tell me, Varenka?"

I could not answer her.

"In the future, would you be so good as to let me be the judge of what's best for me? From now on and always."

Was it her voice that hurt me the most? So cold and harsh that it didn't seem to be hers at all? Or was it the fury in her eyes? She rose and walked away to open a window, letting in loud whistles and cheers, musket shots and bursts of fireworks that greeted the dawn of New Year's Day.

"I wanted to protect you," I muttered. "That is all I ever wanted to do."

I must have wept then, for the next thing I remember is the window closing and feeling Catherine's fingers touching my face.

I didn't have a choice. I told her her own story as seen through the spying hole from the moment she arrived at the palace. I told her of the wagging tongues, of the schemes to defeat her, and the bragging of the seducer. Of the Empress's order to send her lover away from her to Sweden, as soon as the New Year's festivities ended.

Catherine sat motionless as I spoke. Only her fingers moved, running over and over Bijou's fur, twisting it into curls.

"Is that everything?" she asked, when I'd finished.

"Yes," I said.

In the glow of the fire I saw that she was biting her lip so hard a spot of blood had appeared.

I tried to say more, to remind her how far she had come since those dark days ten years before when she could have been sent home at a moment's notice, but she stopped me. "Go, Varenka," she ordered. "I need to be alone."

I obeyed her.

I did not return to the ballroom. Around me, in the cold, drafty corridors of the Winter Palace, merry voices exploded, feet pattered down the wooden stairs. I hurried to my quarters, deaf to Masha's warnings, her talk of God's will, inscrutable in its intent. I slept deeply, and did not remember my dreams.

n the first weeks of 1755, right after *Krieszczenskije morozy*, the icy-cold days of mid-January, talk of the coming war had intensified.

In the New World, the French and the English were testing their hold on the land. These faraway hostilities were casting shadows across Europe. The French had allied themselves with Prussia, England with Austria, though loyalties were constantly shifting. At the Russian court, the English were considered perfidious, the French deceitful. If Russia was leaning to the side of Britain, it was because Elizabeth hated Frederick of Prussia more than she detested the Empress of Austria.

The way she saw it, an insolent bully trumped a scheming hypocrite.

To get Elizabeth's attention these days, a courtier was wise to call Vienna dingy, its narrow lanes full of filth and mud. Or to dwell on the fact that in the Berlin palaces gilded copper passed for gold. In the Chancellor's chambers, clerks pored over spy reports in search of royal name-calling. It mattered when and to whom Frederick called the Russian Empress a whore, a cunt, or a flat-chested bitch. Or how often Maria Theresa declared Elizabeth a shameless sinner who would burn in hell.

In the intrigues of the court, anything was of use if it could fan imperial rage.

On the last day of January Egor received word that his army commission was on its way. Not artillery, as he had been promised, but infantry grenadiers. By then he didn't mind. What mattered was that he would not spend his best years entangled in "the battlefields of the boudoir." He laughed at Saltykov, cooling his heels at the Swedish court, scarcely arrived and already asking when he might be allowed to return. The imperial stud had learned the hard way, my husband said and sneered, what passed for gratitude in the palace games.

It was not Egor Malikin's way.

His honors would come from the heat of battles, from victories that would bring Russia her glory and him the rank of at least Lieutenant Colonel. Advancement was possible at a time when the maps of Europe were constantly being redrawn.

Waiting for his commission papers to arrive, Egor practiced fencing and boxing. He came home from his matches bruised and sweaty, joking about having grown stiff standing guard for years. He was fitted for new breeches, new boots. He bought a brass traveling kit of toiletries and writing instruments that fascinated Darya so much that he allowed her to keep one of the crystal bottles of ink.

He had also ordered a portrait of himself, in full uniform, a sword at his side, standing with his right leg forward, hand cradling a shako. I thought that the artist, a serf who taught himself painting, captured his likeness in the first sitting, but Egor was not satisfied.

"Give me a few wrinkles," he ordered the painter. "And straighten these lips. I don't want my grandchildren to see me grinning like a fool."

In the Winter Palace there was no one Young Court anymore. There was Peter's court and Catherine's court. His was the domain of the

Shuvalovs, presided over by *Das Fräulein*. Catherine was on her own, and I was her tongue.

"The Empress has to trust you, Varenka," she counseled me. "She has to let you stay with her when others are sent away. Tell her what she wants to hear."

In the Imperial Bedroom, when Elizabeth tired of denouncing Prussian lies, I reported on the Grand Duchess's gambling debts, debts that did little to stop purchases of ruby pendants, or yet another pair of silk shoes with silver buckles. I called Catherine cold and calculating, having time only for those who could do something for her. There was little need for more specific accusations, for any mention of Catherine made Elizabeth's voice harden. An evening spent playing cards or a failure to show up at a palace ball was proof that the Grand Duchess was reckless or too proud. The daily assurances of Catherine's gratitude, her insistent praises of everything in the Imperial Nursery, did not soften the Empress. A smile was as suspicious as a tear.

"We never much like those we have hurt, do we, Varvara Nikolayevna?" the Chancellor remarked.

I want to know everything. However insignificant it may seem to you, Catherine had said.

And so I reported everything I saw. A shallow breath, swollen hands, a nightmare broken by a scream or the frantic clutching of a Holy Icon. Another bloodletting, the surgeon's frown, Elizabeth's dark, thick blood. The pain in the belly, her insistence on looser clothes. She fainted. There were convulsions.

I told Catherine of long visits the Empress made to the chapel, muttering her confessions, bargaining with God. In the middle of the night a hooting owl was chased away with musket shots. Birds were shooed if they even approached her windowsill. A sick valet had been sent home and never spoken of again.

In the Winter Palace the word *death* had been banished from all speech.

⌒

"His words, Varenka," Catherine would insist, when I mentioned Bestuzhev's name. "Tell me exactly what he says."

The war is unavoidable.

The time of war is rapacious, fraudulent, and cruel, calling for extraordinary measures.

A knockout blow is always better than a long war of attrition.

A skillful ruler must do more than react, but for that clear plans and purposes are needed.

Everyone knows that the Grand Duke admires Frederick of Prussia. But is this where his wife's loyalty lies as well?

Tell the Grand Duchess I wish to advise her. Tell her to trust me, to start thinking of me as her friend.

"Should I trust him, Varenka?"

Some thoughts are like shadows, fortified by darkness, multiplying and dancing around, reappearing where they are not expected. Thoughts that never reach the stage when they can be called decisions, though they turn into them.

I didn't decide I would turn my back on Bestuzhev, try to beat the Chancellor of Russia at his own game.

How he wanted her out of Russia, I thought, instead. *An empress of some cabbage field! Does he think his treachery forgotten?*

I told Catherine of the files Bestuzhev kept, whom he thought nasty and toadlike . . . who *had the bearing of a peasant* . . . who was *devious and very slippery.* Who was looking for a protector, a sinecure, or merely a wealthy wife. Who collected money from his estates, and who had to sneak out his back door for fear of creditors. Who held a grudge against the Grand Duke, and who was secretly hoping for the Shuvalovs' fall.

The map of desires, he called it, *written on human skin.*

"He will support you as long as it is in his interest," I said. "He will betray you the moment a better opportunity arises."

Seated at her desk she'd brought from the Oranienbaum palace, Catherine picked up a clean sheet of paper and smoothed it with her sleeve. "I don't know what I think, Varenka," she had told me once, "until I write it down."

Her index finger, I noticed, was blackened with ink. She noticed it, too, for she licked the stain and began rubbing it with her thumb.

"Tell the Chancellor that I'm considering his offer, Varenka. Make him think I need more signs of his loyalty. Let him prove himself first."

When the ice fields on Lake Ladoga began to break up and enormous ice floes rumbled noisily down the Neva, the reconstruction of the Winter Palace finally began. At first only some sections of the building had been cordoned off, far away from the Imperial Suite of rooms. Newly arrived sculptures stood everywhere, bundled in burlap and straw.

For a time the Empress still received visitors in the Throne Room, but soon the hammering and sawing made it impossible. In the courtyard the British Ambassador had slipped on a patch of wet plaster and sprained his ankle. Countess Rumyantseva ruined her shoes when she stepped in a pool of tar. When even Ivan Shuvalov began to complain of headaches from persistent noise, the court began to pack up for a big move.

By the time bird cherries were covered in white blossoms and wildflowers carpeted the banks of the Neva, the new temporary palace at the junction of the Great Perspective Road and the Moyka Canal was finished. It had but one story and an attic. The walls were flimsy. The entire floor shook when anyone walked down the hall. It was easy to foresee problems. The wooden panels would freeze in the winter; the windows and doors would warp. There wouldn't be enough room for all the courtiers to reside there.

"It's only for one year," the Empress said impatiently. She cut off all jostling for space. There would be no more petitions. No more complaints. Having said that, she departed to Peterhof with her ladies-in-waiting. Catherine and Peter moved to Oranienbaum for the summer. Everyone else was ordered to help with the move.

A court in transition, I thought, *considering its options*.

Catherine's new rooms, I discovered, would be far away from the Grand Duke's and the Empress's but close to mine; perhaps Elizabeth was making some amends after my assurances that Catherine had accepted her fate.

Charged with supervising the move of the Imperial Bedroom, I spent the lilac-scented summer days in endless deliberations on what should be put in storage and what should be unpacked in the Empress's temporary suite. Tense days, I thought them, filled with grumblings and complaints, days of trailing the maids and the footmen, of teary investigations when yet another swanskin fan went missing, not to mention the Venetian smelling bottles or the Empress's favorite tortoiseshell comb. *What will be next?* I asked myself. *Her shoes?*

Elizabeth's cats, brought to the temporary palace, promptly disappeared. But a few days later I saw them come back, one after another, to scrape their faces against the furniture and doorframes, to lie on one of the Empress's shoes, or on her pillows.

My new bedroom was too small for anything more than a bed, a dresser, and a chest of drawers. Most of my wardrobe had to stay in trunks in the attic, brought down only when necessary.

The move exhausted me. At night, when I closed my eyes, I was haunted by the images of hands groping for crates, burlap, and braids of straw.

Oblivious to all this, Darya rejoiced. In my daughter's imagination empty palace rooms turned into oceans, shrouded ottomans became deserted islands. In the attic where the washerwomen hung the laundry to dry, she loved to watch the cats rolling in the baskets of freshly folded linen. "Look, Maman," she would call, pointing out their antics, but I took note instead of loose boards and the chinks in the attic floor.

How easy for anyone, I thought, *wishing to spy on those below.*

If there was emptiness in these days, I refused to dwell on it. Right before our move, Egor's papers arrived. His departure was swift. One moment he stood in our parlor in his new uniform—gold buttons gleaming against his green coat—complaining that the collar was too tight. Darya was trying on his shako, and Egor bent over her to explain that the letters EPI crowning it stood for: *Elizaveta Petrovna Imperatriza*. Masha, red-eyed and sniffling, was hanging a Holy Icon around his neck. There were promises. There were jokes. There was Egor's newly shaved face, flushed and happy, when he adjusted the red leather belt of his sword. There was a smile of triumph so clearly meant for me.

And then he was gone.

Every June 29, on the Feast of Saints Peter and Paul, the court celebrated the name day of the Crown Prince. It was always a lavish day filled with music, dancing, and military parades, a day without end, for during the white night that followed, the sun dipped beyond the horizon only to rise again almost immediately, dissolving darkness into a foggy mist of blue and violet. In 1755, Peter's name-day celebrations were more spectacular than ever. That year the Crown Prince shared his name day with his new son and heir.

"Go to Oranienbaum, Varvara," the Empress ordered. Nothing more than three words were needed for a tongue.

By the time I arrived, the yard of the Oranienbaum palace had been fitted with a vodka fountain and barrels of German beer. An orchestra played in the garden, a violin quartet in the palace courtyard. Footmen made their way through the throng, balancing platters of crayfish and mounds of roasted meat, replenishing the food that vanished as fast as it was placed on tables. On one of the sideboards rose a turreted fortress made entirely of pastries and fruit. The Grand

Duke was there, wearing a smart-looking emerald-green jacket with gold trim instead of his usual blue Holsteiner uniform, graciously acknowledging another round of musket salutes. *Das Fräulein*, I noted, was delighted to stand by Peter's side to greet the visitors.

There was no sign of Catherine.

I walked across the courtyard toward the palace in search of her. Around me, lagging conversations became lively only when something disparaging was said. So-and-so made herself look ridiculous with too much Valenciennes lace. So-and-so spent five thousand rubles on a dinner party and yet the food was revolting. So-and-so was lusting for another man's wife.

Enough gossip to keep the Empress satisfied, I thought.

In the palace hall the Chancellor stood by an open window, watching the courtyard outside.

"Spectacular entertainment, wouldn't you say?" he said gleefully, seeing me. "The flower of the court. The old players and the new." His shrewd eyes missed nothing. *Das Fräulein*'s sharp laughter, my anxious looks at the door where Catherine should appear at any moment.

"Look at the British Ambassador. He is trying so hard to impress our Empress these days." The Chancellor leaned over the windowsill. "My old friend has brought reinforcements."

Sir Charles Hanbury-Williams, the British Ambassador to Russia, his ankle still not fully healed, hobbled beside a slim young man in a cherry velvet frock coat. No wig, I noted. The young man's hair was frizzled and powdered, a black braid tied with a satin ribbon.

"Count Stanislav Poniatowski," the Chancellor told me. "Straight from his European grand tour. He's Sir Charles's private secretary. And his protégé."

Count Poniatowski, the Chancellor said, was taking his first steps into politics. His uncles had sent him to St. Petersburg to advance Polish influence at the Russian court. He had already been received by the best families. After an audience in Peterhof, the Empress gushed over his shapely calves so much that Ivan Ivanovich began to sulk.

In the courtyard Count Poniatowski gracefully returned someone's bow, accepting a glass of champagne from a passing footman. Sir Charles was introducing him to Field Marshal Apraxin.

Beside me, Bestuzhev chuckled.

"The Shuvalovs think him quite dangerous, Varvara Nikolayevna. The dashing count should take it as a compliment."

The medals on General Apraxin's chest glittered. Count Poniatowski extended his hand.

"I should warn you that Countess Shuvalova has already started hinting at unnatural inclinations between master and pupil." The Chancellor chuckled. "So don't be surprised when the Empress becomes curious about our handsome Polish newcomer."

So there is gossip already, I thought, listening to the rest of the Chancellor's account of Count Stanislav's first days at court. The French faction was eager to disgrace the British by whatever means.

I ignored the questioning look in Bestuzhev's eyes. *Tell him I change my mind every time you talk to me*, Catherine had said. *Let him grow desperate.*

The time of war, I told myself, *rapacious and fraudulent. Cruel.*

When I entered her rooms, Catherine stood in a dazzling flood of sunlight, surrounded by her maids-of-honor, a constant buzz of talk around her. She was still being dressed. The maids were lacing up her stays, adjusting the panniers, tying the pockets around her waist. One of her maids was powdering Catherine's hair, curled in elaborate locks for the occasion; another attached a beauty spot above her lip. A court gown of ivory silk was laid out, its skirt frosted with intricate silver lace.

"Varenka," Catherine exclaimed, as I curtsied. She gestured for me to rise. "Is the move complete? Is the new palace as ready as everyone says it is?"

I wondered if it were belladonna or laudanum that made her eyes look so wide and so blue.

It was her son's first name day. Had she at least been permitted to embrace and kiss him? Or did she have to hold back tears and speak of her gratitude for his well-being? Had she had to force herself not to reach for her baby, even when he extended his hands to her? The "darling boy," the Empress ordered, must be spared the undue agitation of his mother's presence. Longing for her son, I'd heard Elizabeth declare, would make Catherine's womb more receptive for another pregnancy.

"The palace is awaiting Your Highnesses' arrival," I replied.

Catherine raised her hands so the maids could slip on her petticoats, inner and outer, and her stomacher. By the time she was ready for the gown itself, I had answered all her questions. The palace was small but clean. The Great Perspective Road was noisy in the morning, but her windows were facing the canal. Besides, Monsieur Rastrelli swore we would all be back at the Winter Palace a year from now.

The silk gown rustled softly as Catherine made a slow turn. The silver lace sparkled. The maids were now on the lookout for the smallest of imperfections, a loose thread, a fold too supple or too tight, a smudge of rice powder on her neck.

I thought Catherine hadn't looked so fine for quite a while.

Outside, in the Oranienbaum yard, someone shouted, "Long live the Crown Prince!" The cheers that followed lingered. I thought of *Das Fräulein*'s eagerness to seize Catherine's place beside her husband.

Another round of musket shots rang in the air.

I was relieved when after a moment of silence, tense and uncomfortable, Catherine smiled and told me that she was ready to join the Grand Duke at the feast.

"Who is he, Varenka?" Catherine wanted to know.

From a bowl of fruit Count Poniatowski picked out a pitted plum and slipped it into his mouth. Then he took another.

I repeated the Chancellor's introduction. *Count Poniatowski . . . the British Ambassador's Polish protégé . . . his private secretary . . . but more like his friend and pupil.*

"He seems to like plums," Catherine observed. "Does your plum-loving Polish count have a Christian name?"

"Stanislav."

"Has *she* seen him?"

I said that Count Poniatowski had been officially presented to the Empress several days before.

"Did she like him?"

"Yes."

"More than her Shuvalov?"

"I don't think so. He made a grave mistake."

"He ate all her plums?" A playful flicker came into Catherine's eyes.

"No." I stifled a smile. "I heard that he quoted Voltaire before Ivan Ivanovich had a chance to do so."

Out of the corner of my eye, I saw Count Poniatowski bow in front of the oldest of Prince Kurakin's daughters and lead her to the dance floor. The Count's turns and steps showed the mastery of practice and a delight in his own dexterity. Each time he bent toward his partner, a warm smile softened the fine lines of his face. Not a smudge of Sergey Saltykov's arrogant manliness, I decided, hoping Catherine would see it, too. Just the worldly ease of someone who feels at home everywhere.

It was then that the Grand Duke motioned for me to approach him.

"She doesn't like my ensemble, Varvara," Peter complained, pointing at *Das Fräulein*, who was hanging on his arm, sulking. "Tell her what you heard."

He sounded like Darya when she needed my approval.

"Everyone remarks Your Highness looks especially fine today," I said. "The Grand Duchess and Chancellor Bestuzhev particularly praised the choice of the jacket."

Countess Vorontzova gave me a scowl.

"What do you have to say to that now?" the Grand Duke asked her with glee.

By the time I returned to Catherine's side, she was standing by the refreshment table with Count Poniatowski, Sir Charles right beside them. Count Poniatowski was laughing at something Catherine had just said. Her lips were parted, and I thought her beautiful then, in that rare way joy can suddenly rearrange a plain face and make it sparkle.

"You are luckier than I've been," I heard Catherine say. "I arrived here in the middle of the Russian winter, which is not for the faint of spirit." She didn't acknowledge my presence; I didn't mind.

Sir Charles Hanbury-Williams limped away from Catherine and Stanislav and gestured for me to join him. The Empress, I recalled, liked to mock the Ambassador's stout frame and full lips.

"It was entirely my fault, Madame Malikina," the Ambassador said when I expressed my concern over his injured foot. His French, though fluent, carried the slight awkwardness of an English speaker who took to it too late in life. "I had been warned of the perils of renovations. I should've watched my step."

It pleased me that he remembered my name. We had exchanged a few polite words when I came across him in the Empress's antechambers, but this was the first time we talked without others present.

Sir Charles eagerly reported the details of the official introduction that had happened in my absence. "I called Count Poniatowski my political son, the child of my heart," he informed me, "and the Grand Duchess most graciously congratulated me on my taste."

Around us the din of voices melted into laughter. At the other end of the room, Chancellor Bestuzhev was explaining something to the Austrian Ambassador, placing his hand on his shoulder, a friendly gesture meant to be seen. Sir Charles didn't hide how much he was taken with Catherine. "What intelligence, what grace," he gushed. "No one else in this room can measure up to that smile."

I let Sir Charles speak, but my thoughts drifted to Catherine and Stanislav. Not so much to what they said—for only snatches of their words reached me—but the subtle message of their gestures. Cathe-rine's fan touching her lips, a glitter in Stanislav's eyes.

"I've been in Poland long enough," Sir Charles continued, "to see the possibilities. A country half as large as France, intended by nature to be the granary of Europe, is rotting away in obscurity. Waste is not in Europe's best interests. This is what we talk about with Count Pon-iatowski every day, Madame Malikina."

Glancing at his protégé, who was bending his head toward Cath-erine, Sir Charles spoke of the balance of power needed to keep all players in check. France was reaching for more than was her share. France, who liked to form factions in every country with much pas-sion, only to abandon them with levity. Poland had learned it already, to her detriment. Poland was looking for more solid alliances now.

"Poland and Russia, Madame, linked by common interest and common good."

These were an Ambassador's words, I thought. Sir Charles was planting the seeds of his mission, seizing opportunities whenever he could. To whom did he wish me to repeat his words? Elizabeth? The Chancellor? Or Catherine?

In the sunlight of the white night I heard Catherine's voice, joyful, teasing, entangled in Count Poniatowski's soft chuckles.

When the feast ended, I went into Catherine's bedroom. In Peterhof the Empress awaited my report of the celebrations, and I needed to know what Catherine wished me to say to her.

But Catherine refused to talk about the Empress.

The chambermaids had left the windows open, and the curtains of thick crimson velvet billowed, letting in a breeze of cool, fragrant air from the sunlit gardens. I could smell lilac and heavy jasmine blooms.

"I asked Count Poniatowski about Paris, Varenka. Do you know what he said? That he loved its radiance. That cities are like people: They emanate their desires. Paris, he said, lives for pleasure."

My carriage was waiting. I rose to leave, but Catherine stopped me.

"Do you ever think I will go there?"

"To Paris?" I asked stupidly.

"Yes."

"If you truly wish."

Her eyes narrowed and then softened, two shining pools of light. "I cannot live any longer without love, Varenka. Not one single hour."

I smiled. "It seems to me you won't have to," I said.

The Empress sent me to Oranienbaum once more before the court came back to St. Petersburg for the winter.

This time it was the Grand Duke whom Elizabeth wished me to see. There have been complaints of the new regiment her nephew had summoned from Holstein. Unwelcome and annoying, when Russia was on the very brink of war with the Prussian King.

"Tell this fool, this nephew of mine, that my patience doesn't last long, Varvara," the Empress raged.

The Holsteiners in their blue uniforms camped at the outskirts of the Oranienbaum grounds. Food had to be carried to them from the palace kitchens. The footmen charged with the task were bitter about having to serve "these snotty Germans." The Empress had already been approached a few times, begged to interfere.

I watched Elizabeth's face, blotched and reddened with fury. I watched her circle the room, the sound of her heels on the floor punctuating her words. The problem was to go away. She didn't care how.

"Make sure I don't hear another word of this matter, Varvara."

I curtsied and took my leave.

In Oranienbaum I asked to see the Grand Duchess. It was important, I told the haughty maid who tried to make me wait.

Catherine was in her study, writing, with just little Bijou for company. A bouquet of red roses stood in a crystal vase on her desk, with water stains around it, for the maid's vigilance did not extend to bringing a doily. Seeing me, the Grand Duchess put the quill away. Too quickly, for she let a large drop of ink fall.

"Varenka," she exclaimed, sanding the page to stop the stain from spreading. "Just the person I wished to see!"

I attempted to give her an account of my mission and of Elizabeth's displeasure, but she hardly listened. Her skin glowed, her hair, left unpowdered and tied with a simple yellow ribbon, shone.

"He is here, you know," she said. "Again!"

"Count Poniatowski?" I guessed.

She nodded. Count Poniatowski had been a frequent guest at Oranienbaum, she told me, for the Grand Duke wished to hear of his father's military exploits. Forty-six years ago, at the Battle of Poltava, old General Poniatowski had fought at the side of Charles XII of Sweden against Peter the Great.

"War! That's all they talk about," Catherine said, rolling her eyes.

It was not the famous Russian victory over Sweden that excited her husband, not his grandfather's strategy, nor his political vision. All he wished to know from his Polish guest was how the defeated King of Sweden managed to fool the Russians and escape from the battlefield with General Poniatowski's help.

It was becoming too easy, I realized, reporting on the Grand Duke's blunders.

"This is not quite what the Empress should hear now," I warned.

"Why not, Varenka?" Catherine shot me a playful look. She bent over Bijou and scooped him up. "Perhaps this is exactly what she should hear!"

Tossed and tumbled, Bijou began to bark with excitement.

This hilarity was getting too loud. I put my finger on my lips.

Still laughing, Catherine set the dog down and embraced me. "I'm only teasing you, Varenka. Don't be so serious, please. Let's go to them now. Let's have some pleasure, shall we?"

"May we join you, gentlemen?" Catherine asked, as we entered the Grand Duke's study.

In the corner, *Das Fräulein* jumped up as if she saw a ghost.

The Grand Duke was tracing a line with his finger on a military map. He was back to wearing his blue Prussian uniform. I had seen his valet singe holes in it with burning coals, making them look like musket shots. Count Poniatowski stood beside him, nodding at something he had just heard. His colors were earthy, the warmth of clay and rust, his elegant fitted jacket lined with flecks of gold. At the sound of the Grand Duchess's voice, both men turned toward her. Two faces, one pockmarked and reddened with excitement, the other handsome and composed.

Count Poniatowski bowed. The Grand Duke flapped his hand, waving us in. *Das Fräulein* was staring at the floor.

I wondered what pleased Peter more, our unexpected visit, which—judging by his triumphant glare—he took for the manifestation of Catherine's marital interest, or *Das Fräulein*'s annoyance at it.

Catherine turned to Count Poniatowski.

"My husband assures me that you tell most amusing stories."

"I try to please." Count Poniatowski made another bow.

"Tell my wife of the *maire* of Paris," the Grand Duke demanded, chuckling.

Such exchanges must have happened before, I thought. There was a note of amused indulgence in Count Poniatowski's voice, a promise to please his host, even at the cost of repeating himself. His hand, emerging from a lace cuff, made sweeping movements as he spoke.

The mayor of Paris had received him in a pink bonnet, the Count told us, then led him to a room where chamber pots stood in a row, each half filled with sand. Every few minutes, the mayor begged his pardon and attempted to relieve himself. Each time into a different chamber pot.

The traveler's charm, I thought, listening to the waves of laughter that followed these stories. Stories meant to please. Stories interspaced with praises of Russian warmth, Russian hospitality, the glories of St. Petersburg, the beauty of Russian women.

An hour passed, giddy and fading fast. The dark paneling of the

Duke's study softened with early August sunshine; from the Oranienbaum gardens came the smoke of burning twigs.

It was Catherine who firmly took *Das Fräulein*'s arm and proposed
a stroll in the gardens. She wished to show Count Poniatowski her
new aviary. She had a pair of Chinese pheasants, she told him, some
quails, and the birds the Oranienbaum birdman had been trapping
for her all summer. Thrushes, magpies, orioles.

"You go," the Grand Duke said, ignoring the plea in *Das Fräulein*'s
eyes. "I've seen it already."

I, too, declined to join the party, eager for my chance to speak with
the Grand Duke alone.

On the following day, in Peterhof, I assured the Empress that there
would be no more complaints from anyone in the Grand Duke's retinue. My success was the result of a simple discovery. The Grand
Duke's servants had not been compensated for delivering food to the
Holsteiner troops. Once the Grand Duke agreed to remedy his over-
sight, the patriotic fervor of his footmen had died out and "serving the
Prussians" became just another duty in their daily rosters.

The Empress was pleased.

She didn't ask me about Catherine, and I didn't mention the
Grand Duchess or the Oranienbaum visitor. I didn't mind being ordered back to St. Petersburg, either. The temporary palace was still
half empty. The Imperial Suite was shrouded in linen coverings. The
thought of Darya there, alone, with no one but Masha and the servants for company was enough to make me uneasy.

In mid-August, Egor returned to St. Petersburg for the first time
since assuming his commission. Leaner and quieter, more of a guest
than a man of the house as he inspected our new quarters.

Through the windows came the sounds of the street, the beat of
horses' hoofs, the rattling of carriage wheels, the enticements of sellers. The floors were bare, smelling of pine resin, squeaking under each
step.

I watched Egor run his hand over the wooden wall of our small parlor, rub it with his finger. He knocked at it, judging its thickness.

"It's only for one year," I told him. "This is not home."

"Still better than the soldiers' barracks."

I could see the tensing of my husband's jaw when he said it.

During the day, Darya followed her father around, demanding stories of his army life, or showing him what she had learned in his absence: a cross-stitch, a French verse, a curtsy. Egor took her for walks along the Great Perspective Road, from which they returned with bags tucked under their arms. "Let me do it, Papa," Darya insisted, as she fished their treasures out to show me: a china doll with black shiny eyes, birch-bark boxes with dried fruit and comfits, a length of pearly pink satin for a dress, a string of red beads.

"For me. For you, Maman. For Masha."

The afternoons were still too mild for fires, too bright for candles. On the table in the parlor, Masha spread her treats: *bliny*, dumplings, bowls of steaming borscht, slices of smoked sturgeon. For Egor, for the visitors who flocked to our rooms, eager for the news.

War, I heard, demanded careful preparations. Gathering of strength. Loyalty. Fortitude. Strategy was paramount. One did not fight on a whim; one imposed the conditions on the enemy.

They listened, Egor's former comrades, most of whom I recognized from my husband's days in the guards. Among the newcomers were two Orlov brothers, Grigory and Alexei from the Izmailovsky Regiment. Both barely over twenty, both tall and powerfully muscular. Grigory was the more handsome of the two, though only because Alexei's face was disfigured by a scar that ran across his cheek. They moved into a house on Millionnaya Street, I had learned, ever since their parents died, and brought the other three Orlov brothers to live with them. Egor praised them for being "thick as thieves."

Crowding our small parlor, sprawled on the ottomans, perching on windowsills like some giant green birds, they all listened to my husband's words.

It was the politics that Egor found an irritation. The ever-changing orders. Having to tell his troops that yesterday's enemy had overnight become an ally. Soldiers needed a simpler world, clear-cut differences, plainly visible goals. They needed one voice issuing commands.

"Hear, hear," I heard when he finished.

Egor's former comrades did not lower their voices. They did not hide their tight smiles, the discontent in their eyes.

Bears in a pit, I thought. *Oblivious of the foxes intent on outsmarting them? Or ruthless enough to ignore the peril?*

On Egor's last evening, after Masha had put Darya to bed, my husband and I finally sat together alone.

It was of Darya that we spoke first, how her French improved, how her drawing master praised her talent for capturing likenesses of people and animals. How Egor's commission and my living at court now allowed us to put money aside for her dowry.

The possibilities flew quickly between us, without effort. A future added up, hopeful, expectant. But then silence came, hesitant at first, then darkening and swelling in the dusk.

One of the candles began to smoke. I rose to trim the wick, but Egor stopped me. His hand was cool and dry on mine.

"Please," he murmured, as if I intended to leave him alone.

I sat beside him.

A shadow flickered across Egor's face, making him look worn out, as if he had merely paused during some long trek he would soon have to resume.

In the quiet of the evening, his voice sounded hollow.

It was not just the politics that he could not understand, Egor told me. Not just the alliances, shifting from month to month, as if Russia had no one in charge.

Army sword belts fell apart after first washing. The last batch of new recruits had to practice with wooden muskets, for there was a shortage of real ones. There were limits to sacrifice. What was happening in the palace? Was Mother Russia forgetting her sons?

I stirred and cast my eyes toward the door.

"Hush, Egor. There are no safe rooms here," I whispered. "No one is ever alone."

He gave me a long look of bewildered hurt. As if my words were an accusation. As if I did not know him at all.

"You didn't marry a coward," he said.

I felt the grip of his hand on mine. Stronger than I'd remembered it.

Later, after Egor had left, I recalled these words every time I slipped into my bed at night, snuggling in the familiar spot beside my daughter's warm, dreaming body. I turned them in my head, assessed their weight.

A boast?

Or a promise?

There is one more memory of this summer—of Darenka, in the Oranienbaum aviary, among parrots, parakeets, canaries, helping Catherine feed them, holding out her small hand, hoping they would come and peck at the seeds she held. The memory of my daughter asking Catherine if she could let the birds out, into the garden, where they could fly where they wished to.

I recall Catherine's warning.

When she was a child, she, too, once wanted to free birds from her aunt's aviary. And so she'd left the door to the cage open.

"And what happened?" Darya asked her.

I froze, knowing too well that Catherine would not indulge my daughter's desire for smooth and joyful endings.

"To me or to the birds?" she asked. "I was sent to bed without supper, and that was that. The birds did not fare so well."

I watched Darya's face as she pictured the images of Catherine's story. Parrots pecked to death by other birds. Sparrows and thrushes her aunt had saved from death an easy prey for cats and neighborhood boys. The bloody scraps, the feathers flying. A cat with a limp bird in its mouth, surprised, perhaps, by the lack of struggle.

"You won't ever do that to my birds, Darenka, will you?" Catherine asked.

I saw my daughter shake her head, stern and pensive.

In September, the court returned to St. Petersburg and settled down in the temporary palace on the Great Perspective Road. The entire east wing of the palace was taken by the Imperial Suite, the nursery, and the rooms of Elizabeth's ladies-in-waiting. The Grand Duke and his entourage were allotted an apartment right beside the Imperial Bedroom.

Peter was not pleased. His Holsteiner officers had been billeted in the house across the street. *Das Fräulein* and his maids-of-honor had to share one room. He had no place for his military displays and his maps.

The walls were thin. If he sneezed, the Empress would hear it.

There was no room in the temporary palace for the government offices, either. The Chancellor and his clerks took over a house on Millionnaya Street. "Noisy," Bestuzhev complained when I inquired of the new quarters. The hammering and the sawing in the old Winter Palace went on day and night. Monsieur Rastrelli was determined to move the workers inside before the first frosts.

In the palace on the Great Perspective Road, Catherine's suite— four large antechambers and two inner rooms with an alcove—was in the west wing, close to mine. The Empress, I thought, still wished to keep her far away from her child.

With the arrival of the court, the calm of the summer months ended. Once again I was at the Empress's beck and call. A servant and a spy.

On the day the Empress arrived, a thief had been caught in the palace yard, his pockets bulging with silverplate. The fireplaces smoked, the floors squeaked. The antechambers teemed with visitors and petitioners. Ambassadors, Envoys, foreign visitors rubbed shoulders with portrait painters and carpenters, nobles and merchants, hoping for a commission. Wisely, Monsieur Rastrelli was keeping out of sight.

"Send them all away," the Empress ordered.

I did.

By the time I returned, the Empress was lying on her bed, propped up by two fat pillows. Her hands and feet were swollen, her face oily with sweat. One of her maids was sweeping broken glass from the carpet. Another was trying to draw the curtains tighter.

"Where is my rosewood dresser, Varvara?" the Empress screamed. "I want it here. Right now."

She didn't wish to hear any explanations.

I sent the footmen to the attic for the dresser. I waved the frightened maids away.

I spoke of good omens. A litter of kittens, a new moon, a four-leaved clover. The cuckoo who counted out the twenty years still left to her. I kept my voice soft and soothing. Next door, in the nursery, the Grand Duke Paul was whimpering, protesting some ministration he would have to submit to. The gossip was that the baby was easily terrified and woke up screaming at night.

Sir Charles Hanbury-Williams was as frequent a visitor at the Great Perspective Road as he had been in the old Winter Palace. As everyone expected, the colonial war between England and France had spilled into Europe, whipping up old conflicts, forcing new alliances. The British Ambassador was trying to secure a treaty between England and Russia, a treaty that Chancellor Bestuzhev was ready to support but the pro-French Shuvalovs tried to kill.

It always came to this, a battle for Elizabeth's mind, a battle in which all moves were permitted. Visitors followed visitors, all armed with flattery and gifts, all hoping to sway her in their direction. To Masha's delight, even my paltry position in the Imperial Bedroom merited baskets of delicacies and toiletries, gifts of kid gloves and ostrich feathers, lengths of lace and fancy ribbons. All to buy a chance to cross the Empress's path, a hint when to come and when to wait.

Sir Charles flattered the Empress shamelessly, declared himself smitten by her beauty, longing for her presence, quoting her own words, which he claimed were "unforgettable."

I had seen her take this in like an eager puppy.

Sir Charles's specialty was gossip from all the European courts he had resided at or visited, gossip he milked for all its worth. I heard him assure Elizabeth that Berlin was a mere hamlet beside the magnificence of St. Petersburg. Without its garrison of fourteen thousand, the German capital was practically empty. And scrawny Prussian women could not compare to Russian beauties.

Polish royal hunts were no match for Russian ones, either. "The sitting-down hunts," Sir Charles called them. In the Polish forest of Białowieża, boars, wolves, and bears were put in cages so that the King of Poland could shoot at them upon their release. "No chase, no thrill. Your Imperial Highness would find it tediously boring."

The Empress made a little snort of pleasure.

Once I walked in on the two of them talking of England. Elizabeth was convinced that the Russian troops could march all the way from St. Petersburg to London in two weeks.

"I'd have to agree," Sir Charles said with a deep bow. He was not going to mention the existence of the sea that would have interfered with Elizabeth's will.

It was after one of Sir Charles's visits that I remarked to him how well he kept the Empress entertained.

"I aim to please, Madame Malikina," he replied, with a twinkle in his dark blue eyes and a flash of his monocle. "Though I would not like the Empress to question me too closely on whose pleasure is most dear to me."

I hesitated.

"You must excuse my directness, Madame," he said. "But your devotion to the Grand Duchess has not escaped me."

"I, too, aim to please," I replied, impassively.

His full face lit up, smoothing the wrinkles around his eyes, an intricate network of laugh lines that gave him the appearance of a naughty boy up to some prank. "Then we have more in common than I could ever have imagined."

I was not surprised that evening when a messenger from the British Embassy delivered a case of claret and a basket of preserves.

By mid-October, the court had settled into a routine of receptions and soirees, Russian Theater nights, broken by frequent trips to Peterhof when the Empress wished for more comfort.

For Elizabeth it was the time of card laying. Seven of hearts: broken promises. Ace of spades: bad news. Six of spades: gradual improvement. Ten of clubs: unexpected gift. For a while the jack of spades appeared in these readings in awkward places, overshadowed by doubt. When she changed to the tarot deck, it was the tower that showed up repeatedly, another sign of tensions brewing, a prediction of a violent release.

Fortune-tellers, bearded *dziady, babas* with toothless mouths, mumbled their warnings of a treacherous woman, a child's life threatened with a sword, a sudden flight of seagulls. The business of the Russian court hung on the Devil's bile and the shadows cast by angel wings. Audiences were canceled at the last moment; urgent documents were left unsigned. A departure was either rushed or delayed, a route diverted, a return postponed.

The Chancellor bristled at the delays. Whatever papers he had brought, Elizabeth had me tell him, could wait for another day. Ruling the Empire had been reduced to a waiting game. Swooping on the moment of Elizabeth's benign mood, softened by an auspicious card, a dream.

Many a time I saw him walk away, dismissed abruptly from Elizabeth's rooms, his shoulders stooped, rolls of papers under his arm. Once when we found ourselves alone, he could not restrain himself any longer.

"Did you manage to remind the Grand Duchess of my profound respect for her?" he asked.

I said I did.

"What did she say?" he demanded.

"Nothing."

He was waiting for me to say more, but I didn't. Anticipating his disappointment I slyly glanced at his face, but all I saw was a little light of contempt.

By the end of October, the evenings were windy and icy-cold. Horses, their backs covered with blankets, spewed soft mist with every breath. On the Great Perspective Road, coachmen in long sheepskin coats stomped their feet, slapped their palms together, casting anxious glances at the palace doors, waiting for their masters to emerge. Every so often a hand dipped inside a coat to extract a flask for a quick sip.

"What are they doing?" Catherine asked as we slipped secretly out of the palace.

"It's vodka. To keep them warm."

"The Grand Duchess deserves to live a little, too," Prince Lev Naryshkin had said. It was his idea, these evening gatherings of friends in his sister's house on the embankment, as soon as the imperial carriage left for Peterhof. "No one needs to know."

I saw the flash of childish joy in Catherine's eyes at his words. Leaving the palace without permission from the Empress? In disguise?

"Will you help me, Varenka?" she asked.

I swore to her that I would keep her safe.

I kept my word.

I still smile at the memory, our hands hastily undoing the buttons of our gowns, letting the petticoats fall, lacing our stays tighter to flatten our breasts. Hers refusing to yield until I remembered the length of wide linen ribbon the midwife had given her after the *accouchement* to wrap herself with. I had smuggled the uniforms of the Preobrazhensky Guards into Catherine's room, and now we both donned our disguises: white breeches, black jackboots, the fitted tunics of dark green woolen cloth that made us look so lithe and light.

An officer and his escort, ready for their night on the town.

I remember Catherine, standing at attention, clicking her heels, saying, "To think that everything might become useful"—meaning the hours she had spent practicing Peter's drills, presenting an imaginary musket, learning to walk with the arrogant wide stride of a man.

I remember a knock at the door, a moment of panic, then the unsure voice of Madame Vladislavova asking through the door if she would be needed again before the morning.

"No, no. Go to sleep. I have everything," Catherine assured her.

The service door, warped already, opened with a piercing squeak. Shielding the candle flame with my hand, I led Catherine through the corridor, past a hall where a sleeping groom opened his eyes, gave us a dull glance, then turned away into his dreams. We hurried into the street, the frigid winter air pricking our lungs. The rays of the moon lit up the fresh layer of snow.

On the Great Perspective Road a rattling carriage made the horses raise their heads. One of the coachmen, well warmed by the vodka in his veins, crooned:

Be so kind, oh joy of mine
As to try an apple from my tree

The singer's large mustache was frosty white.

"A night out, officers?" he muttered. He looked down at our jackboots, unable to decide if we were trouble or an opportunity.

"What do you want for a few good sips from your bottle?" I called up to him.

Before I could stop her, Catherine fished a coin from her pocket.

The bottle changed hands quickly. It was a vile concoction. A fiery snake, a viper going straight into our brains.

Catherine's eyes flamed with joy. Her gloved hand grabbed mine, strong and firm.

They were waiting for Catherine at Princess Naryshkina's palace.

"My sister brought your *bijou* here." Prince Naryshkin meant Count Poniatowski. "Anna and I expect a hefty reward for my powers of persuasion." In the next room someone sang "Awake Awake." Someone else demanded more champagne.

I turned to leave, promising to wait for the Grand Duchess at the palace. To make sure no one saw her return.

"No, Varenka," Catherine said. "I want you here, at my side."

Hesitation flickered in Prince Naryshkin's eyes. A warning for a bookbinder's daughter to beware of recklessly crossing boundaries. But the warning died as swiftly as it had appeared.

"Madame Malikina is most welcome."

I followed Catherine into the Naryshkin parlor, taking note of the velvet burgundy curtains drawn over the windows, the opulence of the soft carpet and gilded armchairs. On the marble mantel a golden clock chimed nine, the simpering cherub perched on top glittering in candlelight.

The guests all gathered around Catherine, maids-of-honor, princes and counts, raising champagne glasses, laughing as Prince Naryshkin did his imitation of the Grand Duke playing the violin, struggling not to fall down.

Count Poniatowski was their guest of honor. Impeccable in his white jacket trimmed with silver thread, he rose at the sight of Catherine. A smile lit his handsome face.

"Your Highness," he said.

"Catherine," she corrected. Christian names only tonight, she demanded. No titles. No fuss. No ceremony. Just Stanislav, Anna, Lev, Varvara.

I took a step back, into the shadows.

"I'll call you by your true name, then. Sophie," Count Poniatowski said, bowing to kiss Catherine's hand.

Was it the uniform? The boldness of disguise? The freedom from hooped dresses and petticoats? The swirl of vodka in her head?

Clicking the heels of her jackboots, Catherine lifted Stanislav's hand to her own lips.

For an instant he hesitated. Then his look of surprise melted in sheer delight, erasing the clanking of food trays, glances of other guests straying toward them, erupting in knowing smiles.

The hostess kept ringing for the servants, summoning more and more food. *Botvinia* with salmon and parsley, honeyed cucumber, *bliny* dipped in sour cream. Borscht and fish soup. Quails. Stewed mushrooms. Astrakhan grapes.

Catherine in the Preobrazhensky uniform, seated in a chintz-covered armchair, ankle crossed on her knee, seemed both recognizable and unknown. It was Stanislav she spoke to most often.

"So what else have you learned from your travels?"

"That people have far more in common than they believe. That all societies, no matter how different, tend to call good what they consider useful for their survival."

Her questions were the most pressing. Her laughter the most resonant.

They read the same books; they admired the same *philosophes*. They agreed that wars could often bring about unforeseen progress. They declared their fascination with paradoxes: A man says, "I am lying." Is his statement true or false?

True.

Then he is not lying.

False.

Then he is lying.

Neither true or false? But how is that possible? How can something be true and false at the same time?

Their heads, his dark and powdered, hers black and shiny, leaned toward each other. I listened to their voices and to a crack of silence between them. I watched them withdraw from the safety of the gathering, melt into shadows. Over a glass shelf covered with curiosities, by the window with a view of the Neva, I heard them exchange words that signaled the quickening of danger.

"Must duty wipe out all happiness?"

"Should marriage be a prison?"

It was well past three in the morning when, heavy from food and wine, Catherine and I set off for the Great Perspective Road. Stanislav and Lev Naryshkin insisted on seeing us off. By the embankment, the shores of the Neva had frozen already, the northern night broken only by the fires the sentries lit, in search of warmth.

Catherine and Stanislav walked slowly ahead, stretching the remnants of the night. Lev Naryshkin, forced to keep me company, tried chasing me with his groping hands and vodka breath, until I pushed him away.

I thought of Egor, freezing in some distant camp. *No rashes or itches so far,* he had written in one of his short letters, *for which the Russian soldiers can thank the heat of the banya.* One of the letters contained a drawing for Darenka, showing her Papa shoeing a horse. *Trying to learn everything,* the caption said. *To be ready when the need arises.*

The Great Perspective Road was deserted by that hour, the sleighs all gone, leaving behind trampled snow and hardened balls of horse dung, but I insisted that Stanislav and Lev must leave us and let us walk on alone.

"The things Stanislav has seen, Varenka," Catherine told me as we hurried together toward the palace. "The people who love him!"

He had seen the pink dawn over Île de la Cité, the blossom-lined paths of the Tuileries, the tamed cranes in the *ménagerie de Versailles.* The birds follow the visitors there, he had said, for they want to be noticed.

"Do you know what else he said, Varenka? 'Just say the word, Sophie, and I'll take you to see them.'"

Catherine and Stanislav. When he smiled, she smiled; when she frowned, he became thoughtful. *So why do I also remember sadness?*

Accounts of the Lisbon earthquake were trickling in every day, hushed, impossible. A hundred thousand perishing amid the debris. Homes crumbling, crushing those inside. Bodies piling up, mountains of twisted limbs, cast aside by the surgeons as they tried to stave off gangrene.

"How can it be, Maman?" Darya asked me, afraid to fall asleep. "How can the earth move?"

I held her in my arms, wishing her never to know the swiftness with which life can turn upside down. I whispered promises that earthquakes did not come to St. Petersburg, that such grand upheavals happened far, far away. "I'm here with you," I promised my daughter. "I won't go anywhere."

It soothed her for a few days, but then came the night when she woke up screaming, "Papa is far, far away!"

Nothing I did or said that night would console her. It was Masha's voice that finally lulled her to sleep with the old song she used to sing to Egor when he was little:

In the night, when the seas are rolling in
In the night, when the stars are shining clear

All Catherine's escapades that winter began with furtive signs exchanged among her small coterie led by Prince Naryshkin. A tap on the right shoulder at the opera, a beauty spot on the chin. No words were necessary. She perfected the art of feigning fatigue, locking the door to her bedroom, demanding to be left alone, so that she could sneak out in disguise.

Whenever I could, I helped her. But there was only one more time that December that I accompanied Catherine to the Naryshkins' parlor.

Stanislav was already there when we arrived. I caught a whiff of violet water, mixed with snuff. Behind him, Sir Charles hovered.

"Look at them, Varvara Nikolayevna," the British Ambassador said to me, drawing me aside.

Catherine and Stanislav had moved across the room, into the shadows beyond the circle of candlelight. That night her disguise was a simple maid's dress, hair tied into a knot, so plain-looking beside Stanislav's elegant court jacket, the color of ripe aubergines. Deep purple, I decided, suited him better than white and silver. Their heads touched.

At least they were away from the palace, I thought.

"Our children," Sir Charles called them.

It was impossible not to look.

Outside the parlor, the Neva, frozen solid, snowbanks lining the streets; inside, the warmth of the tiled stoves, the smell of melting wax, and the flurry of voices. It didn't surprise me how quickly the talk turned to the news from Lisbon.

"Fate," I recall Stanislav saying that evening in the Naryshkin parlor. "The divine plan for which there is no remedy."

"But surely God teaches us lessons," a voice argued.

Stanislav shook his head. "Lessons for which we are not ready and which we cannot comprehend. In spite of all the signs, premonitions, the movements of the stars and planets."

"Let's drink to ignorance, then," Prince Naryshkin quipped, raising his glass. "My virtue of choice." At the other end of the room, someone giggled.

Catherine was shaking her head.

"No," she said. *Too loud*, I thought. *Too impatient.*

There was a hush.

"A catastrophe is not merely an act of blind fate," she continued. "And we *can* learn from it."

Her eyes brightened as she spoke; her voice soared. Her argument was simple: Those in Lisbon on the day of the quake were doomed, but not by fate. Mankind could think ahead, prepare for contingencies. If those who planned the city believed in smaller settlements, in living closer to nature, in lighter houses, evacuation would have been possible.

"It is in the human power," she insisted, "to limit suffering."

"Hear, hear," Sir Charles echoed. The British Ambassador, too, believed in the power of human will. "We have faculties of reason," he said. "We have traits of character we can change."

I watched Stanislav's cheeks flush. "Fate does not free us from trying," he countered, "but we are not omnipotent. Think of the stray bullet that ends a soldier's life. How can his will stop it?"

Voices rose, some puzzled, some adamant. "What if he ducks?" I heard someone ask. Someone quacked in response. Someone else called for more civility.

I was no longer listening.

Was it will that took me out of the bookbinding workshop on Vasilevsky Island into this fashionable salon filled with people for whom my father would have been nothing but a tradesman? Or fate? Was it will or fate that placed me, a bookbinder's daughter, among these perfumed counts and countesses? What would I hear about myself if I were listening through the panels of their elegant salons? For them, was I a nobody always trying to put herself in the Grand Duchess's good graces? A guard's wife desperate for advancement? A spy?

The parlor shrank and expanded, dimmed and brightened. Unwanted, other thoughts rushed in, too. Was I Elizabeth's only tongue in this room? Was anyone else watching? Reporting the many indiscretions committed so very recklessly? And to whom? To the Empress? To the Chancellor?

In a corner Lev Naryshkin was amusing his guests with a crude imitation of Elizabeth's walk, his chin held up to hide the "turkey's throat." Who was making note of those who were laughing?

"You've grown pale, Barbara." Stanislav's voice broke into my thoughts. "Is anything the matter?"

Barbara, he called me. My Polish name.

"Be careful," I whispered, dizzy from my thoughts.

"I am careful," he replied.

He knew what could happen to a foreigner who lets himself go too far with the Grand Duchess of All the Russias. He knew of Elizabeth's wrath. Of the knout that breaks the back. He knew of the frozen fields of Siberia.

He brushed my hand with his. He smiled.

No one will find out, I promised Catherine. Not the Empress, not Bestuzhev. Catherine and Stanislav became my secret.

Alone with the Empress, watching her cradle Catherine's son in her arms, I began mentioning Lev Naryshkin's name.

"He meows," I said, "before he knocks on the Grand Duchess's door. This is their secret sign. That's when she lets him in." I wished the Empress to believe that Naryshkin was Catherine's lover. Stanislav, I wished her to think, was of no importance. Merely a foreign guest in awe of Russian splendors. Amazed and humbled by everything he saw.

"Should I tell the Grand Duchess that Your Highness is not pleased?"

"No, Varvara. Let her play."

There was more, I told the Empress. Lev Naryshkin was a philanderer. Catherine was on course for another bitter disappointment; she was wasting her time on the intrigues of the boudoir. Time, I hinted, she will not have for politics.

Elizabeth listened, still deciding what use all this was to her, what sordid details she could still get out of me. I could see it in her eyes, watery blue, shiny, studying me.

I thought how the guards raged when they heard that at the *banya*, *Das Fräulein* now called Catherine "a scheming bitch."

"She slips out at night in disguise," I told the Empress. "In a guard's uniform . . . or in a maid's dress. He waits for her in the street. They go to his sister's palace. She never even asks me about her son now. . . . She told the Grand Duke she had a headache and could not visit him. She doesn't sleep much."

Elizabeth looked me up and down, making her calculations. This is how it was: Women had to be watched. The one overlooked could be the most treacherous of all.

A soft, malicious chuckle, spiced with jealousy. "And what does my nephew Peter say about Naryshkin's latest conquest?"

"Peter doesn't know."

"Then he should."

"Yes, Your Highness," I agreed without hesitation. "I'll make sure the Grand Duke is informed."

Another pause, another chance to slip in a few chosen words. I spoke of good omens: Darya's dream of a baby with a golden crown. A baby just like the Grand Duke Paul. The future revealed?

"Only to the eyes of innocent children," Elizabeth said and sighed.

The mere mention of the baby Grand Duke always altered the Empress's voice, made it gentle, unsure, almost puzzled. The Tsarevitch smiled in his sleep. He cried when she picked him up.

In his great-aunt's arms, Paul blew bubbles of spit and pulled at her hair. He was declared musical, like his father, for he moved his hips to the sounds of the fiddle as he crawled and he loved banging cabinet doors. He was brave, for he no longer shrieked with fear when the nursemaids sat him on the big rocking horse that stood in the center of the nursery.

Catherine was not allowed to witness her son's first smile, nor when he raised his head or sat up by himself. In the first year of Paul's life, she had seen him nine times only, and never alone. Her presence did not make his face light up with recognition. Her voice did not lull him to sleep.

"You cannot do anything about it," I told her. "But you can bear it in mind."

A bargain had been forced upon her. As long as the Grand Duchess did not try to take her son back, Elizabeth would let her have her trivial indiscretions.

In the winter of 1755, Catherine no longer cried about it.

One morning, in the first week of December, I entered Catherine's bedroom and smelled the sweet scent of violet water. This is when I knew that I had not foreseen everything.

"Was Stanislav here?" I felt my throat tighten.

"He loves me, Varenka," Catherine said, her eyes besotted, glowing. "And I love him."

"Oh, Catherine! When did he come here?"

"Lev brought him. He pushed him in." She giggled, her hand resting on her lips. "It was all his fault."

She sprawled on the bed, in her cream-colored satin nightdress with pink ribbons, her black hair loose and tangled.

"Did anyone see him?"

"No, Varenka," she answered. "He left through there." She pointed to the window.

I prayed Stanislav was wearing a hooded cloak that hid his face.

I didn't tell Catherine of the attic above the rooms, the loose boards that made it easy to see what was happening below. I scrutinized the bedroom for the traces of the night. The stained sheets, that sweet smell of his eau de cologne.

My face must have revealed my terror.

"It was late. No one saw him, Varenka. There is no need to fret!"

I sprayed the sheets with Catherine's own perfume. I made her sit at her escritoire and write a note to Lev Naryshkin. *Beloved friend . . . your most precious visit . . . still thinking of you.* It would be left on the desk for the maids to see.

She watched me, bemused, shaking her head.

"If we are lucky," I said, shivering, "we might fool the spies—this time. But only just."

There is nothing that divides the court more than the frenzy of approaching war. Prussia, lean and hungry, was casting its eyes toward its neighbors. Everyone agreed that this was dangerous for Russia, for it upset the balance of power. But this was the extent of agreement.

Depending on whom one listened to, restoring this balance called for different steps.

Arguments sparked.

In the New World the British were relentlessly pushing the French from the colonies. Should Russia cast its lot with France—as the Shuvalov faction advocated—or should she sign a treaty with England, as the Chancellor argued? Who would be more likely, when the time comes, to help clip soaring Prussian wings?

The inner rooms of the Imperial Suite turned into a war cabinet, each faction trying to sway Elizabeth's mind. Ordered to keep all visitors away, to watch out for anyone trying to sneak within earshot, I heard muffled voices behind closed doors. Bestuzhev's, Vorontzov's, the Shuvalovs'. Angry words, threatening, pleading, faltering into resigned silence: *a deal . . . a treaty . . . salvation . . . treason.*

The Chancellor was winning. With Sir Charles's help, the Russian treaty with England had been negotiated, written and ready for the royal and imperial signatures. But as the papers were couriered between London and St. Petersburg, another seismic shift ripped the shadowy mesh of diplomatic possibilities. Without warning, the King of England withdrew from an alliance with Russia and offered his support to Prussia and Frederick the Great.

The palace seethed with injured pride, and Elizabeth hotly declared the British Ambassador an unwelcome guest.

The Shuvalovs rejoiced.

The Empress was getting restless. Was it because of the British treachery? I wondered. Or the inevitability of battles that could be lost? In one of her dreams, someone whose face she could not see handed her a note. *You have taken what was not yours to take. Your days are numbered. Russia will pay for your sins.*

"It was him. It was Ivanushka." She muttered the name of the deposed Emperor. "The guards say that lights and shadows come to him, that he sees the future."

At midnight, having sent her Favorite away to his rooms, she demanded plates of food: *selyodka*, the fat herring from the White Sea; Russian bread smeared with Altai honey; sugared plums dipped in brandy; nuts in drops of chocolate.

Unable to sleep, she wanted to hear of Ksenia, the heartbroken young widow who gave away all her possessions, put on her late husband's uniform, and roamed the streets of St. Petersburg. Massaging Elizabeth's swollen feet, I told her stories of Ksenia's miracles: A baker from Mieshchansky Street who gave her some bread began to prosper himself. A hackney driver who offered her a lift made more money in a day than he had made all month. A mother followed Ksenia with her little son, begging her to bless him, and when she did, the child recovered instantly from rickets.

My rewards were a sigh, a few words muttered under her breath, or her imperial hand, wrinkled and swollen, extended so that I could kiss it before she sent me away.

The Chancellor's diplomatic failure had been the source of much merriment among the Shuvalovs' supporters. The Old Fox was losing his famed touch. His rabid distrust of France had clouded his political judgment. Where were his spies when Russia needed them? How much had the British paid *him*?

Stories flowed of Bestuzhev's servants dispatched to the taverns to search for their drunk master. Once, a hackney driver brought him home at dawn, half-naked and dripping with water, muttering curses about some Gypsy's tricks. Ivan Shuvalov's uncle called the Chancellor a "has-been" in the Empress's presence, although she had pretended not to hear.

The Old Fox, I heard, was spent and tired.

He would stop me in the corridor, smelling of camphor and expensive musk, asking if the Grand Duchess was still infatuated with Naryshkin.

A sense of exhilaration was urging me on. A spymaster can be deceived, too.

"Oh, yes," I assured Bestuzhev. I told him how the Grand Duchess and Prince Naryshkin sat together in the opera box, laughing at *Das Fräulein*'s derriere swaying as she walked. "Like a horse the Paris brewers would love," I said in my best imitation of Lev's crackling banter. "Not that Naryshkin has ever been to Paris."

The Chancellor managed a faint, sour smile. Powder could no longer mask the bloated, ruddy skin of his face.

"He wears a blue waistcoat when they are to meet at the opera," I continued. "Green for the Russian Theater. It's not love, though the Grand Duchess likes to say she loves him. She is still young. She wants to dance. She wants to be told she is pretty."

I met his eye.

I smiled.

The spymaster's own lesson: Good liars look you in the eye and smile.

He'd taught me well.

"Talk to her of love if this is what she wants to hear, Varvara Nikolayevna, but keep reminding her that her husband does not know what it means to rule. The Empress is not going to live forever. Politics is Catherine's game, and she knows that."

"Tell her I'm on her side."

"Tell her she only has to give me a sign."

"Tell her she needs me."

Among the daze of tulle, lace, and ribbons, I covered my lips with a fan and mouthed my promises before turning away.

For me, Sir Charles's disgrace at the Russian court brought many discreet invitations to the British Embassy.

Sir Charles needed a go-between to carry his words to the Chancellor and Catherine. I needed stories about him to tell the Empress. For, having banned him from her sight, she now craved gossip that would justify her anger.

Our own private treaty, we called it. Our alliance.

The hours we spent together were rare islands of calm in these fe-

verish days, for the Ambassador cared as much as I did for keeping
Catherine and Stanislav's secrets. In the Skavronsky palace he rented
on the Great Perspective Road, liveried footmen came and went, carrying refreshments, while we talked.

He had made inquiries about me, I was to discover, for he kept
referring to Egor's military achievements and his prospects. "Field
Marshal someday, perhaps?" he would say with a nonchalant gesture
of his hand.

Listening to Sir Charles was like listening to a prophet who demanded that I follow him to the top of a mountain to see beyond
what I'd ever seen before, to survey all the roads I could take.

"The Grand Duchess will not stay the Grand Duchess forever,
pani Barbara," he said. Like Stanislav, he now used my Polish name.
"But she will always need friends."

The court in St. Petersburg was but one player on the chessboard
of Europe, he told me. Russia was like Lisbon before the earthquake—on the surface, people went about their business, but underneath, great forces were shifting, ready to collapse or explode. The
outcomes could surprise us all.

"The land of your father is in need of a wise ruler, so that no one
ever again will have to leave Poland in search of prosperity elsewhere."

He knew how to find words that went right to my heart.

Catherine the Empress of Russia. Stanislav the King of Poland.

Some dreams are more seductive than love.

We hardly ever spoke of ourselves during this time, though Sir
Charles did get me to confess the forced circumstances of my marriage, and he acknowledged the existence of Lady Frances, with whom
he exchanged dispatches as if she were a business partner rather than
his wife. In the cut-crystal tumblers, Hungarian claret shimmered
ruby red as we drank to our ambitions.

To the future Empress!

To the future King!

To their friendship!

To their love!

"My political son," Sir Charles called Stanislav. Saturn was in the ascendant when he was born. The sign of the return of the golden age, of triumph over obstacles. Some saw a crown over his head. A double crown.

"Stanislav is not a dreamer. He knows the limitations of your country, Barbara. He wants an enlightened leadership, and an end to corruption. He is not alone. He has the support of his uncles, the Czartoryski clan. This is why he is here in St. Petersburg—to learn what is possible."

To make sure the servants didn't understand us, we always referred to the Empress as "the Great Obstacle" or "Yesterday." Catherine was Colette, Stanislav "*Le Cordon Bleu*," the Grand Duke "the Soldier." The Chancellor was "the Old Fox," or simply "the Devil." "The Dream" meant a strong Poland and an enlightened Russia walking together hand in hand.

In these tête-à-têtes it all seemed possible: Catherine becoming the Empress of Russia, using her influence to have Stanislav elected the King of Poland. The two of them, united in love, bound by trust, ruling two great nations, in unity and peace. We hardly ever mentioned Peter, as if his withdrawal into oblivion was already certain. Sometimes I could almost see him in Oranienbaum with *Das Fräulein* and his fiddle, building a model fortress or marching his Holsteiners in perfect formations, a child left to his own happy amusements.

How many times we drank to "the Dream," buoyed by the signs that Providence itself supported us in these chilly days of winter! Empress Elizabeth was fading. Her shortness of breath was growing worse. Once I saw her surgeon's assistant leaving her bedroom with a big bowl of yellowish liquid. I didn't need to ask. Her swelling belly threatened to burst and had to be tapped.

Catherine told me that Ivan Shuvalov had come up to her and asked why she avoided him. "Let me take this very moment to express my admiration for you," the Empress's lover had said.

Stanislav told Sir Charles that the Polish King was dying, which meant another royal election. His uncles wrote from Warsaw that he should consider returning to Poland, "for such opportunities will not last forever."

By March clouds swept in from the Gulf of Finland, dumping more snow on the streets and frozen gardens of St. Petersburg. Sir Charles and I were still carrying on our feverish conversations, the consultations of the demiurges bent over the blueprint of their new world.

Dangerous delusions, I say now, for we were merely trying to cover our own impotence with these plans for those we held so dear.

In the first week of March, Monsieur Rastrelli declared that the old Winter Palace—which only months before was still to form part of the new structure—had become an obstacle to his grand vision. The ceilings were too low, the foundations too flimsy. If he was to deliver what was expected of him, everything would have to be razed.

"Another year," he said, pointing to the model two attendants carried into the Imperial Suite, drawing Elizabeth's attention to the magnificent windows he envisioned. "Some might call it a significant delay, Your Highness," he said, his vigilant eyes scanning Elizabeth's face. "I would call it an unavoidable necessity."

The Empress paced the room in anger.

Monsieur Rastrelli was not pleading for time. He pleaded for a chance to make the Russian palace grander than Versailles. Everything in it would draw a visitor's attention. Quadratura techniques would "open up" walls and ceilings, turn flat surfaces into domes and galleries filled with golden light. Sculptures would capture movement in stone. Paintings and tapestries would entice with scenes of passions so grand that no eye could glide over them unseeing.

Rich, he promised. Golden. Bright.

Work would go on through the winter, he continued. Stoves would be installed as soon as the external structure was ready, so that the plasterers and carpenters could move in, come the first frosts.

"The jewel of Your Majesty's palaces," he crooned. "A tribute to Russia's power. A setting worthy of the victories that will soon come."

The silence that fell was long and tense. On the Empress's face, promises of glory battled with her impatience; her hand flexed like a cat's claws.

But then Elizabeth smiled, and I knew that the temporary palace would have to serve the court for a long time.

For Darya's name day, Egor sent her a headdress embroidered with tiny pearls. *To adorn my dark-eyed flower,* he had written.

As hard as a helmet, I thought, as I watched my daughter put the headdress on, slipping it over her hair, as black and shiny as her father's.

"Will you take me to the Empress?" Darya asked, holding the headdress in place with her hand. "I want to show it to her." She was twisting her body in front of the mirror, trying to see herself from the side. Catherine had once told her that she had a Grecian profile.

"Why would the Empress wish to see it?"

"Because she is my friend."

"Who told you that?"

"She did."

"When?"

"When I was playing in the yard. She called me. She gave me a sweet apple. She said I could come to see her if I wished."

"Did she say it, or did you ask?"

The signs of impatience: eyes cast to the ceiling, fingers clutching at the hem of her dress.

"I didn't ask. But I *wanted* her to say it."

"You must never bother Her Highness, Darya. The Empress has little time for trifles."

A moment of calculation, doubt, washed out of my daughter's eyes as swiftly as it had appeared. "Papa's gift is not a trifle."

"No, it isn't. But you are just a child."

"I'm older than baby Paul. And I don't cry as he does."

"You cried when you were his age."

"That I don't remember."

"But I do," I said, wishing for Egor's presence, for his words to add weight to mine.

The headdress, carefully wrapped in twill, went back into its box. I tried to think how soon Darya could wear it. On Sunday, perhaps? To church?

I hid a smile as my daughter made a stern face. "You are just a child," she murmured in imitation of me, a finger raised in the air. "When will Papa come back?"

"Soon."

"Tomorrow?"

"No, not tomorrow."

She turned away quickly, to hide childish tears, her hand clasping mine, and I suddenly remembered my mother's tapered fingers curling around mine.

To make the temporary palace habitable for at least another year, carpenters reinforced the weakest walls, added a few partitions, replaced boards crusted with mold.

There was much grumbling at the announcement of the delay in construction, but I liked anything that made it easier to hide Catherine's love. I blessed the chaos, the constant flutter of plans, abandoned and resumed. Orders were forgotten almost as soon as they were issued. The hairballs gathered in the corners; half-packed trunks stood abandoned in the attic; rooms were reassigned at an hour's notice to escape leaky walls.

The Empress may have granted her permission for the delays, but that did not make her less irritable. For days after Monsieur's Rastrelli's visit, anything could trigger a vicious fit of temper. She dismissed a chambermaid who tarried with teacups. She slapped a hairdresser who took too long curling her hair.

I, too, felt her anger when I could not come up with instant answers to her constant questions. A pinch of my arm. A shove. "Is *she*
still with Naryshkin?"

"Yes, Your Highness."

"She goes to see him at his palace?"

"Yes."

"Does he think I might make her Regent? Does he want to rule
with her, that clown?"

"I don't know, Your Majesty."

"Then find out, you fool. Are they plotting against me? Is this British traitor helping her? I want to know what she is thinking."

I ducked to avoid a snuffbox hurled with a scream.

"Hurry up! You are not the only tongue I have!"

Some stories pacify more than others: lowly horseboys leaving the
British Embassy at dawn with cheeky smiles, goldplate under their
coats. Sir Charles cursing his own king. Saying that Britain was making a big mistake by kissing the Prussian Frederick's ass.

Anything, I thought, to hide those near-misses that Catherine
would tell me about with such reckless amusement. Stanislav took
her for a ride in his sleigh. A sentry in Peterhof stopped them. Stanislav said he was a musician the Grand Duke had hired, while she, in
man's clothes, could hardly stop herself from laughing. Their sleigh
hit a stone, and she was thrown out into a snowbank. She had been
knocked unconscious, and he despaired over her senseless body.

Catherine let me see the bruises on her ribs from that fall. A deep
purple patch I touched with my fingertips, fearful she might have
cracked her bones.

It was nothing, she said.

She was strong.

Stronger than I'd imagined.

"I saw Stanislav cry, Varenka," she told me that day. "He vowed he
would've killed himself if I died. He swore he didn't want to live with-

out me. He promised that if there is ever a choice between his happiness and mine, it's my happiness he'll choose."

And then, at the end of April, Catherine's dog, Bijou, showed me how easy it was to expose the truth. Stanislav and Count Horn, the Envoy of the Swedish King, arrived at the palace to pay their respects to the Grand Duke. It didn't take them long to find a plausible excuse to visit Catherine's rooms.

"I hope this is not an intrusion, Your Highness," Stanislav said, with an elegant bow.

"A welcome intrusion, dear Count," Catherine replied sweetly. "We rarely do anything of importance here."

They talked for a while of the last ball, of the astounding progress of the renovations—the envy of the Swedish King, as Count Horn repeatedly declared.

The conversation between Catherine and her guests took its courtly turns, and my thoughts drifted toward Darya, who was next door, playing with Bijou. Recently my daughter's questions had begun to worry me. "What does *uppity* mean?" she had asked, her smooth face pensive, fingers tugging at her black curls. "Why has Countess Shuvalova called you a bookbinder's daughter?" She was almost seven, still just a child, so easy to hurt.

The door to the room swung open, and Bijou left Darenka's side to greet Stanislav with a show of exuberant joy. The dog began barking wildly at the only stranger among us.

Count Horn said nothing, but his thin smile suggested that the significance of this moment was not lost on him.

I scooped Bijou up and carried him out of the room, taking Darya with me.

Count Horn was not deceived. Later, Catherine told me that he gave Stanislav a lecture on the usefulness of little Bolognese dogs in spying on their mistresses. He himself was in the habit of giving one to any woman with whom he fell in love. When a suspected rival appeared, all he had to do was watch the dog's behavior.

Horn assured Stanislav that he was a discreet man and wouldn't do any harm to him or the Grand Duchess, but neither Sir Charles nor I was comforted by this. Too many people knew the secret. Elizabeth would soon learn the truth.

"If anything happens to Stanislav," I warned Catherine, "you will never forgive yourself."

I armed myself with arguments. If Stanislav were accused of seducing the Grand Duchess, I reminded her, nothing would protect him from Siberia. A diplomat would be expelled, but the Count was just a private secretary, a foreigner at the St. Petersburg court. Stanislav must go back to Poland and return to Russia as a diplomat, protected by the Polish King.

"Couldn't he stay one more week?" Catherine begged. "Or just a few days more?" But she knew there was no other way.

As soon as Stanislav departed for Warsaw, Sir Charles sought every chance he could to soothe Catherine's grief. He entrusted me with his letters to her, and Catherine showed me some of them: *Your future is bright, and so is his. Love him with all your heart, and you'll find a way to bring him back to your side.*

In May of 1756 French troops attacked a British garrison at the island of Minorca. The war had finally come to Europe.

England was Prussia's ally.

The King of Prussia was Russia's enemy.

Even an Empress's tongue could no longer risk a visit to the British Embassy.

Once again jeweler Monsieur Bernardi began smuggling letters.

EIGHT

1756–1757

W e were all holding our breath, waiting for Russia to declare war, for letters from a lover to arrive, for death to shift the treacherous balance of power.

In the summer of 1756 I moved to Tsarskoye Selo with the Empress's entourage, glad to get Darya away from the heat and noise of the city. In spite of Monsieur Rastrelli's assurances, the rebuilding of the Winter Palace had not been smooth. Rumors swirled of thievery and chaos. Carpenters ran out of lumber, plasterers of sand and lime. Bills exceeded estimates twofold or more.

"Another curious inconsistency in these accounts, Your Highness," I heard the Chancellor point out to the Empress. He spoke of deliveries accepted without checking against the orders, workers sitting idle for lack of supplies, sheets of gold leaf missing.

A mistake, I thought.

Excess never offended Elizabeth. Frugality was good for the Prussian King, for his world of thin soups, melted candle ends, a round of cheese measured every evening. Inspecting the ledgers? Searching the workers as they left the site? "Petty actions, worthy of a monarch without vision," Ivan Shuvalov said, sneering.

If he wanted the Empress's attention, the Chancellor should have spoken of another winter spent in the cramped palace on the Great Perspective Road.

Of daring to keep the Empress of All the Russias waiting.

Of not trying hard enough.

In the garden of Tsarskoye Selo, Darya was running in search of butterflies through the unmowed patch of meadow behind the pea-tree hedge.

I heard uneven steps behind me, crunching the gravel.

I turned.

The Chancellor of Russia was coming toward me, limping, his right knee stiff, his swollen right hand gripping the handle of his cane. My daughter's joyful voice trailed in the distance. I stifled the urge to warn her away.

"Proud of yourself, palace girl, aren't you?" Bestuzhev muttered, with a dark glimmer in his steel-blue eyes.

Catherine has told him, I thought, as we began walking together along the hedge.

"There are some mistakes you cannot afford, Varvara. Underestimating me is one of them."

I savored the bitterness in Bestuzhev's voice. Catherine must have been blunt. My thirst for revenge tempted me with possibilities: *No, it was never Naryshkin. . . . Even the Chancellor's spies can be tricked to sniff at the wrong path. . . . If you wish to be my friend, prove it.*

The Chancellor's voice broke through my thoughts. "I can be of more use to her than your British fop who thinks he can teach her how to become Empress."

I quickened my steps. "Sir Charles wants the Grand Duchess to be happy. As do I."

"This is not about happiness, Varvara," the Chancellor said, and sniggered. "This is about power. A British Ambassador has his reasons to wish for her rise. Do I have to spell them out for you?"

By then Bestuzhev was breathing hard, his face reddening, but he did not ask me to slow down. And he didn't stop speaking.

"I did tell you once, Varvara Nikolayevna, that I wasn't a man without a heart. Remember, we are backing the same horse. I've come to warn you. You are forgetting the lessons I've taught you. You've begun trusting people."

"Leave me," I said.

The fury in my voice startled even him.

"Please," he said. "Not so loud. We are having a pleasant little stroll through the garden, not a spat someone on the other side of the hedge might want to report. And do slow down, will you?"

Darya was waving to me from the meadow, her butterfly net raised in triumph. I stopped and waved back.

"Remind the Grand Duchess that I'm trying hard to do what she wants," the Chancellor wheezed. "Tell her to be patient. Tell her that what she wants is not easy to achieve."

A flock of the palace peacocks passed us by, stately, indifferent, their folded tails trailing in the gravel. I stifled the urge to scare them into flight.

"She wants me to persuade the Polish King to send that handsome Pole of hers here as his Envoy. This is not hard to do. But it is Stanislav's mother who also needs persuading. He fails to mention that in his letters, but my Warsaw spies have been more forthcoming. Countess Poniatowska doesn't trust the Grand Duchess of Russia."

His voice rose in a crude imitation of a woman's plea: "Don't go back there, I beg of you, my son. She is a manipulator. She cares only about her own pleasure. . . . She will trample over you once she has what she wants. . . ."

My thoughts clung to the memory of Catherine and Stanislav, the remnants of their supper pushed carelessly aside, tracing some imaginary journey over a beautiful old map of Russia. *Imperii Moscovitici*, I read the words on the hand-colored copper etching. *Why don't we just run away?* Catherine had whispered to her lover.

"Countess Poniatowska is wrong," I told the Chancellor.

"In one of those cozy moments when you mistake our Grand Duchess for your sister, Varvara, do whisper to her shapely little ear that I, her lowly servant, will do everything to bring her beloved back to her, but that she should still work with me, even if I fail. Tell her love is not that important, after all, in the scheme of things. She knows that already, even if she is not quite ready to admit to it."

"Why should I help you?"

"Now?"

"Now or ever again."

"Now, because she needs me to succeed. Later, because I know what you still don't."

I wondered what I hated him more for. The turns my life had taken from that day when I arrived at Elizabeth's decaying palace, an orphan believing in the power of imperial grace? Or the doubt his poisonous words let creep into my heart?

I looked at his face, blank, inscrutable, aging.

"Maman," Darya cried from behind the hedge. "Look what I've caught!"

As I hurried toward her, the Chancellor of Russia limped back to the palace, the cane that supported him making deep, hollow scars in the gravel.

The thespian side of Elizabeth's soul! Hunger for the awe lighting up visitors' faces when they reached her presence, having passed through the enfilade of staterooms connected through carved and gilded portals. Hunger for the gasps of astonishment at the soft browns and yellows in the Amber Room. Shades of ebony touching on the color of dark honey, through which she, the queen bee, floated in her luscious dresses, her high heels sliding on the polished mosaics of the floors. "How vulgar, Varenka," Catherine had murmured. "She has the taste of the Russian peasant she will always be."

When the Grand Duchess came to Tsarskoye Selo, the Empress greeted her with affectionate inquires: "Have you slept well? Is your migraine gone?" Catherine responded with compliments. The subtle grace of Elizabeth's dance steps took her breath away. In her newest ball gown, the Empress looked as beautiful as she had on that winter day in Moscow when Catherine had seen Her Highness for the first time.

Elizabeth returned to calling the Grand Duke and Duchess her beloved children who had pleased her by giving her an heir to the throne. Now she was waiting for them to repeat the act.

Paul was almost two and still walked with cautious, wobbly steps. The nursemaids dressed him in loose smocks and tied his golden baby curls with a blue ribbon. Two of them always hovered over him, ready to hold him up if he merely tottered. Every morning Elizabeth made them bare their breasts for her inspection; any blemish, even the smallest one, was cause for instant dismissal.

And now, when the Grand Duchess came to Tsarskoye Selo, the Empress allowed her to visit her son.

Odd visits, cruel, I seethed, so unlike anything I wished for mother and child. The Empress laid out her conditions: *in the afternoon . . . not longer than half an hour . . . never when I am away.*

The nursery turned into a battlefield.

The stage of triumph had been carefully charted, the roles cast. Elizabeth walking into the nursery, the nursemaids shooting anxious glances at her, hoping she would notice their zeal. Behind her, Catherine, with downcast eyes, mindful of every step, every word she uttered.

"*Tyotya,*" Paul shrieked, as soon as he saw the Empress, flailing his arms with excitement, like an awkward bird learning to fly.

He wriggled out of his nursemaid's arms to rush toward her. Elizabeth swooped him up, tickled his belly, laughed when he reached for the pearls in her hair.

Every kiss, every word, measured and weighed, hurled at Catherine's heart.

"My dove . . . my prince . . . Show me your little eye . . . your little nose . . . your little toe."

Catherine stood motionless, in her pale yellow gown embroidered with flowers, hands clasped behind her, lips arranged into a faint smile. I saw her twist the rings on her fingers, as if one of them held a fairy-tale spell, would let her fly into the air, change into a mouse, a cat, a hawk.

Would render all poison harmless.

"Do you know who has come to see you? . . . Do you recognize your Maman . . . Where is she? . . . Where is your Maman? . . ."

"Maman," Paul repeated, but the word was an empty husk. Coaxed to look at Catherine, he buried his face in his aunt's bosom.

"You want her to go away, don't you, little man. . . . You want her to leave you alone."

I hoarded it all: the simpering imperial voice, the knowing smiles of triumph. *One day,* I thought, *you might come to repent what you are doing. One day those you have hurt might haunt you.*

That summer Elizabeth had commissioned a portrait of the Grand Duke Paul in the Preobrazhensky uniform, sitting on his rocking horse, a wooden sword in his hand. The painter had asked for only two sittings. He vowed, "A child with such remarkable features I can paint from memory."

In the picture, Paul's face looked bold and determined against the leafy-green tunic of his uniform. The Empress had been particularly smitten with the pink hue on his cheeks and the touches of silver paint that had rendered the wooden sword real.

She liked to hear the courtiers declare how Paul resembled his great-grandfather. How the Romanov blood flowed in his veins.

The portrait, its gilded frame studded with diamonds, hung in her bedroom, next to her own likeness as a round-faced little girl resting on an ermine throw, a miniature of her father in her right hand like a trophy, her white naked body curving gently, her hair adorned with pink flowers.

Two children, beside each other.

Would she name Paul her successor? I wondered. Would she pass Peter by?

At night when the Empress could not sleep, she called me to her side.

Unsure when these summonses would come, I took to sleeping in my clothes, the stays loosened, the hooks of my bodice half undone.

"Where have you been?" the Empress snapped, no matter how quickly I arrived. Often I noticed that cold glimmer in her eyes, the only sign of drinking I could detect then. Ivan Shuvalov was never there on these nights. He'd been dismissed, I presumed, to his own rooms.

"Who comes to see her, Varvara?"

In the shadowy darkness, stretched on her bed, the Empress wanted to hear about Catherine lost in the mazes of jealousy and lust, in the glitter of jewels, in the heat of summer nights. She still wanted stories that would justify taking a son away from his mother.

"Princess Galitsina is her best friend now, Your Highness. They see each other every day, I hear. Princess Dashkova, too. The Grand Duchess always sends everyone away when they come. Then the jeweler arrives, and they look at necklaces and earrings."

"Does she buy anything?"

"Oh, yes. She likes big stones. She wants them noticed."

"Is she still borrowing money?"

"Monsieur Bernardi has advanced her more credit."

"What else does she do all day?"

"She has started writing a Russian play, but this is still a secret. A surprise for Your Highness. It's about the Time of Troubles, but I don't think it's very good. Far too long, and there are too many speeches. She also wants to give a big party at Oranienbaum this summer. For the Grand Duke. She wants all the ladies to wear white taffeta with flowing tulle and the gentlemen blue velvet with white."

"Does the Grand Duke lie with her?"

"He does."

"And she is still not pregnant?"

"No. She has put on weight, though. The maids complain that it is harder and harder to lace her properly. And her right shoulder is crooked. Her teeth are beginning to hurt again, but she refuses to let the dentist see her. She says that all doctors do is cause more pain, so she chews cloves instead."

"Who else comes to see her? Bestuzhev?"

"Yes."

"What does that old bastard want from her?"

"They close the door when they speak, but I know she wants him to find her a new lover."

Among all the Grand Duchess's visits to Tsarskoye Selo that summer, one stays in my mind.

In the garden pavilion, dahlias and nasturtiums spilled out from stone planters, and flowering vines climbed on wrought-iron grilles. In birdcages suspended from the ceiling, canaries and parakeets chirped and hopped about, breaking into song. Embroidered shawls covered the tables and shelves, on which lacquered boxes, birch-bark baskets, and candy bowls crowded. In the corners, in big copper watering cans, red and yellow begonias bloomed. The iron furniture had been replaced by gilded armchairs and cushions embroidered with images of the firebird.

On the trays that footmen carried about, many colored vodkas glittered in crystal carafes: beet, cranberry, lemon, horseradish, plum, cherry. The guests were offered *sushki*, pirozhki stuffed with cabbage and wild mushrooms, smoked pork-belly slices arranged in the shape of a horn of plenty, adorned with grapes.

Such were the Empress's wishes. "Just like in a *skazka*," she had demanded. Elizabeth always craved the simplicity of fairy tales, good triumphant, a wise cat fooling a conniving magician, an overlooked princess rewarded with the throne.

"Another grand delusion," the Chancellor had quipped. I rubbed the place on my arm where he had held me before I wriggled away. In

Warsaw, Stanislav was still awaiting the King's orders. The Old Fox was not trying hard enough, Catherine had told me. Last time he pleaded with her to be given more time, she told him that if he could not bring Count Poniatowski to St. Petersburg, perhaps the Shuvalovs might be of more use to her.

Sprawled in her gilded armchair, chewing on a pork-belly slice, the Empress surveyed the scene of her making. Her feet rested on an embroidered footstool; folds of her purple dress framed her like soft drapery. "Keep everyone away from me, Varvara," she had ordered. Her red-rimmed eyes were nobody's business. Even a sleepless night, I thought, had become a state secret.

I hovered behind the Empress, a guard dog and a spy, knowing that what she wanted from me was a story to her liking. A bad mother and a good aunt . . . a foolish prince unworthy of his inheritance . . . a blessed baby who would save the Empire.

The Grand Duke, having taken a seat underneath a birdcage, to the Empress's right, clasped his hands tightly to stop them from fidgeting. Catherine had persuaded him to wear the Preobrazhensky greens. He had been with her to the nursery once—a reluctant visit, for, as he told Catherine, what can a father do with a child who is not old enough to march?

The Grand Duchess praised everything. The flowers, the birds, the breeze coming from the garden carrying the scents of roses and honey. Her dress was plain, a summer dress of white muslin and satin ribbons, but all eyes naturally turned toward her. Even Ivan Shuvalov leaned to whisper something, words Catherine acknowledged with a graceful nod and a flutter of her fan. As she moved from one group of guests to another, she offered nods and smiles, a touch of her hand, a kind comment.

It was only the Chancellor whom she visibly ignored, her eyes sliding past him when he bowed to her, darting in the opposite direction if he made the slightest effort to move closer.

He frowned. He shook his head.

He tried again, and again was snubbed.

It turned into a game, an amusement for the court: Catherine's half-smiles, her swift turnabouts, the Chancellor's persistence, Ivan Shuvalov's chuckles.

The Empress wiggled in her chair. She didn't like attention to flow away from her. I propped up her pillows. The one behind her back was damp with sweat.

I was relieved when the Imperial Favorite stood up and—hand resting on his chest—began reciting an ode to the Illustrious Minerva of the North:

May the Lord to the end of our days
Multiply your cherished years
To the joy and defense of the world!

A lively round of applause brought a smile to Elizabeth's lips. When the applause faded, Count Razumovsky, his voice rich and low, intoned one of his Ukrainian *dumas* about lovers parting in sorrow.

The Empress tossed him a handkerchief. He kissed it before sliding it into his breast pocket.

The Chancellor stood next.

"A speech would be too long, Your Highness," he said, "so I'll be brief."

He was brief. Russia was ready to teach Frederick of Prussia a lesson he would not forget. The troops reported their readiness; peasants gathered at the recruiting stations, singing songs to the Empress's glory. Field Marshal Apraxin was waiting for the chance to prove himself to His Beloved Sovereign and his Motherland.

I stifled a temptation to laugh. A few words, maybe, but none idle.

At the mention of his beloved King of Prussia, the Grand Duke lowered his head. Beside him, Ivan Shuvalov winced when he heard Apraxin's name. He was still hoping the Empress would not appoint the Chancellor's protégé to the post of supreme commander of the Russian army.

"The whole nation, Your Highness, is ready," the Chancellor continued. "We merely await your command."

The Empress slapped her hand on the arm of her chair. In her eyes I saw a flicker of dark glee.

"If Russia has to enter the war," she announced, the purple sleeve of her gown shimmering with diamonds, "I'll lead the troops myself."

There was a moment of uncertain silence, but it ended as abruptly as it began. Praises flowed, just as Elizabeth wished them to, lavish, exuberant. She would be magnificent. She would astonish the world.

Our little mother.

Beloved.

Merciful.

Virtuous.

I didn't see the Grand Duke rise. His voice made me look at him. It was piercing and high-pitched, a shiver in the marrow of the bones. There is something deadly in foolishness that takes no notice of the dismayed faces, faces that hide in the shadows the instant your eyes touch them.

"How can Your Majesty even think it possible?"

The Empress cocked her head, puzzled, as if her nephew spoke some foreign tongue whose meaning had to be pieced together word by word. A patch of color appeared at the base of her neck.

"My father headed his troops," she seethed. "Do you think I'm not as good as my father?"

I watched Peter's scarred face turn crimson. He flung his long hands about him. Such is the bitterness of a foolish prince, I thought, the disappointment of the one less able. Like a marsh, deep and treacherous, reeking of rotting leaves.

"He was a man, and Your Majesty is a woman," Peter shrilled.

Before the Grand Duke managed to say anything else, Ivan Shuvalov pulled at his sleeve so hard that the seam tore.

Too late.

I saw the footstool overturn; I saw the kick that sent it flying. I saw the Chancellor rise and lunge toward Elizabeth, as if his touch could contain her rage.

It was Catherine's voice that stopped them all.

"Please, Your Highness! Promise us you will not put yourself in the path of danger. We beg of you, in our times of trouble, have mercy on your children."

A voice soft and pleading but irresistible.

The Grand Duke opened his mouth again, but Catherine didn't give him a chance to speak. "We may not be your soldiers," she continued, throwing herself to her knees in front of the Empress, "but we need your guidance. Rule the generals who lead the troops, but stay with us here, we implore you."

The Empress sank back into her cushions. Two tears rolled from her eyes. She let them trickle down her rouged cheeks.

The foolish prince from the Russian skazkas *is always saved by a wise princess,* I remembered.

"Enough, my child," the Empress said. "Get up."

I rushed to help the Grand Duchess to her feet. I felt her hand squeeze mine. If she expected her husband's gratitude, it did not come. "I'm not like Madame Resourceful," Peter had said to me before he left, recalling his old name for Catherine. There was a dangerous note of resentment in his voice when he said it.

At the rare moments when we found ourselves alone that summer, Catherine questioned me about Elizabeth's fluttering heart, the smell of rot coming from her womb. Was there any truth to the rumors of fainting spells? Had she started avoiding stairs?

"She's been like this before," I answered. "Don't believe all you hear."

Catherine's face sharpened in disappointment.

"It's all this talk of the war," I continued. "She is afraid."

The imperial terror of reckoning, I called it. The judgment card of the monarch's tarot deck. This is what brought drops of sweat to Elizabeth's forehead, darkened the puffed skin under her eyes. In the Empress's mind, God decided a nation's fate by weighing the sins of its ruler. Which would matter more—French sloth, Prussian greed, or Russian pride? "Have I not been merciful?" I heard the Empress mutter as she prayed.

In one of the letters Catherine showed me, Sir Charles urged her to give up the part of a friend and take up that of heir of Russia. *You are more powerful than you think*, he had written. *You can have all you want.* At night, with Darya tossing in her sleep, still grinding her teeth in spite of Masha's wormwood infusions, I savored the promise of his words.

In the sparsely furnished guest suite at Tsarskoye Selo—a reminder of the Grand Duchess's position at court—Catherine continued her questions.

"Does she sleep at all, Varenka? Is she often in pain? Does she talk about me?"

I looked at the room: two gilded chairs, a small table, a bed, a chest of drawers. A window overlooking the kitchen garden, from where a scent of something unexpected floated in—cinnamon and cloves, as if it were Christmas.

Catherine, in her light summer gown, stood by the open window, her fingers twisting the gold tassels of the curtains.

"You miss him," I said softly. "Have you not had a letter?"

She turned her head toward me, and I saw the glitter of tears. "I don't want to talk about Stanislav. Please, Varenka. I can't."

So I spoke of the Imperial Bedchamber instead. Of peasant singers, bandura players, children with voices the Empress might call "angelic." A roster of ladies-in-waiting eager to amuse her with gossip until suppertime, when the Imperial Favorite arrived. Well rested, glowing, like her cats.

"The Empress refuses to be alone," I continued, pleased when my words made Catherine smile. "So I make sure she isn't."

At night, when Ivan Shuvalov was sent back to his rooms, when the palace slumbered, I found the Empress leafing through the *St. Petersburg Gazette*, scrutinizing the caricatures of the Prussian King through her magnifying glass. Frederick II on a stool, a sack between his knees, packing the lands of Silesia, Bohemia, and Saxony into a grab bag with one hand, picking bits that have fallen to the ground with another. Frederick, in his scanty frock coat, licking his lips as he peered through a spying hole at the naked flesh of reclining Austria.

"What do they write of him now?" the Empress asked, pushing the newspaper into my hands.

A bandit and a thief, I read, *treacherous . . . conniving . . . insatiable . . . claims that his army of two hundred thousand men can be at his enemy's throats in three weeks.*

Elizabeth bit her fingernails when I read, and then rubbed at them, as if she could make them longer. Underneath her dressing gown, a frill of Belgian lace revealed the etchings of blue-green veins under the paper-thin skin.

So that Frederick might rob a neighbor whom he had once sworn to defend, black men are fighting on the coast of Coromandel and red men scalp each other by the Great Lakes of North America.

I spiced the essential with pinches of the trivial. *In the Prussian army, officers eat on tinplate. Silver spoons are forbidden.*

"A miser," Elizabeth muttered. "A highway robber with no conscience."

There was hatred in the Empress's face, hatred like fire to be fanned and kept burning. She would never forget that the King of Prussia had once called her "an illiterate cunt ruled by pricks."

In spite of the Shuvalovs' displeasure, the Empress granted Field Marshal Apraxin full command of the Russian army. The orders that followed brought many changes. My husband had assumed the duties of a receiving officer for new recruits. It would be harder for him to get away, he told me when he came to Tsarskoye Selo for a week, a harried week of rushing about.

We, too, talked about the war.

The price of salt soared from *twenty* to *fifty* kopecks per *pud*. The price of liquor doubled. The Russian treasury was raising money.

"Not fast enough," Egor said.

Now that the Prussian King had the backing of the British, the Prussian army would go on the offensive. "Russia doesn't have much more time to get ready," he said.

Masha kept the tally of chores. Master's dress uniform had been torn at the sleeve and had to be mended. His pockets were stained, for he had carried carrots and lumps of sugar there, for his horse. He needed fresh handkerchiefs. He needed a few jars of her own shoe polish, which she concocted from wax, tallow, and tar, so much better than what the army could provide.

Our bedroom smelled of saddle soap and snuff. I'd return after my shift in the Imperial Bedroom to hear Egor's triumphant grunts as he counted out the last of the hundred push-ups with which he started his days. Next door, where his valet slept, my husband's trunks were filling up, but the things he always kept with him were neatly lined on the side table. The toiletry set, his saber, his pistols, all in cloth covers that Masha had washed and ironed, all tied with string.

During the day Darya never left his side. She carried a doll he had bought for her, refusing to part with it, even when Masha was giving her a bath.

"Flowers have roots that drink water from underneath the earth. Birds eat seeds, Papa." I heard her voice, serious, insistent. She never stopped, as if every thought had to be turned into words, every mystery examined.

"Masha says that swans lose their feathers every spring and then they cannot fly. Is it true?"

"Yes."

"Can they not find them?"

"They have to grow new feathers. They have to wait."

"Why?"

"It takes time to grow."

"How much time?"

With Egor there was no shyness in her, I thought, no hesitation. She either knew something and announced it or did not know and wished to find out. If an answer did not satisfy her, she would not stop. Precision pleased her, certainty of facts that fitted together snugly.

"Sometimes she is no longer a child," Egor said.

"Only sometimes," I said, laughing.

Evenings that August were chilly. On Egor's last night at home, we sat on the garden bench, watching the deepening shadows. Darya, the doll propped beside her, was drawing something in a sketchbook Egor had given her, the tip of her tongue extended in fierce concentration. She was already trying to contain his looming absence, asking when he would come back. "How many weeks?" she would ask, spreading the fingers of her right hand, hiding her left hand behind her.

The birch leaves were already beginning to yellow. Soon the earth would be carpeted with amber and gold.

I told Egor about the dancemaster I intended to hire soon, to give our daughter dancing and deportment lessons. I wondered if the one hour a day I now made Darya walk in high heels, with a book on her head, was enough to keep her spine straight.

The gardeners had been burning twigs and dead leaves, and the air carried the sharp bite of smoke.

"It's not right," Egor said, as if he hadn't heard me.

I fell silent.

He lowered his voice as he spoke, staring at the polished tip of his jackboot. "Bribery and soul-buying," he muttered.

On his knee, his hand curled into a fist. On his tensing jaw, a shadow of black stubble quivered.

He had seen deserters, he told me. Many more than he'd thought possible. Men were poking out their eyes, crushing their toes, cutting off their fingers, or knocking out their teeth. Anything to avoid the army.

The Yaroslavl' villagers had been caught buying serfs in another village to serve in their place. "Three hundred and sixty rubles," Egor continued. "That's the going rate for a good recruit."

The villages that did send their own recruits did not give them adequate provisions, often less than half of the flour required for the simple bread the soldiers baked in earth ovens. How long would it last them? A month? Two? How was he to keep his men strong on flour and water? Soldiers needed vegetables and some meat or fish. The Russian army would starve even before the marching orders came.

Why was there money for a new palace when the soldiers didn't even have enough bread? Why had Apraxin been made Field Marshal? That old fart who forbade his aide-de-camp to wake him up before ten?

He was struggling to understand.

He was failing.

He believed that virtue, not fickle fortune, made the army.

"Remember the Orlov brothers, *kison'ka?*" he asked, his fingers skimming over his chin.

I remembered the two young officers who had listened to Egor so intently at the gatherings in our parlor. Grigory, the handsomer of the two, Alexei with the scar on his face. The Orlovs were no longer in St. Petersburg, Egor said. They had followed his example and had applied for active duty with the army.

"Excellent officers, both of them, but only Alexei shares my worries," my husband continued. Alexei didn't have Grigory's devil-may-care conviction that everything would turn out well in the end, that victory came to those who dared. "We rage," Egor confessed, "while Grigory is chasing another mistress. Time will tell who has got it right."

He halted for a moment to seek my eyes. I looked at the weathered skin of his face, at his thin lips, set tight, steeling for a bad situation to become worse.

"True nobles . . . service nobles." I heard Egor's bitter voice. The likes of the Shuvalovs and the Vorontzovs on one side, the likes of the Malikins and the Orlovs on the other. The old distinctions refused to go away. True nobles grew up hearing stories of great deeds done by those whose names they bore, whose flesh made theirs. Service nobles rose up the ranks through merit or favor, not birth, accused of pandering to the Sovereign's passions, using base means to acquire the Empress's goodwill.

Allowed to imitate their betters but not to be one of them.

"Until we force our way," Egor said, words spoken too loud, making Darya flash us a quick look before returning to her unfinished drawing.

I placed my finger on my lips, but Egor shook his head. "You know that, too, *kison'ka*," he said. "You have always known it. Haven't you?"

I felt a knot of tension dissolve in my throat when his hand touched mine.

In the morning, after Egor's carriage left, Darya was silent and pensive. "You have to be strong," Egor had told her. "You are a soldier's daughter." She nodded nervously when I assured her that Papa would be back soon, but she didn't ask when it would be.

It was the absence of Egor's things that I recall, the empty bedroom table, the fading scent of saddle soap and snuff. And the thought that Russia is not yet at war. The belief that a recruiting station is out of harm's way.

Five days after Egor's departure, news came that Frederick of Prussia had crossed the Saxon border, his army pouring through Leipzig into Dresden. In September, by the time the court moved back to St. Petersburg for the winter, the Prussian army reached Dresden. In October, at Pirna, the Saxon army surrendered.

The Empress wished to hear of little else. Saxony was an Austrian ally. Maria Theresa of Austria may be a liar and a hypocrite, but she had been wronged and slighted. The Prussian bully had crossed one line too many. Russia wouldn't stand idly by.

The Chancellor of Russia was no longer kept waiting in the antechamber. I'd hear his voice from Elizabeth's inner room, praising the wisdom of her decisions. Field Marshal Apraxin was reporting the Russian army ready for combat. As soon as winter was over it could start marching west. "The whole world awaits Your Majesty's command."

Catherine was growing impatient. The Chancellor still had no news for her about Stanislav's appointment, and the invasion of Saxony meant another delay.

"I'm asking for so little," Catherine had told him. "If you cannot do this for me, what is the value of your help? Perhaps I should listen to Ivan Shuvalov, after all? Consider *his* offer of friendship?"

There had been no offers, just hints, but Sir Charles's letters made Catherine bold. She would show them to me. Letters in which she underlined whole sentences: *Claim the throne of Russia, and make Stanislav King of Poland. This is a destiny worthy of your talent.*

I turned the pages in my hand, hoping Sir Charles did not keep copies and that Monsieur Bernardi was not losing his touch. It did not soothe my worries to notice the old subterfuge: Sir Charles had addressed the Grand Duchess as Monsieur. I resolved to urge him for more secrecy next time I saw him.

"Please burn these letters," I pleaded with Catherine. The lock in her escritoire could be picked with a flick of a hairpin. Her secret drawer opened with a push of one of its wooden columns.

"Sir Charles is quite sure the Empress doesn't have long to live," Catherine said, ignoring my plea. "Do you think he is right, Varenka?"

I shrugged. "I don't claim I can predict the future. But I know she is thinking of Christmas. She is being fitted for a cream satin dress, with ermine trim."

Finally, in November, the Chancellor told Catherine the good news.

The King of Saxony and Poland had appointed Count Poniatowski his Envoy *extraordinaire* to the Russian court. Stanislav set off for St. Petersburg at the beginning of December, promising in his letter to Catherine to arrive before Christmas. But Christmas came and Stanislav still was not here.

Catherine tried not to worry. Winter was harsh; delays were inevitable.

Every day I sent a servant to the Saxon mission, only to be told that Count Poniatowski was on his way. Then, on December 28, at midday, he arrived.

The boom of the midday cannon still lingered when I rushed to Catherine's room. The day was very cold but bright, the snow piling up alongside the Great Perspective Road. The Saxon mission was a short carriage ride from the temporary palace.

"Take this to him, Varenka," Catherine ordered, placing a sealed letter in my hand. "Tell him I'll come as soon as I can."

The footman took me to the receiving room, kept warm by a blue-tiled stove and a fireplace. The windows were covered by elaborate curtains. On the wall hung the portrait of Augustus III, *by the grace of God, King of Poland and the elector of Saxony.* A big man with an arrogant stare and full, ruddy cheeks, his body barely contained in a blue jacket, embroidered with gold. I recalled Sir Charles's stories of his "sitting-down hunts" in the Polish forests, wolves and bears pushed from scaffolding so that he could shoot them from his chair. "Saxony would have to suffer his bloodline," Sir Charles had told me once. "But Poland doesn't have to. There are advantages to being a country that elects her kings."

Stanislav was still wrapped in furs when he entered, as if unable to believe that his long journey was truly over. A powdered wig made his handsome face leaner than I recalled it, older and more thoughtful. His hands were warm when he held mine and raised them to his lips.

"Dear friend," he said. "How is she?"

"Better. Now that she knows you are here."

I handed him the note from Catherine and watched him break the seal with trembling hands. He kissed it after he read it.

"You surely kept us waiting," I teased.

"I had to take a longer route." He turned his face toward the fireplace, toward the dancing flames. "I had been warned of an ambush ... right after I crossed the Russian border."

"Warned?" I asked, concerned. "Who warned you?"

He gave me a bemused smile. "Let me tell her that myself."

I felt a pang at these words, a reminder not to feel more important than I was.

Outside the receiving room, something heavy was being dragged along the floor. We heard footsteps approaching. The door opened, and one of the mission servants appeared, asking if refreshments would be required. Stanislav looked at me, but I shook my head. I had to hurry back to the palace.

Stanislav waved the servant away and offered to walk with me along the Great Perspective Road.

The glittering winter sun had been swallowed by a heavy cloud, and now big flakes of snow were falling on our faces as we walked. He asked me many questions, and I answered them all.

Catherine was well. She was wearing her hair shorter but still unpowdered, just the way he liked it. No, he could not go to see her right away. It was too dangerous. She would come to the Naryshkin palace as soon as she could. Not earlier than eleven, though.

He should wear a disguise and come through the service door. A musician's costume would be best.

I would tell her he was well. I would tell her he would be counting every second that kept him away from her.

I did not let Stanislav walk with me for more than a few minutes. Even in the street, too many curious eyes lurked.

When it was time for him to turn back, I watched him walk away, slowly. A beggar stopped him, and Stanislav extracted a coin from his pocket. A moment later, the beggar's wail turned into a loud litany of blessings.

With the anticipation of Catherine's joy came the thought of my own unease. Egor had sent a note that he'd been ordered to take his recruits west, in the direction of East Prussia. The Orlov brothers, he assured me, had sworn to take care of me and Darya, should anything happen to him.

That night, when I escorted Catherine to the Naryshkin palace on the embankment, I caught a glimpse of Stanislav through one of the ground-floor windows, a pale, serious shadow of a face, a waving hand.

In the light cast by a lantern, Catherine's face wavered. Impatience suited her. Her cheeks, reddened with frost, needed no rouge; her eyes needed no belladonna to glitter.

No more loneliness for her, I thought. *No more waiting.*

Catherine glanced at me only once before hurrying inside. "Thank you, Varenka," she breathed, smiling. "I'll never forget what you've done for us."

Something about her troubled me, but I couldn't think what it was. Only later, I realized that her lips were drawn in what looked to me surprisingly like her mother's selfish smile.

How droll, I thought, *and how impossible.*

The court welcomed the new year with fireworks and cannon salutes. The Empress held the New Year's ball in Peterhof. Before she left St. Petersburg she prostrated herself in front of the Holy Mother of Kazan. She prayed for forgiveness. *Please*, I heard her mutter, *do not punish Russia for my own sins.*

Seventeen fifty-seven would be the year of victory.

I thought of Egor, in the army camp, of his letters, simple and spare. *Winter is harsh, but I'm of good thoughts. Tell Darenka that I like her drawing of a horse best.*

After the New Year celebrations ended, I often saw Stanislav in Elizabeth's antechamber, standing among other Envoys and Ambassadors, awaiting an audience.

Elizabeth never made him wait long. He had pleased her with his first official speech, with which he assumed his Envoy duties. Invasion of Saxony was not just an outrage but a sign of the future, he had said. Frederick of Prussia was *a Hydra with many heads*. If one of them was chopped off, two more grew in its place. This was why Prussia deserved no mercy.

The Empress liked that.

She was not the only one. A fluid, passionate speech, I heard it described. Loud enough to be heard but calm enough not to be dismissed as a young man's rant.

As soon as I had the opportunity, I congratulated Stanislav on his success. "The Empress talks of little else."

"The Empress is very kind," he replied. "I watch the Russian court and I learn. Each day a new lesson."

Lessons tailored for a star pupil, I thought. Sir Charles had begged Stanislav not to try to see him. Not even in secret. Ever since Prussia invaded Saxony, the British Embassy had been under tight surveillance. Every embassy servant was a Russian spy. *It is with a heavy heart that I stay away from both of you now, Monsieur, hoping it won't be for long,* Sir Charles had written to the Grand Duchess. *One day Catherine the Empress of Russia and Stanislav the King of Poland will rule together, and I'll be able to offer my help and friendship to both. But for this to happen, I cannot have other masters. This is why I've submitted my resignation, and I'm now awaiting a letter from London freeing me from my embassy duties.*

Stanislav called Sir Charles *La Sagesse*—Wisdom—and a true friend. Catherine told me that she would always consult him like the Delphic Oracle.

And I?

I thought of the force of words, repeated, mulled over. I thought of how they swelled, turning possibilities into desires. The Philosopher

Queen. The Philosopher King. Vanity replaced by wisdom, sloth by hard work.

A better world. A world more just.

What else could be more worthy of my efforts?

By the end of February Catherine was again with child. Her appearances at the court functions became joyful occasions for concern. Maids were ordered to fetch cushions and place them under her feet. The Empress reminded the Grand Duchess of the importance of avoiding drafts and of the virtues of foot massage. The blood had to flow freely. The body needed to store strength. Baskets of delicacies for the Grand Duchess arrived daily from the palace kitchen, blancmange tortes with pineapples, boned quails, silver tureens with rich, creamy soups. The complaints about new debts or Peter's drinking were replaced with loud praise of the strength of Romanov blood.

The ancient lineage, I heard, could not be suppressed for long.

I saw the Empress place her hand on the Grand Duchess's belly, smiling as if she could already feel the child kick. Fears and ill humor ebbed from her. Birth trumped death, banished it to the shadows. Elizabeth never asked who was responsible for Catherine's "delicate condition." Appearances had been kept. The "moon children" shared their marital bed. Peter could not deny that the child might be his, and in the Winter Palace, that was good enough.

Stanislav, the Envoy *extraordinaire* of the Saxon King, attended all required audiences and receptions. In Elizabeth's presence the Count used every opportunity to draw her attention to Saxony's plight: Dresden destroyed by cannon fire, released criminals setting fires to houses and fields, Frederick issuing false Polish coins to buy supplies for his army.

The Empress praised Count Poniatowski's deportment, his youthful charm, his impeccable elegance. If any of the Shuvalovs hinted at his passion for Catherine, the Empress changed the subject. She had more pressing matters on her mind.

In June, at Kolin, Frederick suffered his first defeat. He had not been such a great strategist, after all. The Austrians had forced him into an attack. His flanking strategy failed. It was the perfect time for Russia to deliver her blow.

The Chancellor spent more and more time with the Empress. I saw him enter her inner room with rolls of maps under his arm and papers to sign. Field Marshal Apraxin was marching the Russian army toward East Prussia. Egor would not come to St. Petersburg this summer. His letters were even briefer now—lighthearted accounts of blisters upon blisters, the long-forgotten joy of sleeping in a haystack. There was always a drawing for Darenka: *Papa by the bonfire, drying his breeches. Papa picking wild blueberries for dessert.*

I heard the Chancellor's voice quieting Elizabeth's doubts: Her officers were the best in Europe; her soldiers would die with their Tsarina's name on their lips.

At dawn, drunk on cherry brandy, Elizabeth demanded my stories of Lev Naryshkin disguised in a musician's garb, his carriage stopped by the Oranienbaum sentries. The Prince declared himself a member of the orchestra in the service of the Grand Duchess.

"What do you play?" the guards had asked him.

"A flute," he responded.

"Show us your instrument, then."

Imperial laughter, I thought, was as good as permission, as good as a truce.

In July, Sir Charles received an official confirmation that his request to resign his position as British Ambassador had been granted. His replacement, a Mr. Keith, would arrive in a few months. Until then, George Rineking, Sir Charles's onetime secretary, was to perform his duties.

He bade an official farewell to the court. He was a free man.

"I don't intend to leave, *pani* Barbara," he told me. "Please assure the Grand Duchess that I'll do everything to be around when she requires my counsel."

It was Sir Charles's choice, the tavern where we met, beyond the Anichkov Palace. The windows were steamy, the floors sticky from spit and spilled beer. On my way there, I saw dogs fighting over kitchen scraps and neighborhood boys pelting them with stones.

Sir Charles's enthusiasm was contagious. On his lips, even the sordid accounts of Peter's drinking bouts carried a tinge of promise about them. Debauchery was shortening the Grand Duke's life. If he died, Catherine and Stanislav would be free to marry.

"I advise the Grand Duchess to watch and wait, assess all options, but hide her cards," Sir Charles said. "To improve her relations with the Shuvalovs. To cultivate everyone. Not to reveal her position too early."

In the murky corner by a window smeared with oily fingers, I nodded my agreement. On the thick wooden table, someone had carved a crooked heart pierced with two arrows. In his last letter, Egor had mentioned that his regiment had crossed the border of East Prussia, without even a skirmish. He had missed the siege of Memel by a few days, arriving in time for the victory celebrations. *We are heading west soon*, he had written, *though I won't know when and where for some time yet*.

"The Grand Duchess can count on me," Sir Charles continued. "Now that I am free, I intend to postpone my departure until I'm needed."

He bent toward me, his eyes shining. "We are not soldiers, *pani* Barbara." There was urgency in his voice. "You and I don't fight a war. But we can improve the world our children will one day inherit."

That summer I, too, thought myself indispensable.

I did not see us for what we were. A cabal of a former Ambassador and a bookbinder's daughter turned imperial tongue, two figures willing the future to bend to their own grandiose wishes, while the truly important events of the time were relentlessly unfolding in their own way.

In the Imperial Bedroom thick wax candles never stopped burning. There were the nights when I found Elizabeth in front of the mirror, in her negligee, staring at the lines on her face, adjusting the lace around her cleavage. Without a wig, her head looked small and naked, almost childlike, and she would run her fingers through her hair, cut short ever since it began to thin. Her cats were squatting in the shadows, lounging, pouncing on dust balls, rolling over to expose their bellies, licking their hind legs thrust in the air.

I never knew what the Empress wanted from me when I entered her bedroom. Would she talk or would she want to listen? To judge or to plead? Sometimes she insisted I search her maids' trunks for a missing comb, a bottle of infusion, a hairpin, or a ring. Sometimes she announced some newest order, such as forbidding court ladies to include pink lace and ribbon in their finery, for she wished to be the only one wearing it. One night she asked me if I ever dreamed of my father, but before I could answer she hid her face in her hands and began to sob. Once I found her sniffing the inside of her shoe, wrinkling her nose with disgust. "Is anything the matter, Your Highness?" I asked, but she looked at me as if she did not see me. "How difficult," she muttered, "to keep the past away from the present."

I thought of sand silently trickling in an hourglass. *Perhaps Sir Charles is right*, I thought. *Perhaps death and change are not that far away.*

The court had returned from Peterhof at the end of August. In the Empress's inner rooms, opened trunks smelled of cedar and rosemary. The Empress had been restless, pacing the rooms, searching for distractions, awaiting the news from East Prussia. It wasn't often that she cared if her tapestries had been aired.

I had just unfolded a pink damask dressing gown, one of Elizabeth's favorites, when the Chancellor walked into the room, a dispatch in his hand. The Empress closed her eyes and clasped her hands in a silent prayer.

"Smashed, Your Majesty," he cried, beaming with joy. "Decimated. And this is just the beginning. Your Majesty's absolute victory is now assured."

The Russian forces had defeated Frederick of Prussia at the village of Gross-Jägersdorf.

"Field Marshal Apraxin promises a proper report with next post. For now he sends a summary."

"Read it," the Empress ordered.

The Chancellor read slowly, each sentence a triumph. The Prussians attacked first. The Kalmyk cavalry and the Don Cossacks lured them into a trap, under artillery fire. The battle lasted the whole day. The surrounding villages had been set on fire to further disorient the Prussians. In the smoky fog the Russian bayonets had been far more lethal than Frederick's muskets. Elizabeth Petrovna, the daughter of Peter the Great, had taught Frederick his first lesson. Now Prussia stood naked and helpless before the might of the Empire of the East.

When the Chancellor finished, the Empress ordered everyone in the room to pray with her to the Virgin of Kazan.

To give thanks for Russia's triumph.

I was alone in my small parlor in the temporary palace when the messenger arrived with the news that Egor was one of the forty-five hundred Russian soldiers killed at Gross-Jägersdorf.

I listened but did not respond, in the strange, unreal way one hears such news. The messenger had perfected the somber look, the respectful glances, the bows and discreet withdrawal, and when he departed, I sat on the ottoman, too heavy to move.

In the room next door I heard steps followed by the governess's voice. A plea to try harder. Darya was practicing her deportment.

I stood up and opened the door. My hand was trembling.

"Look, Maman," Darya said when she saw me. She was walking across the room in her high heels without stumbling, her back perfectly straight, her curls tightly tucked under her laced cap.

I motioned for Mademoiselle Dupont to leave us alone.

Then I told her that her Papa was dead.

Darya stood motionless, frowning, trying to make sense of what I'd said. She knew of battles and wars. She had seen paintings of slain soldiers, hands still clinging to their muskets, left behind as their comrades charged bravely on.

She stepped out of her high heels gingerly.

"I must put my shoes away," was all she said. She picked them up and wiped them against her sleeve.

I took her in my arms. I waited for her tears, but they did not come. Through the thin wall I could hear Masha scolding the maid.

"Cry, Darenka," I whispered. "Cry."

But she wouldn't. Not until she heard Masha's wailing, piercing and raw.

Only then did tears come, hers and mine. Silent and hot.

I stayed at Darya's side that night until she fell asleep, one hand cradling her doll, another softening in mine. Our small rooms smelled of *ladan*, the Russian herbs of mourning, sweet and pungent, meant to dull the pain.

In the streets of St. Petersburg there were so many of us—wives, mothers, sisters, daughters, all swathed in mourning. We recognized one another through the newness of our black clothes, how we averted our eyes when the glorious victory was triumphantly proclaimed.

"Battlefields stink like a dunghill," Egor told me once. "The dead soil themselves. Men and horses."

Among the things returned to me were my husband's sword, his seal, his pistols, and a wooden box with the two jars of Masha's shoe polish.

They found his body three days after the battle ended. The army surgeon informed me that a bayonet gash had split Egor's right thigh.

There was a bullet wound in his left arm; the bone was smashed. If my husband had survived, he would have lost both his arm and his leg. I was to consider this very carefully, to think what kind of life would be his, had he lived.

"Oh, Varenka," Catherine said. "My dearest girl."

She had brought lace and satin ribbons for me, black for my mourning dress. She hung a golden cross around Darya's neck. "I'm not even allowed to come to the funeral," she told me, hand resting on her growing belly. "*She* says that a cemetery is not a place for me now. But why should I be surprised, Varenka? Did *she* not forbid me to wear mourning for my own father, for he had not been king?"

There was such warmth in her embrace when I sobbed.

Egor's embalmed body arrived in St. Petersburg for the funeral, waxy and pale. A gash on his forehead had been sewn tight. One of the eyebrows looked crooked. His neck shriveled as if he was tensing his shoulders even in death.

In the Court Journal my husband's name was inscribed well below Prince Trubetskoy's youngest son, who had also died at Gross-Jägersdorf. A true noble and a service noble would never be equal, I thought with bitterness. I had been granted two months' leave from my duties. The Empress did not wish a fresh widow around her. In the Imperial Palace, death was considered contagious.

With Masha's help I turned all mirrors in our rooms against the wall so that my husband's soul would not get trapped. We tied a black crepe ribbon at the corner of Egor's portrait. As custom demanded, I sent out mourning cards, their border ornamented with a death's-head and crossbones, announcing Egor's passing, inviting visitors to pay their respects.

My daughter held my hand all through the service. A tight grip of a child's small hand. I did not have the heart to scold her for her chapped knuckles, her bitten nails. Before the casket was closed, I kissed Egor's cheek. It was hard and cold. I lifted Darya so that she could kiss it, too.

"You are a hero's daughter, Darenka," Catherine had told her. "You have to be brave."

At the St. Lazarus cemetery with so many fresh graves, we prayed by the simple headstone with brass letters: *Egor Dmitryevich Malikin, May 15, 1725–August 30, 1757. May the Lord grant him eternal rest.*

On our way back, the city smelled of refuse and pine resin, of wet cloth and smoke. By the embankment the scaffolding around the new Winter Palace had been mostly cleared, but workers still carried lumber inside, and the courtyard was littered with bricks and broken tiles.

When we got home I cradled my daughter's small body in my arms, and she clung to me as if she were about to drown. Later I discovered bruises on my arms where she had dug her fingers into my flesh.

"A soldier's widow, Varvara Nikolayevna, will never be alone," Alexei Orlov assured me.

He had come to St. Petersburg as soon as he could after hearing the tragic news. Grigory, too, was on his way. They had not been at Gross-Jägersdorf, and their leaves were short, but the eldest Orlov brother, Ivan Grigoryevich, had already pledged his assistance. The house on Millionnaya Street was at my disposal. A messenger from the temporary palace could reach it in minutes.

I let Alexei speak. The last time he had seen Egor, the three of them went to a *banya*. My husband had just received the marching orders. He was in excellent spirits. He spoke of me and of his daughter. He had asked Grigory's advice on what gift to get for me on his return. He joked that he was asking a man nine years his junior. "But my brother, Varvara Nikolayevna"—Alexei flashed a pale smile—"is quite a ladies' man."

He had promised Egor that no harm would come to me or Darenka. I must remember that. Always.

My eyes rested on Alexei Orlov's scar as he spoke, a wound now completely healed.

That day, before leaving, Alexei Orlov asked to be allowed to say one more thing. He had made inquiries and learned that Colonel Zinovev, Darya's godfather, had been dead for three years.

"You would do me a great honor, Varvara Nikolayevna, if you would think of me as Darya Egorevna's godfather."

I nodded.

He clasped my icy hand and pressed it to his heart.

Before I could think of what assistance I might need, Alexei Orlov had brought two guards to stand at attention by our door. "A great loss," I heard his voice, greeting visitors in the corridor leading to our rooms. "The tallest blade of grass is the first to be cut by the scythe." The two youngest Orlov brothers, Fyodor and Vladimir, had been directing the footmen who took care of the constant stream of hats, canes, gloves, and calling cards. The Orlovs' servants served refreshments and tea. The flowers that kept coming had been placed in vases; the scent of them was everywhere.

The honey Masha sweetened our tea with came from the Orlovs' country estate. So did the chunky white cheese and cured hams. "Day after day, without fail," Masha said, as baskets from Millionnaya Street arrived at our door. "Always with a kind word."

All five Orlov brothers signed the notes that came with the gifts: *Ivan, Grigory, Alexei, Fyodor, Vladimir.*

Dressed in black, I sat on the ottoman in my tiny parlor, my thoughts slowed with laudanum. At times the visitors resembled marionettes, powdered heads bobbing on their shoulders in some grotesque dance, each repeating its scripted phrase. *Consider your blessings. Submit to God's will. The hammer shatters glass but forges iron. Think of the strength of friendships and the consolations of motherhood.*

It was the laudanum, I thought, that made me wish them all to leave. Laudanum made me long for sleep, night and day alike, with Darya beside me, my knee touching the tender crook of her leg.

And yet on the day the mourning visits ended, I found the empti-

ness unbearable. Masha had taken Darya to the market, and I had no
duties to attend to. I tried to read, but the words swam in front of my
eyes.

In the street someone laughed. A horse snorted and neighed. I
closed the window and drew the curtains. By then Grigory and Alexei
Orlov had already left the city, assuring me that my husband's name
would not be forgotten.

I sat in the empty parlor in my widow's weeds, staring at Egor's
portrait, the bright reds and greens of his uniform. The painted face
resembled the original vaguely. Was it the fault of the wrinkles on his
forehead Egor had demanded? Or was the nose too straight? The chin
too rounded?

I thought of the palace girl I had once been, orphaned, lost, hugging myself in the dark, shivering for attention. I thought of the palace
spy seduced with promises of her own importance, her eyes set on the
life that wasn't hers. I thought of a young bride blinded by grand
thoughts of her own destiny, unable to see happiness within her grasp.

I thought of what might have been but never would be.

The agony of loss that washed over me was unstoppable, like an
ocean wave after the earth shakes.

I hardly recognized Sir Charles in the man who waited for me by
Egor's grave one afternoon in late September. A day still warm, although I had already seen the first twirls of withered leaves scattered
by the northern wind.

Seated on a small wooden bench, he cut a poor figure. Bloodshot
eyes, razor nicks on his chin, his gray traveling coat crumpled and not
too clean. Sir Charles rose and extended his arms when I approached,
as if he meant to embrace me, before dropping them abruptly.

Darya's hand tightened in mine.

"He is an old friend," I whispered to my daughter. "It's all right."

"Papa's friend?" she asked, still doubtful.

"Yes," I said, lifting the black muslin veil from my face. "And ours."

Sir Charles offered his condolences and apologized for not visiting me earlier. "I had not been well. I hope I can make up for it now." His voice was hoarse, feverish, almost.

This is not why he came here, I thought.

But it was only on our slow walk back to the carriage, with Darya ahead of us, that Sir Charles asked me to warn the Grand Duchess.

"Tell her not to write to me, *pani* Barbara. My letters are being opened. My servants have all been bribed."

The Shuvalovs were poisoning the Empress's mind against Field Marshal Apraxin. The victory of Gross-Jägersdorf paled beside the rumors of the Russian commander's massive incompetence. Supplies missing, detachments sent into the wrong towns, orders signed too late, for the Field Marshal refused to be woken up before ten in the morning.

I winced at the mention of Gross-Jägersdorf, but Sir Charles was not looking at me. He spoke in short, abrupt sentences.

"I only hope that the Grand Duchess didn't do anything rash," he said. She had been seen with Bestuzhev far too often. What was the Chancellor pushing her to do? She wasn't foolish enough to show her support for Apraxin, was she?

I felt a pang of impatience. Is that all that mattered? Palace rumors? Intrigues? Is nothing more important?

In front of us Darya skipped, only to stop and cast me an uneasy look. *Can Papa's soul see me?* she had asked that morning.

"Will you remind the Grand Duchess that Apraxin is thought of as Bestuzhev's man?" Sir Charles continued anxiously. His fingers toyed with the silver buttons on his coat. I smelled the mustiness of wool.

"Yes," I said, not trying to hide resentment in my voice. "I will."

Beside me, Sir Charles stopped abruptly and gripped my arm. He was not wearing gloves, and I caught sight of his whitening knuckles.

"You haven't been in the palace, *pani* Barbara, so you don't know," he said, and I felt the fine mist of his spit on my face. "The Empress is dying, and no one but Catherine is capable of ruling Russia."

I put my finger on my lips to warn him to lower his voice, grateful that only a few steps separated us from the wrought-iron gate of the Lazarus cemetery.

"Tell the Grand Duchess," Sir Charles continued, ignoring my gesture, "that I'll never abandon her. I'll help her when the moment comes. And, dear *pani* Barbara, that moment is coming soon."

"Sir Charles is warning you to be careful," I told Catherine that evening. She had sent her maid away and was resting on an ottoman in her bedroom, a book propped over her protruding stomach, her feet buried in a bearskin. The woodstoves in the temporary palace gave little heat.

She closed the book.

"I don't need his warnings, Varenka. I'm not witless. I'm sorry he put you through so much trouble on my account."

I looked at the mound of her belly. The baby was due in two months.

An image flashed through my mind, a gardener in Oranienbaum with his bucket of brine, plucking the snails from a bed of dahlias and drowning them. Catherine, straightening to ease her back, complaining that the Lower Gardens had been infested all summer.

"*The Empress is dying? When the moment comes?*" I repeated Sir Charles's words. "What was he talking about?"

Catherine motioned for me to sit beside her. "Sir Charles has been odd in the last weeks. I didn't tell you, for you have enough of your own troubles."

"Odd?"

"Forgetful. He ordered his china plates to be packed, and then accused his servants of stealing them. Stanislav, too, is worried."

I waited for her to say more, but Catherine took my hand and placed it on her belly, so much bigger than it had been when she was pregnant with Paul.

"The midwife tells me to keep warm, Varenka. Do you think there might be twins inside?" she asked with a smile.

In November, the court celebrated Elizabeth's accession to the throne, the thirteenth year of her reign. She was forty-eight years old.

I had turned thirty, a widow of three months, with an eight-year-old daughter and no family. Only a few friends and an old servant to look after her if I died.

I resumed my court service. The chambermaids let it slip how in my absence the Imperial Bedroom had not functioned as it should. This or that lady-in-waiting had not come when she was meant to, another left too early, as soon as the Empress dozed off, and was not there when the Empress awoke. Cats had been locked out, left meowing in the cold. Candles smoked. Another thief had been caught hiding in the closet, his pockets padded with the Empress's silks.

"Madame Malikina," the hushed voices of the chambermaids trailed me. "A terrible loss," they called Egor's death, while their faces urged me to remember their sympathetic words, to judge them worthy when the time came to assign duties, distribute rewards.

The Empress let her gaze slide over my black dress.

"Bring Darya to the nursery," she told me. "The Tsarevitch knows that soon he will have a little brother. He is jealous. Darya can play with him."

"My daughter is not well yet, Your Highness. She won't eat," I said, thinking of how Darenka's bony shoulders stuck out of her dress.

You are contradicting me, the Empress's face said. I waited for her voice to harden, but to my surprise, it didn't.

"Bring her tomorrow, Varvara," she said gently. "Children need to play."

With the accession banquet over, the palace readied itself for the second imperial birth. No one would mention the cause for the planned feasts—it would have been unlucky before the baby was safely delivered—but I watched whole carcasses of lambs, calves, and pigs carried into the house opposite the temporary palace, rented for its deep cellars. Hares, pheasants, and capons arrived in huge baskets. Barrels of wine and beer were rolled inside. In the palace itself, right above the kitchen, the smells of baking wafted every time the windows were opened.

The banquet room was scrubbed and polished. No chip in the gilded chairs went unnoticed, no crack in the paneling unpatched. The maids burned sweet perfume pills to infuse the room with the scent of roses. The footmen, in felt slippers, walked on the giant banquet table, waxing and buffing the surface inch by inch.

In the churches across the land the Russian people prayed for the safe delivery of the Grand Duchess and for another grandchild of Peter the Great.

"I want Stanislav to be with me when it happens," Catherine told me.

"Think of a way, Varenka," she ordered, when I raised my eyebrows. "You do everything *she* asks of you, don't you?"

"He'll have to hide."

"Then he'll hide. I don't want to be alone! Not this time."

The bedroom in the temporary palace where she would give birth was large and drafty. It was not difficult to persuade the Empress that it needed a screen that would make it warmer. With a few adjustments, a small closet attached to the bedroom could be easily turned into an antechamber, with a narrow bed Stanislav could use. This is where Catherine's lover would hide, in the closet, behind the screen, able to come out the moment Catherine was left alone.

"It has started," I told Stanislav, when I rushed to the Saxon Mission on the night of November 29 with the news of Catherine's labor pains.

In the mission parlor, with its portrait of Augustus II, the Elector of Saxony and the King of Poland, proudly displaying his double chin, Stanislav made a sign of the cross: "May the Lord keep her in his mercy," he murmured.

He fixed his solemn black eyes on me, as if I knew what the next hours would bring. Around his neck there was a golden chain, but whatever pendant it carried was covered by the folds of his cambric shirt.

"Please hurry," I urged him.

As he was getting ready, I walked to the window and parted the curtain just a crack. Down in the street an open sleigh sped by, its harness bells ringing softly. Moonlight glittered on the thin layer of fresh snow. Egor loved to bring it to Darya, the first snowball of the season, melting in his big hands.

I didn't wait long. In the last days, Stanislav had kept his clothes laid out, his carriage at the ready. All he had to do was gather a few things. Books to read to Catherine, paper and quills. Smelling salts.

"She is strong," I promised him. "The second time is always easier."

He gave me a grateful look, but I could tell my words did not reassure him.

During the short carriage ride along Great Perspective Road, the lifted curtain revealed the fleeting spectacles of the streets: a squealing pig escaping its owner, *murziks* in coarse knee-length sheepskin coats hauling bales of wool from the ship.

"I wish he were here," Stanislav said, as we passed the British Embassy, its brown façade lit by smoking lanterns.

A month before, in spite of all his promises, Sir Charles had exhausted all means to postpone his departure. In the end even a feigned illness didn't work. Now he was somewhere on his way back to London. There had been no letters.

"Did you see him before he left?" I asked Stanislav.

"Only for a hurried moment."

"Did he seem odd to you?"

"Odd?" He laughed. "No. Sad, perhaps. Resigned. Why? Have there been more malicious rumors?"

The carriage swayed. If the snow holds, I thought, we would soon change into sleighs. I pulled the fur blanket over my lap, feeling the soft warmth of sable on my feet.

"There are always rumors," I said.

The maid who opened the door to Catherine's bedroom gasped with relief. "The Grand Duchess is waiting for you. She won't let anyone else in."

Only one candle burned in the candelabra, casting restless shadows on the wall. Catherine was lying in bed, her knees bent.

"Is he here?" she demanded, lifting herself up on her elbow. I saw her wince in pain. The contractions were getting stronger.

"Outside," I said. "In the carriage. I'll send the maids for the midwife and bring him in."

Her face lit up with relief, but her hand when she squeezed mine was hard and moist, like a whetstone.

The waters broke after the midwife made Catherine drink some rhubarb tea, and soon the whole palace learned of the imperial confinement. Elizabeth arrived, surrounded by her ladies-in-waiting, and, after exchanging a few words with Catherine, demanded to see the soiled sheets.

"Are they pink?" she asked, holding them to the light for everyone to examine them. "Will it be another boy?"

"Pink," the ladies-in-waiting assured her one by one, telling the Empress what she wanted to hear.

Elizabeth nodded and asked how long it would take before the new Tsarevitch would arrive.

"A few more hours, Your Highness," the midwife said. "Your Highness should rest."

The Empress asked three more questions. Was the Grand Duke told? Why was he not here? When was he coming?

As I hurried with answers, from behind the screen I heard Stanislav's muffled stumble. I breathed a prayer, hoping that there was too much commotion in the room for anyone to notice, but the Empress turned her eyes toward the screen.

This is when Catherine gave a yelp of pain and rose from the mattress.

"Please," she stuttered, her teeth chattering. "Please. It hurts."

The Empress turned toward her with some soothing words. Moments later, she was gone and the midwife was waving everyone away. We were taking up too much air. The Grand Duchess needed to breathe. The Grand Duchess needed to concentrate.

In the room next door, among the throng of restless courtiers, I thought of Stanislav. The folly of Catherine's need for him suddenly terrified me. *What if he cannot stay hidden?*

But he did.

He stayed there, silent when the Grand Duke came to tell Catherine of a great parade he was planning as soon as he had another son. A hundred cannons firing all at once.

He stayed there when he heard the midwife say the word *breech*, and Catherine's sobs that followed.

I wondered if his presence was helping her. If when the pains gripped her she looked in the direction of the screen.

Hours passed. Long, sweaty hours of birth. Hours of pain and fear and uncertainty. It was ten o'clock the next morning when the midwife opened the door and screamed for someone to fetch the Empress.

I ran across the length of the palace to the Empress's inner rooms. I found her in bed, propped on pillows, covered with an ermine-lined mantle. Her arm had been freshly bandaged. The bandages were stained with blood.

The bedroom maids were evasive in their answers. The doctor said it was nothing, just a fainting spell. The doctor bled her right away, and Her Highness had been resting ever since. They were not to talk about it to anyone.

I approached the bed.

"Your Majesty," I said.

Elizabeth stirred.

"The midwife says it's time," I continued. "Is Your Highness able to walk?"

The Empress opened her eyes. Her sagging cheek was reddened where it had pressed on the pillow.

"Why wouldn't I be?" she asked.

When she sat up, I saw that the maids had not removed her evening gown but merely opened it at the back. I fastened the hooks as quickly as I could. When I extended my hand to her to help her from the bed, Elizabeth slapped my hand and told me to stop fussing.

By the time the Empress reached Catherine's bedroom, the baby had already slipped out.

"Your Highness. Paul Petrovich has a sister!" the midwife exulted, as she washed the slime and blood from the tiny body.

"A sister?" the Empress repeated.

The baby gave a soft squeal.

The midwife had not been able to keep the spectators away. Elizabeth's ladies-in-waiting had poured in behind the Empress. Now they huddled, craning their necks. Keys, seals, looking glasses suspended from their chatelaines, tinkled softly.

I heard Catherine moan.

I held my breath.

"Perhaps this is for the better," the Empress finally said. "Paul won't be so jealous of a girl."

A murmur of applause followed, whispers of approval.

I cast a quick look at the Grand Duchess. Her skin was blanched, her lips pursed to stop her teeth from chattering. She looked frail and feverish.

I was still hoping that the Empress might let Catherine hold her daughter. I thought of the sweetness of the moment when I'd cradled

Darya for the first time, so small, and so very much mine. But as soon as the baby girl was swaddled, the Empress took her away from the room, her cooing voice fading in the distance. She didn't even wait for the afterbirth, which did not come on its own and had to be extracted by hand.

The courtiers followed.

Go with them, Varenka, Catherine's eyes pleaded. *I need you to tell me what you have seen.*

I left.

Anna Petrovna, the Empress called Catherine and Stanislav's daughter, named after her beloved sister, Peter's mother. She ordered that the baby would stay in the Imperial Bedroom, at least for the first month of her life.

It was an endless day. Footmen had to fetch cots from the attic for the wet nurses. Furniture had to be rearranged, the place for the cradle found, not too close to the fireplace but away from the draft.

The visitors thronged to see the baby, delivering their predictable praises. "Beautiful . . . graceful . . . angelic . . . her face just like her aunt's."

Elizabeth beamed. Other than the bandaged arm, I thought, her fainting spell had left no trace.

No one mentioned the Grand Duchess. I comforted myself with the knowledge that this time, Catherine was not alone. Stanislav would wipe the sweat from her brow. He would hold her in his arms when she wept for their child.

I thought the Christmas celebrations that year particularly loud and lavish. Fireworks lit the December sky; laughter poured out of brightly lit rooms as the Empress announced the last Christmas at the temporary palace and the first Christmas for the new Grand Duchess.

In our small parlor, Masha hung a paper star and tied fir branches to the backs of chairs. In a leather-bound notebook Catherine had given her, Darya had drawn a manger with the Holy Mother and Child, surrounded by the shepherds and the animals who came to visit them.

It was our first Christmas after Egor's death. I thought of Catherine's baby, who would never feel the closeness of her own parents, and of my daughter, who would grow up without a father.

Elizabeth's heart, I told myself, had known no laws but her whims. Her heart craved secrecy and deceit, for in secrecy and deceit lay her power. As long as she ruled, more soldiers like Egor would die, more children like Darya and little Anna would grow deprived of their parents' love.

Death, I thought. Death has to take the Empress away and give a new Empress a chance. A crack in the darkness, a mere slit, but the new Sovereign will make good use of it. She'll force her way, and I'll follow in her steps. Her helper. Her friend.

If she succeeds, Darya and I would never go without.

For a moment I glimpsed it: a world beyond deceit and malice, beyond fear. A new world, where words like *a bookbinder's daughter* or *a service noble* were not the shackles that bound our steps. The vision may have been fleeting, but to me it shone like the tooled letters of gold on the spines of my father's bindings.

NINE

1758

Every morning Elizabeth's ladies-in-waiting visited Catherine's rooms.

Anna's crib was carved out of an ancient oak, they said, her clothes sewn of the softest cambric. When Anna cried, the Empress carried her in her arms, murmuring endearments. *My little soul, my life, my joy. Grand will be your dresses, your jewels. You will be beautiful and full of grace.* The Imperial Favorite was constantly at her side, declaring himself smitten by both the aunt and her grandniece.

"A blessed angel child," they murmured.

"*Her* cabal," Catherine called the ladies from Elizabeth's entourage. "Sent here to spy on me, Varenka."

By January she had seen her daughter only three times, and each time the baby was damp with sweat.

The questions she asked me were angry, smoldering with hurt. Didn't the Empress ever allow air in the nursery? Wasn't there anyone among the courtiers to put one good idea into her mind? Was that so difficult?

Ever since Anna's birth, Catherine had kept to her bedroom, pleading ill health. Stanislav often stayed there with her, the little closet always a convenient hiding place when anyone came. Prince Naryshkin and his sister Anna, as well as Princess Dashkova, were also frequent visitors. Sometimes I'd hear their laughter, followed by the low murmurs of courtiers well accustomed to eavesdroppers.

"The Grand Duchess is eating for twenty." The maids winked and giggled as they cleared empty plates. I warned them to keep their lips sealed if they wanted to stay with their mistress.

They swore they would.

Monsieur Rastrelli—so often chastised for the delays—proudly announced that the Winter Palace would soon be ready for the court to move in. In the meantime, to ease the waiting, he invited the Empress and her Favorite to inspect his progress.

Elizabeth didn't mind that her visits were accompanied by the incessant hammering and banging of the carpenters and masons. She didn't mind when pieces of plaster stuck to the soles of her shoes, or when her ladies-in-waiting tripped over pieces of tile and discarded stucco moldings. Leaning on Ivan Shuvalov's arm, trailed by the courtiers, she swept through the finished chambers, gasping with pleasure.

"More light!" the Empress had demanded of her chief architect when he had brought her the plans ten years before. Monsieur Rastrelli obliged with big windows that let in the sun, gilded frames, and the sparkle of precious stones. He gave her gilded ornaments on white walls, mirrors reflecting candlelight, gleaming mosaics, and the rich, translucent glow of amber.

"The Russian baroque," he told her as she inspected yet another glittering room, "has purity unknown anywhere else. This light will be Your Majesty's lasting gift to Russia. This sparkle will make all of Europe take notice."

The Empress liked that.

Monsieur Rastrelli was once again called a genius, even when it became clear that the sections or rooms he presented as finished were far from it. After the Empress left, teams of masons, bricklayers, carpenters, and painters descended on them to replace faux walls, to finish the rough floors hidden beneath carpets, or to swiftly dismantle what the Empress disliked.

Catherine was not impressed by the Russian baroque. "Gaudy and passé," she told me, after she had accompanied the Empress on one such visit. I tried not to dwell on the venom in her voice. "Wait until another winter, Varenka. When these giant windows freeze over and crack."

In the steppes of Ukraine, Egor told me once, a single cloud on the winter horizon foretold a blizzard. A traveler could count on a mere few hours to seek shelter before all roads vanished, carriages turned into awkward humps, like grave mounds in a white desert without signposts.

In the first weeks of 1758 the news from the front was greeted with growing disbelief. The spectacular victories of the previous year did not bring the expected offensive farther into East Prussia. Instead, with the first snow, Field Marshal Apraxin had ordered a halt of all army movements for the whole winter.

"He says it's because of the breakdown in supply lines?" Ivan Shuvalov's voice soared with a thespian flourish. "How can a victorious army be short of supplies?"

I described it all to Catherine. How when Apraxin's reports were read aloud to the Empress, Countess Shuvalova raised her eyebrows. How her brother sucked in air through his blackened teeth. "Why is Field Marshal Apraxin giving the Prussian King a break? Is it incompetence or treason?" he asked. "And who is telling him to? Bestuzhev and one of his new friends?"

He means you, I warned Catherine, but she did not look concerned. She had nothing to hide, she assured me. Bestuzhev was forever trying to interest her in some of his schemes, but she always refused to take sides.

"Let the Shuvalovs talk, Varenka," she said. "There isn't much more they can do."

She was right, I thought. St. Petersburg was preparing for Prince Naryshkin's wedding. The bride was his mother's choice, for the son had been taking too long to make up his mind whom to propose to. In the Imperial Bedroom the government papers awaited Elizabeth's signature, reports lay unread. The Empress sent back dozens of pandoras that modeled her ceremonial gowns before she settled for a sky-blue silk gown with wide hoopskirts, on which garlands of muslin vines sparkled with diamond grapes.

"You can always count on our help," Alexei Orlov had assured me in these painful days after Egor's death. He repeated his promise every time he called on me during his visits to the capital.

He would bring gifts for Darenka, a china tea set for her dolls' house, a silver brush set for her hair. He'd stay to a simple dinner. "Uncle Alexei," Darya agreed to call him.

Very proper visits they were, chaperoned by Masha's mute presence, her good eye catching mine when the subject of our conversations strayed to what she didn't understand, warning me against what she judged to be too much joviality, a gesture too free. For no matter how she liked Alexei Grigoryevich Orlov of the Izmailovsky Regiment, how often she called him Master Egor's true friend, she would not allow me to become a target of malice.

"People talk," she grumbled, refusing to tell me what she had heard. "This is how people are. You are a widow."

One such evening, for Darya's amusement Alexei Orlov was coming up with one outlandish story after another. The scar on his face, he assured my daughter, came from a unicorn's horn. It gave him special powers.

"Close your eyes and count to five," he told her. "And I'll go to the moon and come back."

I watched Darenka fight disbelief when our guest presented various proofs of his moon trips: a stone, a feather, a smooth piece of driftwood.

"Is it true, Maman?" she asked. "Do birds fly that far away? Are there trees on the moon?"

"How would I know, *kison'ka?*" I asked her back, not wishing to extinguish the sparks in her eyes. "I've never been there."

Amid all this merriment, I waited for the conversation to turn to Catherine. I never forgot that the guards were called "the makers of the Tsars."

The Grand Duchess handled her horse superbly. Her command of Russian was a source of marvel; so was her poise and good humor, especially in *Das Fräulein's* presence.

There was no need for words more direct than these. The winter freeze had suspended the hostilities, but Russia was still at war. The time was not right, but that did not mean that it was being wasted. The Shuvalovs were not the only ones making plans. In the games of the court, there were those who—in the hour of need—would stand at Catherine's side.

On the morning of February 13, Stanislav came to my rooms at the temporary palace shaken and distraught.

"Bestuzhev has been arrested," he told me, once I'd sent Masha away. "Yesterday. Right outside the Imperial Bedroom." Fear made his voice waver and break.

I could not believe his words. I'd been at the palace all day. I saw no one running, no signs of agitation that would indicate an event of such magnitude.

"Keith told me," Stanislav continued, trying to steady his voice.

The new British Ambassador had kept Sir Charles's allegiances, but he didn't tell Stanislav much beyond the basic facts. Bestuzhev had been stripped of his office and his rights, and questioned about his friendship with Field Marshal Apraxin. Bernardi, the jeweler who carried Catherine's notes to Sir Charles and to Stanislav, and Abadurov, Catherine's Russian tutor, had been arrested as well.

The old spymaster beaten at his own game?

I felt a thump of fear as my mind rushed to consider the conse-
quences. My heart was racing. The Shuvalovs were no fools. They
knew I was Catherine's friend. Bernardi used to carry my letters, too.

Catherine didn't know anything of these events, Stanislav continued. He'd wanted to warn her himself, but her maids told him she was
with the Grand Duke. In the temporary palace, the Grand Duke's
room was next to the Imperial Suite. Stanislav didn't want to go there
himself. He didn't want to cause Catherine more trouble. He pressed
a folded note into my hand and closed my fingers tightly around it.
His fingers were sweaty and cold. "You have to warn her, Barbara," he
urged me. "Please, hurry."

I asked him to wait for news at the Saxon Mission.

I slipped the note into my pocket. Darya was calling me from the
other room. On my way out I motioned for Masha to go to her.

Before we parted, Stanislav put his hand on my arm.

"Tell Sophie that all will be well—in the end."

I walked along the corridor in measured steps, anxious to hide my
own terror. I recalled the Shuvalovs' contempt for Apraxin's reports.
"Let them talk," Catherine had said. She was wrong. I knew that now.
The Shuvalovs had the Empress's ear.

As I moved along the hallway, I passed old tapestries depicting
familiar hunting scenes: A stag pierced by an arrow. A bear, upright
and bloodied, tearing dogs off its chest. Through the window, I saw a
water carrier rolling a large barrel through the path cleared of snow,
whistling a loud tune. By the palace kitchen a beggar woman with a
bandaged face and two slits for her eyes stood patiently for her share
of stale pies and hardened bread.

I recalled the anguished face of Madame Kluge, her loud screams,
her limp body dragged to the scaffold.

When would the guards come for me? At dawn, so that no one
would see? No one but my child.

Before the Grand Duke's suite I pinched my cheeks to get some
color in the pale face I glimpsed in the ornate mirror.

The Grand Duchess was having a private breakfast with the Grand Duke. The papers they had been working on still covered part of the table. She brightened at the sight of me.

"It's Varenka, Peter! What a lovely surprise."

"I told you she would come by." The Grand Duke brushed bread crumbs from the front of his silken waistcoat. "We were just talking of Lev Naryshkin's wedding feast. Have you heard that the bride's mother demanded twenty barrels of oysters?"

"Twenty-five," Catherine said, laughing.

I walked toward her. When Peter motioned for one of the footmen to bring more coffee, I slipped Stanislav's note into her hand.

"My stockings are ruined again," Catherine complained, bending, so that the table would hide her from her husband's sight. I saw her unfold the note and scan it quickly before slipping it underneath her garter. Her face did not change.

"How is sweet Darenka?" she asked. "Will you let her stay with me in Oranienbaum this summer? Tell her she can help me take care of the birds. She'll like that."

The servants brought another plate for me. Would I have *bliny* with caviar? Cucumbers with honey? There was no hurry in Catherine's voice, no note of alarm.

It was only when we reached her room that I saw the white knuckles of her clenched fists.

For the next hour, in silence, we fed the fire with her papers, all of them, no matter how innocuous. Letters, receipts, pages of her writing. Notes on her readings. She opened her drawers one by one and handed me the contents.

I recognized Stanislav's handwriting, but mostly I recognized that of Sir Charles. Many of the letters from him were pages long. Catherine had not destroyed them, as I had urged her to.

How slowly paper burns, I fretted, as the flames licked the edges of the sheets, as singed words turned from brown to black, soot flowers I shattered with the poker until only ashes were left.

There would be no sudden change of plans, we agreed. Catherine and Peter would go to Naryshkin's wedding. There would be no note for Stanislav. Just a message I was to pass to him in utter secrecy: *Keep silent at all cost.* Deny everything, until she learns more.

"Tell him there is nothing he can do to help me. Tell him not to do anything without word from me. Tell him to trust me, Varenka."

I hurried to the Imperial Bedroom. It seemed to me that the guard at the door gave me a vacant but irritated look, as if struggling to recall who I was.

I tried to pay him no heed.

The chambermaids informed me that the Empress had left for the day, and that she had taken the baby with her. Ivan Ivanovich Shuvalov was with Her Majesty. They didn't know more than that.

Awaiting the Empress's return, I couldn't keep still. Restless, I ordered a thorough cleaning of the fireplace in the Imperial Bedroom. I sent the footmen outside with the carpets, to spread them on the snow and beat the dust out.

I was praying the Empress would allow me to stay with her that night, to entice her with my stories. I would tell her of a woman on Moskovskaya Street, her swollen breast flattening, the ugly tumor melting into nothingness after Blessed Ksenia touched her. The same Blessed Ksenia, I would tell her, who had given away all she owned to the poor and now walked barefoot through the streets of the city, dressed in rags. Then I would mention Bestuzhev's name and watch Elizabeth's face, read the shape of her frown.

But the Empress did not come back. That evening one of her ladies-in-waiting dropped by for the brushes and combs. I arranged them on a silver tray, adding a jar of Elizabeth's favorite cold cream. The lady-in-waiting took the tray and said that the Empress would stay in Count Shuvalov's suite for the night.

When she left, I sat down at the Empress's dressing table. My body felt as though it were made of stone. In the gold-framed mirror, my own face stared back at me, haggard-looking and strange. My black mourning dress was speckled with ashes from the fireplace.

I thought of the Chancellor, locked in some room, answering or refusing to answer questions. I thought of Catherine's calm and of her clenched fists.

The chair underneath me moaned as I rose.

I walked to my own rooms swiftly, through the long corridor of the temporary palace, my black-clad figure duplicating in the mirrors as I passed.

The rumors ranged from plausible to ridiculous. The accusations were vague but serious: misrepresentation of imperial orders, conspiring with the enemy, treason. The most serious ones spoke of the Chancellor ordering General Apraxin to stall the Russian offensive against the King of Prussia. Someone had heard him say that the Empress had only weeks to live, that it was now up to the Young Court to secure Russia's future.

Depending on whom one listened to, Bestuzhev had acted at Catherine's request or out of his own conceit. He was tortured or he was not tortured. They'd found incriminating papers or they'd found nothing. He'd confessed or he'd insisted on his innocence.

The rumors grew wilder, but there were no more arrests.

We had no choice but to think of this time as a time of trial.

We were watched. We had to act our parts.

Stanislav stayed home, feigning illness. Catherine and Peter went to Lev Naryshkin's wedding, where she laughed heartily when Count Nebalsin rejoiced that he would not have to pay Bernardi for the necklace the jeweler had delivered to him the day before he had been arrested.

The Empress returned to the Imperial Suite two nights later. She paid no heed to the brightness of the freshly brushed carpets. She did not wish me to massage her feet. When the evening came, she sent me back to my rooms.

Countess Shuvalova, she told me, would stay with her at night from now on.

I went about my daily duties and held my daughter close every night. The Grand Duchess and I kept our conversations brief and trivial when we met. A week later, I saw her in the corridor with one of her maids-of-honor. When I passed her, Catherine murmured, "It's not as bad as I feared, Varenka."

I stopped.

Catherine motioned for her maid-of-honor to move on.

The news was vague, but vagueness, too, could bring comfort.

Catherine had asked Prince Trubetskoy, the Procurator-General charged with conducting the inquiry into the affair, what the charges were against the Chancellor. The old Prince had a soft spot for the Grand Duchess ever since word reached him that she had cried when his youngest son was killed at Gross-Jägersdorf.

He told her, "The Shuvalovs had Bestuzhev arrested. Now I'm supposed to find out why."

The message from the Chancellor came hidden inside a snuffbox. The messenger who brought it insisted on handing it to the Grand Duchess herself. She was not in her rooms, and he didn't want to ask any of her maids-of-honor where she could be. The person who trusted him with the note mentioned my name, so he came to me.

In the palace chapel, where I took him, Catherine was bowing in front of the icon of the Lady of Kazan, touching the ground with the fingers of her right hand, the Orthodox way.

The messenger placed the snuffbox in her hands. As soon as he left, she opened it and extracted a note from the double lid, reading it quickly.

I saw the relief on her face.

"The Chancellor managed to burn his papers before they came for him, Varenka," she murmured. "The Shuvalovs have nothing but gossip."

She rolled the note and used it to light a candle of thanksgiving for a favor granted.

I nodded, but I could not coax a smile onto my lips. In Elizabeth's bedroom, gossip could still maim.

"Cheer up, Varenka." Catherine squeezed my hand. "Now I know what to do."

That evening everyone in the palace who passed by the Grand Duchess's rooms heard her anguished sobs. Her maids-of-honor rushed in and out, fetching laudanum and smelling salts. The Grand Duchess fainted, I heard. The Grand Duchess asked for her confessor.

Someone was trying to destroy her reputation, Catherine sobbed when Father Semyon arrived. Someone was trying to drive a wedge between her and Her Majesty, Her Benefactress.

Her voice wavered and broke: "If only Her Majesty would hear me out. . . . I cannot live like this anymore. . . . I want to fall asleep in a snowbank . . . . I've heard that it doesn't hurt to die from the cold."

Before Father Semyon left her room, he made a sign of the cross over her and ordered the maids-of-honor to pray for the souls in despair.

At midnight on April 13, a month after Bestuzhev's arrest, I heard the Empress dismiss her ladies-in-waiting and her maids.

I thought of Catherine, about to receive her summons. I thought of the power of gossip. I looked at the ceiling. Even above the Empress's rooms, the carpenters had not been too thorough. After the summer heat, the cracks in the floorboards had grown wider. Enough moonlight would come through attic windows for me to see my way.

In the service corridor I dipped a handkerchief in a bucket of water. Then I took off my shoes and crept up the narrow steps to the attic.

I lay on the dusty floor, my nose covered with a wet handkerchief to stop myself from sneezing. I did not move. Below me, I could see the marble tabletop lit by two candelabras, unfolded papers spread between them. The Empress was sitting in her armchair, a fan in her hands. I could tell she was not alone. In the dark, behind screens brought in for the occasion, shadowy figures crouched. *Some of the Shuvalovs?* I guessed. *The Grand Duke?*

I didn't have to wait long before the door opened and the guard announced the arrival of the Grand Duchess.

Before Catherine had time to utter her greetings, Elizabeth pointed to the papers on the table.

"What do you have to say about these?" she asked.

Catherine made a step toward the table. Her skirts rustled.

"These are my letters," she answered, a moment later. In her voice there was no hesitation and no fear.

"Letters to whom?"

"To General Apraxin."

"You have no right to send letters to my general. I expressly forbade you to concern yourself with politics."

"I merely congratulated the general on his victory, Your Majesty. I wished him a successful campaign."

"Bestuzhev says there were other letters."

"The Chancellor is wrong. There were no other letters."

"Should I have him tortured for lying?"

"If Your Majesty wishes."

I held my breath. In the cellars of the Secret Chancellery, there were many ways of ensuring confessions. Its chief, one of the Shuvalovs, had bragged of blows that left no traces on the skin. Elizabeth could order Catherine tortured, too. She could, like the Great Peter had once done to his own son, grab the knout from the executioner's hands to strike the first blow.

Behind one of the screens, someone moved.

I heard Peter's voice. "Don't believe her, Your Majesty. She knows how to twist the truth so that everyone believes she is right."

So the Grand Duke, too, had been summoned. What had the

Shuvalovs promised *him*? A triumph over his wife? A triumph he feared was slipping out of his grasp?

The Grand Duke emerged from his hiding place, his movements jerky and agitated. "*Elle est méchante*," he stammered, and stamped his foot.

He was calling his wife mean and deceitful.

Catherine fell to her knees. "I displease you, my Benefactress. I displease the Grand Duke, my husband. Your Highness can see it for yourself. There is nothing for me here. No one at this court will speak to me. No one trusts me. All I do is wrong. Every day I pray for Your Majesty's health and for the health of my children. I pray for Russian victory in this war. I don't know how else to please you and my husband. Let me go back to my family. Let me do some good with what is left of my life."

Was it Peter's clumsy abruptness that tipped the scales? Or was it Catherine's ultimate act of surrender that Elizabeth could never resist?

I heard a softening in the Empress's voice. "How can I send you back? What will you live on?"

"Anything my family can spare. I have no great needs. There is nothing here for me."

"You have two children."

"They are in excellent hands, Your Majesty. I'm not allowed to see them, anyway. Please let me go. It'll be best for me to go."

"You won't go anywhere. This is your home."

Peter grunted in disbelief. The floorboards squeaked under his shifting feet. *It is over*, I thought, as I watched the Empress motion for Catherine to stand up, extending her hand to be kissed. Catherine had won. She would again be welcome in the Imperial Bedroom, asked to soirees and games of cards.

Behind one of the screens, someone stifled a cough.

"You can see your children. . . ." I heard Elizabeth pause, negotiating the extent of her magnanimity. "Every other day."

There is distraction in relief. Time to notice the smudges of dust on my sleeves, to feel how my hands grew stiff from cold. To hear something move, scurry along the wall, underneath the white sheets hanging on strings, like giant sails.

The Grand Duke had been dismissed. Below me, Catherine was explaining something to the Empress, but I couldn't hear what she said. Once or twice it seemed to me that she uttered Stanislav's name.

Every time the Empress laughed.

There were more night summons to the Imperial Bedroom, sudden, urgent, unpredictable. Elizabeth did not like to give warnings. She trusted tears, confessions by candlelight, oaths on the Holy Icons. Catherine took to sleeping in her clothes, shoes by her bed, a basin with cold water nearby to wash the sleep from her eyes.

I didn't dare climb to the attic again. During the days that followed, I didn't seek Catherine's company, either, but when I did see her, she seemed calm and composed. We didn't talk about much other than our children and books, though she did mention Sir Charles. He did not write to her. She knew he had reached London only from his daughter's brief note of thanks. The presents the Grand Duchess of Russia had sent Lady Essex through her father were exquisite, and she was very grateful for them. Sir Charles was not well, she wrote, quite exhausted after his long journey and unable to hold a quill.

Neither of us mentioned Stanislav's name.

I didn't know if Stanislav had tried to see her, or had even tried to smuggle a letter. Once, passing by the Saxon Mission, I thought I saw him looking through the upstairs window. I stopped the carriage and told the driver to wait, thinking Stanislav might send his servant for me, but no one came.

In the Imperial Bedroom I was again ordered to massage Elizabeth's feet. *A good sign*, I told myself. After relaying the choicest of the palace gossip, I regaled the Empress with the rumors of the streets. The Chancellor's fate was the source of many wild speculations. Was he a Prussian spy in Frederick's pay? An English toady? An old court-ier past his prime trying to force her hand?

The Empress hardly listened. *Not as swollen as he had hoped,* her eyes mocked, as she twisted the rings on her fingers, her hand holding an emerald ring she had slid off her finger as if it were a die to be cast.

Once she ordered me to stand by the window and tell her what I saw there. The Palace Guards marched in formation. A carriage sped by.

"Nothing else?"

"Nothing, Your Highness."

Sometimes it seemed to me that we were not alone, that behind one of the screens that now always stood in the bedroom, someone was hiding, listening to my every word. But I never saw anyone.

Soon the news from the Prussian front replaced the rumors of the Chancellor's fate. After Apraxin's arrest, the imperial soldiers were again beating the Prussians, proving to Europe that Russia was not to be ignored.

Catherine was back in Elizabeth's favor, and the court took notice. The bows that greeted her deepened; the smiles grew wider; the in-quiries about her health became loud enough for everyone to hear.

It was a muted, gray morning in early May when I entered her room, the day's sudden chill signaling the annual breaking up of the ice fields on Lake Ladoga. In a few days the whole city would turn out to watch the ice floes noisily grinding against one another as they piled up on their way to the sea.

Catherine was hugging Bijou in her arms, letting him lick her hands. Old faithful Bijou, wheezing and smelly, more and more wob-bly on his feet.

She had bad news.

Two letters from Stanislav, Catherine told me, had been discov-ered among the former Chancellor's papers. They were formal letters of little significance, yet they reminded the Empress that it was Chancellor Bestuzhev who insisted on bringing Count Poniatowski back to St. Petersburg as the Saxon Envoy.

Stanislav, she said, had been ordered to leave.

"When?" I asked.

"Before the end of August."

"Could he not resign his position and stay?" I asked, knowing it was impossible. *Poor Stanislav,* I was already calling him in my thoughts.

Catherine gave me an unseeing look and lowered Bijou, letting him settle on his velvet pillow.

I can still hear her voice, terse and somewhat stiff, as if she had practiced her reply for too long and had grown tired of it already. "The Empress cannot do anything else, Varenka. The Empress must consider the future."

In the spring, the newly laid ceiling stuccos in the Winter Palace had begun to crumble and would have to be replaced. The long-promised move had been postponed once again. The Empress raged. Rastrelli was declared an incompetent liar, his workers a bunch of deceitful thieves. For weeks we all tiptoed around her, mindful of every word. Catherine and Peter were relieved when the time came to move to their Oranienbaum palace for the summer. I was not that lucky. When the Empress departed for Tsarskoye Selo, I was ordered to go with her.

The aftermath of Bestuzhev's fall was felt in St. Petersburg for some time, even though his interrogation yielded no results. Bestuzhev was not tortured. He would have said too much, gossips said.

After months of Apraxin's interrogations there were no proofs of treason, but no exonerations, either, only suspicions allowed to fester. Then, at the beginning of August, the Field Marshal died of a stroke. Bestuzhev was stripped of his position and banished from court to his country estate. He was forbidden from contacting anyone in the capital.

He left St. Petersburg in the second week of August. No one dared to see him off. His name would never again be mentioned in Elizabeth's presence. It was not the first such banishment. Nor would it be the last.

After a few postponements blamed on illness, in the third week of August, in Tsarskoye Selo, the Saxon Envoy presented his final report to the Empress and offered his profound thanks for the Russian hospitality.

The Empress presented Count Poniatowski a snuffbox with her portrait on the lid, studded with sapphires and rubies, and wished him a safe journey home. That same day, Stanislav traveled to Peterhof. Catherine had slipped out of Oranienbaum to be there with him for a few stolen days. They stayed in the Monplaisir Pavilion by the sea. Alone.

I saw Count Poniatowski at the Saxon Mission in St. Petersburg on the morning he left.

It was the last day of August. The day promised to be beautiful, in spite of the chill brought by the northern wind. In the courtyard of the Saxon Mission, two of Stanislav's servants were checking the straps on the coffers and trunks. Another was spreading a travel rug on the carriage seat.

I walked past them, into the mission.

Stanislav was waiting for me in the parlor. The portrait of Augustus II was in its usual place, but darker patches of color marked places from which paintings from Stanislav's own collection had been removed.

"This is not how I imagined leaving," he said.

"No," I replied, fighting an urge to place the palm of my hand on his forehead, the way I did with Darya when I wanted to test for fever. He was wearing the cambric shirt Catherine had given him when he came back last December. It had a letter *S* embroidered on the collar. No one else called her Sophie.

I had brought him presents. A basket holding Masha's preserves, and a drawing Darya had made for him, a cat in a velvet outfit, bowing in front of a Queen.

"Tell Darya that I'll put it in a gold frame when I get to Warsaw." Stanislav's voice was strained.

"I will."

"I'll be back, Barbara. I'll be with her when she needs me most. Don't let her forget that, will you?"

I walked with him to the yard. The horses neighed when they spotted him. He had a chunk of apple for each of them.

The carriage door was opened, the step extended.

How can you help her? I thought. *What can you do for her? What can she do with your love? Go. It'll be easier for her if you are not around.*

Stanislav put his foot on the carriage step, a polished tip of a black jackboot with silver trim. Inside the carriage I spotted an open trunk filled with books for the long journey to Warsaw.

In the end, he couldn't stop himself. Some thoughts are like aching teeth one probes with one's tongue.

"She wants me to come back, doesn't she?"

"Yes," I lied.

It was not for me to reveal Catherine's hand.

"Will you let me know if anything changes?"

"Of course."

I waited until the carriage started to roll away into the busy street before I walked back to the palace. I thought I would never see him again. Nothing else—no other future—seemed to make sense.

In the streets of St. Petersburg the beggars who sang war ballads and ditties were filling their pockets with coins. *Old Fritz, who lost his wits. Can't beat the Russians, he admits.* At the Tartar market vendors hawked battle scenes on which the paint had not yet dried, studded with miniatures of the new war heroes: By the fall of 1758 Grigory Orlov was among them. A hero from the Battle of Zorndorf.

"Orlov?" the Empress asked. "Handsome?"

"Yes, Your Highness."

"Tall?"

"Yes."

"A hero?"

The war was not yet over, but the Orlovs' army career had proved a disappointment. "Still a Lieutenant, though others became Majors and Colonels," his brother Alexei had said, bitterly, when he called on me at the palace. "Hiding from creditors and licking his wounds." His own commission had ended, and he was back in St. Petersburg, at the Izmailovsky Regiment. He would not seek another. It was back to the palace duty for him.

"Lieutenant Orlov captured the King's adjutant," I told the Empress. "He refused to leave the battlefield in spite of seventeen slashes of a saber on his body. But then there was this scandal."

"What did our eagle do?"

"He seduced his commander's mistress. Princess Kurakina. Ran away with her, but then he gambled away all his money and the Princess went back to her parents. His brother had to pay his debts."

"Tell me more," the Empress said, and laughed.

A soldier, brave and reckless. Strong enough to stop a runaway horse with bare hands. Eyes brimmed with glee when he walked into a room, dulled with dismay when he left.

Just like the men she always wanted to hear about.

"Give it to him." The Empress took a small ring off her finger and tossed it to me. The ruby, I noted, would not be worth more than two hundred rubles.

The limits of the imperial attention. "Advancement in the Russian army does not come on merit," Alexei had said. "It is either favor or bribe."

TEN

1759–1761

On the morning of March 8, the Grand Duchess Anna Petrovna woke up with a piercing scream. She would not suckle. She would not stop crying when the wet nurses carried her in their arms, and when they put her down she waved her arms and legs like a beetle stuck on its back.

She was fifteen months old.

The Empress rushed to the nursery, but even her favorite lullaby would not soothe Anna for more than a bewildered moment, a painful pause between wails. The doctor ordered a fresh chamomile infusion, but the baby vomited it all. Her eyes were glassy with fever. She was scratching herself until she bled; her face was covered with hot patches of raw skin.

When the nursery cat began to screech, the Empress ordered the room searched for anything suspicious. Nothing was found, no bones, no hairballs, but one of the wet nurses wept and admitted dreaming of a snake swallowing a frog. With its small legs, the frog clung to whatever it could grab, a stick, a branch, but the snake wouldn't let go.

The Empress stared at the nurse, her hand tugging at the hem of her sleeve; her face stiffened, furrowed with dread.

Rain pelted the windowpanes. Water dripped from the cracked frame, staining the white wallpaper. I thought of Catherine in Oranienbaum, making plans for her new garden, in preparation for the Young Court's annual move to the country. In the grayish stillness I saw Anna's hand twitch, her tiny fingers clasping and unclasping the air.

"Send someone to fetch the Grand Duchess, Varvara," I heard Elizabeth's strained voice. "Tell her to hurry."

What I recall next is a blur. I must have hurried to the guards' room, for I remember my relief at the familiar sight of Alexei Orlov's scarred face. Such a giddy feeling of relief it was, almost joy, as if one man could stop death, as if one man could make things right. I must have blurted something incoherent, for he asked me to repeat what I wanted before he understood. "Messenger," I remember saying, "quickly."

"I'll go right away," Alexei Orlov offered. He said something else, but, to me, his lips seemed to be moving without forming a sound. I sagged against his chest and cried.

When I got back to the nursery, the Empress sat by the cradle, dipping cloths in icy water to place on little Anna's forehead, giving her attar of roses to smell. She rocked the cradle gently. She promised her angel child a diamond as big as her beautiful eyes, if only she would get well.

The baby gave no sign that she'd heard.

The wet nurses and the ladies-in-waiting were praying in front of the icon of the Lady of Kazan. I, too, joined in the prayers.

Anna died three hours later. She had closed her eyes forever before Catherine entered the nursery, her mantle soaked with rain. There was no need for words. The Grand Duchess took one look at the Empress's frozen face and began to sob.

Dawn was breaking when I passed by the guards' room again. Inside, Alexei Orlov paced from window to door, the massive frame of his body rigid with tension. Three other guards sat squeezed on a wooden bench, watching the spectacle of the Orlov rage.

I leaned against the doorframe, my eyes smarting from crying, from sleepless hours of prayers.

Alexei lurched toward me. I felt the floor shake. I smelled the acrid foxy odor of his sweat. A tale came to me, an old Orlov family story I had heard once. Alexei's grandfather, condemned to death for mutiny, stepping on the scaffold and kicking the head of the man beheaded before him out of the way. Earning Peter the Great's pardon.

"She should've been sent for sooner. Who keeps a mother away from her child at such a time, Varvara Nikolayevna?"

My eyes trailed the scar across his cheek, the open collar of his tunic, hands clenched into fists. For a moment I, too, longed for a simpler world, where all wrongs could be avenged. An eye for an eye, swift and sure.

"I made the Grand Duchess leave the carriage behind and mount a horse. We rode like the devil. Still, we were too late."

Behind me, at the end of the corridor, something stirred. A maid in search of the secrets of the morning? I put my finger on my lips.

Alexei raised his voice. "I'm not afraid."

Inside the room, one of the guards cheered. Another one clapped his hands.

"I have to go," I said. My heart was heavy with the memory of Anna's waxy face, a child of such perfection. I needed to hold my own daughter in my arms. But before I could leave, Alexei Orlov caught the ruffle of my sleeve.

"The Grand Duchess has many friends, Varvara Nikolayevna. Let her know that, will you?"

Catherine and Stanislav's daughter was buried in the Alexander Nevsky Monastery, Peter the Great's gift to Russia. At the funeral, the Empress, in a plain black taffeta dress, without her jewels, ordered two of the strongest footmen to stand by her side, to hold her up if she began to falter.

Catherine had hidden her face under a thick black veil. She lifted

it only once, when she kissed Anna's cold hand before the priest closed
the lid of the tiny coffin. After the funeral she was silent and pensive,
preoccupied with her grief. I tried to console her, but nothing I did
dispelled her pain.

There was more bad news in the weeks that followed Anna's death.
First a letter came from Paris, to inform the Grand Duchess that
Princess Johanna had died. Catherine had been writing to her mother
for some time, so she knew of the Princess's most recent illness and
her growing debts, but the news was still a blow.

Then another letter, this one from London, announced the death
of Sir Charles Hanbury-Williams. *My beloved father*, his daughter
wrote Catherine, *did not find peace after his return from Russia. Nothing
here satisfied him; nothing could compare with what he had left behind.* In
the antechambers the rumors were less reticent: *a fine mind ravaged*, I
heard, *syphilitic confusion . . . an actress attacked with a knife.*

The end of old dreams, I thought, hurtful but necessary. Like purg-
ings, like drawing dark blood away from the body, the only way to let
the healing begin.

After Anna's funeral, Monsieur Rastrelli ordered thick canvas curtains hung to block off unfinished sections of the Winter Palace. Day
and night, his workers painted, laid carpets, and moved furniture.
Stoves were always banked up to the full, so that paint would dry
faster. By the time the Empress was brought to see her new bedroom,
only a scent of varnish bore witness to the frenzy that had ruled there
mere hours before.

"Here it is, Your Highness. The jewel worthy of you and of new
Russia. May it bring you everlasting pleasure."

Sculptures wrapped in burlap still crowded in the smaller ballroom. In what would become the servants' quarters the carpenters
stored lumber and glass panels. But Monsieur Rastrelli made sure the
imperial eye did not miss the precious wood floor, the gilded walls,
the crimson upholstery.

The Empress gave her architect a faint smile.

It won't be long now, I thought.

She was breathing hard, each breath drawn painfully out of her lungs. Her hands were too swollen for her favorite rings. Her feet were spilling out of even the most comfortable shoes.

When the Empress moved to her newly finished suite, only five of her twelve ladies-in-waiting followed. The chambermaids slept on cots in the alcove. Everyone else left the Winter Palace at the end of their shifts.

In the grand bedroom the old Imperial Bed looked small, a ship cast adrift on the sea.

When did I know the Empress of Russia was dying?

Was it at *Kanun* of 1761, the time of fasting and prayers after the January freeze, the preparation for the midnight Baptism of the Lord? The day before, *poslushniks* who serve the Nevsky monks cleared the snow from the river and cut a *Jordan*, a hole in the ice shaped like the cross, where the faithful would plunge, naked, to purge their bodies of sin.

"Silence!" the Empress screamed when we pleaded with her not to go to the *Jordan* that year. She stood there in the bitter cold when the bells tolled, when the monks led the procession to the ice hole.

In profile she looked as stern as her own face on a coin.

One by one, the faithful climbed out of the frigid bowels of the Neva, their hair frozen into icicles, and, shivering, joined the chorus of prayers. Swaddled in furs, cloaked in darkness, Elizabeth Petrovna, the daughter of Peter the Great, whispered, "Lord forgive me my trespasses as I forgive those who have trespassed against me."

By *maslenitsa*, the last week before Lent, when eating meat is forbidden though cream and butter are still allowed, the Empress was no longer able to sleep.

Her favorite cats—brought from the temporary palace—lounged with her on the bed, tucked along the curves of her body, purring under her caresses. When Bronya began growing big with kittens, Elizabeth ordered a birthing box for her to be placed by the stove.

At night twenty thick candles were to burn at all times in every room where she went. She was rarely left alone—visitors, courtiers, lovers, old and new, kept arriving. If she sent them away, one of her ladies-in-waiting was always ready to take their place. If the chatter of voices tired her, she called for her Cossack singers.

For a time there was hope of new cures: kalgan roots, which re-sembled a tiny human; Marcial waters from the Karelia that had once cured Tsarina Ksenia's barren womb; or the velvety black shungit rocks. Elizabeth chewed the roots, drank the waters, held pieces of rock in her hands. She prayed. On better days she even ordered a fit-ting for a new gown or asked to see jewels from the treasury. She'd dip her fingers in heaps of precious stones, caressing the rings and neck-laces, recalling the balls or masquerades when she had worn them.

When Gypsy women and the soothsayers arrived, the Empress no longer wished to hear of her future. It was the Tsarevitch's destiny she wanted revealed.

At seven years old, Grand Duke Paul was small and fragile, but no one ever said that to the Empress. His visits were scheduled for late afternoon, when she felt most alert. His gray eyes looked about her room without settling on anything. Sometimes he lifted his thumb to his lips and then dropped it before it reached his mouth. He called the Empress "Auntie," and ran to hide in her arms if anything frightened him, a door banging, a crow shrieking in the courtyard.

The cards released from their wrapping of black silk were laid in semicircles or crosses. "Spit on your hand and touch this card, Your Highness. Put a coin on that one. Knock on it. Tap it with your index finger."

The cards were elusive. One Gypsy woman saw Paul with a wife and children, many children; another saw him set off on a long jour-ney that would reveal what had been hidden. Most often the cards merely spoke of forked roads, uncertain promises, periods of danger.

"What kind of danger?" Elizabeth kept asking.

"The kind that will pass," the fortune-tellers replied carefully.

I, too, weighed my words with care.

I didn't tell the Empress when I found Bronya's whole litter of kittens dead in the birthing box. The maid swore they were all fine just hours before. Only one of them seemed to have had a runny nose, she wept in terror.

I didn't tell the Empress that the Blessed Ksenia had disappeared. Hackney drivers no longer spotted the bent figure in red and green rags who used to bring them good luck every time they gave her a lift. She did not sit at the entrance to the church of Apostle Matvei, and bakers waited in vain with her favorite cinnamon-spiced buns. No one could tell where she had gone until a novice monk saw her in the open fields, outside the city, crossing herself and bowing in prayer.

Instead, I brought stories of miracles. I told the Empress of holy men whose touch shrank tumors, of monks whose blessing cleansed the blood, of holy relics whose very presence made the crippled throw away their crutches, rise from their sickbeds, and walk away in grace. I told myself that I needed to please her, just as I always had. For had she ever asked about Bronya's kittens?

And then, on one moonless night lashed by the northern wind, the Empress ordered me to bring Anna's clothes and toys to her bed. She kissed the folds of the tiny dresses, smoothed the lace of the white baptismal gown, lifted the dolls, one by one, and stared into their lifeless eyes.

"God's will is sometimes so hard to bear, Varvara," she said.

I bent my head in silence.

For a long while the Empress sat motionless, with folded hands, muttering a prayer for the dead.

I, too, prayed with her. I prayed for forgiveness of my own sins and for my own dead. I prayed for my parents, and I prayed for Egor. I prayed until the Empress asked me to help her to her bed.

Soon, nestled in the splendor of the imperial silks, Elizabeth looked as if she were asleep. I rose to slip out of the room, but then I heard a small, frightened voice: "Does it not matter that I spared his life? Is mercy not enough?"

It took me a moment to realize she meant Ivanushka, the baby Tsar she had deposed twenty years before. The mad-room Prince, locked safely in his prison cell, was still able to chase imperial sleep away.

It was in these dark spring days that Catherine's *révolution de palais* began.

First came the guarded steps, words tossed like bait, unexpected visits that ended with fingers touching the lips in caution.

In the temporary palace, the Grand Duke claimed the now-empty Imperial Suite. Where Elizabeth's bed once stood, he spread a model of the Battle of Zorndorf, for which *Das Fräulein* had made intricate papier-mâché trees and replicas of peasants' huts. "A disputed Russian victory," the Grand Duke informed his visitors, rubbing his hands as he presented his calculations. The Prussians lost 12,800 men, while the Russians lost more than 18,000. Although the Russians kept the battlefield on the following day, they were the first to retreat.

How can the Crown Prince say such words? I wondered then. Whose side was he on? Was he a fool or a traitor?

I was not the only one posing questions.

"Remember, Varenka, how Peter marched me like one of his soldiers," Catherine recollected. "How he wouldn't even let me touch those dolls he always played with?"

Remember how he lashed his hounds until they howled?

Remember when he executed a rat, for it dared to upset his toys? This, too, is a memory of these days. That snigger, raw and razor-sharp, every time Catherine mentioned her husband's name.

"The Grand Duchess has many friends, Varvara Nikolayevna," Alexei Orlov had said. But it was Grigory Orlov who crossed our path one

May morning in the gardens by the Summer Palace, where Catherine had given birth to Paul seven years before.

Grigory had been away for so long that I had almost forgotten how much he resembled Alexei. The same towering frame, the same raven-black mop of untamed hair. The same flaunting gestures, one hand on his chest, another holding the dusty coat over his steel-blue Izmailovsky tunic. But where his brother's cheek was marred with a scar, there rose but a darkened shadow of yesterday's shave.

"Hear me out, Your Highness," Grigory implored in a loud voice, his eyes alight. "I am no stranger. Varvara Nikolayevna here can vouch for me."

I nodded. "A friend," I told Catherine. "Lieutenant Orlov and his brothers have been most kind to me after Egor's death."

"Leave us, then, Varenka," Catherine ordered. Amused curiosity brought a sheen of color to her cheeks. She tossed her head and smiled.

I stepped aside.

I could see Grigory Orlov from where I retreated, a giant on his knees, clasping Catherine's hand. Rising, bending his head to hear her out, shaking his head, repeating his plea.

The words that reached me were broken fragments: . . . *your husband . . . not worthy . . . If you don't, we will.*

I looked around but saw only a bird skittering in and out of a hedge, a worm writhing in its beak. I plucked a fresh leaf from the hedge and tore it into tiny pieces. It left a scent of musk on my skin.

When Catherine called me back to her side, there was no trace of Lieutenant Grigory Orlov of the Izmailovsky Guards, only a hollow in the gravel path where he had knelt.

"If anyone asks," Catherine told me, "a hero of the Battle of Zorndorf wanted to pay his respects."

The rumors swirled, less and less cautious, less and less hushed. Who will be Elizabeth's successor—Peter or his son, Paul? Will Catherine rule with Peter? Or will she be made Regent for her young son?

As the Empress of Russia sickened, the Shuvalovs and the Vorontzovs closed ranks and threw their support behind Peter. At functions
that called for his wife's presence, *Das Fräulein* began showing up at
her lover's side. Catherine ignored these slights, until the much-
awaited premiere at the Russian Theater when Peter announced that
there was no room for her in his carriage. "You can go tomorrow," he
told his wife, relenting only when the Grand Duchess threatened to
walk.

In the imperial sickroom, when at the Empress's request I brought
Darya to visit her, the ladies-in-waiting eyed me with open hatred.
"That sneaky bookbinder's daughter," I heard Countess Shuvalova
mutter, "and her brat."

"Why doesn't she like me, Maman?" Darenka whispered to me,
when the Countess had swept by us, her wide skirts rustling, her be-
jeweled hand pushing my daughter out of her way.

"I'll tell you when you grow up."

"Why not now?" I felt Darya's fingers tighten on mine.

I knew she was not convinced when I explained that only then
would she understand.

No spy can afford to ignore a mask of forced indifference, a moment
of pensive silence where a simple answer would suffice. I saw it all: the
infinitesimal hesitation when Catherine mentioned Grigory Orlov's
name, that instant when she looked out the window and waved at
someone, her fingers covering a smile.

"A valiant soldier and a true friend. But unlike his younger brother,
he has been reckless," I warned the Grand Duchess. I mentioned the
abandoned mistress, the debts Alexei had to pay.

"We've all been reckless at times, Varenka," Catherine said, and
smiled.

Rumors flew. Grigory had won a thousand rubles at faro. He'd
spent it all in one evening, buying vodka for anyone willing to drink to
the Grand Duchess's health. He'd sworn that she was surrounded by
miserable scoundrels, rouges and milksops, half-men who would fall

over if he pushed them with his little finger, tremble if he stomped his foot.

"Why is Uncle Grigory always in such a hurry when he comes to see us?" Darya asked me when Lieutenant Orlov cast impatient glances at the clock.

Some faces do not need to be studied, I thought. They speak with each pore of the skin. Their vocabulary is simple; their blunt sentences form indisputable conclusions: Act first, think later. Strength forces submission, assures power. Lust demands the sweetness of release.

"One of the Orlovs?" Princess Dashkova shook her head, scowling. "Vulgar boors who forget their place, Your Highness."

I saw Catherine nod her agreement.

Princess Dashkova had openly declared herself to be on Catherine's side. "You are already my Empress," she had said.

But power does not come from public declarations. It has to be wrenched out of the hands of people whose hearts are narrow and whose appetites for it are vast. Power needs the half-light of service corridors, the concealed movements of the hand.

It needs soldiers and spies, not figureheads.

In the back alleys of St. Petersburg, passions grew red-hot, fierce as bears that hurled the dogs against the walls, smashing their limbs and skulls. The guards were picking fights with the Holsteiners. Again and again, this or that officer asked aloud where the Crown Prince was when Russian heroes had died on the battlefields.

At the temporary palace, Catherine's rooms had always been far from the Grand Duke's, but now—with the constant chaos of room swaps that followed every move to the new quarters—it was even easier for her to stay out of sight. Whole sections of the service corridors, boarded off, needed but a little tinkering to create secret pathways. In rooms rotting with mildew, with rats chasing one another along the walls, disappearing under the floorboards, Catherine's visitors could come and go as they pleased.

In Catherine's bedroom, I smelled the scents of wet leather and soldier's sweat.

"Please, Varenka," Catherine murmured. "Just make sure no one knows." On her face I saw that half-smile of anticipation, that impatience with anything that slowed her down.

I did what a friend would. I changed the stained sheets before the maids could see them. I opened the windows to let the fresh air sweep away the musky odor of her lover's sweat. I wiped the muddy traces of his boots. I picked up whatever he had carelessly left behind: a belt, a brass button, a spur.

"Does Grigory at least tell you that he is ready to die for you?" I asked Catherine, laughingly. "Or maybe even give up gambling?"

There it was, always, a blush of pleasure on her cheeks.

"So you approve of recklessness, after all?" she would tease.

Stanislav was in Warsaw. Sir Charles lay buried in his English grave. Twenty years ago, Elizabeth had been made Empress by the Palace Guards who carried her in their arms to the throne of Russia.

Recklessness served the guards well. Weren't they called "the makers of the Tsars"?

Two of the Orlov brothers held all the regiments in their hands.

In the Imperial Bedroom of the new Winter Palace the windows were never covered. The Empress wished to see the barges floating down the Neva, the golden spires of the Petropavlovsky Fortress, the squared tower of the Kunstkamera on Vasilevsky Island.

"What are they doing now?" she asked querulously, every time she heard the hammering or sawing. Sent to inquire, the maids came running back with accounts of chandeliers hung in the Grand Ballroom, marble balustrades fitted along the landings, or sculptures rolled through the corridors to their final destination.

"Show me," Elizabeth demanded.

Four footmen carried her chair. Big, strong men in powdered wigs, with faces that did not smile or grimace, placed the poles of the chair

on their shoulders and took the Empress through the wide new corridors of marble and intricate mosaics to admire yet another chamber,
glittering like the inside of a jewelry box.

In the Imperial Bedroom, visitors crowded around the Empress,
on footstools, ottomans, armchairs, bringing gifts and gossip. Ivan
Shuvalov sat beside the Empress, on the bed; Count Razumovsky
took the spot at her feet. Both made sure they did not touch her arms
or legs, scarred from frequent bleedings. Catherine came with accounts of her visits to the nursery: Paul had grown another inch.
She'd found him sprawled on the floor, waving his wooden sword.
"Do I look fearless?" he'd wanted to know.

Only the Grand Duke Peter stood by awkward and silent, his fingers nervously playing with the hem of his sleeve. In the taverns of St.
Petersburg, his Holsteiners called the Russian army a mockery. The
serf soldiers are cowards at heart, they said, and only their fear of the
knout forces them to fight. In return, the guards mocked the Holsteiners' tricorne hats. And the Crown Prince of Russia, they grumbled, resembled Frederick of Prussia like an orangutan resembled a
man.

"Why this long face, Peter?" Elizabeth asked. "Can't you at least
pretend that you enjoy my company?"

He never knew what to say. His protests were lame and brittle,
easy fodder for her sneers.

"I can . . . I mean, I don't pretend . . ."

"Don't fidget, then. Stand straight. Stop staring at me with that
stupid grin on your face."

When Count Panin—the Grand Duke Paul's official Governor—
brought his charge for his daily visit, Elizabeth made her voice cheerful. She always had a surprise for *the child*, a Siberian apple, a toy, a
bird on a string. She asked him to recite his lessons, show her his
drawings. Sometimes she'd tell him to play quietly, for she wished to
talk to Count Panin.

I didn't know what they talked about. The new Imperial Bedroom
was big, and they always kept their voices low. Rumors said that the

Empress had changed her last will, naming Paul her successor. Some whispered that she had designated Peter to be his son's Regent; others insisted that she had chosen Catherine.

No one dared ask her. No one dared speak of death.

I did not believe the rumors. In Elizabeth's eyes I saw hesitation, not resolve. A child needed to grow up first. One baby Tsar in the Schlüsselburg Fortress was enough; she didn't wish for another.

Her calculations were simple. Peter she thought a fool of no use to anyone. Paul she loved with all her heart. She didn't care much for the Grand Duchess, but Paul needed her help.

Paul was the only reason why Elizabeth didn't want Catherine destroyed.

"Help me, Varenka," Catherine said in the autumn of 1761, placing her hand on her belly. "I need you now more than ever."

She was carrying Grigory Orlov's child.

There had been no bleeding for a month. She woke up feeling ill, just as she had with Paul and Anna. But this time Peter would not believe this child might be his. Since Stanislav's departure, *Das Fräulein* had made certain the Grand Duke had not been to his wife's bedroom even once. Countess Vorontzova didn't intend to be an imperial mistress forever.

To me, Catherine didn't have to spell out the dangers. She had already caught a wardrobe maid going over her bedsheets. No tongue of the Shuvalovs could be allowed to guess her secret, give the Grand Duke a reason to disgrace her.

I didn't curse Grigory Orlov's carelessness, his cheerful conviction that *his* Catherine, *his* Katinka, could find a way out from all difficulties. But there could be no *révolution de palais* before Catherine's child was delivered. Once again, the future hung perilously on secrets. On a swelling belly and the midwife's skills.

I smoothed Catherine's black hair. I wiped tears from her cheeks. I promised I would protect her. I kept my word.

Every month, with the help of two trusted maids, I dipped her cloths in fresh blood, so that the Shuvalovs' spies would think she was having her menses. I washed away the evidence of morning sickness, helped her cover her growing belly beneath folds of cambric petticoats. I smuggled pickles and dark bread to her bedroom at night, tightened the folds of her dressing gown to hide the rounding of her pregnant belly and the silvery sheen of her swollen breasts.

I sent to the Oranienbaum greenhouses for fresh flowers the maids arranged in a vase by Catherine's bed. Fragrant blooms to dampen a whiff of sulfur in the air that made her queasy. Since the last fumigation, her bed curtains were finally free of bugs.

By November, Catherine began her morning walks along the banks of the Neva to steady her nerves, strengthen her constitution, and escape prying eyes. Winter promised the respite of loose woolen shawls and fur-lined pelisses. *By the time Catherine's favorite snowdrops come back to the banks of the Neva*, I thought, *it will all be over.*

When we were alone, I told her of the Empress's bleedings, her fainting spells, the nightmares that made her scream. Of the day when the Empress asked, "Have they burned the stubble in the fields after the harvest already, Varvara?"

"Yes, Your Highness," I said, but my answer did not satisfy her. "What are these fires, then?" she wanted to know.

I leaned out the window, seeing nothing but the gray waters of the Neva.

"The gardeners, Your Highness," I lied. "They are burning last year's leaves."

She looked at me as if my words made no sense.

"How have I displeased God, Varvara?" she asked.

I hesitated.

If she asks me again, I thought, *she really wants to know.* But she didn't.

Princess Dashkova went about St. Petersburg prattling about the need for a new Russia, one no longer ruled by the knout and the Prus-

sian hangman. She was nineteen years old and believed herself Russia's savior, a young woman leading the Grand Duchess and her people
to a glorious revolution. "You have only to give the order and we will
enthrone you," I heard her tell the Grand Duchess. She could not
fathom why Catherine, this "best friend" who "trusted" her in everything, begged her to wait.

A royal skill, I thought with pleasure. Tell them no secrets, but
make them think you have.

"That oaf," Catherine said loudly every time Grigory Orlov's name
was mentioned near her in public. The palms of her hands ran over
the folds of her dress. It was still possible to hide her belly, but time
was running out.

The Empress could barely make a few steps through the room,
grasping the ivory handle of her cane, the tusk of an elephant long
dead. There were more and more nights when she would look at me
with the searching, bewildered gaze of someone whose thoughts were
wandering into the next world, but still she asked me about Catherine.

"Does Count Poniatowski write to her, Varvara? Does she answer?"

"The Count writes. The Grand Duchess answers. But not immediately. She makes him wait for her letters."

"Does she write about me?"

"No, Your Highness. She tells him that he has to be patient. When
the Count writes that he wants to come here, she begs him not to."

"They tell me she has a new lover. Is it true?"

"Yes, Your Highness. Lieutenant Orlov. He eats pineapple and
parsley before coming to her, for he wants his sperm to smell sweet."

"Does Count Poniatowski know?"

"No, Your Highness. She is afraid he might return here if he hears
of it. But she doesn't want him to stop writing. She doesn't want Orlov
to be too sure of his place."

Every morning Catherine sent her maids to the Winter Palace to inquire about the Empress's health and to beg to be allowed to come to her side. Every morning she was thanked for her concern but told to wait.

In the first days of December, Monsieur Rastrelli declared the Young Court quarters in the new Winter Palace finished. The Grand Duke had already set the day of his move, but Catherine did not. The shooting pains in her back, she claimed, would make climbing Monsieur Rastrelli's grand stairs too difficult.

In the corridors, *Das Fräulein* began to rush past the Grand Duchess with only the slightest bow. The Grand Duke asked Princess Dashkova why she bothered to visit his wife so often. "Does Grand Madame Resourceful make you pray to her icons?" he had asked.

Former Chancellor Bestuzhev, banished to his estate at Goretovo, sent me a crate of honey with a note that he hoped I would pass to Catherine. He signed it: *a man reduced to judging disputes over trodden cabbages and slain sheep.*

The Empress still clung to life—greedily, the way she lived.

"Don't oppose her," Doctor Halliday cautioned. "Try anything that calms her down."

I remember the entertainment summoned to her rooms. The juggler who spun colorful ribbons, a Chechen girl who could bend backward to touch her calves with the top of her head, and a monkey dressed in a pink frock, carrying an umbrella and a pocket watch.

By the second week of December the Empress could no longer keep down the foxglove brew that once relieved the shooting pains in her chest. News of further victories at the Prussian front—news she would have relished even a month before—now brought only a flicker of interest in her distracted eyes.

She pushed away the food the servants brought but emptied glass after glass of cold, frothy kvass.

The Blessed Ksenia was seen back on the city streets, telling everyone to make *bliny* and pots of sweet *kissiel* for a big funeral.

On one of these December nights, when the winds blew over the frozen Neva, raising a misty dust of powdery snow, I saw the Empress of All the Russias lift her reddened hands to her eyes. She moved them to the right, then left, but her eyes did not follow.

As if she were going blind, I realized.

The hands fell down on the bed. Pushok, the white tomcat who slept settled in the crook of her neck, began to snore. I moved him gently, and the snoring stopped. The room seemed deeply cold, in spite of the well-stoked stove and thick curtains. I bent over her to adjust her pillow.

"Do you hate me, Varvara?" the Empress asked in a hoarse whisper.

"Hate, Your Majesty?"

"Stop repeating my words."

"I do not hate Your Highness."

"Because I'm dying?"

"Your Highness is not dying."

"Don't lie to me, Varvara. I know what you think. That I married you off to a guard. That you deserved better."

"It's all in the past now," I said, taking a breath to calm my racing heart.

"The past doesn't let go of the present that easily. . . ."

A fit of coughing overtook her, and she could not finish. I fetched a glass with water for her to sip from. I held her shoulders as she shook, flustered and grimacing with pain. I wiped her mouth with a handkerchief.

Hate can be as brittle as a wishbone.

By the time the coughing stopped, I could no longer hold on to the memories of her anger, her vanity, the searing pain of her dismissals. My resentment crumbled. *An old woman facing death,* I thought, as she fell back into her pillow. In the end we are all alone with fear.

She knew. She saw it on my face, the yielding of compassion. In the silence that followed, Elizabeth pointed at the wall where her oldest portrait hung, that little naked Princess in her father's court.

"They wanted to kill me, but I lived. I want him to live, too. You have to promise me that you'll keep my grandnephew safe. Swear to me that when I die you won't let anyone harm him."

I moved uncomfortably. "Who am I to make such a promise?"

"You are her tongue."

I began to protest, but the Empress silenced me with an impatient wave of her hand.

I still wonder what she knew in these last days of her life. Had her spies told her of the plot to overthrow Peter? Of Catherine's pregnancy?

"Give me the icon, Varvara."

I put the Holy Icon of Our Lady of Kazan in her hands. "Will you swear on your daughter's life that you will keep him safe?" Her faded blue eyes were pleading.

I kissed the Holy Icon. I promised to protect Grand Duke Paul Petrovich.

Exhausted, the Empress closed her eyes. When she extended her hand again, I felt her hot, swollen fingers touch my cheek, slide down toward my chin, a phantom of caress.

"Tell the Grand Duchess I'll see her now," she muttered.

No one was allowed to stay in the Imperial Bedroom after Catherine arrived. Before the doors closed behind me—wide, gilded doors crowned with the double-headed Russian eagle—I caught a glimpse of Catherine's bending figure and Elizabeth's hand raised in a blessing.

When the Grand Duchess opened the doors an hour later, her eyes were red from crying.

I wondered if she, too, had sworn to keep her son safe.

From that day on, Catherine refused to leave the Imperial Bedroom, even for an instant. "My place is at Her Majesty's side," she'd say when we urged her to rest. Sometimes I was able to persuade her to doze on the chaise, but she would not go back to her rooms in the temporary palace. When the priest came to say his prayers, she knelt with all of us on the floor, clustered around the Empress's bed.

The Grand Duke arrived each morning, stood by his aunt's bedside for a short while, listening to the doctor's report, and hurried out.

From the anterooms came the sounds of raised voices. The Shuvalovs had settled themselves there already, receiving petitioners eager for new positions. Through the prayers that filled Elizabeth's room, we heard the sounds of bargaining. Someone called for more food, glass shattered, a kicked dog wailed.

There is but a thin line, I thought, *that separates an Emperor from a fool.*

The end, when it finally came, was bathed in blood.

First a thick, red stream appeared under the Empress's nose and wouldn't stop. Father Theodorsky intoned a prayer. He was asking God to be merciful to His daughter, to deliver her from the pain of this earth. A moment later the Empress was suffocating, coughing up blood, gasping desperately for a drop of air, her face, breasts, all splattered, stained, reddened.

Catherine did not recoil. Her hands and her dress spattered with blood, she ordered more candles, water, rags. She asked the surgeon to give the Empress another sip of laudanum. I watched her for any sign of faintness, but there was none.

An hour passed, and Elizabeth was still fighting. She tore out the dressing from her nose, upset the bowl filled with blood and bile, spilling its contents on the carpet.

Dying is not easy, I remember thinking. The mighty Empress of All the Russias, her hands restless, grasped everything—the doctor's arm, the towel, the sheets. She was growing weaker, slumping back on the pillows, staring at us as if we were all strangers, a pale, livid, blotched face with stricken eyes.

Then, after the frenzied rush of the last efforts to bring Elizabeth some comfort, the room fell silent. Someone ran to fetch the Crown Prince. I rushed to the window to let in some fresh air. I meant to open it just a crack, but the window frame swung out of my hand. A freezing gust extinguished the candles.

"Close it!" I heard Peter's piercing voice. "Do you want me to catch my death from cold?"

He was rubbing his hands like a merchant closing a long-anticipated deal.

I closed the window and drew back the curtains.

Peter leaned over the bed. The muscles in his pockmarked face twitched. "Is she really dead?" he asked, giggling nervously, as everyone in the room, including Catherine, fell to their knees before him. In the corner of my eye I saw one of the cats arch its back and rub its cheek against his leg.

It was four o'clock on Christmas Day, 1761, when Prince Trubetskoy, the Procurator-General, with tears on his wrinkled and powdered face, threw open the doors to the antechamber to announce: "Her Imperial Majesty has fallen asleep in God. God save Our Most Gracious Sovereign the Emperor Peter III."

In that stifling death chamber, I felt a strange longing to run out into the freezing cold of the streets. It was not the Great Perspective Road that beckoned me but the backstreets and out-of-the-way lanes of clay houses where animals lowed after the day's labor. Where people huddled behind their thin walls and groaned.

This is her route, I thought, my mind racing past the dingy taverns by the Fontanka River where the fiddles ruled; where Cossacks danced, jutting out their legs in a show of prowess; where old men told stories of Mongol horses whose nostrils were slit to make them breathe easier. This was the route the soul of the Empress surely wandered before leaving this world, while, on her bed, she lay with eyes closed, hands folded, a stiffening body, absent and indifferent at last.

In the Grand Throne Room of the Winter Palace, Peter—in the

green uniform of the Preobrazhensky Guards—received homage from the Archbishop of Novgorod, who invited him to ascend the Romanovs' ancestral throne. No one had been sent to fetch Grand Duke Paul from the nursery; no one had brought Catherine from Elizabeth's deathbed.

The new Emperor was going to rule alone.

Inside the palace, courtiers thronged and lined up to pay their tributes. Outside, all regiments of the guards gathered in the torch-lit courtyard, waiting for their turn to swear their allegiance, to lower their standards in salutes and cheers.

On the morning of December 26, at the stroke of six o'clock, the thunder of cannons from the Petropavlovsky Fortress proclaimed the beginning of new Russia.

ELEVEN

1762

he dead come back, brush against me, thieves breaking into my nights, waking me up with a jolt of my heart, knocking about in the chimney. The wrong dead, unwelcome, unwanted, while those whom I love stay away.

Go back to eternity, I say to their shadows.

But they do not leave. They know that I cannot bear their pleading. That my skin is too raw, my own doubts too grave, that I, too, am suspicious of the betrayals we who called ourselves Catherine's friends delivered in these first six months after Elizabeth's death.

In the corridors of the Winter Palace, where Elizabeth's embalmed body lay in state, clothed in silver and crowned in gold, as her weeping subjects passed by the open casket, I felt like a gambler who had bet everything on one throw of dice: *Let it be fast, so that what is new can begin.*

But it didn't begin, not for an agonizingly tense while. Those who had shrieked in horror at Peter's antics when he was the Grand Duke were now fawning over him. After thirty-seven years, Russia was again ruled by a man! As if all that had gone wrong with Russia could be blamed on women and their whims.

There was no grand ceremony, no coronation at the Moscow cathedral. At the Senate Council, Peter III, the new Emperor of All the

Russias, flanked by the Shuvalovs, fired off his orders. From now on, no noble would be forced to serve the Tsar against his will. No soldier would be flogged with the knout. Speaking against the Emperor would no longer be a crime, and it would not have to be reported. The Secret Chancellery would be abolished. The Good and Merciful Tsar, the true father of Russia, had no need to spy on his children.

Not a day passed without an announcement, a proclamation, a ukase, and yet another appointment.

Ivan Shuvalov, no longer satisfied to be a mere curator of Moscow University, was put in charge of the infantry, marine, and artillery corps in St. Petersburg. Two of his uncles became Field Marshals, though neither of them ever smelled powder or drew a sword. Most of Elizabeth's ladies-in-waiting left the court for their estates, but the ones who stayed received positions within Peter's inner circle. The Emperor, I heard, wished to assure the future of everyone who had been of use to his *beloved* aunt.

In the temporary palace, I waited for summons, but none came.

"Ask Peter to assign you to my entourage, Varenka," Catherine urged me. "Beg him if you must."

Dressed in her taffeta mourning dress, a black fichu over her hair, Catherine never spoke about her own waiting for invitations that never came. "My friends haven't deserted me, Varenka," she told me once, when I brought her another letter from Stanislav. "Even if I couldn't have been as true to them as I had wished."

The Stewardess of the Household gave me a hesitant glance when I listed my old positions: the reader to the Grand Duke, the Chief Maid of the Imperial Bedroom. I kept my voice even, not too insistent. The large carved desk that separated us was covered with files tied with green ribbons. Behind her, her ashen-faced attendant was taking notes.

"I have been of use," I said.

The new Winter Palace still smelled of paint, varnish, and wet plaster. *Das Fräulein* had claimed Ivan Shuvalov's apartment, right

above the Imperial Bedroom, from which carpeted private stairs led
to the Emperor's suite. Her entourage was twice as big as Catherine's,
who was not yet invited to name her own ladies-in-waiting. The day
after the state funeral, the new Emperor's official Favorite was seen
wearing Elizabeth's jewels.

The Stewardess of the Household sighed and told me to come
back in a week. But when I did, she had no time for me at all. It was
her assistant who assigned me to the Imperial Wardrobe. The Chief
Seamstress, she lisped, needed help. The late Empress left fifteen
thousand ball gowns alone. There were shoes and silk stockings. There
were purses, parasols, gloves, *kokoshniks,* and fans to sort through.

"If it suits you, Madame Malikina, that is," she said in a brisk voice.

"I'm most grateful," I replied.

The assistant cast a quick glance at her notes, avoiding my eyes.
My daughter and I could remain in the temporary palace for the time
being, she told me, but I should soon start looking for my own lodgings. The quarters at the Winter Palace were not for everyone.

The memories of the days that followed come entangled in brocades,
patterned velvet, and embroidered silk. They take the shapes of caf-
tans, sarafans, and tulle veils. Panniers and wigs. Skirts and over-
dresses. Entire chests of drawers are filled with panels for the sleeves,
trains, and bodices, ready to be assembled into an evening gown at a
day's notice. Baskets overflow with silk undershirts. Whiffs of sour air
mix with faint scents of rose water and almond milk, and everyone
repeats stories of the new Tsar.

In the evenings, I crossed the corridor to Catherine's rooms armed
with words that stained.

"Inspections," the Emperor insisted, "unexpected and unan-
nounced," were the essence of governance.

He swooped down constantly on the army barracks to check the
state of uniforms, on the mint to weigh the coins, into the government
offices to find which senior official valued his morning sleep more
than his duties.

"I didn't think that they had so much love for me," he said of the Palace Guards saluting him as he rode past.

He made faces at the crows circling the snow-covered fields. He lolled out his tongue at the Celebrant during Mass. He played his fiddle for four hours straight. He called Russia "an accursed land." He threw himself on his knees before the portrait of Prussia's Frederick the Great, vowing, "My brother, we will conquer the universe together!" He pushed the prettiest of his ladies-in-waiting into a room with the Prussian Envoy, urging them "to improve this barbaric race with some good blood."

A moth, I thought of him then, drawn to the flame, blind to anything except the flickering candle. Such was our Tsar. Such was our future, if nothing was done to stop it.

Catherine listened as I spoke, looking up from her books and papers. The ample folds of her mourning dress hid her belly, heavy with child. Her dangerous secret was well kept, wrapped in excuses of migraines that demanded lying flat in a darkened room, with just old wheezing Bijou for company.

"Does he speak of me at all, Varenka?"

"I hear that he calls your mourning for the Empress 'theatrics.' Who is my wife fooling, he asks everyone, with these black shawls of hers? How long is she going to stand in the chapel like an ugly black crow, crossing herself?"

"Does anyone laugh?"

"A few."

Quite a few, I knew but did not say.

The Shuvalovs cast their nets wide. Word had been sent out: Join us and you will be rewarded. As soon as it became clear Peter was not going to consult his wife on anything, those who had declared their support for Catherine began to waver.

At the new Winter Palace, Catherine's name evoked frowns of concentration, as if the memory of her had to be dragged out from somewhere deep. *The Emperor's estranged wife*, I heard dismissive whispers, *hiding away. What shall it be for her? Some distant country estate? Or a monastery cell?*

Ailing, I heard, pushed aside, visited by only a few.

Her ills were of little consequence. Like her friends. For what did they have to defend her? Stories of blunders repeated in desperation?

Was that all?

For the second time in my life, I thanked God for the Orlovs.

The Palace Guards, Grigory and Alexei assured me, did not forget their misgivings. They never failed to notice when the Emperor appeared in public not in the Preobrazhensky greens but in the blue uniform of a Prussian colonel. When he replaced the Russian Order of Saint Andrew with the Order of the Black Eagle, a treasured gift from the King of Prussia.

"Our time is coming, Varvara Nikolayevna. As soon as the baby is delivered. As soon as Katinka is well enough!"

The Orlovs' time, I called it in my thoughts, heady, dangerous, and rushed. Grigory and Alexei on the prowl, gathering allies, promising, threatening, cajoling, haggling for support. Ivan, Fyodor, and Vladimir awaiting orders in their big house on Millionnaya Street.

The five Orlov brothers, thick as thieves. All behind Catherine, pregnant with one of the brothers' child.

Grigory and Alexei didn't care if anyone watched them. In the temporary palace, emptier with each passing week, the floors shook under their swaggering steps. Every evening, they brought news of yet another disgruntled officer, another member of this or that noble family pledging their support. When Catherine's voice faltered, when she paused, when her hands rested for too long on the swell of her growing child, the two brothers would exchange glances and break the seriousness of the moment with one of their skits: *The Orangutan and his Prussian Master, The Last Oranienbaum Feast.* Not much more than youthful merriment, I decided, but enough to make Catherine laugh.

"We'll push him to his knees . . . teach him a lesson he won't forget."

I, too, could not stop myself from giggling when Grigory Orlov, his voice turned shrill, waved his hands madly or marched with stiff legs in the imitation of a Prussian goose step.

Ever since the Secret Chancellery had been abolished, men calling themselves former spies peddled denunciations by the dozen or traded in seedy tales. Sins once entrusted to a priest at confession were sold by the dozen. "If you do not buy yours," the sellers whispered, "someone else will."

From his exile in Goretovo, former Chancellor Bestuzhev no longer complained that crows fighting over carrion provided his only entertainment. He had written to the new Tsar, begging to be allowed back at court, but his letter had gone unanswered. To me he offered the wisdom of country proverbs, which, he was sure, would also please the Grand Duchess: *When the cat is away, the mice will play. When harvest is weighed, one cabbage can tip the balance.*

I threw his letter into the flames. For me, time had assumed the shape of Catherine's rounding belly, the tightening of her skin, the steady kicks of a baby's foot.

A woman's time brings its own conclusion, hopeful but unsure of its end.

By the end of February, Catherine only visited the Winter Palace to see her son.

Paul would turn eight in September. He was wetting himself at night and had started to suck his thumb again. On the day Count Panin told him that his father had become Emperor, Paul blinked his eyes and asked only what happened to his aunt's cat Pushok.

The new Imperial Nursery with its view of the winter road across the snow-covered Neva was three corridors away from the Emperor's suite, and Catherine could come and go without being seen by anyone except Count Panin, his Governor.

She told me of these visits when we were alone, her voice strained with pain. *Did you sleep well?* she would ask her son. *Did you like the book I brought you? Will you show me your drawings?* Paul would hide his face in the folds of his nurse's apron and shake his head. If Catherine implored him to look at her, he would lift his head long enough to reveal his florid face and then hide it again.

"This is Peter's doing, Varenka," Catherine seethed. "He wants to keep me away even from my own son!" I didn't like to see her eyes flare, her fingers snap. There was a baby in her womb. Babies were shaped by their mothers' thoughts, harmed by them.

Nothing Catherine said or did in that nursery made any difference. Her son's small face puckered in a stubborn grimace at the sight of her. What could she do but leave in tears?

"Can you go to Paul, Varenka?" she asked me after one such disastrous visit. "And take Darya with you?"

The thought enticed her, softened her face.

It would calm her greatly, Catherine continued, grasping my hand in hers, bringing it to her heart. The mere thought of our children playing together. The chance, however slight, I or Darenka might have to assure her son that he had a mother who loved him.

I can still hear Catherine's plea. So fervent with hope.

"We have been friends for so long, Varenka. We both have witnessed the power of malice. We know how much has been destroyed already. We know what is at stake."

How could I not agree?

By March, nightmares came. Dreams of bellies splitting open, of waters flooding the room. "As if sent by the Devil, Madame," the trusted maid who had come to fetch me blithered.

I hurried across the corridor to Catherine's bedroom. Her teeth were chattering; her lips were livid. She muttered about babies swaddled in cobwebs, babies with fins and flaps, babies with no mouths, with no eyes.

She, too, had been to Kunstkamera. She, too, had seen Peter the Great's monsters.

Having sent Masha to Millionnaya Street for the Orlovs, I'd offer her tea sweetened with white honey, a glass of *malinovoi*, raspberry kvass. When these didn't help, I'd suggest a brisk walk along the empty corridors.

By the time we returned to her rooms, Grigory Orlov would be waiting. "Silly Katinka," he'd mutter, scooping Catherine up in his arms as if she weighed less than a feather.

I'd wait until the doors to her bedroom closed, and then I'd leave.

In the first week of April, Peter III, the Emperor of All the Russias, came to the Imperial Wardrobe on one of his famous inspections. He was dressed in Prussian blue. *Das Fräulein* was clinging to his arm, her black eyes gliding through the dresses spread on tables, assessing their worth.

"That was all *hers?*" she exclaimed. On her finger, a garnet ring flickered in the light. Blood-red, set in white gold. Elizabeth's favorite. Her eyes passed me as if I did not exist.

The Emperor of Russia took off his wig. His thinning scalp was covered with blistering wounds, the result of constant scratching.

"So this is where you are now, Varvara," he said, turning toward me. "I was wondering what happened to you. Have you been treated well?"

He put the wig back on, glancing at the dressing mirror to see if it was straight, but right away he noticed a basket filled with wooden dolls, Elizabeth's pandoras. He picked up one of them, naked, with twisted limbs, and waved it over his head, like a trophy.

"Yes, Your Highness," I answered. "I've been treated very well."

"Good," he said, tossing the pandora back into the basket. "Show me the ledgers, then."

The Chief Seamstress handed me the heavy bound ledger and stepped back, marred with resentment for being overlooked. The other seamstresses bent over their sewing, trying to steal glances at the Tsar. I could already imagine their gasps after his departure. *How handsome, how elegant, how splendid, how kind.*

I opened the volume at random, pointing at the lists of evening gowns, morning dresses, costumes from Elizabeth's masquerades.

Das Fräulein yawned, but Peter paid her no heed. He licked his thumb and turned the pages, staring at some of them longer than others. I wondered what caught his attention. The description? The price paid? The names of new owners beside the dresses that Elizabeth had given away as gifts?

He closed the ledger, frowning.

"It's all in Russian," he complained.

I kept silent. Would he order us to keep the books in German? Or French?

He didn't. He handed me a sheaf of papers instead. Letters, I noted, petitions. In one of them, Mr. Porter, a St. Petersburg cloth merchant, complained of not being paid for his last delivery. In another, a wardrobe maid asked for a silk chemise the Empress had promised her before she died.

I said I would look into them right away.

"Good," Peter said. There was a broad grin on his face. I could see *Das Fräulein* lean toward him, her fingers picking something invisible from his shoulder. A hair? A thread?

The inspection was over.

I was waiting for the Emperor to leave, but he turned to me one more time.

"You were my friend once," he said, in a subdued, boyish voice I recalled from the time I used to read to him.

"I am still your friend, Your Majesty." I tried to make my own voice steady and firm.

He looked at me with sharp intensity, as if considering my answer, but his next question had nothing to do with me anymore.

"I hear that the Grand Duchess is still writing to Count Poniatowski? Is this true, Varvara?"

I muttered some elaborate protestation, only to see it dismissed with a snap of his fingers. When his eyes narrowed, my heart skipped a beat. When he spoke again, his voice had changed. It was prickly and sharp.

"Some call me a fool, Varvara. But it is safer to deal with honest fools than with great geniuses. My wife will squeeze you out like the juice from an orange, and then throw away the rind!"

It was her third baby, and it came out without fuss. "I've gotten good at it, Varenka," Catherine murmured, as the midwife fiddled with swaddling clothes.

On Thursday, April 11, I held Grigory Orlov's newborn son, red-faced, sucking on my finger, but falling asleep as soon as I handed him to his mother. He was the first of her children that Catherine had been allowed to hold.

Outside the birthing room, Grigory Orlov was pacing the floor, waiting.

I opened the door. Grigory rushed toward me and grasped my hands. "Katinka?" he breathed. "Is she well?"

I nodded. I tried to tell him he had a son, but my voice choked with relief. I merely stepped aside to let him in and stood at the door, waiting for Catherine's sign.

They didn't have much time. Enough for an embrace, a few endearments. The letters Catherine had written to be delivered in case she died in childbirth were now burning in the fireplace, their seals intact.

Alexei Orlov had promised to protect us, and he had kept his word. With a few fellow guards—all members of the conspiracy to put Catherine on the throne—he had set fire to an abandoned house near the temporary palace to prevent anyone from hearing Catherine's screams. It was a grand fire, I heard it described later, flames leaping through the walls and out of the windows. The ceilings crashed, the beams fell among the sparks and billowing smoke. Chickens flew from a coop, their feathers singed; squealing pigs ran madly around the courtyard. The throng of onlookers guaranteed that no one leaving the palace on the Great Perspective Road with a bundle in her arms would be followed.

It was Catherine who named the baby Alexei Grigoryevich.

She kissed her second son on his sweet lips before giving him to me and turning away. I bundled him in a beaver skin and took him to the couple who had agreed to keep him. The former valet and his childless wife cooed with happiness when I placed the baby in their arms. "Until his mother can take him back," I told them. "Only until then."

As soon as Catherine had delivered safely, *révolution de palais* was all we thought about.

The Orlovs had been right. Five months into Peter's rule, the conspiracy was growing bigger than the suspicions of the Palace Guards.

In May, the Russian army under Suvorov took the fortress of Kolberg. The victory was considered decisive. Everyone spoke of crushing the Prussian forces and occupying East Prussia.

At first Peter did not hide his displeasure at the Prussian defeat, but then he did something much worse: He offered Frederick peace. "The miracle of the House of Brandenburg," the King of Prussia would call it. Peace without strings, without demands, a turnaround that saved Frederick's tottering kingdom.

St. Petersburg tensed with disbelief.

Is this our payment for the husbands, sons, brothers slaughtered in the battlefields of Gross-Jägersdorf and Zorndorf? people asked.

As more accounts of the Prussian rejoicing at their unexpected good fortune arrived, Alexei's months of cajolings and promises began to pay off. Count Cyril Razumovsky, the brother of the former Emperor of the Night, pledged his support for Catherine. So did Prince Trubetskoy and Prince Repnin. Only Count Panin, the Imperial Grand Duke's Governor, hesitated. He admired the Grand Duchess, he said, but he didn't want another woman on the Russian throne.

"Not even as Regent for her son?" Alexei enticed him.

Every time I came to deliver my reports, Catherine looked more radiant. It didn't matter that she woke up at dawn and stayed up late into the night. Her reading abandoned, she was sending requests for loans, negotiating securities, soothing the impatient with assurances of rewards. On Vasilevsky Island, a printer who had remembered my father and promised me utter secrecy was printing Catherine's proclamation: . . . *freedom from all dejection and offense . . . freedom from force and from fear.* The promise that her Russia would be ruled by reason and law. Count Panin—finally convinced that Catherine would rule as Paul's Regent—had joined Catherine's conspiracy.

My daughter spent every Monday afternoon in the Imperial Nursery, playing with the Grand Duke Paul. Masha or I would take her there, and the maids let us in without fuss.

Darya delighted in these visits. There were charades to solve, spinning tops, whistles, a big rocking horse to climb. She and Paul ran along the corridors of the palace or played hide-and-seek in the empty rooms around the nursery. Sometimes Paul asked her to read him a story; sometimes she taught him a dance step she had just learned.

"Did you tell the Grand Duke that his Maman misses him?" I asked Darenka whenever I could.

She did, but her words never merited more than a shrug of shoulders or an embarrassed look.

It did not surprise me.

Paul doesn't need words but time, I thought. Time with his mother. Time together. The quiet time filled with childish trifles. The time that healed.

But there was no point in telling Catherine what she already knew only too well.

In June, with the white nights, impatience set in. By the embankment, sunlit even past midnight, stray dogs roamed, filling the air with their snarls, growls, and yelps of pain. On the Great Perspective Road, smells of frying lard wafted in the air at all times, mixed with the aroma of bread baking and of malted barley.

At the Imperial Wardrobe, Elizabeth's gowns that had not been claimed by *Das Fräulein* or the ladies-in-waiting were being disassembled, turned into panels of fabric and trims. Dressmakers of St. Petersburg's fashion houses were making their bids, assuring the best lengths of ribbons, lace, and embroidery for their outfits. What wasn't bought vanished. Scraps of imperial fabric were already sold in the stalls of the Tatar market, and soon Elizabeth's favorite pink would flash in the trims of dresses merchant wives wore to Sunday Mass.

In the temporary palace, Catherine's maids began packing, but it was not for the annual summer move to the country. This year, the Emperor announced his intention to go to Oranienbaum with *Das Fräulein* and his son. If the Grand Duchess wished to escape the heat of the city, she could stay in the old Monplaisir Pavilion, on the grounds of the Peterhof palace. And in August, as soon as the court is back in St. Petersburg, Catherine would have to move to her four rooms at the Winter Palace, five corridors away from the Imperial Suite.

The temporary palace had been an eyesore far too long. It would be razed to the ground.

In our own rooms, Masha had swathed Egor's portrait in old sheets; she had gathered Darya's old toys and dresses, ignoring my pleas to make presents of the ones she had outgrown to the scullery maids. "Never know what becomes useful," she muttered, her lazy eye sliding away as I looked at her. Besides, there was no need to be stingy with space. She had heard that in the new Winter Palace even *Das Fräulein*'s maids had quarters twice as big as those we lived in.

"Isn't it where we are going?" she asked. "The palace?"

I didn't say anything.

I didn't believe in tempting fate.

The *révolution de palais*, I knew, was a gamble, like all palace games.

What would it be, victory or destruction? I asked myself when I looked at my daughter at her lessons or at play. In the last months, her body began to reveal her grown-up shape. And yet she'd often give me a soft, pliable look, as if she were still a small child. On the table beside my bed lay a book of fairy tales, beautifully bound and gold-tooled, a present from Count Poniatowski. He was hoping for news, however trivial, asking if I reminded Sophie of his promise to come back. *Some dreams*, he wrote, *cannot be abandoned, without losing part of your soul.*

I shuddered and chased the future away.

I didn't want to think of my daughter having to live with only the memory of my touch.

And then, on the eve of the court's departure to Oranienbaum, a troubling incident took place.

A the state banquet, Peter began the celebration with a toast to the Imperial Family. Everyone at the table rose with boisterous enthusiasm, ready to drink. Everyone except Catherine.

"To the health of the Imperial Family," Peter repeated, staring at his wife.

Guests and courtiers froze, unsure of what they were witnessing. Did the Tsar want Catherine to stand up when he himself was seated? Weren't they drinking to her health as much as to his? Surely he was not telling Catherine that she didn't belong to the Imperial Family?

The silence that fell was long and uneasy.

"To the health of the Imperial Family," the Emperor repeated, finally taking a sip of the wine, and everyone drank with relief.

The banquet continued, cups skating in their saucers, napkins soiled with trickles of butter and dark mushroom sauce, glossy lips opened wide. But as soon as the toast was complete, *Das Fräulein* had turned toward the Emperor. She shook her head and stroked his arm. He leaned toward her, craning his neck.

Moments later, one of the Emperor's generals made his way toward Catherine. In a voice loud enough for everyone to hear, he said, "His

Majesty wishes to know why Your Highness did not rise from your seat."

"Doesn't the Imperial Family consist of Your Majesty, myself, and our son?" Catherine had become very pale, but her voice showed no trace of hesitation. Everyone fell silent.

"*Dura!*" the Emperor screamed.

Fool. The Emperor had called his wife a fool.

I learned all this a few hours later, in Catherine's room in the temporary palace, from Alexei Orlov, who had begged me to help his brother calm the Grand Duchess. "He'll pay for it, Katinka, I swear." Grigory Orlov's enraged voice broke through Catherine's sobs. "I won't let him humiliate you like this."

She was still in the same mourning dress she'd worn to the banquet, the milky-white skin of her shoulders gleaming through the black lace. Her sobs were muffled by Grigory's broad shoulder.

"That coward. That milksop." Her lover's voice bounced off the walls freshly stripped of draperies. "He'll beg for your pardon. For your mercy. You'll see, Katinka. You'll see."

I added my voice to Grigory's.

"Your friends are all behind you," I told Catherine. "We are watching. We won't forget anything."

But Catherine would not be consoled.

"You'll go to Peterhof, Katinka. You'll wait there until we get everything in order. I'll come to you with news every week."

I saw Grigory's big hand caress Catherine's back, slide down the shiny taffeta of her mourning gown, linger at the base of her corset. "At the end of August, when he comes back to St. Petersburg, we'll arrest him at the gates. We'll bring him to you in chains."

When she still did not raise her eyes, I prayed that we wouldn't have to wait that long.

In the morning of June 28, the eve of the Feast of Saints Peter and Paul, the name day of the Tsar and his son, Alexei Orlov burst into my parlor at the temporary place with the news: Our Lieutenant Passek had been arrested.

The Emperor was staying in Oranienbaum with *Das Fräulein* and the Grand Duke. Catherine was in the Monplaisir Pavilion on the outskirts of the Peterhof gardens, where, on the following day, the splendid feast would begin.

In his well-worn riding trousers and a tight-fitting jacket, Alexei looked like any young veteran of the Prussian War, unsure of what to do with himself. I smelled vodka on his breath.

"There is no more time left, Varvara Nikolayevna," he told me. Passek knew the location of the printed copies of Catherine's manifesto announcing her accession to the throne. One round of torture might be enough to expose our conspiracy. Catherine must be brought to the capital immediately. She must claim the throne now, while the Emperor was still in the dark.

Sweat was moistening the crease of my underarms and beneath my breasts. Through the crack in the curtains the morning light was streaming into the room as it might into a prison cell.

I studied Alexei's face, the jagged shape of the scar across his cheek. A memory came of his joking explanations for its presence: a Prussian saber, a touch of the unicorn's horn.

"I've taken him where he is safe," Alexei said.

He meant Grigory's son, his little nephew, who gurgled with pleasure when I bent over him. Last time I visited I'd heard his wet nurse call him "our golden *Tsarevitch*." She'd given me such a pained look when I told her to watch her tongue.

I noted the flash of pride when Alexei pronounced his nephew's name: Alexei Grigoryevich. Son of Gregory.

Did I guess it already? The depth of the Orlovs' ambition? The weight of debts she would owe them? If I did, I wouldn't admit such thoughts. Not even to myself.

Egor flashed to my mind, his bitter voice complaining of the court intrigues that sapped the strength of the army. "As if Russia didn't have true enemies," he had told me. Thrusting our copy of the Court Calendar into my hands, Masha asked me to look for the names of soldiers from Egor's regiment who had been decorated or promoted. There were so precious few of them. What could I tell my servant when she wondered what her master would've been had he lived? Still a Lieutenant? Still in debt?

I thought of Paul, in Oranienbaum, of the feverish chaos that would greet the first news of the coup. Empty corridors, distraught nurses. *Promise me you'll keep him safe,* Elizabeth had said on her deathbed. *Swear it on your daughter's life.*

"I'll go to Oranienbaum," I told Alexei Orlov. "I'll take Darya with me. Paul knows us well. He'll go with us when I tell him to."

Alexei flashed me a quick, sharp glance. "You are not afraid?"

"No," I lied. "Where is Grigory?"

Grigory was with his regiment, assuring the Izmailovsky support. The other three Orlov brothers were in their Millionnaya Street home, awaiting his orders.

In the other room, Darya was asking Masha, "Is it Uncle Alexei? So why can't I see him, too?"

"I have to go, Varvara Nikolayevna," Alexei said. "Tell Darenka I'll come back."

I told Masha to bring our traveling clothes. "Fast," I urged. "We are leaving right away."

I calculated the distance: twenty-eight *versty* from St. Petersburg to Peterhof. Fifteen more to Oranienbaum. Six hours in the carriage, if I changed horses twice on the way.

My old servant gave me a long, dark look with her good eye. She knew what was happening, for I had no choice but to trust her with our secrets. If the coup succeeded, I would bring Catherine's firstborn son to the Winter Palace. There, guards from all regiments would protect him. If the coup failed and I was arrested, Masha would take Darya and go west, to Warsaw. Hidden in the double bottom of a leather trunk, beside gold ruble coins, there was a letter addressed to Count Poniatowski, a plea to take care of my child.

I heard Masha murmur a blessing. I felt her hand on my forehead. My servant's fingers, I noticed, were beginning to bend at odd angles. I had seen her struggle to thread a needle.

Darya sensed that this was not an ordinary outing. "Where are we going, Maman?"

"To Oranienbaum," I replied, trying to make my voice cheerful. "To visit the Grand Duke Paul."

But I thought, *To keep an old promise, an oath I gave on your life.*

At the Oranienbaum palace I ordered the driver to take us to the back entrance. I hoped no one would pay attention to an unmarked carriage that would leave the moment we were safely inside.

As soon as we alighted, I straightened Darya's dress and took her hand in mine. "Slowly," I told her. "We don't have to hurry now."

We made it through the service hall, onto the back stairs to the second floor. At the top of the stairs I stopped to take a look at the corridor we had to walk along. It was deserted.

We walked past the portrait of Peter the Great on a horse, piercing a bear with his lance, past the billowing tapestry of Adam and Eve in Paradise, surrounded by cavorting lions and lambs.

From behind the nursery door came Paul's laughter followed by a happy squeal and the patter of feet. Then, suddenly, the door banged open and the Emperor ran out, hands over his head. A pillow came after him but missed and landed on the floor. My heart thundered wildly.

"You didn't get me," Peter sang in a funny opera voice.

The nursery door closed with a loud thump. Inside, Paul screamed, "I did. I did."

I hesitated, but we were too close to turn back unnoticed, and there was nowhere to hide. Not with Darya beside me, already antici-pating Paul's delight at seeing us.

The Emperor, in his worn blue housecoat, without a wig, was still laughing when he noticed us. "Varvara Nikolayevna. What are *you* doing here?"

I curtsied and pulled at Darya's hand, and she followed my example. But the Emperor waved his hand.

"No need for ceremony. This is not the Winter Palace." He winked at Darya, motioning for her to approach him. I let go of her hand, and she made a cautious step forward.

"The Grand Duchess sent me, Your Majesty," I said, pointing at the nursery door. On the other side of the door came the thumps of someone running. "With a name-day present," I added, quickly. And then I cursed my own stupidity. Anyone would notice that my hands were empty.

I wondered if the Emperor even heard me, for he was busy pointing to his pocket. I saw Darya's hand dive there and retrieve a handful of bonbons.

"It's a secret," Darya chirped. "You have to promise you won't tell anyone we are here." She popped the bonbons into her mouth before I could stop her.

"Your Majesty . . ." I corrected her.

The Emperor giggled and raised his hand to his heart. "I promise."

Then he turned to me. "So Madame Resourceful has come up with a surprise for her son?"

"Yes," I said.

"Go inside, then," he said carelessly, and walked away. I cast one last look at him as he left, a gangly, awkward figure, waving his long arms, muttering to himself.

Before I knocked on the nursery door, I peeled off my gloves. Only then I realized how damp my palms were. And how cold.

On the eve of the coup, Darya played with Paul, helping him erect fortifications from blankets and pillows. After a supper of pineapples and ice cream, he pretended to be a soldier storming a fortress while

Darya happily played a captured princess rescued from attacking bears. "Don't move," Paul screamed his warnings. "Pretend to be dead."

I looked at his face, reddened with exertion, eyes set wide apart, narrow lips, nose short, upturned. Peter's features, I thought. To counter my growing unease, I recalled the night he was born, eight years before, and his mother's pain when she could not even touch him.

In Peterhof, by then, the gardeners must have already moved the giant pots with citrus trees from the orangery and lined them up along the paths in preparation for tomorrow's feast. This year's imperial name-day celebration was to be particularly festive.

After the maids had put Paul to bed, he asked me to sit by his side. He closed his eyes and said nothing for a long time, but when I assumed he had fallen asleep and rose to snuff the candle, he spoke.

"She has come to me in my sleep." He meant Elizabeth Petrovna, his great aunt. "She told me not to be afraid."

"Why would you be afraid?" I asked him.

"I don't know. I am sometimes."

"Everyone is afraid sometimes."

"Even Lieutenant Orlov?"

"Even he." I wondered who had mentioned Orlov's name to him and when.

In the Oranienbaum gardens, lilacs were in bloom, making the air heavy and almost sickly sweet. In the distance someone was plucking at guitar strings.

"Do you want to pray with me for Empress Elizabeth's soul?" I asked the Grand Duke.

Paul gave me a sideways glance and nodded. His eyes began glistening with tears.

Give rest, O Lord, to the soul of thy departed servant. . . . I intoned the prayer for the dead, but it was atonement I prayed for, and hope.

So that all Elizabeth had destroyed could be repaired, all that she had filled with secrecy could be illuminated by the truth of the new reign.

While I watched over the sleeping children in Oranienbaum, two hours' ride away, in Peterhof, an ordinary street carriage with two post horses waited in the small Monplaisir courtyard. In the silvery twilight of a white night, Catherine was dressing in haste to the sound of Alexei's restless steps outside her bedroom. The maids had laid out her clothes: stays, chemise, petticoats, stockings, shoes, and her simple black mourning gown.

"All is ready for the proclamation. You must get up," Alexei said when he'd knocked on her bedroom door.

"Now?" she asked. "Why?"

On the other side of the garden, the dogs had already caught the scent of a stranger. Their frenzied barking brought out the lights. Someone whistled loudly. A yelp of pain was followed by a whimper.

"Passek has been arrested. There is no time left." Alexei's voice was sharp with tension.

As the maids watched, Catherine crossed herself and bowed in front of the icon. Twenty-one years before, in a moment like this, Elizabeth had vowed that if God made her the Empress of All the Russias, no one would be sent to death on her orders.

If Catherine made a vow that dawn in Monplaisir, she never told me. She ordered the maids back to sleep and drank a few sips of water. Her carriage had to be on its way before anyone noticed Alexei's presence.

Kozlov, her hairdresser, arranged Catherine's hair as her carriage sped toward St. Petersburg. Two hours later, Grigory met her at the halfway point with fresh horses, just when hers were beginning to falter. They sped toward the barracks of the guards.

Alexei and Grigory had done their part. By the time Catherine rode into the barracks that dawn, the guards awaited her.

She alighted from the carriage and stood before them, solemn in black, her mourning dress a reminder that—unlike her husband—she didn't wish to forget the late Empress. Her voice did not falter, her face did not flinch.

"The Emperor," she told the guards, "is listening to the enemies of Russia. He has given orders to arrest me. I fear he wants to kill me and my only son."

A barrage of angry shouts followed, shouts Catherine allowed to ring before she continued.

"The Emperor is denying me and my son our rightful place beside him. You, the best sons of Russia, know what our beloved Motherland needs. I have come to you for protection. I'm placing my fate in your hands."

So much can be weaved into a voice: a sovereign's assurance, a woman's plea.

Wild applause greeted her words, a torrent of cheers rising from the barracks. "No one will touch you," the guards shouted. "Not while we live."

When the first *Vivat* sounded, Catherine knew she had won. Lit up, glowing, she stood tall and triumphant as, one by one, the regiments of the Izmailovsky, Semyonovsky, and Preobrazhensky guards swore their loyalty. Soldiers kissed her extended hands, the hem of her mourning dress, still dusty from the journey. They fell to her feet, trembling like mercury in a child's palm, calling her *Matushka*, their Little Mother. Their Empress.

On their knees, their cheeks aflame, their eyes locked on her as if she were Russia's only hope.

"A frenzy of joy, as the word spreads, Varvara Nikolayevna," Count Panin told me when he arrived at Oranienbaum at noon to escort us to St. Petersburg. "Emperor Paul," he referred to the Grand Duke, still convinced Catherine would rule merely as her son's Regent.

You see what you want to see, I thought. *You believe what you want to believe.*

Count Panin did not hide the raw urgency in his voice. We had to hurry before the news of the coup reached Oranienbaum. It was one o'clock already. We had at least six hours of the carriage ride ahead of us.

I crossed myself.

It has happened.

Catherine is safe, I thought. *Her son is safe. We are all safe.*

I walked to the window. Outside, the fountain in the Oranien-baum garden had just been switched on. The sun was weaving rainbows into the streams of water. On a stone bench, a group of musicians was playing a festive piece. From the open windows of Peter's suite came screeches of laughter. *Das Fräulein* must have given her lover another name-day gift. For a moment I saw Peter himself leaning from the window, a blurry figure waving his hand.

The Emperor of Russia did not know he had already been deposed.

He'll be a happier man than he'd be as an Emperor, I thought. *Exile will please him in the end.*

In the courtyard, horses stomped their feet. Carriages were lining up, ready to depart for Peterhof. A gull cried.

"Are we going to see my Papa now?" Paul asked me, anxiously, when the maid led him in. His morning tutor had been teaching him a poem he was to recite at the name-day feast, and he still stumbled over the lines.

"No, Your Highness," I answered. "We are going for a ride."

"Is this a surprise?" Paul's eyes opened wide in anticipation.

"Yes," Count Panin said cheerfully. "Very well put, Your Highness. This is a wonderful surprise."

Paul laughed. "It's a surprise," he said, giving Darya a conspiratorial wink. "For Papa's name day."

Darya jumped up and down. Paul began jumping, too.

"But it's your name day as well, Your Highness," Count Panin cut in, demanding his pupil's attention. There was a tinge of irritation in his voice at having been ignored, and I should have paid more attention to it. I had been at court too long to underestimate the warning signs of jealousy.

"I have to practice my poem." Paul's eyes were still fixed on my daughter.

"I'll help you," Darya offered.

I saw the astonishment blossom in my daughter's eyes when Count Panin ordered her to be quiet. A crimson blush rushed from her cheeks. "What did I do, Maman . . ." she began.

But there was no time to reassure her.

As our small party rushed toward Count Panin's carriage, I blessed the comings and goings that preceded even the shortest of imperial journeys: seamstresses busy with the final fittings of the court dresses, footmen lugging trunks and boxes. Skittering cats and whining dogs.

MAKING OF THE EMPEROR

The Lord took the strength of the mountain
The majesty of a tree . . .

These were the lines the Grand Duke began to recite as we sped along the St. Petersburg road, his voice small, unsure.

"*Added the calm* . . ." Darya prompted, but Count Panin didn't let her finish.

"Please, Your *Majesty*," he said, his plump hand descending on the Grand Duke's bony shoulder.

Paul cast him an uneasy glance.

"Did I make a mistake?" he asked.

"No, Your *Majesty*." Panin's voice took on the solemn, affected note of a courtier. "There is no time for poetry now. I have something very important to tell you."

I tried to warn him. "Perhaps his mother should be the one to do it," I said softly.

"Will you let me decide what is proper, Varvara Nikolayevna?" Panin snapped. *The bookbinder's daughter should mind her place*, his eyes warned.

I fell silent.

Paul's shoulders hunched. He looked at me. A child does not understand silence, cannot yet sift through what has been left unsaid.

I turned my head away. Darya curled deeper into the shadows, bewildered.

We sped toward the Winter Palace. Beside me, Panin was explaining to the Grand Duke what a coup was. And what the difference was between an Empress and a Regent.

It was well past six when our carriage finally rode through the streets of St. Petersburg, past the cheering crowds. Shouts of "Victory!" and "Long live the Empress!" flooded the evening, a white night, as bright as day. *A tidal wave*, I thought, recalling Alexei's promises. Once set in motion, a wave so great it sweeps everything and everyone with it.

Count Panin's restless gaze swept over the crowds. The children had been silent for hours. I was glad when we reached the yard of the Winter Palace and it was time to part.

The carriage door opened. Paul turned to me.

"Go, Your Highness," I told him. "Your Mama is waiting."

He scrambled out of the carriage. A step followed by another, still hesitant but irreversible now. Count Panin went right after, fast, as if he feared I would overtake him.

In a few moments the Grand Duke would be in his nursery, guards from four regiments stationed at the door at all times. Safe.

A hard lump formed in my throat, and tears stung my eyes. Darya and I, too, got out of the carriage. The air was freezing, and I shivered.

In Our Lady of Kazan, Catherine was taking her oath as Empress and Sole Autocrat. She would be nobody's Regent. The Grand Duke would have the time to grow up before he took the throne after his mother's death. As it should be.

I stood in the palace courtyard, suddenly not knowing what to do next.

"Why are you crying, Maman?" Darya asked.

I put my arms around her, too tight, for I could feel her squirm.

I saw Catherine an hour later, on the Great Perspective Road, wearing the Preobrazhensky greens. Saber in hand, oak leaves on her tricorne hat, she was riding Brilliant, her gray stallion, along the cheering street, from the Kazan church toward the Winter Palace.

People fell to their knees as she passed by, imploring her for her blessing, raising their children up in the air so that they would be closer to the Empress, could touch her black jackboots. The old and the sick were helped to the windows so that they, too, could see the miracle of the new reign.

I knelt on the ground, recalling that first time I saw her, a child of fourteen arriving in Moscow, unsure of her fate. I thought of the young woman she became, branded by injustice and pain, singed by humiliation. Much had been taken away from her, and yet her heart had not been broken. *My Empress*, I thought.

Catherine's voice, loud and resonant, rang in the air: "I swear to Almighty God to make Russia greater than it has ever been before."

Alexei and Grigory Orlov were riding right behind her, in the Izmailovsky's steel blues trimmed with gold ribbons. Two brothers-in-arms, big, silent, and vigilant, their sharp eyes constantly surveying the crowd.

Around me hands rose, a sea of hands, waving, pounding the air: "Long live our *Matushka*! Long live our Empress!"

Weeping, I added my voice to these cries.

The streets of St. Petersburg filled with the aromas of roasting pigs, sauerkraut simmering with wild mushrooms, potato pancakes fried in lard. Vodka and wine were offered free in all city taverns. Soon the day of revelry turned into the white night of dancing and love-making, the time when more children were conceived than at the end of Lent.

The June children, I'd hear them called in the months to come.

"The great warrior hid behind the hooped skirts of his mistress." Alexei Orlov laughed as the news poured in.

In Peterhof, Peter, by then the Emperor in name only, could not believe what stared him in the face. With growing annoyance, he surveyed the new orchestra pit, the rows of giant pots with citrus trees along the paths, lanterns hanging on the branches. It was his name day. Why was Catherine not greeting him upon his arrival?

He sent his footmen to the Monplaisir Pavilion with a message that she should hurry. When the footmen came back saying that the Grand Duchess begged for more time to get ready, Peter stood on the terrace of the Peterhof palace and watched the fountains of the grand cascade.

Half an hour later, when Catherine still did not come, he decided to fetch her himself.

Alexei's booming voice rose and thinned when he imitated Peter's cries, "Where are you? Where *are* you?" as the deposed Emperor ran from room to room of the Monplaisir Pavilion cursing the cowering maids, looking under the bed, in the wardrobes, even in the water closet, as if Catherine were a child playing hide-and-seek.

In the Throne Room, everyone desired Catherine's attention. The giant mirrors reflected the silk court jackets and embroidered gowns, the uniforms, the sea of waving hands, the necks craning to get a glimpse of the new Empress.

Victory, I heard. *Blessed day.*

Catherine the Second, the Empress of All the Russias. She had put on a gown of plain ivory silk, decorated with the blue ribbon of the Cross of St. Andrew, reserved for the Sovereign. Beside her, Grand Duke Paul rubbed the green sleeve of his Preobrazhensky uniform, looking unhappy and confused.

I marveled at Catherine's patience with the elaborate petitions thrust into her hands, with the long lines of courtiers jostling to kiss the hem of her dress. When Grigory Orlov tried to push them away, Catherine told him not to stop friends from expressing their joy.

I, too, knelt before her.

"Varenka," she said.

Triumph made her eyes sparkle. Her hair shone; her cheeks glowed.

A throng of people behind me were pushing to get closer.

"Varenka," she repeated.

She raised me and kissed me on both cheeks and then, placing her hand on mine, she asked, "Will you be of even more help to me now?"

I nodded, my voice caught in my throat. Catherine's next words rose over the din of whispers.

"It is thanks to such friends as *Countess* Malikina," she said to the crowd, "that I was able to deliver Russia from the perils of autocracy."

A cheer resounded, then another.

She had made me Countess, and I didn't even have time to thank her, for I felt an impatient pull from behind, a tug of my sleeve reminding me I was not the only one wishing to approach the new Empress. Beside me, Alexei Orlov repeated a plea that Catherine must show herself to the people.

In the streets of St. Petersburg, rumors flew: that Peter had come to the city in disguise to gather support, that the King of Prussia had already sent his troops to help him, that he was planning to kidnap Catherine or even that he had already kidnapped her.

"Right now, Your Highness," Alexi Orlov kept saying, his voice hoarse from strain but still booming. "Please, Little Mother. They need to see you and the Grand Duke. To know that you are both safe from this *monster*."

I remember how harsh this word sounded, and how unnecessary. For a brief moment I even waited for Catherine to chastise him, but then the sparkling, unbelievable happiness at our victory claimed my thoughts.

A coup is a debt, and after it, debts multiply.

Catherine, in the Preobrazhensky uniform, appeared everywhere. She hardly slept; she ate on the run, on the way to inspect the troops or meet yet another delegation. She was graceful and gracious, distributing rewards, bestowing titles, estates, and medals, granting petitions and recalling the banished.

I await you as soon as your horses can bring you here, she wrote to the former Chancellor Bestuzhev. Count Panin—reconciled by then that she would not be Regent for her son—sported a red, sliver-lined ribbon of his newly received Order of St. Catherine.

Grigory Orlov was named Adjutant-General. All five Orlov brothers became Counts. The top conspirators were offered six hundred peasants and a pension of two thousand rubles or twenty-four thousand rubles in lieu of land. I, a bookbinder's daughter turned Countess, too could make my choice.

In the corridors of the Winter Palace, courtiers swirled, their numbers doubled and trebled by the giant gilded mirrors. They bowed when our eyes met, waiting for a chance to assure me of their longtime devotion. Count Panin walked about with brisk, determined steps, his rouged lips creased into a smile. What position had *he* been promised? A Chancellor? *Will he replace Vorontzov?* I heard.

But even the most generous rewards were not enough. Not a day passed without some guard attempting to return the Order of St. Alexander with which he had been decorated, calling himself the unhappiest of men, refusing to be consoled until Catherine took the petition he thrust into her hands, promised to reconsider a past judgment or restore old privileges.

"Every guardsman can say, 'I made that woman,' when he looks at me," Catherine said to me in one of those rare moments when I found myself close enough to speak to her. "How long until they will start saying, 'I can undo her'?"

She didn't say, *I want you to watch them, Varenka. I need you to lis-*
ten to what they say.

She didn't have to.

Here is what I heard in those fevered days.

From Oranienbaum the spies brought reports of a boat waiting,
packed to the brim with supplies. The Holsteiners, they warned, were
charting the shortest route to Prussia.

"No harm will come to him." I still hear Alexei's thunderous promise as he left to arrest the former Emperor and escort him to the
Schlüsselburg prison, where it had been decided Peter would stay
until Catherine decided his fate. "And he will cause you no harm, Your
Majesty."

The dispatches flooded in, as beaming messengers rushed in and
out of the staterooms, heroes of their own stories.

A Schlüsselburg cell was not yet ready, so Alexei took Peter to the
Ropsha palace, thirty-six *versty* away from St. Petersburg. He vowed
to spare no effort to keep the former Emperor comfortable.

Yet Peter had complaints. His room was too small, his bed too
narrow. He had no place to take his morning walk, and without exercise, his legs swelled up.

He was drinking. He refused to eat his breakfast and his dinner.
He cried and asked for *Das Fräulein's* presence.

I'll go away and never come back. All I want is my dog, my flute, my
Negro, and my mistress, he wrote to Catherine. *I renounce the throne of*
Russia. I willingly swear allegiance to Empress Catherine II. I beg her
forgiveness for all I have done wrong.

Amid the giddy promises of those first days of Catherine's reign, I
tried to push away the memory of the lonely wigless figure in his blue
housecoat walking down the Oranienbaum corridor.

Peter has surrendered, I told myself. *He is a better man than he is an*
emperor. A few months in prison will pass quickly. He will be happier
for it in the end.

I still refused to admit that justice might merely be another name for getting even.

On the third day after the coup, at five o'clock in the morning, I waited for my Empress with a pot of fresh coffee, the coveted privilege I claimed as my right. From her new bedroom I heard Grigory Orlov's voice: "Don't think about it, Katinka. Push it from your mind."

At the Winter Palace, Catherine had taken the Imperial Suite: the state bedroom and six adjacent inner rooms, all gold and white. Grigory Orlov moved into the apartment right above hers.

I heard a dog yelp. Old Bijou was no more. Sir Tom Anderson, an Italian greyhound, was now chasing away the palace cats, the few scraggly ones that still kept showing up, in search of Elizabeth. I no longer recognized them, though some had Bronya's tortoiseshell fur and Pushok's eyes.

Sir Tom began to bark.

"Stop it," Catherine shrilled. The dog whined, and stopped.

Catherine said something I could not hear.

The sounds of her steps, fast, circling the room, were followed by Grigory's booted stride.

"You *have* to stop the rumors, Katinka," I heard him urge her. "Alexei says that he will turn his back on you and bite your hand."

In the antechamber to the Imperial Bedroom, I straightened the tapestry on the wall. I picked up a soiled glove from under a chair. It gave off the odor of jasmine blossoms mixed with sweat.

I waited.

It was a quarter past five by the time Catherine walked in. She gave me a wan smile when she saw me. I could tell she had been crying.

"Everyone wants something from me, Varenka. I cannot please everyone."

Before I could say anything, she put her finger on her lips.

The letter from Ropsha arrived on the fifth day of Catherine's reign. The Empress was in the Throne Room, surrounded by courtiers. The messenger threw himself at her feet, bringing with him the rank smell of the road, the rot of the marshes, and rain.

Catherine broke the seal and read quickly, in silence. Her lips tightened. I saw her wipe her fingers on the silken folds of her skirt. She crushed the letter in her hands.

"I'm shocked and dismayed," she said, raising her eyes.

I will never forget a single word on the crumpled sheet. *Little Mother, your husband is no more.* There had been a skirmish in Ropsha, an unfortunate skirmish, wished by no one. An argument turned into a quarrel, too swiftly to extinguish or control. Everyone who was with the former Emperor at that time was guilty, worthy of death. But it was Alexei, Count Orlov, who wrote, begging Catherine's mercy, a pardon or a quick end.

Life's not worth living, for I have failed you.

The jeweled heel of Catherine's foot stomped on the floor. I heard voices rise and fall.

I did not listen.

Peter is dead, I thought.

Murdered.

I don't know how I made it to our rooms in the temporary palace. Seeing Darya's frightened eyes, I managed to smile and spin some lies. Nothing had happened, I assured her. I was merely tired. I needed to rest.

When my daughter left, I felt exhausted, as if I had climbed a mountain. Beads of sweat broke out on my forehead. Even the air I breathed seemed to hurt me. The light was too bright. I told Masha to keep the curtains drawn.

She called the surgeon instead.

I was bled. Bled again. Purged. Blistered. I slept for what must have been day and night, for the maid who brought me a cup of hot beef broth asked me if I knew what day it was. I wanted to answer, but when I opened my mouth, no words came.

I missed it all. The public announcement attributing Peter's death to *hemorrhoidal colic and violent stomachache, with which he was often afflicted.* The sight of the Emperor's embalmed body lying in state at the Alexander Nevsky Monastery, thick kerchief tied around his neck. The whispers: A onetime baby Emperor was still languishing in the Schlüsselburg Fortress. What Empress could afford *two* deposed rulers? How long before some crackpot tried to free one of them?

Catherine wrote to me: *Get well soon, Varenka. I need you at my side.*

Grigory Orlov delivered the note himself.

"Katinka is concerned, Varvara Nikolayevna. Every day she asks me about you."

He lowered himself into the armchair beside my bed, his handsome face serious, drawn.

I listened to his words: *... terrible accident ... Alexei shouldn't have been drinking ... shouldn't have let himself be provoked ... He knows it. ... Katinka knows it. ... The coup was a gamble. ... Not everything can be predicted. ...*

Outside, a newspaper boy was shouting, "Great news in *St. Petersburg Gazette.*" A woman began to sing a ballad I did not recognize. A trumpet blew.

My mouth tasted sour from the fever. My leg hurt from the surgeon's cut.

"He is here, Varvara Nikolayevna. He is leaving St. Petersburg tomorrow." Grigory Orlov cleared his throat. "My brother begs you to hear him out."

I felt my heartbeat quicken as I nodded my agreement.

Alexei must have been waiting right outside the door. He entered as soon as Grigory called his name. He took an awkward step toward me, straightening the steel-blue Izmailovsky tunic.

"I'm guilty, Varvara Nikolayevna."

The scar across Alexei's cheeks twitched as he spoke. His voice broke at times. He repeated himself. Catherine had ordered him to protect her husband, and he'd failed. He wouldn't make excuses. What happened, happened under his command. He couldn't undo what had been done.

The rough floors of the temporary palace squeaked every time Alexei shifted his giant frame from one foot to the other. Beside him Grigory, his hands clasped, nodded vigorously at his brother's words.

"I'm ready to die. I'm a soldier. Soldiers die. But our beloved Matushka refused to punish me. 'Will your death help me rule?' she has asked. So I begged her to send me away. Every time she looks at me, she shouldn't be reminded of the terrible price she had to pay."

A soldier's voice, strong and yet pleading. Simple words, impossible to refute. Words I would turn in my head for days to come.

"A terrible thing has happened, but we can make use of it.

"For the Empress.

"For Russia.

"For us all."

I rang for Masha as soon as Alexei and Grigory left. Katinka, both brothers had said, had a whole empire to run. After years of neglect, so much needed to be cleaned up. Cleared. Repaired.

"Bring Darya," I told Masha hoarsely.

Darenka approached me on tiptoes, my beloved child.

"What have you been doing today?" I asked.

"Nothing."

"Why?"

"I broke a cup."

"Which one?"

"The one with red roses in the bottom."

"We will get another one."

"You are not angry?"

"No."

"I knew you wouldn't be. But Mademoiselle Dupont said I was negligent."

"Were you?"

"A bit. I wasn't thinking of what I was doing."

"Why not?"

"I was listening to what the doctor was saying. That the crisis was coming. But no one would tell me what crisis it was." Fear flashed in her big dark eyes, and I felt a pang of guilt.

"I'm feeling better, *kison'ka*. You don't have to worry anymore."

She smiled, a burst of brightness, pain washing away from her face. She threw her hands around my neck. Clung tight to me.

"I don't like the way you smell," she said, wrinkling her nose, laughing.

By August, when I was strong enough to walk, Catherine's Chief Steward sent word that our new quarters at the Winter Palace were ready. Four spacious inner rooms and an antechamber, just two corridors away from the Imperial Bedroom. Furnished and redecorated according to Her Majesty's wishes. The temporary palace, once emptied, would be razed to make room for a small park.

There was no official appointment yet, only an invitation to join Her Majesty's entourage. The Empress woke up at five and worked alone in her study until eight in the morning. Visitors and petitioners came as soon as she was dressed and coiffed. Five state secretaries took care of the daily flood of solicitations. Petitions had to be examined and filed, gifts acknowledged, impossible requests refused gently, and all that merited her attention prepared for her inspection. The afternoons were reserved for reading. Evenings for the closest of friends.

Her Majesty's Chief Steward trusted that Countess Malikina would make sure this new routine was not needlessly disturbed.

It was an October afternoon, dark and lashing with rain, when a messenger from the British Embassy delivered a letter addressed to Madame Malikina. Someone had crossed off *Madame* and put *Countess* instead.

The letter was from Count Poniatowski.

He had been beside himself with worry. He had received no news from Catherine for fourteen weeks. He feared that his previous letters may have been lost.

Enclosed was a sealed note with *For Sophie* written on it and a request for me to place it directly into her hand.

It was still raining the following day when I entered Catherine's private study with her morning coffee. The cherished moment, however brief, when I could be sure to see her alone.

I barely had time to light the fireplace when Catherine walked in, Sir Tom right beside her, prancing on his hind legs, awaiting his treat. Her face was drawn. The relentless whirl of imperial obligations was taking its toll. By then even the afternoons Catherine so much desired to keep free for reading were broken by constant interruptions.

I placed the tray with the coffeepot on its usual spot, beside the sharpened quills and a neat pile of foolscap paper. I poured coffee into a china cup and waited until Catherine took the first sip before giving her Stanislav's letter. She opened it, glanced at it quickly, and handed it back to me. It was then that I saw it was in cipher.

"Burn it, Varenka," she said. "Before anyone sees it."

I threw it in the fire.

Catherine made room for me at her own desk. "Write, Varenka," she ordered.

I wrote what she dictated: How reason demanded that we have to come to terms with circumstances beyond our control. How she had to guard herself at every step. How she was sorry, more than she could express, but such was the truth. *Farewell, beloved friend. Life often brings strange surprises, but you can be sure that I will do everything I can for you and your family.*

Catherine paused, as if considering something she might still add.

"There is no use fighting what cannot be changed, Varenka," was all she said, slipping the letter, folded and sealed, into my pocket.

From the green velvet cushion beside her desk came the thumping sound of Sir Tom's wagging tail.

Before I dispatched Catherine's letter to the British Embassy with a request to pass it on to Count Poniatowski, I added a few words from myself. *Don't believe everything you hear. When you hurt, it is easy to assume the worst.*

Later that day, when the rain had finally stopped, I took Darya for a walk I had long promised.

We climbed the stairs to the Petropavlovsky Fortress to look at the city below, at the splendid palaces facing the river, white and yellow walls lit by the warm rays. The deep waters of the wide Neva had been tamed, the red Finnish marble lining the embankment postponing the fury of the floods.

"I still talk to Papa," Darya said. Her voice quavered.

"What about?" I asked, but she wouldn't tell me, so I held her tight to my chest and let her weep.

Former Chancellor Bestuzhev had been back at court for more than two weeks, but I'd managed to avoid him. Now he had come to me, frail and hunched after his years of exile. His red-rimmed eyes assessed the burgundy curtains with gold tassels, the thick carpets, Egor's portrait over the mantel.

I didn't like the smile on his face; I didn't like the amusement he didn't bother to conceal in his voice.

"We've won, *Countess* Malikina. We've backed the right horse, you and I."

He kissed my extended hand. I motioned for him to sit down, noting the wig plastered carelessly to his bald head, the yellow stain of egg yolk on his velvet vest.

His new title of Field Marshal was a meager consolation for the glaring lack of an official post. "Cabbage Field Marshal," Grigory Orlov had sneered.

The former Chancellor opened a snuffbox and took a fat pinch of snuff. He offered me some; I declined.

"Curious," he observed. "My doctor swears it is good for hangover, but I have yet to experience that. I go through five pounds of it a month, and the only thing it relieves is my purse."

He placed the snuff on the hollow between his index finger and his thumb, sniffed, and waited for the powder to stir his nostrils. He sneezed and then examined the brown stain on his handkerchief. Then he started to speak.

"Very clever," Bestuzhev called Catherine's appointments. Letting Vorontzov keep the title of Chancellor but giving Panin foreign policy. Making Grigory Orlov preside over a brand-new Chancery for Foreigners, so that no one could say he had replaced anyone. Offering Alexei the imperial pardon but sending him off to the army barracks. Making sure no one was too strong, so that *she* could control them all.

I turned my head toward my parlor window. The sun over the Neva was pale and hesitant.

Bestuzhev gave a heavy sigh and frowned.

"Nothing has changed, Varvara Nikolayevna. You still have only two choices: be indispensable or be insignificant. I've tried a simple life. Its appeal has little allure, believe me."

"Nothing has changed?" I asked, disbelieving. "When have you last seen an Empress work that hard?"

Bestuzhev looked at me carefully, a doctor considering his diagnosis.

"Have you forgotten all I've taught you, Varvara Nikolayevna? Or have you let yourself be dazzled by your new title? Need I remind you that titles come cheap around here these days? A gambling house doesn't turn into a monastery just because there is a new owner."

He leaned toward me, a sneer twisting his face.

"Do you know what some of your new friends call you? Nosy Varvara who needs to have her nose torn off."

I rose.

"You better leave," I said. "I have duties to attend to."

His face reddened at the word *duties*, drops of sweat gathering at the edge of his wig.

"Is bringing her letters from her Polish lover one of them?" he taunted. "What is she telling him, I wonder? That she needs a Polish footstool for her tired feet?"

"I don't see how it is any of your concern."

"But it is," he retorted, with a sudden glee in his eyes. "I find it irresistible to watch how our Catherine gets others to do her bidding."

"God help you." I was trembling. "Always seeing the worst in everyone."

"She got to the top thanks to the people who supported her for their own reasons. Now she is beginning to believe she has done it all by herself. She'll be shedding friends. It'll get ugly very soon, my dear *Countess*. It always does, and you are no longer hidden in the shadows. You'll soon acquire real enemies and you'll wish for something more than memories of friendship to protect you. Are you that sure you no longer need me?"

"Leave," I said, reaching for the bell to summon my maid. I wanted him out of my room. I wanted his voice to stop.

TWELVE

1763–1764

n St. Petersburg taverns, old men with wrinkled faces like to recall the disbelief of their youth when they heard how the vast expanse of flat land, with a few huts of Finnish fishermen scattered across it, would become a powerful, thriving city.

The old men remember the Great Tsar. They speak of Peter the Great's giant steps that made ordinary men run when he merely strolled, the deftness of his hands, the wood he carved, the icons he painted, the shoes he made, the teeth he pulled out.

"Delay means death," they repeat, the Great Tsar's favorite words.

With their blood warmed by vodka, the men whose eyes saw a city raise from the foggy marshes speak of soldiers and serfs whose skulls and bones are dug up every year when the shattering foundations of St. Petersburg are repaired.

There is no bitterness in their voices.

Wouldn't these serfs and soldiers have died anyway? Wasn't it better to die, if death made the future possible? To die for something that would last longer than an ordinary life?

From the crates and trunks that had come with us to our new quarters in the Winter Palace, I had unpacked many treasures: Darya's drawing of a house with a guard standing beside it, tall enough for his head to reach far above the chimney. A note I found on my breakfast tray on the morning my daughter turned eleven: *Maman, at what age did you have your own room? At what age did you start wearing long dresses? Can I now bathe in your bath?* Now she copied the gestures of the court ladies, the careless, languid sway of their steps.

"The Empress is quite smitten by your daughter, dear Varvara Nikolayevna," Princess Galitsina would stop to tell me.

Imperial presents of gowns and furs, invitations to a children's masquerade, ballet lessons with the Grand Duke had all been noted, Galitsina's eyes said. Before the coup, a glance over her shoulder would be all I could merit.

Where were you, I thought, *when the Grand Duchess with no future needed a friend?*

Right after the coronation in the Moscow cathedral, the Grand Duke collapsed, exhausted after hours of standing beside his mother, waving to the jubilant crowds. Carried to his room, hot and sweaty with fever, he screamed that snakes were crawling over him. His right leg was swollen and purple.

I sat at Paul's bedside. I put a cold compress on his forehead. I washed the sweat off his chest. When icy water dropped down his temples, he opened his eyes and gripped my hand painfully.

"Am I going to die?" he asked, his voice small, frightened.

"No," I replied. "Your Maman won't let you die."

He opened his mouth as if to ask me something, but he did not speak.

On the day when the Grand Duke was well enough to show himself to the people, a peasant woman wrapped in a black kerchief flung herself to the ground, shrieking, "Long live Emperor Paul Petrovich! Long live our *batushka!*"

Two guards had to make their way through the crowd before those around her scattered.

By the first anniversary of Catherine's accession, there was no need for the guards' vigilance. Fireworks lit the night with exploding wheels and flowers, and for a breathtaking moment a giant glittering C hung in the sky. The crowds applauded, drank greedily at the vodka fountains, and gasped as tightrope walkers took another precarious step on the rope suspended across the Great Perspective Road.

In the Grand Hall of the Winter Palace, tables decorated with the imperial eagles were lined against the gilded walls. Children ran from one to another, in search of their favorite treats. I saw the Grand Duke creep behind Count Panin and flap his arms like a giant insect. Count Panin pretended not to see it. I saw Darya, lovely in her green satin dress, sneak a glance at herself in one of Monsieur Rastrelli's giant mirrors.

"If only Master lived to see us now," Masha said and sighed. At the Tartar market, butchers now saved their best cuts for Countess Malikina, and the fishmonger put aside the choicest pieces of smoked sturgeon.

In the Imperial Suite, the maids pulled me aside to mention an ailing mother in need of money, a sweetheart who wished to propose if only they had the Empress's blessing. "Just mention me to *Matushka*, our Little Mother," they would plead. "She will listen to you."

Every morning at five, I still waited for the Empress with the pot of coffee and her mail, which I placed on her desk. In the evenings, Catherine sometimes allowed me to linger in the Imperial Bedroom before Grigory stomped down the private staircase. And there were always the precious moments when her ladies-in-waiting were out of earshot, or a walk together in the garden at dusk.

How much can one say in such times?

It was better to listen.

"Whatever I do, Varenka, I'll hurt someone.

"It pains me when even old friends watch me with terrified eyes, as if I were Medusa's head. Does friendship always flee from Sovereigns, Varenka?"

Grigory Orlov was still finding *Das Fräulein's* things in his apartment: a silk stocking, a fiddle bow, a shoe deformed by her limp. He brought them to Catherine like trophies. I saw him wait for her in the Imperial Bedroom, sprawled on an ottoman, flicking cards to pass the time. I saw him lift her off her feet when she arrived and whirl her around, making her breathless. I saw him caress her neck as she bent over her writing, his hand sliding into her hair.

In the marble corridors of the Winter Palace, Field Marshal Bestuzhev, cane in hand, was on the lookout for anyone willing or luckless enough to listen to his long, meandering speeches. Polite excuses were of no use; drunk or sober, the former Chancellor took no notice of hurried steps or impatient grins. Catherine gave strict orders not to admit him into her inner rooms. In the British Embassy, footmen were tipped double for prompt warnings of his approach. Everyone awaited the weeks in which Bestuzhev's penchant for vodka won over his ambitions and he would be too drunk to pay his visits.

"One word, Countess Malikina. One word only," he called in his hoarse voice when he spotted me. The gold handle of his cane, encrusted with gemstones, glittered in the light streaming through Rastrelli's giant windows.

But by then I had learned to look and not see.

"Don't go just yet, Varenka. I want to ask you something about Darya. But let me finish this first. . . ."

Among the many letters I had just brought the Empress on this chilly October morning, there was a note from Count Panin—or Nikita Ivanovich, as Catherine called him now—whom she'd put in charge of foreign policy.

I sat on a footstool by the fire in Catherine's study and waited, listening to the sharp nib scratching over the thick vellum paper she liked the most.

As they frequently did these days, my thoughts drifted toward Darenka. I'd often come to our rooms at the palace to find her gone.

"Summoned again," her governess explained, pointing at the ceiling as if the orders came from God Himself.

When my daughter returned, her face colored with excitement, she was bursting with stories. She had been allowed to carry Catherine's fan. She had been asked to read a passage from an old prayer book. Sir Tom had chased a cat down the service corridor, but she had brought him back.

"Who was there with the Empress?" I'd ask, watching her happy face as she described the visitors. Count Panin shuffled his feet as he walked, Darya told me. Uncle Grigory made the Empress laugh with shadow puppets dancing on the wall.

"What did he say?"

"That the Empress should find me a good husband. With a big house in the country."

"You are too young to think of husbands," I told my daughter, laughing. "You wouldn't know what to do with one."

But I felt a pinch of fear.

In the fireplace, as I waited for Catherine to finish her letter, the flames leaped and flared. I stared into them, thinking of my child leaving me. Next year she would turn fourteen, the age of Catherine when she came to Russia to marry.

I heard the crackle of paper folding, smelled wax melting over a candle.

"Ballet, Varenka," Catherine said, turning to me as she set her quill down. "I want our children to dance together."

The relief I felt brought hot tears to my eyes.

"I'll tell you more," Catherine teased me, "but only if you stop crying."

It was Herr Gilferding—the Austrian dancemaster Catherine had brought from Vienna—who'd come up with an idea for a court performance. A ballet of his own creation, *Acis and Galatea*, would tell the story of a shepherd in love with a beautiful nymph. At its end, Acis, slain by the jealous cyclops Polyphemus, would be turned into a river by Galatea, and Hymen would end the ballet with a solo mourning dance.

Grand Duke Paul would dance the part of the god Hymen, and Darya would be the nymph.

"If her teary mother lets her, that is," Catherine teased as I reached helplessly for my handkerchief, already enchanted by the image of my daughter dancing on the stage of the Winter Palace theater, applauded by the whole court.

"That's settled, then." Catherine waved away my gratitude and turned her attention to the letters I had brought. I saw her pick one and break the wax seal. Before I reached the door, however, she leaped from her chair and jumped up and down like a little girl. Sir Tom abandoned his cushion, barking, and began a mad chase after his own tail.

"King Augustus II of Poland has died," she cried out. "Get Nikita Ivanovich here right away."

But just as I was pressing the door handle, she stopped me and told me not to bother Count Panin just yet. She needed to gather her thoughts in private. Her voice, so joyful a moment before, became serious: "Now that I can finally repay an old debt to a dear friend, Varenka," she told me, "I don't want to make a mistake."

Two weeks later, Count Keyserling left for Warsaw with instructions to assure Stanislav's victory in the Polish royal election. By mid-November, Prince Repnin followed with assurances of more Russian help. He also carried Christmas presents for Stanislav: a box of black truffles, a bronze statue of Minerva, and a jeweled snuffbox with Catherine's profile carved out of ivory.

Hazy with joy, I repeated Sir Charles's words: *Stanislav, the King of Poland; Catherine, the Empress of Russia. Bound by trust, ruling two great nations, in unity and peace.*

An old dream, I thought, and yet how just, how timely, and how wrought with promise.

On the last night of November, unable to sleep, I sat alone in my parlor. I tried reading a book, but my eyes smarted from candlelight, and my thoughts stubbornly returned to my unfinished tasks: a painting from the last Parisian shipment that was still missing, the dwindling supplies of silk thread for Catherine's new passion—knotting ornamental braids that she gave away as coveted gifts.

The clock in the hall had just chimed midnight when I heard a commotion in the antechamber. For a moment I feared Bestuzhev had managed to get past my footmen. In the last weeks he had begun to pester me with letters, all versions of the same request to help him obtain a private audience with Catherine.

But it wasn't Bestuzhev.

The disheveled man, reeking of vodka and garlic, who stormed into my parlor, turned out to be Grigory Orlov. In his hand, he held a bowl of ice cream.

"For Darenka," he told me. "Egor's little sunshine."

"Where did you get ice cream in the middle of the night, Grigory Grigoryevich?"

"The cook likes me," he mumbled, drunkenly. "I don't know why."

I laughed. "My daughter is asleep," I told him.

The ottoman gave a moan when he fell onto it, his arms extended stiffly, his offering melting into a sticky puddle.

Masha had heard the commotion and scurried in, her lazy eye trained on the ceiling. "Take this to Darenka," Grigory slurred, as Masha deftly maneuvered the bowl from his hand and carried it away.

He staggered to his feet. "Why is she making *him* King of Poland, Varvara Nikolayevna? So that she can marry him?"

So this is what stung him, I realized, as Grigory's words flowed like a torrent, curses dissolved in weeping and threats: *Milksop . . . coward . . . plotting to get back at her side.* He made a lewd gesture with his hand. "Is he still writing to her?"

"You have to ask the Empress that."

"She won't talk of him." Grigory Orlov gave me an unsteady, out-of-focus stare. Behind him, a candle guttered out. I sat listening, fatigue weighing on my shoulders, wondering how much longer this jealous tirade would last.

"Alexei sent word that that Polish runt is still writing to her, wanting to come back. . . . Alexei says to watch out . . . that everybody is plotting against us . . ."

Grigory stood, swaying, towering over me, a mountain of flesh and muscle. And then he fell to the floor.

Worried that he had hurt himself, I bent over him. He snored. Masha fetched a blanket and a pillow. Grigory grunted when she took off his boots. "Don't, Katinka. Not now." This is how we left him, in the end, sprawled on the carpet, covered with a blanket, asleep.

I'd hoped we didn't wake anyone, but when I got to my bed I heard Darya's voice asking what had happened. She was sitting up, a slim figure in a white nightgown holding her knees, her nightcap gone, her black curls tangled.

"Nothing," I said. "Go back to sleep, kison'ka."

"You never tell me anything." She sighed with resignation. "Was it Uncle Grigory?"

"Yes."

"Did he really bring me ice cream?"

"Yes. But let's keep it a secret. He had a bit too much to drink."

"I know," she said, yawning. "I'm not a baby anymore."

I pulled her toward me. Her hair smelled musty, even though it had been washed only the day before. I resolved to tell Masha not to spare the egg yolks next time.

Please don't refuse my most sincere apologies and this small offering for Darenka, Grigory Orlov wrote in a note that came the next day. *And please don't mention it to anyone. I don't want my Katinka to know what a stupid fool I can be.*

With the note a whole basket of presents arrived: a set of sandal-wood nesting apples, each enchantingly hidden inside another, a lacquered box with a lid showing a fairy-tale princess wearing a crown of peacock feathers.

My lips are sealed, I wrote back, *and your gifts are too generous for one little girl who likes ice cream.*

The reply came immediately. Grigory Orlov insisted I accept his offering. *In Egor's memory,* he wrote. *A token of old friendship.*

In the months that followed, I didn't think much of the events of that night. I understood Grigory's jealousy, groundless as it was. There is power in an Empress's bed. A widow can marry again. An heir to the throne can die.

I didn't keep Grigory's note, either. Why would I?

Among the constant flurry of hours and days, it was Darya's dancing that occupied my mind.

"I'll be a nymph," Darya kept telling everyone, glowing with delight, always ready to demonstrate a newly learned gesture or passage.

I didn't want to talk of envy. "If you let everyone in the palace see the pieces of the dance before the performance," I said instead, "there will be no surprise."

For the first round of rehearsals Herr Gilferding installed himself in the blue card room in the Imperial Suite so that the Empress could drop in on the children's practice. No one else was allowed to watch.

This is what I remember from these winter days when I fetched Darya at the end of the rehearsals. Paul's delight at his costume, the wig that he insisted on wearing all day. Darya greeting me with most light-footed circling of the room, her face framed in the oval of her hands. Excited voices, fierce frowns of concentration. Stories of near misses and unforeseen disasters averted at the last moment. An ankle twisted, a broken prop.

At the end of March, Herr Gilferding announced that the rehearsals would be moved to the court theater and a select audience would be allowed to observe.

I noticed that Darya did not seem as excited about this news as I'd expected, but I put it down to stage fright. So I was taken by surprise when she came into the parlor on that spring day. "Maman, would you be very upset if I didn't dance in the ballet?" Her eyes avoided mine.

"Why wouldn't you dance?" I asked.

Only the day before, Herr Gilferding had praised my daughter's grace, her endurance, her expressiveness. "She may be only thirteen, but there is more poise in her than in the dancers of the Imperial Theater School," he'd bragged.

"You can tell me," I coaxed Darya when she didn't answer. "Are you worried that you are not ready?"

She shook her head. I saw her bite the tips of her fingers. She had never been a nail-biter before.

I patted the spot beside me on the ottoman. Reluctantly, she sat down.

I told her how there was no need to be shy now. Once she was there, onstage, I promised, all these worries would vanish. Her father would have been so proud to see her dance with the Grand Duke, admired by the entire court. After all, hadn't the Empress often said she wished to do much for her? And wouldn't Catherine herself be in the audience that evening?

It was then that the gold pendant around her neck caught my attention. I hadn't seen it before.

"Where did you get this from?" I asked, fingering it to take a better look at a cluster of gemstones set in the shape of forget-me-nots.

"It's from the Empress," she muttered, still not looking at me.

"Was it a reward for something you did? You don't have to be shy about pleasing the Empress."

She nodded, a nod of such slightness I might have missed it.

"Was it for your dancing?"

"Yes," she said, too hastily, her cheeks turning crimson.

"So why this silly blushing, my love? You might as well get used to praises. If you ever stop slouching, you will be the most beautiful of nymphs."

She straightened herself, immediately.

"So no more stage fright now?" I asked, and was relieved when Darya nodded.

I watched her as she walked away, her spine straight, her shoulders back, her head held high. Herr Gilferding's tutoring had made all her movements languid and poised. A remarkable teacher, I thought. No wonder Catherine had been so eager to keep him at the Winter Palace. She would be pleased to learn he began talking about finding a house in St. Petersburg. Only to rent, his valet reported, but with an option to buy.

I am still not sure how Bestuzhev managed to get into my parlor.

Later, Masha assured me that she hadn't heard anything. The servants swore on the Holy Icon they had not seen him come in, let alone accepted a bribe for defying my orders, but I didn't believe them. It isn't difficult to soften a footman's or a maid's resolve. I had done it many times myself.

The former Chancellor could barely stand up on his own. His breath reeked of vodka. His puffed eyes were glassy.

"You have not responded to my requests, Countess Malikina," he slurred. "Did you ask the Empress to see me?"

I said I had many requests to consider.

"I remember you being far more willing to please me once."

For a moment I thought I had misheard him. Then I saw by the smirk on his lips that I had not.

Blood drained from my face. "Get out of here," I managed to hiss, reaching for the bell to ring for my footman.

But Bestuzhev was faster.

"Why are you so stubborn?" he asked coldly. "Because you are so sure she needs you? An old friend she has always trusted? You still don't know, do you?"

"Know what?" I stared at his sweaty red face, hating my curiosity, unable to stop myself from asking the question the Old Fox so clearly wished me to ask.

"That you were never her only tongue, Varvara. Even then, in Elizabeth's bedroom, there were others." He tapped at his own temple as if prompting me to think harder. "Many others. I often wondered when you'd find out, but you never did."

I felt my knees buckle. A tremor shot up my spine. "Leave before I throw you out," I said, ringing the bell.

"You did her bidding then as you do now, nothing more. You were commonplace, Varvara. Another disposable spy. The only difference with you was that you believed you were *special*."

He blinked and turned away from me.

What is taking that damned footman so long? I raged.

But the former Chancellor was already opening the door, making the man jump with fright.

After he left, I sat alone. When Masha came in, asking if I needed anything, I sent her away.

I soothed myself with the memory of Catherine's dismissive words as she set aside yet another of Bestuzhev's elaborate plans for reforms. The previous batch had concerned foreign policy, which annoyed Panin. The current one proposed reforming the army, and made Grigory Orlov sneer.

This is who he is, I reminded myself. *A has-been. A loser who cannot bear his own defeat. Trying to poison the well he can no longer draw water from.*

I closed my eyes and waited until my heart stopped racing.

The court performance of *Acis and Galatea* was scheduled for the end of May. At the end of April, Catherine showed me the design for the invitations, which were to include a list of the cast members.

I hurried to our rooms to tell Darya the news, but she didn't come when I called her, so I looked for Masha. I found her in the pantry where she stored our supplies, despairing, for mice had gotten there already. The sack of flour was chewed through, and mouse droppings were everywhere.

"Where is Darya?" I asked her.

"Asleep," she said.

"In the middle of the day? Is she ill?"

Masha wasn't sure. Darya had gone to the bedroom, she insisted, saying only that she wanted to rest for a bit.

"How long has she been there?"

"Ever since the cannon," Masha said, meaning the noon blast from the Petropavlovsky Fortress. "As soon as the teacher went away. Our *kison'ka* is tired from all this dancing."

"She has slept long enough," I said, walking toward the bedroom. I pressed down the door handle, but the door did not give in. It was locked.

"Darya," I called. "It's Maman. Open up."

I tapped gently at the door, then more firmly, for there was no answer.

"Darenka! Are you awake?"

There was no reply.

My heartbeat quickened.

I placed my ear to the door, but I couldn't hear anything. Then I banged on it.

It was Masha who stooped and put her good eye to the keyhole.

"She is not there," she reported.

I, too, peeked through the keyhole. In the light that came through opened curtains, I saw an empty bed.

For a dreadful moment, I thought she had fainted and rolled off the bed and was lying there unconscious.

I rattled the door handle.

Again, nothing.

In the next few moments the maids came running. Darya's shawl was gone, they told me. So were her walking shoes, her hooded traveling coat. Finally, Masha found the bedroom key, left in the calling-cards tray.

I grabbed it, rushed to the bedroom, and unlocked the door.

Inside, nothing seemed out of the ordinary. The bed had been carefully smoothed. Darya's slippers were lined up by the footstool.

Then I noticed that my old cedar trunk was opened. She must have searched for something there, for my mother's white muslin dress had been pushed aside.

And then I saw it. Egor's letters untied, a red ribbon cast aside. "*I still talk to Papa. . . .*" I recalled my daughter's words, her pale face drawn and shriveled with sadness.

I guessed where she might be.

I sent the maid to get the carriage. I ordered the driver to take me to St. Lazarus Cemetery.

"Hurry," I urged the coachman.

As the carriage sped eastward, past the Fontanka River, my eyes followed any girlish figure rushing through the streets. I thought of the time when Darya came to me to tell me how she didn't want to dance in the court ballet. I remembered how I'd made her change her mind.

When the carriage stopped at St. Lazarus's gate, I alighted, picked up my skirts, and ran down the gravel-lined paths. I ran awkwardly, in my silly heeled shoes, in my full court dress. I ran until I saw my daughter, a huddled figure at the foot of her father's grave, her face hidden in her hands. On Count Orlov's orders, my husband's plain headstone had been replaced by a monument of marble: an imposing figure of a soldier leaning on a musket, skull and bones under his feet. His face, smoothly handsome, bore no resemblance to Egor.

"Darenka," I called.

She raised her face, her face wet with tears, toward me.

I mumbled my relief, my accusations. Everyone had been so worried. We'd looked for her everywhere. Masha was beside herself.

"Don't be angry, Maman," Darya said.

"I'm not angry," I said.

I took her in my arms and caressed her shiny black hair. No court honor, I thought, merited my child's pain.

"You don't want to dance in the ballet?" I asked, ready to admit my error. "You don't have to, *kison'ka*. We will tell the Empress tomorrow to find someone else to dance your part."

But Darya was sobbing, not at all appeased by my words.

"What is it, my love?" I asked.

Please tell me, I thought. *Please do not hide from me.* I embraced her, thinking how quickly her chest, once so flat and narrow, was taking on flesh.

"It's all my fault," she wept.

I pried it out of her, bit by bit.

At first she had noticed small things. Catherine's glances had made her uneasy, though she didn't know why. Maybe it was because of that silly thing Paul had said, that when he got to be the Emperor he would make Darya Queen of Poland. She'd even told Catherine that the Grand Duke was just saying such silly things, but he didn't mean them. And the Empress said she knew that and that she was not cross at all.

Then the Empress started coming by every day to watch the ballet practice. She applauded and praised both Darya and Paul, and my daughter was deliriously happy. But one day, when the practice ended, Catherine called her aside and started to ask questions. Did she like the ballet they were practicing? Was Herr Gilferding truly happy with the Grand Duke's progress, or did he say so only to her? Would Paul be ready for the big night?

Herr Gilferding thought that the Grand Duke was dancing very well, Darya assured the Empress. She also confessed that while she liked the story of Acis and Galatea, a nymph in love with a shepherd, she didn't like the way it all ended.

"What don't you like about it?" Catherine asked her.

"That the shepherd must die," my daughter replied.

The Empress nodded and told Darya that she had a kind heart. But then the Grand Duke got impatient and began calling her, so Darya had run to join the other dancers.

The Empress came back the next day, and the next, and she always asked Darya something. Odd questions: Did she have her own bed, or did she sleep with me? Did she wake up at night? Was she allowed to stay up, and how long? Finally, Catherine asked, "Does anyone come to visit your Maman at night?"

My daughter answered that she went to sleep early and slept soundly, so she wouldn't know. She didn't even hear when I rose before dawn, as I always did.

"So you never heard anything?" the Empress asked. "Ever?"

This is when Darya remembered the ice cream she never got, and so she told Catherine of Uncle Grigory coming with a bowl of ice cream for her in the middle of the night. Of Masha having to throw it away because it all melted. Of the beautiful presents she got from Uncle Grigory the next day.

The Empress asked her many more questions then. How did Count Orlov look? What was he wearing? What did he say? What kind of presents did he send? And why didn't she ever know about it?

Because Maman asked me not to tell anyone about them, Darya had answered, only then remembering the promise she had given me.

She must have looked worried and unhappy, for the Empress assured her that it didn't matter. Then she gave her the pendant and told her not to tell anyone about their little talk. It would be their secret, she said.

So Darya had promised. She'd felt awful when she had to lie to me about why she got the pendant. And then Uncle Grigory started looking at her in a strange way, so he must know as well and must be angry with her, too.

"And today I found this," my daughter sobbed, pulling something from her coat pocket. A slip of paper, folded in half. I thought she had taken one of Egor's letters from my trunk and wanted to return it, but I was wrong. It was a crude drawing of two figures. A big fleshy man, his face distorted with a cruel smile, was stretched naked on a bed, reaching for the imperial crown with a two-headed eagle. A woman, with her nose torn off, was climbing into his bed.

"It means nothing," I assured her, tearing the paper to pieces. Somehow I managed to keep my voice even.

She had found the drawing under my pillow, Darya confessed. She'd thought I had left her a secret message, like the ones Papa used to hide for her when she was little, to lead her to a surprise.

"I'm not angry with you," I said, wiping tears off Darya's cheeks.

I promised I would talk to the Empress.

I promised that all would be well.

When we returned to the Winter Palace, I questioned Masha and the maids if anyone had been to my bedroom that day. They all swore I had no callers. The day before, the Grand Duke's footman had come to fetch Darya for her ballet practice, but the man was made to wait in the corridor and never crossed our threshold.

I sent them away.

It's a nasty feeling, suspicion. The curse of all spies. The long minutes spent examining the seals on the letters I received. The voice that questions every cheerful smile, flares up at the first display of curiosity. Watches for the unusual and doubts what is routine.

What was the chambermaid doing in my room alone? Why this sudden flow of eagerness to scrape the grate of the fireplace?

I even checked the walls for secret doors. I found nothing.

Spiders spin two kinds of threads, I recalled. A smooth one to walk on, a sticky one to trap.

When Darya finally went to bed that night, teary but content, I hurried through the corridors of the Winter Palace, my figure multiplied in the gilded mirrors. I hurried by the still-unfinished wing, rooms left unpainted because Monsieur Rastrelli, offended by Catherine's order to remove some of the ornate gildings from the Imperial Suite, had departed for Courland.

My heart pounded; I was dizzy with questions. *Does friendship flee from Sovereigns?* I asked myself bitterly. *Or do Sovereigns flee from friendship?*

I thought of Catherine in the Moscow cathedral, in her robe of silver trimmed with ermine and embroidered with two-headed eagles. Of Catherine taking the crown in her own hands and placing it on her head.

Bestuzhev's voice kept encroaching on my thoughts: *She is beginning to think she has done it all by herself. . . . Are you that sure she trusts you? . . . Another disposable spy . . . You believed you were special.*

Darenka's frightened face flashed through these words, my child in pain, coaxed into a betrayal. An innocent soul blaming herself for the court's poisonous malice.

Is this what I want for my daughter?

I swept by footmen snoring over tables, guards squabbling over card games. I recalled the talk of vicious fights in the guards' quarters, smashed skulls, broken limbs, skin slashed with knives. The Orlovs, I'd heard, were on the lookout for any man foolish enough to believe he could replace Grigory in Catherine's bed.

How long had I been fooling myself? *What else have I missed? What have I already lost forever?*

Cats scurried away at the sound of my steps. The maids said that Murka had gone feral. They whispered that they sometimes saw Elizabeth's old cat roaming through the gardens, stiffening at the sight of a sparrow, disappearing into the hedge if any human moved toward him.

It was almost five o'clock when I returned to our rooms to find Masha waiting for me.

She helped me change my soiled dress, despairing over my crumpled silks. I would catch my death from such running about, she scolded. Drag some misfortune home.

"The Empress must be up already," she said.

"There you are, Varenka," Catherine exclaimed when I walked into the Imperial Study, carrying the silver tray. "You've never been late before. I've been worried. Look at you, your hands are trembling!"

There was so much concern in her voice that for a moment it

seemed that all I had learned never happened. That I had to be in the wrong, that Darya must have misunderstood Catherine's intentions. These thoughts were so tempting, so enticing, that I stood motionless, as if in a haze, the words I had wished to say withering in my throat. "Darya is very unhappy," I managed. "She doesn't want to dance in the ballet."

Catherine pushed aside a pile of papers and motioned for me to sit beside her.

"Is this because of the ending?" she asked, softly, when I hesitated. "But I, too, dislike it. Tell poor Darenka I've already spoken to Herr Gilferding. Why bring up these sad feelings in a story? I told him. Don't we have enough problems in our own lives?"

I felt a brief flare of panic. Something was stirring inside me, some dark current of unease, pulling me and repelling at the same time. "It's not about the ending," I murmured.

I did not sit down, but Catherine had not noticed. She was outlining the changes to the tale she had made. Hymen would stop Polyphemus at the last moment. Polyphemus, overtaken by remorse, would hide his face with shame until he is forgiven. It would be a comic ballet. Herr Gilferding said her changes were brilliant. And then, realizing that I was still standing, she asked, "But why don't you sit, Varenka?"

"It's not about the ballet," I said.

Catherine put her quill down. "What is it about, then?" Her eyes met mine, still concerned but already urging me to move on.

I blurted them out, if not the words I had wished to say, then their shadowy twins: "Did you really think I could've betrayed you? Have I not always been a good friend? How could you ask my daughter such questions about me?" Catherine frowned, but I would not stop. "Darya is not as we used to be at her age. She is still a *child*."

Catherine stared at me as if I made no sense. No matter how incomprehensible it seems to me now, I still expected her to explain it all away. Tear what had happened, the way I tore the filthy drawing

Darya had found. But the words I heard were curt and cold. "Aren't you forgetting your place, Varvara Nikolayevna? What is it exactly that you mind so much?"

Tears stung my eyes. "You wanted my daughter to *spy* on me!"

"I merely asked her to tell me what had happened. For *you* did not!"

There was so much force in her voice that, to my astonishment, I began to defend myself, explaining the innocuous circumstances of my silence. "Grigory is jealous of Stanislav. He drank too much, and he came by to ask me if Stanislav was still writing to you. He fell asleep in my parlor. When he awoke, he apologized and begged me to keep his visit a secret. He was ashamed."

"Do you have the note he wrote?" Catherine leaned toward me. Her eyes never left my face.

"I didn't keep it. I didn't think it was important."

"I told you once to let me be the judge of what is important, Varenka."

The memory that came to me then was that of a whip lashing my calves, sharp, biting, cutting the skin. And the bitter taste of my own impotence.

"You are the Empress," I retorted. "You do what suits you."

Catherine sighed, a mother despairing over her recalcitrant child yet ultimately sure of her own victory. "I don't have time for accusations. I know you've not always been happy here. But there is no need for scenes of injured pride. Let's not mention this again. Tell Darenka she will be a wonderful nymph."

"She is not going to dance," I heard myself say.

Catherine gave me an impatient look.

"Very well, Varenka," she said. "Darya won't dance in the ballet, if this is what you both wish. And now, I have important business to attend to, and you need to calm down before we speak again."

I made a step toward the door. Then I could not resist.

"How many did you have?" I asked, gruffly.

She raised her head.

"How many what?" she asked.

"Tongues. In Elizabeth's bedroom. How many besides me?"

I saw her expression, a smile tinged with pity. I fumbled for the door.

Moments later, I was rushing blindly down the wide marble stairs of the Winter Palace, cursing my own tears.

EPILOGUE

1764

t is well past midnight, my Duval watch confirms, its case covered with clusters of diamond petals, one of Catherine's gifts to me.

Dear Varenka, Catherine wrote in her last letter to me. *When are you coming back?* I picture her at her writing desk at dawn, with a steaming coffeepot on a silver tray.

The candle wavers and hisses. A moth has singed its wings and lies writhing in a pool of molten wax. I make sure the quills are sharp, the ink not too thick, and that I have enough plain paper, for I find the glazed one hard on my eyes. The ink gives off a sweet yet slightly sickening smell. Outside, the November darkness is impenetrable, broken at times by the lantern of a passerby and the howling of dogs. In St. Petersburg, Stanislav used to call such time "unguarded." It was during the northern winters, when the nights came early and stayed long, that confessions came and secrets were revealed.

"This unfortunate outburst of yours, Varenka," Catherine had said when she'd summoned me to the Imperial Bedroom later that day. "I won't let it destroy years of friendship."

Her silk skirts rustled as she paced the room; the hem of her golden court gown swept the floor.

I watched her face as she spoke. Her blue eyes were sparkling. Her smile was warm. As if nothing had happened, as if I'd imagined it all.

"What you need is a journey, Varenka. One I would've liked to make myself. Take Darya to Paris, to Berlin, to Warsaw. She should see the world and be away from this place for a while. Let your daughter come back to court in full bloom."

"Maman, what are you writing?" Darya asked me this morning. Darya's Polish is too rolling, too melodious, so clearly touched by the Russian.

She speaks French to me.

I recalled the time when my daughter was five or six, armed with a sack filled with morsels of bread and asking to be taken to the canal by the Summer Palace to feed the ducks. It was November, and the edges of the water were already frozen and slippery. Darya threw bread to make the ducks slide and slither as they rushed greedily over the ice. She thought all these antics were performed for her amusement.

"My thoughts," I answered.

"What kind of thoughts?" she asked.

"Thoughts I do not want to forget."

We went to Paris and to Vienna. We walked along wide boulevards, saw glorious paintings, palaces of immense splendor where we were received with courtesy and curiosity. The rumors about me made me smile. A widowed Russian Countess and her lovely daughter, a close friend of the Russian Empress, for signs of imperial favor are not easy to hide.

In Paris, being Catherine's friend is a coveted distinction. Monsieur Voltaire is trying his best to be considered as such. His letters to Catherine, copied and circulated widely, call her a Philosopher Queen, the Semiramis of the North, the Northern Star that always shows the travelers the right way.

Monsieur Voltaire is besotted by the notion that Catherine is turning barbaric Russia around, undoing decades of *unprecedented neglect and corruption,* as if France knew no vices of the heart. Catherine drains the Russian marshes by digging canals and cutting down the pine forests, he announces. She has opened a hospital and a foundling home. The Russian Senators have never worked so hard in their lives. "Her motto is *Useful,*" he tells those who trail behind him in awe. "Her emblem is a bee."

I was in Paris when the news appeared in all the papers. On July 4, Ivan VI—once the baby Emperor, and for decades Prisoner Number One at the Schlüsselburg Fortress—had been found dead in a pool of blood. I read Catherine's words quoted in every paper. The *serious and dangerous conspiracy was nipped in the bud.* The pamphlets that the scrawny printers' boys pushed into the hands of passersby were less forgiving. *Another Emperor so conveniently dead merely a year since the last one died. How many tragic "accidents" can possibly happen at the Russian court?* Anonymous writers aired more sinister suspicions. *Philosopher Queen, or Messalina who kills and betrays when it suits her?*

"I don't know the Empress that well," I answered when anyone asked me.

Soon other news from Russia overwhelmed these speculations, for Catherine began buying paintings. Whole collections that had been sitting idly in dilapidated castles could suddenly be sold for ready money. The Empress's agent paid very well and asked few questions. His only reservation was that Catherine, His Sovereign, endowed with a woman's soft heart, wouldn't like anything that suggested death or loss.

How touching, I heard. *And how very Russian.*

I reminded myself: *To govern is to understand the weaknesses of the human heart. And to use such weakness to your own advantage.*

I told myself: *You have no right to expect anything else.*

Have you not called yourself her friend, too? Were you not a shrewd keeper of her secrets?

We arrived here in Warsaw in the first week of September, right after the royal election that—just as Catherine had desired—made Stanislav the King of Poland.

A blue, frosty afternoon darkened slowly as we approached the Vistula River through a maze of twisted streets. As I opened the coach window to let in some air, I heard the buzz of voices outside but couldn't make out what they said.

I had been away for almost thirty years, but as we approached the center of the city I was able to point out to my daughter the cathedral spires against the reddening sky, the roof of the royal castle. I was amazed by how much smaller everything seemed. By the time we reached Senatorska Street, where I had rented an apartment, the darkness was broken only by the lights of lanterns, flickering like fireflies.

"The streets are so muddy," Darya complained.

Now, a month later, she is still not impressed by Warsaw. Palaces here do not stretch for the whole block; there are no canals. Parks are shabby and crowded, bridges narrow.

I've heard the two of them whisper in Russian. Masha, trusting my daughter with stories of her longing.

Not for St. Petersburg, not for the life at the court, but for Russia, where the northern wind blows over expanses of dark green forests. For January nights, white not from the sun that refuses to set but from the silver light of the moon. For ice floes screeching as they rub against one another, for rocks in which precious stones look like frozen drops of blood. For sacred places from where, in a solemn moment that comes when you least expect it, you can peek into the other world.

Masha's good eye is sad and empty; her breath carries the sweet scent of vodka. She defends herself against my questioning with a grimace of denial.

"When are we going back?" she wants to know.

I tell her I don't know, and my old servant walks away unhappily, shuffling her feet.

"She wants to die in Russia," Darya tells me. "She wants to be buried in the village where she grew up. Next to her mother."

Masha speaks of death as if it were a return from some long journey. She wants to be buried with her face turned to the sea in the sandy land of the north, where bodies do not rot. She longs for a simple grave with freshly cut branches of fir on the bottom to make the rope slide from under the coffin with greater ease. A grave on which old women from her village would scatter bread crumbs, and where they would come to sit and wonder to what distant roads Masha's life took her and if she ever peeked into that other world.

"Barbara." Stanislav calls me by my Polish name when he comes to see us. "A friend from such a precious past."

Here, he wears his thick black hair tied in the back. Time is kinder to men: At thirty-two, he does not seem a day older than the day he left St. Petersburg four years before.

He doesn't ask for reasons of my journey.

Prince Repnin has just delivered Catherine's official words: Poland chose her new King well. The Empress of All the Russias predicts a grand future for Stanislav, his family, and his country.

"You saw her a few months ago," Stanislav says. "Did she speak of me?"

"Of course," I lie. I cannot bear to hurt him.

In my front parlor, Stanislav sits in silence, his handsome profile lit by a ray of pale sun. *What is he thinking of? Their Dream? Of two mighty Slavic nations ruled by reason, a Philosopher Queen and a Philosopher King working together for the good of their subjects?*

No one whispers in this country. Merchants complain of clients who do not pay their debts; doctors and pharmacists are eager to discuss the details of their patients' cures. Everyone has plenty to say about Stanislav. Income from his estates amounts to no more than fifty thousand zlotys; a certain Szydlowski is pushing his daughter at him. Even the Poniatowskis' coat of arms—*ciołek*, a young bull—is a source of national merriment. The jokes are predictable: the speculations on the courage of cattle, or on turning the Polish court into a barn.

Here, they don't like Catherine.

In the streets of Warsaw the Russian troops, invited by Stanislav's uncles "to assure peace," are no longer blamed only for stolen chickens and broken fences. The Russians are like locusts, I hear. They leave trampled fields. They leave bastards in the bellies of peasant girls.

Russian money, Russian army, Russian diplomacy made him King, I hear. What will his payment be in return?

"The Empress cannot afford to listen to her heart," I tell Stanislav.

He winces at the word *cannot*.

"That I know," he says, in the gallant voice of a courtier. "But there are many ways of being true to what one believes."

"Yes," I say. "Of course there are."

I cannot pass by a bookstall without touching books that hide among French snuff, tonics for renewed energy and abundance of good moods that the street merchants sell here. I pick them up, these old volumes, open their pages, examine their bindings. I comment on the deftness of their gilding, the rarity of their leather. Sometimes I ask where they come from. The booksellers tell me of trailing death in search of such books. The best moment to approach a family is right after the funeral, they say. On the fingers of one hand they can count heirs not grateful for the opportunity to exchange the old volumes for cash.

I'm building a library to sustain me during the long and solitary evenings I anticipate, a library that will help me understand the significance of what I lived through and reinforce me in my decision. *Candide, ou l'Optimisme* has been my latest purchase. Smuggled to

Warsaw with much secrecy, I was told, and offered only to the most discerning and reliable patrons. Its author, the elusive *Docteur* Ralph, is, of course, no one else but Monsieur Voltaire.

But in the evenings, it is Tacitus I lose myself in. I read of decadence that is meant to seduce and dull the conquered, of favors that buy their souls. I read of spies sent out to take note of the sorrow of mourners—for what we mourn betrays us, too.

Holding to power, I read, is like holding on to a wolf.

Pan Korn, who has a small but prosperous bookstore on Krakowskie Przedmieście, has great expectations of the new King. "An enlightened man," he calls Stanislav. "A man who does not just carry books but reads them."

Pan Korn might be considered handsome, with his dark brown hair neatly parted down the center, his brow dark and thick, his eyes calm, smiling whenever I appear with Darya.

A bookseller, I think. Not that far from a bookbinder's daughter.

He offers us tea sweetened with honey and slices of strudel, with walnuts and raisins. He lets Darya roam through the store, to carry off the adventure books she has developed a taste for. Yesterday he presented her with *The Life and Strange Surprising Adventures of Robinson Crusoe,* and she is already halfway through it, lost in the descriptions of the deserted island, days filled with useful tasks.

Like others in this city, *Pan* Korn doesn't mind telling me stories from his life. His family hailed from Germany but left it when he was so young he has but a passive knowledge of the language of his forefathers.

Why?

The thoughts that make a man pack and leave his homeland are always the same, he says with a smile.

He asks me about Russia. The travelers' accounts he has read disappoint him. A traveler, he tells me, notices what seems odd and different. Instances that may or may not be important.

"You had a life there," he reminds me. "Tell me about it."

I had a life there, but I, too, offer him fragments. Cold gusts of wind stunting the growth of trees. The scent of *ladan* that hovers over icons long after the Easter procession. The way the ice darkens with the coming of spring, cracking like parched earth.

"You never speak about people," he points out.

"I don't want to lie."

Stanislav's coronation will take place on November 25. St. Catherine's Day. Like bringing in the Russian troops, the choice of the day is considered excessive.

A wooden pavement covered in red cloth will lead to St. John's Cathedral, where Stanislav will be anointed king. I hope the solemn ceremonial gestures will soothe some of the resentment against him.

Warsaw is eager for the festivities. The passage from the cathedral where Count Stanislav Poniatowski will become Stanislav August, King of Poland, to the center of the Old Town has been decorated with fir trees and obelisks. In the Market Square, where the city will welcome the new King, the royal throne faces a Triumphal Arch supported by figures of Love, Peace, Bravery, and Justice. In a day or two Stanislav's portrait, crowned by the Polish white eagle, will be raised above them, for this is where the new King will receive the keys to the capital.

I note the opportunities that would please Catherine. Here, in the heart of Poland, I could so easily run a salon according to the Parisian fashion. Fashionable, cultivated. Frequented by the King himself. A place to discuss the newest books, meet the best of minds and the most attractive of women. People talk too much here, already; the need to appear important will prompt more indiscretions.

"I'm aware of my weaknesses, Barbara," Stanislav says. "I also know my own strengths. I'm flexible, I'm patient, I do not take offense easily. I know what is still possible."

I think of rivers, the quiet relentlessness of their currents.

"Peter the Great himself wanted Poland to be a buffer between Russia and the rest of Europe," Stanislav continues. "But a weak buffer is of little use. A strong Poland is in Russia's interest."

In the royal castle, for years neglected by the Saxon Kings who had resided far away in Dresden, we walk from room to empty room, our steps bouncing off the crumbling walls, ceilings stained by mold. I think of the old Winter Palace, with squeaking floorboards now replaced by marble from the Ural Mountains.

Warsaw needs court painters and architects of renown, a proper court orchestra and a kapellmeister. A royal palace where the King can entertain visitors without shame, where adversaries can meet and find a common ground, he tells me, warming to his subject. The message Stanislav wants to send to the world is that Warsaw, Poland, and the Polish King are worldly, modern, and committed to a strong government.

"Stay here, in Warsaw, Barbara. I have enough enemies and those who wish me ill. I realize that what I can offer you pales beside the splendors of St. Petersburg, but you will be among friends."

I let him take my hand and raise it to his lips.

I think of spies who've crossed to the other side, who've served one master by choosing what they reported to the other. Treachery, but possible if one has the strength for another fight, if one believes that a monarch can change the nation he rules.

"I can offer you—"

I stop him before he can finish.

"You offered me far too much already," I say.

Outside the house on Senatorska Street, a swarm of birds has descended on a bare bush that leans on the fence. *Samosiejka*, my new servants call it in Polish, for the bush clearly seeded itself. I do not know its name, but I already know it is hard to kill and is forgiving of heavy pruning. Berries are its most attractive feature, pale orange with a small reddish tip, withered now from the cold.

I love the sound of my quill scratching the paper I write on, good paper with a watermark, nib freshly sharpened, black ink drying as I fill the page.

I still have my sources in St. Petersburg. My correspondents, whose names shall remain my secret, offer nothing beyond facts or observations. They are wise. They do not presume.

It is curiosity that compels me to receive these dispatches— curiosity about the people I once loved and hated, whose lives I'll now merely follow. But there is also a good dose of self-interest in this ac- tivity. For only a fool ignores the conditions at sea that might toss a small boat back into a storm. Grigory Orlov is chasing after another maid-of-honor; his brother still keeps a close eye on any handsome young man who tries to approach Catherine. Alexei has already got- ten into a nasty fight with a certain Grigory Potemkin, the Horse Guard who handed Catherine his sword knot on the day of the coup, a fight that cost Potemkin his eye.

Catherine's lavish gifts—smoked sturgeon from Astrakhan and a book by Brantôme—have arrived enveloped in shimmering fabric and tied with green ribbons, sealed at the ends with her emblems: a bee, a pot of honey, a hive. For Darya, who turned fifteen this month, she has sent a marvelous birdcage with a note pinned to an embroi- dered cushion, an order for Prince Repnin, the Russian Ambassador here, to exchange the note for two parakeets whose antics would cap- ture my daughter's heart.

When you return, Catherine writes, *Darya will make a splendid maid-of-honor, ready for a marriage of distinction. Russia does not forget her friends.*

I think of the rain in the darkness outside of the Ropsha palace, pounding the windows. I see trees bent by the wind, weighed down with heaviness, fields soaking up water, churning soil into mud.

That night, on the fifth day after the coup, there had been no un- expected quarrel, no drunken brawl, no accident.

The doors had opened. The scar-faced man who entered Peter's room carried no weapon. He didn't need one. His hands could break a horseshoe in half.

He didn't have to have orders. He knew what the Empress wished for. He knew the price of imperial friendship.

I imagine Peter falling to his knees, sobbing, pleading with the man to spare his life. "Why would she fear a fool like me? All I want is an ordinary life." His voice, raw and shrill with fear, growing louder, more frantic.

I pray that Peter was too drunk to register the moment Alexei Orlov's hands closed around his throat. I hope Alexei was brisk, for in the end, when nothing else remains, a swift death is the only mercy.

I pick up a pamphlet *Pan* Korn found for me. A simple map, a drawing of a manor house with two pillars supporting the front porch. *A small estate with a stable, a carriage house, and an orchard of good quality, ten miles south of Kraków.* The owner died without direct heirs. The distant cousin thinks his inheritance a burden. Money is more to his liking.

The estate is called Vishin, and I bought it.

It's far away from the Russian border, I tell myself. *The future is more important than the past.*

To the hands of the Empress only, I begin the letter I will draft first, then copy in my best hand. *Catherine will welcome it,* I tell myself. Not having to look at me again. I am the face of what once were her own dreams.

Time has been on my side.

After my months of travel, I already am out of touch with what matters to the Empress. I have become a convert to country life, private, lonely, important to the few.

Darya will not be Catherine's maid-of-honor. I will make my daughter understand why. I'll stay in Warsaw until Stanislav's coronation and then leave for my new home. I want to fade, disappear. I want to be forgotten.

I wasn't her only tongue, I tell myself. There are some advantages to insignificance.

I've paid for Vishin with the money I brought from Russia, the reward for my participation in Catherine's conspiracy. So far only *Pan Korn* knows that we'll be moving right after the coronation, and he has kept it a secret.

I begin my letter with a small borrowing from Monsieur Voltaire, knowing how highly he stands now in Catherine's esteem. There is a passage toward the end of *Candide* in which a simple old man declares that since those who meddle with public affairs sometimes perish miserably, all he wishes to do is cultivate his garden.

I've found these lines deeply moving and irresistible, I write to Catherine, requesting to be freed from imperial service.

The words that come to me are simple, though I will have to disguise them in my letter: *I know what power does to your heart. I know the price of fear. Your world is not the world I want for my child.*

The church bells begin to ring. Three times. *Na Anioł Pański,* they call it here, the evening prayers. Darya is back from her walk. In the hall, as she takes off her coat and gloves, her voice is gay and lively.

"Maman, are you there?" she cries. "I've found them!"

She is losing her foreign accent, picking up new Polish words. Once an old man cursed her and Masha when they spoke Russian in the street, a mistake my daughter is no longer making. In a year or so, no one will remember she wasn't born here.

I hear no more complaints about Warsaw. Darya sleeps well and wakes up determined to oversee the unpacking of her trunks. She will soon have to pack them again.

Now she walks into my room with that effortless grace Stanislav likes to praise. Her sleeves never brush against the arms of the chairs; her buckled shoes never tangle in the folds of the tablecloth.

"What have you found, *kison'ka?*" I ask.

My daughter sits on the ottoman and turns her face toward me. With a pang, I am reminded that she has Egor's dark eyes.

"The birds I like."

After looking at a dozen Amazon parrots and parakeets, pink, yellow, green, Darenka has finally selected Catherine's promised birthday present. Her two birds are from the Indies, iridescent green with black ruffs. They don't speak much yet, but she knows how to teach them. The lessons will take place in the evening, always at the same time. First she will have to give them a snack of bread soaked in wine, place a cloth over the cage, dim the lights, and repeat the words or phrases. Then, in the light, she will repeat the words while holding the mirror in front of the parakeets, so that they think another bird is talking.

I watch my daughter's animated features, the smoothness of her cheeks, the glow of her eyes.

"Remember how the Empress feared you might want to free the birds in Oranienbaum?" I ask.

"What silly things you remember about me," my daughter says and laughs, bright and gleaming. She rises and kisses me on top of my head, a new habit of hers that makes me feel small.

I summon all the strength I'm still capable of.

"I have something to tell you," I say.

I poke at the birch log in the fireplace. It breaks into glowing cinders.

"What is it, Maman?" Darya asks. "Is it a surprise?"

I shake my head.

She wrinkles her nose like a rabbit. She is lovely, and my heart sinks.

"Listen," I say. "I want to tell you a story."

"Is this a true story?"

"Yes," I tell her. "It is."

THE RUSSIAN COURT

1744–1765

The Empress Elizabeth Petrovna, the younger daughter of Peter the Great and his second wife, Catherine I.

The Grand Duke Peter Fyodorovich (Karl Ulrich). Later Emperor Peter III.

The Grand Duchess Catherine Alexeyevna (Sophie), Princess of Anhalt-Zerbst. After the coup, the Empress Catherine II.

Princess Johanna of Anhalt-Zerbst, Catherine's mother.

Alexei Bestuzhev-Rhumin, the Chancellor of Russia to Empress Elizabeth: later replaced by Vice-Chancellor Vorontzov.

Das Fräulein, **Countess Vorontzova**, one of Catherine's maids-of-honor, the niece of the Vice-Chancellor Vorontzov and a sister of Princess Dashkova; also Peter's Imperial Favorite.

Princess Dashkova, a courtier.

Ivan Ivanovich Shuvalov, a courtier and Elizabeth's Imperial Favorite.

Sergey Saltykov, a courtier.

Sir Charles Hanbury-Williams, British Ambassador to the Russian court.

Count Stanislav Poniatowski, an Envoy to the Russian court. Elected King of Poland in 1764.

The Orlov brothers, Grigory and his younger brother Alexei, officers in the Izmailovsky Guards.

Francesco Bartolomeo Rastrelli, the imperial architect of Empress Elizabeth.

Count Alexei Razumovsky, the Emperor of the Night and Elizabeth's Imperial Favorite.

Count Lestocq, a French surgeon, made Count by Empress Elizabeth.

ACKNOWLEDGMENTS

The Winter Palace is a work of fiction, inspired and sustained by a number of excellent biographies of Catherine the Great and her court. I am particularly indebted to Virginia Rounding's *Catherine the Great: Love, Sex, and Power,* Simon Dixon's *Catherine the Great,* John T. Alexander's *Catherine the Great: Life and Legend,* and Isabel de Madariaga's *Catherine the Great: A Short History.* The Empress herself also wrote about her early life in her memoirs and letters, which I have often consulted, using her phrases and expressions across the novel.

Kate Miciak at Bantam Books and Nita Pronovost at Doubleday Canada have offered me their outstanding editorial guidance. Their enthusiasm and faith in the novel have been priceless, their advice and insights a lifeline. I cannot imagine better and more generous editors.

My agent, Helen Heller, has been an invaluable source of encouragement, inspiration, and wise counsel.

My trusted first readers—Shaena Lambert and Zbyszek Stachniak—have read the manuscript in its earliest stages with just the right balance of praise and meaningful objections.

Diane Paget-Dellio has made me see the cats at the Winter Palace. I am grateful to them all.

Eva Stachniak was born in Wroclaw, Poland, and now lives in Canada, where she has been a radio broadcaster and college English and Humanities lecturer. Her debut novel, *Necessary Lies*, won the Amazon.com/Books in Canada First Novel Award, and her second novel, *Dancing with Kings*, has been translated into seven languages. She lives in Toronto, where is is working on her second novel about Catherine the Great, also to be published by Doubleday.